My Mother's Rid...
Dati...

Philip William Stover is the author of *The Problem with Perfect*, also from Hera, as well as *The Hideaway Inn*, *The Beautiful Things Shoppe*, and *There Galapagos My Heart*. He lives on the Upper Eastside in New York City and in Bucks County, Pennsylvania. He has an MFA in writing and is a professor in Global Liberal Studies at New York University.

He grew up tearing the covers off the romance novels he devoured so he wouldn't get teased at school. Now he enjoys traveling the world with his husband of over twenty years and would never consider defacing any of the books he loves.

Also by Philip William Stover

The Problem With Perfect
My Mother's Ridiculous Rules for Dating

MY MOTHER'S ~~Ridiculous~~ RULES FOR DATING

Philip William Stover

hera

First published in the United Kingdom in 2024 by

Hera Books
Unit 9 (Canelo), 5th Floor
Cargo Works, 1-2 Hatfields
London SE1 9PG
United Kingdom

A CIP catalogue record for this book is available from the British Library.

Print ISBN 978 1 80436 729 2
Ebook ISBN 978 1 80436 728 5

Look for more great books at www.herabooks.com

Printed and bound in Great Britain by Clays Ltd, Elcograf S.p.A.

1

*For my husband, WBC, who puts up with my ridiculous rules
and loves me no matter what.*

Chapter 1

Today, I am a 'normal'.

At first, I thought it was just something I would pretend to do. But as I look at myself in the mirror on the back of the bathroom door, I'm realizing how easily I slip into the wardrobe – khaki pants and the most basic blue Oxford shirt I could find with sensible loafers. 'Normals' go to an office from 9 to 5, take vacations twice a year, and are productive members of society. Nothing wrong with it. Some of my best friends are 'normals'. I just never thought I'd become one.

When I first took a job at Brands to the Rescue, I told myself it was only to supplement my ghostwriting gig with the doyenne of romantic women's fiction, Justine Jasmine. But last year she retired to some tropical island and I needed to find another body to haunt. Somehow I got it into my head that I should go out on my own. I had my agent shop around the manuscript I thought would be her next book. But, dramatic pause, under my own name. I'm trying to become my own ghostwriter, so now the calls are coming from inside the house.

Or rather, not coming at all.

I check my phone for notifications, but the screen is the same as it was thirty seconds ago. My agent, Loretta, said she hoped to hear something from Hurlington Press by the end of the summer, and with Labor Day this weekend, time is running out. An offer from them could mean quitting my side gig as a 'normal' and maybe becoming a real writer.

For the past four months, I've endured a series of painful rejections from editors who called my work 'old-fashioned'. One even had the uncanny gall to say it was too much like Justine Jasmine's work. It *was* Justine Jasmine's work, but thanks to the NDA, I can't tell anyone that. I knew what I was giving up when I started working with her; I just thought it would be easier to get it back.

Luckily, the summer hasn't only been about rejections from publishers. I've also had periodic feelings of abandonment brought on by being dumped almost nine months ago by my on-again, off-again lying boyfriend of more than two years. One evening when I thought he was going to ask me to move in with him, he instead told me he was leaving for Los Angeles to 'try and make it work' with his recently separated husband. I told myself I would be over it by the end of the summer and exploring my not-so-hidden daddy issues with a brand-new guy, but I'm still in the fake-it-till-you-make-it phase.

I grab the last part of my normal cosplay, a canvas satchel with leather trim, throw it over my shoulder, and squelch the desire to check my phone one last time before heading out to attend a meeting at the soul-crushing headquarters of the normals – Brands to the Rescue.

Right as I'm reaching for the door, someone knocks. I open it. 'Mom, what are you doing here?' I slide my phone into my pocket.

'That's a terrible way to greet the woman who gave birth to you,' she says, pushing past me despite the fact that I've barely opened the door wide enough for a cat to slink through. Her small meteorite of a purse is on her shoulder, and she's wearing a floral blouse, pale peach culottes with aqua Converse high tops that I am one hundred per cent sure she has lined with comfort inserts. A turquoise studded headband keeps her curly copper-brown hair under control.

'I'm sorry. Hello, Mom,' I say, closing the door and following her into my microscopic living room. I bow toward her so she can place a kiss on the top of my head. She smooches me and then presses her lips together.

'Feels like less hair,' she declares. 'Are you using the minoxidil I got you in bulk from Costco? It's generic but it has the same ingredients. Don't poo-poo it.'

I panic and immediately check the top of my head with my hand. The thick locks of dark brown hair all seem to be there, but I should be more regular about the treatment. How does she know? She's barely through the door and I'm already being criticized.

She throws her arms around me. 'Hello, my beautiful boy.' She beams and then spits on her fingers to smooth my cowlick. 'I had some business in the neighborhood and I...'

'Business in the neighborhood?' I ask. 'You're a retired schoolteacher who lives at the foot of the George Washington Bridge in New Jersey. What kind of business do you have in Hell's Kitchen?'

'Samuel, I know you think your mother's life starts when I open the door and ends when I leave, but I have professional responsibilities just like other people.' She points to her enormous purse and then places it on the table. 'I did not come over to discuss that. I came over to show you what's in this package. You can also get it in black, but I thought the rainbow made more of a statement.'

Impromptu visits from my mom have been on the rise ever since Aunt Shug died almost a year ago. It was a sudden and tragic loss for both of us. One thing I've learned this past year is that everyone grieves differently. My mother grieves by showing up at my door unannounced or texting me articles about social causes I've never even heard of and admonishing me for not being more engaged. She has always wanted to heal the world, whether the world wants it or not. And even though she won't admit it, staying busy keeps her mind off the loss. I've dealt with the loss by dating emotionally unavailable men and having publishers remind me that I'm not nearly as talented as my mother thinks I am.

'Mom, I was in the middle of something.' Telling her I have to get to work will only make her bristle, which is what she does any time I mention Brands to the Rescue. She thinks I should be doing something more meaningful than writing copy for drugs that promise to ameliorate your seasonal allergies or house paints that will last long into the next century.

'Oooooooh,' she sings with a mixture of curiosity and elation. 'Are you writing? Working on a short story? I was thinking you should write something about that woman who subbed your Spanish class in high school when Mr Garcia was having his knee operated on. She was a very interesting person, and I was just talking about her to our neighbor Mrs Simpson.' She pauses for a second to put her hand to her chin. 'Oh wait. She died.'

'Mrs Simpson died? She used to babysit me.' My lip begins to quiver.

'No, not Mrs Simpson. The woman who subbed your class died. Or was it Mr Garcia? Oh, I don't remember.' She waves her hand to shoo away the thought and my lip steadies. 'Anyway, what are you working on? I'm sure it's wonderful. I'm so glad you're writing again.' Her voice floats with joy.

'I am not writing,' I say. When I was a kid I made the mistake of telling my mom I wanted to write a book. The next thing I knew she started introducing me as 'My Son, The Writer'. I was six and still sounding out words but that didn't stop her. Writers are people who have characters speak to them effortlessly in their minds or imagine marvelous ideas about compelling situations and then turn those thoughts into books that people then buy. Stephen King is a writer. Danielle Steele is a writer. Sam Carmichael is not.

'But you're so talented.' she says knitting her eyebrows together. She says this all the time, the way some people say hello. I guess she means it, but I'm not sure I believe it. I don't feel very talented, and certainly not lately. I may soon have to accept the fact that the world has finally discovered I'm a fraud.

'Why don't you show me what you bought?' I ask, changing the topic. The sooner I see what's in the package, the better my chances of getting to my meeting on time.

'I saw this on the Internet.' She places the package on the table. 'I was scrolling through pictures of queer Dalmatians and—'

'Wait. What? What are queer Dalmatians?' I ask, tilting my head toward her.

'You know, the dogs with the black and white spots. They're so sweet.'

'Yes, I know, but how do you know they're queer? They're dogs.'

She puts her hands on her hips. 'Sam, I did not come over here to debate identity politics with you. Some people are queer. Some animals are queer. Some Dalmatians are queer. Get used to it. Okay?' She sighs at me. I've never met another person who can use a sigh like a spear, but my mother can.

'Anyway, I was scrolling and I saw this ad and I thought it would be perfect for Pride.' The woman is obsessed with Pride. She treats it like New Year's Eve, Halloween and Arbor Day rolled into one event. I treat it like PrEP. It's a nuisance but I don't want to know what will happen if I stop it.

She pulls out a pink rhinestone pocketknife from her purse and uses it to stab the over-stuffed plastic envelope like it's some kind of sacrifice. She removes the bubble wrap and tells me she's going to send an email to the company about their excessive use of packaging with some links to stories about micro-plastics in the water. Her heart is in the right place even if her mind is often in a universe far, far away.

'Look at this,' she says.

I cover my eyes like Jamie Lee Curtis waiting for Michael Myers to attack her. Slowly, I peek between my fingers.

It's worse than I thought.

She is holding up a hideous tangle of rainbow-colored straps and silver cock rings. I think it's called a harness but while the standard issue is black and seen on the chest of some hairy leather daddy, this one looks like it was dragged through the dyes at an Easter egg factory. It's a rainbow nightmare of pleather straps and plastic pieces.

'What is that thing?' I ask, my hands at my cheeks.

'I'll have you know these are very expensive if you buy them in a store. I got such a good price on it.' My mother would rather lay down on Fifth Avenue and get run over by the M3 bus than pay full price for something. My entire childhood is a blur of coupons, discount stores and BOGO sales. She shakes the colorful web until some of the pieces separate and then she holds it up by one of the silver rings. 'You really need to get out more. I mean, what does it say about you that you've never been in a harness before?'

'It says I'm not a trashy slut,' I quip.

She gasps. 'Stop it right now, young man.' Her arms lower so the harness is limp on the table. 'You are slut-shaming.' She wags her finger.

'I'm not. I support sluts. I support trashy sluts. I just happen not to be one.' I don't tell her it's not for lack of trying. This past summer my sex life was as steamy as an episode of *Little House on the Prairie*. I look back at my mother and her frown. Do other gay sons have mothers like this? Nice suburban moms on the outside but relentless social justice warriors on the inside? The kind who shame their sons for slut-shaming?

I pick the harness up from the table with two fingers like it's a soiled diaper. It's hideous. Not even a trashy slut would wear this and, again, no offense to trashy sluts. #Teamtrashysluts.

'Mom, forget it. There is no way I would walk down Fifth Avenue in the middle of the day wearing this.' I wrinkle my nose and let the contraption dangle from my fingers. This thing says, *Look at me. Look at me*, when my usual motto is *Would you mind looking elsewhere?* 'I'm sorry, Mom. I appreciate that you thought of me but…'

She grabs the harness from my hands. 'Of you? What makes you think this is for you?'

'Isn't… I mean… ah…' I stammer.

'This isn't for you, Samuel. It's for me.' She says this like it's the most normal thing in the world. 'I'm going to be wearing it for Pride next year.' She holds it against her petite curvy figure and adjusts her headband in the mirror. 'I wonder if I could glue some sequins on?' She holds out a strap for me to examine.

'You can't be serious. Mom, you can't wear that to Pride.'

'Sam,' she says to her reflection, 'loosen up. People are there to express themselves.'

'People? Yes. Mothers? No.'

She rolls her eyes and ignores my comment.

'I'm worried about chafing. If you had experience with these you'd know how to prevent chafing. Maybe I'll wear something underneath. Like my swimsuit,' she says putting her hand to her chin. 'But I keep that at the Y. I guess I could bring it home after my aqua aerobics class, but I'll need to make myself a note to remember to bring it back.' She starts to rummage through her purse and pulls out a Post-it note and a Sharpie the size of a large carrot and begins to write herself a reminder for something that's not going to happen until almost a year from now.

'Mom, you can't wear…' I start to say and quickly realize I'm wasting my breath. She's going to do what she wants to do. It's actually one of the things I admire about my mom. She's someone who truly doesn't care what other people think, which is a good thing because I think most people think she's out of her mind. But the fact is, she knows her own mind better than anybody I've ever met.

8

I start shoving the harness back into its packaging so I can get her on her way. 'I'm sure you'll be the hit of the parade *next year*,' I say. 'But you don't want to miss the bus back to New Jersey.'

'I thought we could make plans for your beep-beep next week.'

Almost a year ago, my mother started pestering me about my big thirty-fifth birthday, and I forbade her from saying the word *birthday* around me until a week before the actual event. My mother loves a loophole so she started saying beep-beep instead. She still had the same questions and nags but remained within the letter of the law, if not the spirit of my decry. Technically she could start using the word today, but I'm not going to tell her that.

'Lunch wherever you want, Mom. Really. It's fine,' I say, trying to get her out the door.

'On your beep-beep day I thought I could come here to give you your big surprise.'

I freeze.

'What do you mean, surprise?' I ask, halting my push to get her to the door. A surprise from my mother is not good. It's never good. I'm still getting over the surprise of my mother wearing a rainbow-colored sex harness during a parade down Fifth Ave.

'Saa-haam,' she sings, her Jersey accent surrounding the slightly nasal notes. 'If I told you what it was, then it wouldn't be a surprise.' She could have any number of atrocities ready for me wrapped up as a surprise. When I turned ten, I had my first all-boy birthday party. I was convinced it would help me fit in for the rest of the year. Then she surprised me with a cake that she had custom ordered from the grocery store with a picture of Joan Crawford on it. I've worshiped her since I was born but

9

explaining who she was to a bunch of boys who had their cakes decorated with baseball team logos and race cars was not how I imagined spending that day. A surprise from my mother is never a good thing.

'Fine, fine,' I say, opening the door for her.

'And can you come over on Thursday evening? The thingamabob broke again and I need you to fix it.'

'Sure, did you try to tighten the do-hickey...' I start to say.

'Yes, but it still is jammed and I can't get the other thing to do the thing.'

'Yeah, Mom, of course.' I bow my head down so she can reach it with a kiss.

'I love you times a million billion,' she says and we hug goodbye.

'I love you a billion more,' I say and close the door.

With a mother like mine, I'm not sure being a 'normal' is even a possibility.

Chapter 2

'Finn Montgomery,' my boss at Brands to the Rescue says pointing to the name on the screen that takes up most of the wall in his office.

'Who?' I ask. I may be wearing my 'normal' costume, but my mind is still preoccupied with getting a phone call from my agent. I straighten my spine and try to shift gears.

'We just closed a deal with a blue-chip gallery,' Robert says as he fiddles with the monitor. 'Big players in the art world. They're looking to get some more buzz for one of their artists. I thought Finn Montgomery would be perfect for you.'

'What about Surentox?' My job involves developing media campaigns for individuals or businesses seeking to establish or transform their brand. All summer, I've been working with a pain medication that causes hives, intestinal dysfunction, and vomiting in addition to treating migraines. I'm writing profiles of Surentox users who have had their lives changed by the drug despite the scratching and frequent trips to the bathroom. I was hoping Surentox would be my last campaign before the publishing world took a chance on me, writing under my own name for once. I don't want to start on a new campaign for some pretentious art gallery.

'Sam, you've done great work there. When people hear Surentox, they no longer think of explosive diarrhea. Thank you.'

'My pleasure,' I say.

'But I need you on the Carlos Wong Gallery and Finn Montgomery. He's an up-and-coming artist.' Robert begins to click through the deck. 'His last project was a series of portraits of queer people in New Orleans.' The first shot is a striking photo of two people embracing. One is bald with full rainbow-glitter painted lips, and the other has a beard, a top hat, and a sign that says, *One Month and Ten Days*. The next photo has a similar structure but this one is a solo queer-presenting person with a sign that says, *Twenty Hours*. He shows me a few more, and each time he clicks, I want to stop him and tell him to go back. The photos are mesmerizing. They incorporate text, images, and some colorful abstract elements in a complicated but harmonious collage. I want to spend more time with each one and try to understand what exactly is going on and who these people are. Each photo makes me want to jump inside and understand it. But before I can do that, Robert clicks to the final slide.

Gorgeous hazel eyes and a warm, laughing smile emanate from the image. The guy appears to be in his twenties and he's holding a 35mm camera with a strap around his neck. He's outside somewhere in the South with those trees that grow in the water. There isn't a sign like in the other images. In a brooding artist sort of way, he's handsome as hell, but he's precisely the kind of guy I don't want to be working with at my day job. I've met more than my share of self-involved artists and they only lead to trouble.

'This is Finn,' Robert says, letting the presentation come to a full stop. 'His work has a social justice angle. The gallery director thinks he can become the next big thing, but he needs to get out there more. Connect with his audience and not just the art world. Get the right kind of coverage. Take him to the next level. He was just on *Art Today*'s "Thirty Under Thirty" list.' I hate those lists, and not just because I'm past the eligibility age. They make no sense and are just the product of some weird editorial decision or, worse, the influence of people like me. Still, it's an impressive credential.

'One issue,' Robert says. I'm listening, but I can't help staring at the image of Finn still on the screen behind him. 'He hates promotion. He's a little obsessed with work according to the people at the gallery. I thought you'd be the best person to convince him since you're both, you know...' Robert struggles for the word. 'Queer? Is it queer now? I always forget. Are you gay or queer? Both? Maybe?' I roll my eyes without trying to hide it. Sounds like someone missed the required training on respecting diversity. I don't answer him and let the awkward silence go on.

'Sam, this is an important client for us.' He looks from side to side as if someone might be eavesdropping. 'Not to put any pressure on you but we're hiring a new full-time position in January. I could see you going from part-time Brand Associate to full-time Senior Brand Manager.'

Full-time Senior Brand Manager? Why doesn't Robert just come over and beat me with his laptop and tell me I'm a failure. There is nothing wrong with being a full-time Senior Brand Manager. It would be an amazing job. Thousands of people spend years working toward this very goal. It's just that it was never my goal. It was just something to do until my writing took off.

'Isn't that something you'd be interested in?' Robert asks.

'I don't know,' I say. I can't tell him how I really feel.

'Think about it and we can chat later.'

The intercom buzzes and a voice says, 'Robert. I have Mr Montgomery here for his appointment.'

'Great. Please ask him to wait in Conference Room A. I'm finishing up with Sam and will send him over.'

'He's here? Now?' I ask. I was hoping I would have some time to come up with reasons why I'm not right for the project but instead I walk with Robert out of his office and down the hall to meet Finn.

'He was in the area and wanted to do a vibe check,' Robert says as we walk. 'Just say hello and tell him about all the good work we do. He's not expecting any kind of formal presentation.'

We walk into the conference room and Finn is looking out the window with his back to us. Some guys are so sexy you can tell they're hot from the back and not just because they look great in tight jeans. This guy has a presence that I can sense before he even turns around. I was impressed by the picture of him I saw only a few minutes ago but being in the same room as Finn makes it clear he's someone with tremendous charisma.

He turns around and as I suspected he's even more handsome than he was in the photo. Finn is wearing a pair of black denim skinny jeans and a V-neck T-shirt that shows off a curated collection of necklaces that sit on top of the small nest of chest hair seductively peeking out the sides of the collar of his shirt. The thick sunglasses on top of his head keep his dark blond hair with natural streaks of lighter blond off his face and he has the same camera at his side. If you were going to make an emoji for a hip, edgy artist you could use this guy as a model. In sharp contrast I could be a catalog model for the terminally dull in my Brands uniform of khaki pants and boring shirt.

Robert introduces me to Finn and tells us both how excited he is about the project and heads out of the room to what I am sure is a much more important meeting. I'm finding it hard not to stare at Finn's hazel eyes, but I remind myself this is work, and I need to keep a professional distance.

'Sorry to keep you waiting.' I keep my voice level and calm.

'That's okay. I was early. I could look at this for hours.'

His gaze is fixed on the view from the over-sized windows. We are about as far south as you can get in Manhattan and on the fifty-second floor. It's something I try not to think about when I'm in the office. I'm not sure anyone is meant to be emailing press materials at this altitude. 'I'd forgotten how spectacular the view is. I've seen it so often that I've just taken it for granted.'

On one side of us, the Brooklyn Bridge feels close enough that you could touch it, and on the other, sunlight reflects off the Hudson River, turning the ripples in the water into shimmering diamonds. Manhattan lies before us like it's something a person could contain and not the all-encompassing organism it is from the ground. I'd forgotten how it felt to take in this view and be in awe. I take a second to stand next to Finn and soak it up.

'Is this your first time in New York?' I ask.

'Just moved up about a week ago. Everyone up here says I talk funny.' He has the slightest hint of a Southern accent but it's not enough to make me think he popped out of an Anne Rice novel. There's a deep but playful honeyed-whiskey quality to his voice that fills the room.

'Where's home?' I ask.

'It's wherever I'm working. I grew up in Texas and Louisiana. Went to art school in California. Had a photo studio in Miami for a few years. Just finished a project in New Orleans and now I'm here. Sort of a Southern Fried Nomad. How 'bout you?'

Instinctively I stretch my arm across my body and point. 'There.'

'You grew up in the river?' he asks. He lays on the accent, making his playful question even more light-hearted.

'No, the other side. New Jersey.'

'Wow. As in *fuhgeddaboudit*?' he asks with the worst Tony Soprano impersonation I've ever heard.

'Just on the other side of the GW Bridge.' I nod.

'That's amazing. I loved N'awleans and Miami is a pretty big city but it's nothing like this place. New York is a lot. Carlos thinks this is the place for me to be right now, and I had an idea for a project, so here I am.'

'Robert agrees with Carlos. He thinks Brands can really help you get more recognition for your work.'

He turns from the window and shrugs. 'I don't really care about recognition. I want to tell people's stories, and I want to bring them to as many people as possible. To have an audience. That's all I care about really.' He looks at me with those penetrating eyes and asks, 'What do you do?'

'I'm a Brand Associate. I work with clients to establish a desirable brand. I'm part-time but I work with all the full-time people if you're worried about that.'

16

'I mean, what do you do? Robert said you were a painter.' He squints, maybe trying to imagine me holding a messy palette of watercolors.

'I'm not.' Why would Robert say that? Maybe he was trying to woo the client. I'm not sure I can expect people to think of me as a writer when I struggle to use the description myself.

'I didn't think so.' Finn shakes his head and his hair falls in front of his face.

'Oh?' My voice rises at the end. His assumption annoys me. It's correct, but still, I find it irritating.

'I know a lot of painters. You do not give painter vibes.' He looks me up and down and pushes his bangs back behind his ear. 'You're a writer I bet.' He stares right at me and I quickly move my eyes away from his.

'I'm a Brand Associate. I write the material that goes along with the branding.' Two minutes with this guy and he's sticking a needle in my deepest wound. I've written multiple books for Justine Jasmine as her ghostwriter and she's a best-selling author. Countless words for clients at work. I have a degree in creative writing and graduated with honors but I still don't think of myself as a writer. My best friend Omar thinks I have imposter syndrome, but every time he brings it up, I point out that you need to have actually had success to think you are an imposter. I'm just your garden variety nobody. I quickly change the subject.

'I saw a few of your images and they're extraordinary.' I'm not just flattering him. They've been in my mind since I saw them. 'Robert showed me a series from New Orleans. The people are holding signs with days or weeks... what do they mean?'

Finn looks off to the side for a second and puts a finger on his chin. 'Everyone thinks being out is so easy now because you can buy a rainbow flag at a big box store, but the fact is, it's still hard for people to be who they want to be out in the world. Those signs are how long it's been since the last time they were harassed or in some cases violently attacked for who they are.'

The images alone were very powerful but hearing Finn's explanation takes this to a new level. He's right. We think the world has become so much more tolerant, and maybe it has, but that doesn't mean that every day people aren't hurt for being who they are.

My mom is always telling me I don't do enough social justice work but I tell her she does enough for both of us. I think I do my part but when I hear Finn talk about his work I realize there is more I could do, more I should do. I think about the one image I saw and the length of time was something like twenty hours. It must have been a day after an attack.

'It's painful to know how dangerous it is out in the world for queer people,' I say and turn to look at him. 'That's why you need me.' When Robert first presented this campaign a short while ago I didn't want to work on it at all, but after seeing his photographs and hearing his incredible explanation, I can't help wanting to be the person that helps get the message out.

'I need you, do I?' He tilts his head to the side. I can tell I've gotten his attention.

'Yes.' I nod my head. 'Your work is deeply personal and incredibly important. But I'm sure generating publicity for it feels... wrong.'

'That's exactly what I told Carlos. I'm not comfortable selling myself.' Finn stuffs his hands in his pockets and looks at the floor.

'I'm not going to do that. I wouldn't.' I try to make eye contact by turning my head to meet his gaze. 'I want to amplify your work. We have the same goal – to make people aware of the issues. I want to help you tell the story.'

He doesn't respond immediately. He turns away from me and looks out the window again, and I give him a moment to think about what I just said to him. He turns back and smiles. 'You aren't what I expected,' he says with a laugh in his voice. 'I told Carlos I'd have an open mind because he's been good to me and I want to help the gallery, but I was sure I'd turn down whoever I met. A lot of these corporate types don't understand how important a story can be. How powerful it is. But I think you do, don't you?'

'Yes,' I say softly. I can barely squeak out the word. I feel a tug in my heart and a little voice reminds me I want to tell my own stories just the way Finn is through his work. I want to write stories that make people feel the way I felt growing up and getting lost in wonderful old classic Hollywood films with fabulous locations and characters that fell in love despite trying their hardest not to. That's why this summer has been so painful watching doors close, one after another.

But then I catch Finn looking at me the way he might study a subject through his lens and I snap back to the moment. 'I thought so,' he says and a wide grin spreads across his face. He grabs his camera from the table and puts the strap over his shoulder. 'So how does this work? Do I call you or do you call me?' He's made a decision.

I explain some of the logistics and we make a plan to meet next week. We say goodbye and he starts to walk away but turns back before he's out the door. He looks at me and then gazes out the windows once more to take in the magnificent view before he leaves.

Then I become aware of something happening below my waist. It's not a stirring in my loins, although that's not out of the question. My phone buzzes with an alert. This must be it. The call from my agent. I dig my hand into my pocket, but before I look at my phone, I take a few seconds to look out the window and enjoy the view.

Chapter 3

I take a deep breath and swipe open my phone, my heart racing. My entire future could be determined by the next few seconds.

The text reads: *Can you bring my fave water bottle?* followed by a bunch of emojis that make no sense, including the taco and the flag of a country I do not recognize – a typical communication from my best friend Omar.

Sure, I send back. My heart descends from my throat back to my chest. I guess my future will need to wait a little longer, or at least until after I pick up his water bottle and we head to the gym together.

Omar and I met in college. We were both on work-study scholarships and spent countless hours in the library's basement talking about what we wanted to do when we graduated and the guys on campus we had crushes on. I was the first person Omar came out to, and he was the first person I let read my senior thesis. We trust each other with our secrets.

I decide to walk home after work since it's such a beautiful day and seeing the city through Finn's eyes this morning has renewed my appreciation for the metropolis. He gazed out the window like he was peering out of the Millennium Falcon across a sea of new galaxies. A guy like Finn can have that limitless optimism, that sense of hope that anything is possible. I guess I felt that way once. Maybe right after college when I won the Seggerman Award for my short story. Or when I saw the first book I wrote for Justine in a bookstore. But it's been a long time since I've felt that way. Hope may be a thing with feathers, but it can also be a rusty gear in a car that won't start anymore.

Summer is holding on to the city but a cool breeze makes the late afternoon air bearable, although I know part of my decision to enjoy the outdoors is influenced by the fact that if I don't get on the subway, I'll still have a signal on the commute home in case I hear from my agent.

After a few blocks, my phone rings and I'm glad I'm not underground, but when I look at the screen, I see my mom is calling. I don't immediately send it to voicemail because she's learned that if it does that after one ring, it means I have actively denied her, so now I have to let the call bleed out, which is super annoying. Instead, I just pick up the phone.

'Hello, Sam is that you?' she asks.

'Yes, Mom. You called me.'

'I know that. It's just that you never pick up on the first ring. Is everything okay? Are you okay? Did you think I was a boy?'

'Your picture literally shows up on my screen when you call. Granted half of the image is the rainbow flag you're holding but I would never mistake you for a boy I like.'

'Oh, so there is a boy you like?'

'No, Mom. There is not a boy I like.' The woman is constantly hoping I will have a bestselling novel or find my soul mate. Sadly, both of those things seem very, very unlikely at the moment.

'Are you okay?'

'Yes, I'm fine.'

'Are you sure?'

'Yes, Mom. I. Am. Fine.' I say each word slowly and deliberately. Maybe she can hear in my voice that I'm preoccupied. I haven't told her a thing about the book project I have on submission. I don't want to let her know that the reality of my career is so much more depressing than she could imagine.

'What's up?' I ask casually trying to hide any concern that might reveal itself.

'I wanted to know if you are driving or taking the train for Thanksgiving and if it's the train which one and if you are driving I wanted to tell you not to take Highway 17 because they're doing construction.'

'Mom, Labor Day is this weekend and you want to know how I'm getting to your house for Thanksgiving. I have no idea. It's months away.' She's always planning events that aren't due to take place for months or sometimes years. I swear my mother will eventually loop herself.

'*Next* Labor Day is months away. Thanksgiving is right around the corner. You have to plan for these things if you want to be prepared. Do you know when they start planning the Macy's Thanksgiving Day Parade? The second after one parade ends, they start working on the next one. I saw that on the news. Technically, I'm behind. So, train or drive? I think train because the construction might not be done, but you decide. It's your choice.'

'Mom, I have no idea.'

'But which would you prefer? The train or driving in?'

'I told you. I don't know.' My mom constantly asks me questions to situations I haven't even considered and the answer 'I don't know' is meaningless to her. I tell her I don't know and she just keeps on asking as if doing so will somehow create a new answer. The phrase 'I don't know' is like ammunition to her.

'You don't know when you'll know or you don't know how you'll get here? Because I could have someone pick you up. Let me make a few calls today.'

'I don't know!' I say again but with more force.

'I'm just asking a question,' she says and I immediately feel guilty. I know Thanksgiving is going to be hard for her. It's going to be hard for both of us. The first one without Aunt Shug. I love the holiday but I remind myself that this one will be a challenge and change my tone with her.

'Mom, let me think about it and I'll get back to you,' I say as I arrive in front of Plant Daddy, the cafe on the ground floor of the building I live in. I stop in front of the window boxes with their late summer zinnias and marigolds to wave to Omar who is finishing his barista shift. He waves back and I point to my phone and roll my eyes. He knows this is code for *I'm talking to my mother*. 'Mom, I have to go.' I hope I can make a quick exit from the conversation.

'We can finalize things when I see you for your big birthday surprise this week.'

Big. Birthday. Surprise. Three simple words that fill me with fear. Images of the Joan Crawford Cake fill my head. 'I have to go, Mom. I'll talk to you later. I love you,' I say and hang up before she can ask another question.

Omar's apartment is just upstairs from mine. He found the building first, and as soon as an opening became available I moved in two floors below him. After a quick stop at my place to change out of my 'normal' clothes and into my gay gym 'uniform', I head two flights up and key into his apartment. His place looks like a fabric store exploded. There are tissue-paper patterns covering the floor, mannequins with lace trim pinned to the edges, and a table covered in gears and small pieces of robotics that he uses to animate his fashions. When Omar is not serving coffee downstairs, or at the gym, he's at his sewing machine making some marvelous creation. I grab his purple water bottle with the sparkles on it and head downstairs to Plant Daddy.

When I walk in, Kai is watering a bushy Boston fern perched on a stand between two cafe tables. He's not only the proprietor of Plant Daddy, but he also owns the building, so he's our landlord as well. He comes over to me and puts the tin watering can he was using on the tray of his wheelchair. 'Any news from your agent?' he asks, biting his lower lip.

'Nothing,' I say.

'They shouldn't make you wait so long,' he says gruffly. 'I found a blossom on the peace lily by the espresso machine. I heard that's a good omen. Maybe it can help us both get lucky.' He tapes a 'Help Wanted' sign to the front window.

'I thought Mitzi was covering Hanzhang's shifts.' Hanzhang works at Plant Daddy in between tours. She got cast in a regional production of *Close Encounters of the Third Kind: The Musical*. She's playing an alien and super excited.

'She was until Mitzi broke her arm at a protest for trans healthcare. Now she needs to stay down in DC. Silly old fool. I told her not to wear high heels.' He scratches the grey stubble on his chin and shakes his head.

'Oh, that's awful. I hope she'll be okay.' I really like Mitzi and to be honest she pulls a much better espresso than Hanzhang. She also has great stories about her and Kai working on the front lines of the trans helpline decades ago. She's sweet and kind which is not how anyone would describe Kai at first meeting. He is sweet and kind but he does his best to hide it.

'Don't worry about her. I'm the one who has to fill these shifts. Who in the world wears kitten heels to a protest march? She has plenty of friends taking care of her.'

'That's good,' I say. Kai saves most of his outward kindness for his plants but everyone knows underneath his crusty exterior is, well actually, more crust but underneath that layer I believe there is something sweeter. 'Let me know if you know someone. Omar has too many hours pattern cutting at Vanata and Maggie can't change her schedule at the yoga studio. Angelika said not to worry because she pulled the Page of Cups.'

Madame Angelika is a regular who reads Tarot cards at one of the tables near the large potted fiddle leaf fig tree. She says the tree has an amazing life source. Kai grumbles about how woo-woo it is but whenever he has a problem he always asks Angelika to pull a card.

'What does the Page of Cups mean?'

'A big happy surprise. So, no thanks. The last time she pulled that card the cappuccino machine broke down and I had to buy that new fancy one,' he says shaking his head.

The previous machine was awful. Everything tasted like the engine of an old Toyota Camry. 'But everyone loves the new machine and you're selling more espresso than ever Kai.'

'You're always able to look on the bright side when it's someone else,' he says and rolls his eyes at me. 'Just let me know if you can think of anyone.'

'Will do,' I say. I wave to Damola, who has his head-phones on and looks up from his laptop for a second with a short wave and then goes back to his screen. I'm sure he's in the middle of some scheduling emergency with one of his dog walkers or mixing some amazing beat or both. I smile at a few other regulars I recognize and head over to the counter where Omar is wiping down the steam wand of the cappuccino machine.

'Anything?' he asks. He knows how anxious I am about hearing from my agent. I shake my head. 'I'm sure it will be good news.' He pulls his apron off over his head.

I shrug. 'I doubt it. Each passing minute makes it seem more unlikely.'

'I wish you believed in yourself more,' he says walking out from behind the counter. *So do I*, I say to myself. So do I.

Chapter 4

We head out of Plant Daddy and down the block toward
our gym, Flex Lab. House music pounds softly in the
background syncopated by the occasional clash of weights
dropping to the ground. We wind our way through the
maze of people, mostly well-toned men, and Omar smiles
and flirts with every single guy. I am the opposite. Head
down, baggy T-shirt and raggedy shoes. Omar is wearing
shorts so short I'm not sure you can call them shorts and a
tank top that shows off his perfect, hairy body. He lives for
the attention. The more invisible I am, the better, which
is easy at the gym, where most guys look right through
me to get a better view of Omar and I'm fine with that.
He knows I prefer the equipment way off in the far corner
so we make our way there.

Without speaking, we load up the bar and begin taking
turns on the bench. We have done this thousands of times
since we met in college. Omar is a muscle god. I am
more a Christmas and Easter worshipper. I don't mind
going to the gym but I miss more workouts than I make.
Technically, I am some form of bear, although I don't
really call myself that. I'm a little thicker than some guys
and hairy in the right spots and if being a bear means I
can eat an extra slice of pie without feeling guilty, call me
whatever you want.

'What do you think of the guy in the sleeveless shirt?' Omar asks. He pushes a massive kettlebell up over his head.

'Omar, this is a gay gym in Hell's Kitchen. Everyone is wearing a sleeveless shirt.'

'The guy with the red shorts,' he adds. 'Isn't his name Steve or Sean or something like that?' He keeps his eyes focused on his target and I squint to get a closer look.

'That's Sven. Maggie knows him,' I say rolling my eyes. 'A total narcissist, she said.'

'He's hot,' Omar says, smiling like he's imagining something dirty.

I shrug. 'Maybe, but did you hear that part about Maggie thinking he might be a narcissist?'

'So what? If I had arms like that, I'd be a narcissist too.'

'As a matter-of-fact, you do have arms like that. Almost exactly and you aren't a narcissist.'

Omar puts down the kettlebell and kisses me on the cheek. 'You are the sweetest best friend any guy could ever hope for. The fact that you think my arms are hot enough for me to be a narcissist means the world to me.'

I pick up a much smaller kettlebell and begin my set. Omar counts but his attention is on the other side of the room.

'Holy shit! What the hell is he doing here?' Omar's angry. I can't imagine who could set him off.

'Who?' I ask, unable to turn my head in the middle of the set.

'No one,' he says, shifting from heated anger to feigned innocence. 'Hey, let's get smoothies. My treat.'

'Who is here and what's going on?' I put down the weight and before I can turn around, I see *him* in the mirror.

'What's he doing here?' I cover my face with my hands.

'Screw him,' Omar says. 'I'm going over there and telling him to get out of our gym.'

'We don't own it.' Omar is fiercely loyal, and I love that about him, but I don't want my ex-boyfriend Paul to think he has any impact on me at all. I pull Omar behind a pillar so that Paul has less opportunity to see either of us. Somehow his reflection bounces around the mirrors so I can stare at him without him seeing me. He's wearing workout clothes but Paul has a way of making even the most casual clothes look formal. His salt-and-pepper hair is slicked back a bit and parted on the side. There's even more grey in his beard than when he left which only makes him look more debonair.

My heart is pounding. Am I angry or happy? Pissed or horny? I can't tell. Maybe I'm just in shock. After two years of dating, I thought Paul and I were headed toward something serious. He told me he was getting divorced and I believed him. He told me it was just a matter of time and that his relationship with Todd was over and I believed him. He told me he loved me and I believed him. Then he told me he was getting back together with his estranged husband and moving to Los Angeles with Todd, and I didn't believe him.

'I really think I should go over there and tell him to screw all the way off,' Omar says.

I try to get a better look at him in the mirror. He's wearing a pair of tight blue shorts and an even tighter grey Under Armour polo that shows off his mature dadbod.

'He can come in here if he wants. We aren't going to hide from him. I'm sure he'll be back on a plane to California after Labor Day. Who knows what he's doing here, and who cares?' Inside I'm answering my own question with a silent, *Me! I want to know!*

Omar and I go back to our workout and I try to appear nonchalant, although I'm sure I am giving off very chalant vibes when Omar says, through clenched teeth and without moving his lips, 'He's coming over here. Locker room escape?' He tilts his head toward the showers.

'No,' I say without moving my lips or head. I can feel Paul's eyes on me and his body getting closer with each step. He's at my side but I refuse to turn my head to look at him.

'Sam? I thought I saw you,' he says. His sweet avuncular voice wraps around me and for a second I melt but then I remember how he just up and left me with barely an explanation. My heart is ice again.

'Hello, Paul,' I say without an ounce of emotion. 'What are you doing here? Aren't you and Todd living in Pasadena now? Bit of a commute, isn't it?' Omar stays silent but I can tell it's hard for him.

Paul smiles and says, 'That's not working out.' He looks down at the ground and pushes his lips to the side.

'Oh?' I ask, my voice suddenly full of hope. I immediately regret my tone.

'I was going to call but I figured you blocked my number.'

'Exactly,' I say although I would never block Paul. I can't block anyone. There's a telemarketer who calls trying to sell me computer virus protection once a week and I can't even block him. It feels so final.

'I figured you and Omar would make your way here eventually. Hi, Omar,' he says. Omar shoots him a look, and before he can say anything I ask Omar to give me a few minutes alone with Paul.

'Are you sure you want to be alone with this liar?'

I nod.

'I totally deserve that,' Paul says.

'That and a whole lot worse. I'll be at the calves machine,' Omar says and then points at his eyes with two fingers and then at Paul. Paul knows Omar is a pussycat despite looking like an action hero. He can put on a good show, even if it is a tad dramatic.

Once we are alone, Paul turns on the charm. 'Sammy, you look great. Bet you spent some time on Fire Island this summer. You've got those adorable freckles across your nose.'

I immediately cover my nose with my hand. This man broke my heart over and over. I do not need or want his compliments. But then I see him smiling at me and my hand slowly drops to my side. He has this way of looking at me that makes me feel protected. There's no denying I have a thing for older guys and Paul fits the bit perfectly. More than a decade older. A professional who knew exactly what he was doing all the time. He knew how to fix a clogged drain, and he filed his taxes on time. He was able to get things done, and I found it very compelling.

'Sam. I owe you an apology and explanation. Can I take you to dinner next week? Any day. You choose.'

I stare him straight in the face. 'Next week is my birthday,' I spit the words out at him. Paul would forget that.

'Of course, what I meant was for your birthday, but of course you have plans,' he says, trying to cover his mistake.

The truth is I don't have plans at all. In the past I made my birthday a self-imposed writing retreat. I'd turn off my phone and refuse to see more than a handful of people. I would spend the day trying to write. This year I don't know what I'll do besides try to survive whatever horrible surprise my mom has planned, but I know I'm not spending it with Paul. He told me his marriage was over. That they hadn't been together in over a year and then one weekend it all dissolved into air. Suddenly he's been transferred to the LA office and he and Todd are going to counseling to rebuild their marriage.

'Paul, you come back here after leaving me to go back to your husband.'

'Ex-husband,' he interrupts.

'So you say.' I continue, 'And you expect me to just forgive and forget and go out to dinner with you? Just pick up where we were, what, nine months ago?' I pretend to be searching for how long ago he left but the truth is I know exactly.

'No, I don't expect that. I just want you to hear me out. Let me explain what was going on. I made some terrible decisions. Please, Sam. I'm only here for a week this time but I'm moving back at the end of the year once things are settled. I know I made a huge mistake. I can't stop thinking about you and what we almost had. Please, Sam,' he says. His eyes are focused on mine searching for a way to connect and it makes me want to let him in. Then he slowly reaches for my hand and holds a few of my fingers in his palm. He gently squeezes and says, 'Please.'

I should say no. I should shake his hand out of mine, unscrew the water bottle Omar left behind and throw the contents in his face. I've always wanted to throw a drink in the face of someone who wronged me but I can't. It's not me. I want to be Bette Davis but I'm more Doris Day. He looks so sincere, standing in front of me, almost begging. Why shouldn't I let him explain himself? If I agree to see

33

him, it wouldn't be to start anything up again. I'd do it for closure. The pain has been an open wound that never quite healed correctly. If I meet him maybe I'll finally be able to put all of the 'what ifs' to bed. But I know once I walk in through that door, it's so hard for me to walk out. I can't say yes, and I can't say no, so I say the only thing I can think of.

'Goodbye, Paul.' I walk away. I can see his eyes following me in the mirrors. Paul is not one to give up so easily and I wonder if my goodbye is only temporary.

Chapter 5

Over Labor Day weekend, I received six voicemails from my mother about my 'big birthday surprise', three from Paul begging me to meet him for a drink so he can 'explain', one from my boss Robert with a dozen questions about Surentox, and zero from my agent, Loretta. Not that I expected to hear from my agent over the holiday but that didn't stop me from hoping she'd call. My birthday is tomorrow and if I don't hear from my agent soon, I might have a stroke as I walk back home from Brands to the Rescue.

Last year I spent the week before my birthday in the Hamptons with Paul. During the day, he worked with clients at their fancy mansions while I poked into small shops and searched for the best lobster roll. We spent the evenings together, watching the sunset and feeling the cold ocean water on our toes as we walked along the beach. Things were perfect. At least I thought they were. Was I so desperate to be in a stable relationship with a grownup that I couldn't see the reality of the situation or were we truly happy and things got off track? I haven't been able to stop debating the question since seeing Paul at the gym. His timing couldn't be worse. It's like he knew I was finally moving on and had to come back to make me doubt myself.

So, when my mother calls, again, during my walk home, I pick up simply to have the distraction. 'Hello,' I say trying not to sound too discouraged.

'What's wrong?' she asks as soon as I answer. It's how she says 'hello' these days.

'Nothing,' I say, which is the exact opposite of the truth.

'I just wanted to make sure you're wearing sunscreen.'

'You mean right now?' I can see the sun beginning to set in the distance.

'Yes, right now. I just saw a post from a dermatologist that the only time you should leave your house without sunscreen is if you leave in the dark and return in the dark.'

'So only vampires are exempt,' I say as I wait for a light to cross Seventh Avenue.

'Make fun all you want but that's not me talking. A board-certified dermatologist said this.'

'Fine, I will wear sunscreen the next time I leave my apartment.'

'What SPF?' Another question. There is always another question with my mother.

'I don't know.' I know what SPF is, but at this moment, I can't remember how it's rated, so I just say ten and turn on to my block.

'Ten? You need an SPF of eighty. At the very least. Promise me you won't even buy ten. Ten is like spitting on your arm. It wouldn't protect you at all, and with your hair thinning on the top, it's taking your life in your hands.' She sounds mildly hysterical.

'Fine. I will wear an SPF of three million.'

'Well, don't be ridiculous,' she says. Right. I'm the one being ridiculous. 'I'll see you tomorrow morning at your apartment for your big birthday surprise.'

'Mom, I've told you I don't like surprises.'

'I know and I've told you that you'll like this one.'

I look down at my phone and see a missed call from my agent. I have no idea how I missed it. I have to catch her before she leaves for the day.

'Mom, I got to go. I'll see you tomorrow.' The words shoot out of my mouth. I run the last half block to my building and zoom past Plant Daddy barely waving to Kai and Omar, who are at one of the tables out front. I skip the elevator to climb the stairs to my apartment. I throw my bag on the table and sit on the couch to dial my agent.

'Hey, Sam. I was about to head home. Thanks for calling back so quickly,' Loretta says. Her voice is always neutral so I don't even try to interpret.

Surely she knows she holds my future in her hands. I want to just scream in the phone, 'What did they say?' But I continue with the niceties and then gently ask, 'So did Hurlington get back to you?'

'I just got off the phone with the acquisitions editor when I left my message. She's really a very nice young woman. She's new but I think she'll be promoted soon.'

'That's nice,' I say but I really do not care at all about this woman's future in publishing unless it involves me.

'Sam, there's no easy way to say this. They passed. I'm sorry. I'll forward you the email,' she says. I hate when she does this. She has already forwarded me a small pile of rejections. I never ask her to but she always sends them along no matter how thorny they are.

'Please, don't,' I say. It's too much for me to handle. 'I just don't understand. It's the same stuff I've been writing for Hurlington. They loved this type of book when it was under Justine's name. They just don't know that I was ghosting it.'

'I know,' Loretta says and I can hear her taking a puff on the cigarette I'm sure is dangling from her mouth. 'I wish Justine didn't have such a strict non-disclosure.' The only people who know I worked for Justine are Loretta and Omar and he's sworn an oath. I've almost slipped with my mom a few times but that would be a disaster. She'd not only leak it, she'd take out an ad in the local paper announcing, 'My son has written a book!' Now, she won't even get a chance to say it out loud. I sink deeper into the couch.

'I don't think they feel comfortable with a guy writing women's fiction,' Loretta says with a cough.

I'm silent. I don't know what to say. I had a major hand in the last six women's fiction books Justine wrote. The first one even made a bunch of notable lists and the sales were always excellent, although they had started to decline over the past few years.

'Sam, there's a reason Justine retired. There just isn't an appetite for that kind of stuff anymore. It's becoming old-fashioned. Maybe you should take some time off. Write your own stuff. Something new from your own point of view. Your own story, not hers. Find your own voice.'

My own voice? I don't even know what that is anymore. Have I been Justine Jasmine for too long?

'And update some of your references. Even I don't know some of those old movies.' I hear her take another puff and then cough. 'I'd be thrilled to look at something in your own voice when you finish it.'

'Thanks,' I say. I appreciate her support but I'm not sure I can handle any more humiliation by continuing the call. I say goodbye to Loretta and we hang up.

I turn off the screen on my phone and slump down onto the couch. My mind tries to step in and tell me this is not a reflection on me as a writer, but my heart is already overriding any logical conclusion. I start to feel a hazy, uncontrollable sensation around my eyes. I let out a wail, and then the tears just pour down my face like a tropical storm. Small sobs lead to big torrents of rain.

It's been almost a year since Justine retired. When you're a ghostwriter, and your author retires, what happens to the ghost? Does the ghost retire too? I thought I'd be able to move on and keep writing the same stuff I was writing for her. Over the years I became so good at being the invisible force behind her writing that I think I disappeared completely.

I hear the door open. It's either a burglar or Omar and I don't think either could get me off this couch. 'I saw you run past. What happened? Are you okay?' Omar asks, rushing to the couch.

'No. Not at all. Loretta called. Hurlington passed.'

'Oh, Sam, I'm so sorry,' he says. 'You'll get the next one.'

'There isn't going to be a next one.'

'Of course there is.' He gently rubs my shoulder.

'Loretta spent all summer submitting my work and that was the last one. I thought I had a real shot at Hurlington since they were Justine's publisher but they think it's too old-fashioned. I feel like such a failure.'

'You are not. You are one of the best writers I know. Look at all the books you've written.'

'Those don't count. Those were under Justine's name.'

'So what? You still wrote them. And *The New York Times* said that the short story you wrote after college that won the Seggerman was…'

'I know. I know,' I say cutting him off. 'A promising voice with a great future,' I repeat the quote that has had to sustain me for more than a decade. 'But that was so long ago. It doesn't even count anymore. *The Times* has been pretty quiet with praise since then. Not that I can blame them – I haven't had anything in my own name in years and years.'

'Let me get my samovar and make you some tea.' Omar only uses the heirloom samovar he brought from Iran in times of celebration or crisis so it signals he's taking this seriously. He dashes out of my apartment to his and is back before my next round of sobs.

'I can't keep at it,' I say to Omar in the kitchen from the couch where I am now completely horizontal. 'I can't deal with all the rejection. For years I write book after book for Justine but when I try going out on my own it's nothing but failure. Maybe I just can't do it. Maybe all I could ever do was parrot her prose.'

'That's not true. You just have to find your own voice.'

'That's what Loretta said. But apparently, my voice is old-fashioned.' The term old-fashioned really stings. I've never been the hippest or coolest guy at the party. 'Omar, you know I'm more likely to quote Katharine Hepburn than Katherine Kardashian,' I shout.

Omar pops his head back in. 'Kourtney, Kim, Khloé, Kendall, Kylie,' he rattles off. 'There is no Katherine.'

'Really, who's the mom again?' I ask.

'Kris,' he says like I'm asking him simple arithmetic.

'See, I am way too out of it to write anything that would sell in today's market.'

Omar brings in two cups of steaming tea, and despite the fact that it's still late summer outside, I drink mine down greedily like each sip will make me feel better.

'We've all been there, Sam. This is just a bump in the road. You know how many times I show my portfolio to a designer or buyer and they reject it.'

'But you know you have what it takes. You know your work is good.'

'I'm not everyone's cup of tea,' he says raising his mug.

'You know it isn't you. It's them. I know the problem is me.'

'That's a problem,' he says. We sip more tea and it does help take the sting out of the rejection just a little bit. 'Oh, I know what will cheer you up.' He grabs his phone and I hear a social media notification on my phone. Ping. Ping. Ping. 'I found the cutest videos of these baby kangaroos. They're so adorable. If they can't make you smile nothing can. I'll send them.' Baby animals do have a way of raising my spirits. I go to open my socials, but before I can see my messages, I see something else that is not adorable at all.

'No way. Are you kidding me?'

A featured post on Tom Colucci my college rival, nemesis, and frenemy. The headline reads, 'Colucci Turns the Tide in Hollywood with Smart, Funny Scripts that Make Inclusion Fun'.

'Arrrrgh!' I scream and send the piece to Omar.

Tom and I lived on the same floor first year of college and from the first competition for floor fire monitor – which he won – to the final contest for graduation speaker – which I won – we were constantly at odds. He has had a string of lucky breaks since then. He parlayed a weekly column at our corrupt student paper into a book deal, which was immediately optioned by a major studio. Then he became a screenwriter finishing scripts the way I finish bags of Doritos. Each time I see his name I get a pit in my stomach and have to remind myself that he churns out horrible, trendy crap that just exploits whatever social media cause is trending.

'He was a marketing major!' I say, although Omar has heard that complaint from me more than once about Tom.

'He never checked the fire extinguishers freshman year. Not once. I looked into it. It was very dangerous. He's a very bad man,' Omar says in a show of solidarity.

Tom may or may not be a bad person. Maybe he got lucky. Maybe he's a genius. Who knows? One thing is for sure. He's incredibly successful. The issue isn't Tom. People love his work. Good for him. I'm more upset about the state of my life. The rejection is just a big moldy cherry on my crap milkshake.

Maybe I should just apply for the full-time position at Brands to the Rescue. It's not a terrible job and going full-time would mean I'd be too busy to even pretend I'm still a writer. Maybe it's time to not exactly give up but change lanes?

'Oh, I almost forgot,' Omar says. 'I saw your mother in Kai's office today and she said—'

'Wait a minute. In his office. What was she doing there?' Kai and my mom know each other enough to wave and chit-chat but why would she be in his office? I don't even go into the office.

Omar shrugs. 'No idea. I made her usual hot water and lemon with a Sweet'n Low and she took it back to his office. She was in there for at least twenty minutes,' he says like it's the most normal thing in the world but I know there is nothing normal about my mother. 'When she came out she told me that she has a big birthday surprise for you. So that's something to look forward to.'

He takes the mugs back into the kitchen. I don't see how my birthday week could get worse but I have a feeling it's about to.

Chapter 6

The morning of my birthday, I lie awake in bed staring at the ceiling. Thirty-five. When I was a kid this age seemed so far away like it existed in another universe. I thought I'd have my life together by now. I pictured a garden apartment with a balcony overlooking Central Park where I'd sip a glass of wine after a long day of writing my next bestseller. My husband would be in the kitchen cooking some fabulous meal after he walked our twin Basset Hounds, Bogart and Bacall. Very *First Wives Club* but without the messy divorce.

That's not the reality I face today.

My romantic life is a series of failures with Paul being the most recent painful example. My career took a left and then a U-turn until it drove off a cliff. My life is a thrift-store jigsaw puzzle with missing pieces someone dumped on a table and forgot.

I look down at my phone for a jolt of serotonin. Birthday messages and posts from friends make me smile. But then I see a message from Paul: *Happy Birthday, Sammy. Enjoy your day. I'd love to celebrate with you.* My first instinct is to delete it and not reply but I'm feeling so low. Some attention from Paul may be exactly what I need. My defenses are down. *Thanks. Sure,* I reply, and he immediately gives me a thumbs up. *Thumbs up?* What have I done? I'm contemplating sending some kind of reply that would reverse my decision to see Paul when there's a knock.

I walk over and open the door. My mother shouts, 'Happy birthday!'

'Thanks, Mom,' I say and we hug. My mother has always been the best hugger in the world. She was designed for hugging. Her ample cushioning allows her to squeeze tightly and make it feel like nothing could ever get in the way. She has an uncanny ability to transfer her love to the hug. Countless times, I've witnessed strangers comment on the high quality of my mom's hugs. She squeezes just right. Once a cashier was in tears after my mom hugged her for accepting a coupon they both knew had expired.

She brushes my hair behind my ears and whispers, 'Happy birthday,' again but this time it's less of an announcement and more a way of saying, *I love you*. She sits down in the chair next to the couch. 'Alright, *Pumpkin Pie*.' She pats her lap. 'Come here.'

'Mom, I'm thirty-five years old now. I think we can do away with…' Before I can get the final words out my mother holds her fingers to her mouth and fake spits.

'Pooh! Pooh!' she says. 'This is tradition and tradition must not be broken.'

I walk over to her and, as tradition dictates, sit on her lap. I try to balance myself with my arms on the side of the couch so I don't crush her. She begins: 'It was the middle of the night and I was staying at your Aunt Shug's.' I look at her face and see that even saying her name is still hard for my mom. It's hard to hear. I wonder if maybe she wants to stop but she pats my head and in my mind I can hear her reminding me that when Aunt Shug was in hospice she kept telling us, 'Life is for the living.'

I lean my head on my mom's shoulder and settle in to hear the story I've heard exactly thirty-four times before. 'It was the middle of the night and I was having this wonderful dream. I was boarding an old-fashioned steamship for a long journey. I carried a large leather valise but I couldn't remember having packed it. When the ship left the dock there were streamers and a big celebration, but I felt sad and lonely until...'

I feel about eight years old, but in a good way. 'The suitcase,' I say. 'The suitcase!'

'That's right.' My mother nods. 'The suitcase starts to move and I open it and there's a beautiful baby smiling and laughing at me, and that baby is you. I knew right then that neither one of us would ever be alone again.' Corny as it sounds, tears come to my eyes. I love my mother very much. As if she knows what I am feeling, she kisses my cheek and then continues, 'When I woke up from the dream I had such a pain in my belly, and I knew you were ready. We called Daddy, who was on a business trip in Albany, and your aunt drove me to the hospital, and six hours and twenty-three minutes later, we were holding the most beautiful baby boy in the entire world in my arms, and his name was Sam. That was exactly thirty-five years ago today and I love that little boy just as much today as I did the day he was born. Even more.'

For a second, I think about how much our little family has changed since I was born. I'm sure my mom thought it was going to be her and my dad and my aunt forever. But Dad died when I was an infant, and now, with my aunt gone, it's really just the two of us. I pick my head up from her shoulder and give my mother a kiss on the cheek. 'I love you, Mom.'

'Happy Birthday,' she croaks – my weight on her lap is suffocating her so I stand up.

'Let me get you some hot water and lemon, Mom.' I head to the kitchen where I keep a ziplock bag of artificial sweetener separate from anything I might eat.

'Thank you, pumpkin, but I want to give you your present,' she says. 'I've been waiting twenty years to give you this.' Twenty years? Has she been malting her own scotch in the basement? I assume I've misheard her and go back to the living room. My mood of tenderness quickly evaporates, giving way to my usual mood of suspicion. I know she has some big surprise planned, and I'm trying to put it off.

'Are you sure you don't want to wait for the water to boil?' I ask.

'I'm sure,' she says. I go back to turn off the stove and then sit on the couch next to her. She hands me the package, with pink and yellow ribbon curling in every direction on top. I shake it a little.

'Is it breakable?' I ask, stalling.

'Don't worry. You can't break it by dropping it on the floor.'

She's a sphinx in a Chico's pantsuit. I shake the box again and I realize it's very light. There's almost no weight to it, so the good news is she hasn't found some hideous rainbow mother–son matching harness for us to wear. A gift card would be great but my mother would never consider a present that allows me the freedom to make my own choices. I realize the only way I can stop her riddles is to open the gift.

'That wrapping paper has only been used a few times, so be careful,' my mother warns me. When she says wrapping paper has only been used a few times she means she bought it when Obama was in office and has used it every birthday and Christmas since. With my mother you get to keep the gift but not the wrapping. I carefully run my finger between the tape and the paper's edge. Mom takes the intact sheet from me and tries to smooth out the creases with her hand on her lap. I slowly take the lid off the box and reveal a slightly yellowed envelope with what looks like a child's bubbly handwriting on it. I turn the envelope over and it all comes back to me.

Chapter 7

I was in eighth grade and had a crush on Matthew Davidson, the gay kid who lived a town away and was two years older. Matthew was cool, aloof and had black spiky hair that looked like he was an anime character. He went to a private school and altered his uniform by cutting out holes in the clip-on tie and stapling anarchy patches on the sleeves. I thought it was the most creative thing I had ever seen. Matthew hated anything conventional so that meant I hated it too. I'd search for information about emo bands on Netscape and wait as our painfully slow router downloaded images of Death Cab for Cutie or Jimmy Eat World. I'd post them to MySpace, hoping Matthew would see them. Secretly I still loved old Hollywood movies and watched Hallmark Christmas specials like they were instruction manuals, but I wanted him to like me.

I had been out less than a year. I know many people struggle to tell their parents they're gay but I didn't have any hesitation. My mother was thrilled. She gave me one of her vise-like hugs and said, 'You're my son. I love you no matter what. Now if you don't clean up your room no *Will and Grace* for the rest of month.' Just like that I was out.

In an effort to be the world's best ally, my mother immediately became the activities chair of the Parents and Friends of Lesbian and Gay Youth (PFLAG) at our regional LGBTQ center. She has always been more into being gay than I've been. I'm gay. I like it. Totally on brand for me. But I don't really think about it.

The center was having an alternative prom for kids from all over the area. My mother was in charge of decorations and the entire house was covered in colorful tissue paper flowers she had been making for weeks. The theme was 'Rainbow in Paradise' which sounded more like a religious cult than a decorative motif. Matthew thought the whole thing was dumb but said we should show up dressed all goth as a kind of protest. I wasn't sure what we were protesting. Color, I guess? People were planning to wear prom attire to match the Rainbow Pride theme, but Matthew told me to dress entirely in black to stir things up, so when my best friend and personal LGBTQ ally, Patty Perkins, came over, we went to my room and closed the door to get ready away from my mother's prying eyes. Mom hated my goth phase and never missed an opportunity to tell me I looked like I was going to a funeral instead of nineth-grade algebra.

Patty was wearing the gorgeous pink taffeta vintage cocktail dress we had spent weeks searching for at local thrift stores. I had found a totally ironic powder-blue tuxedo that I had been planning to wear. My mother kept saying, 'You'll look very handsome in it,' which only made me want to wear it less. I kept it hung up in my room so she would think I was changing into it, but when the door closed, I showed Patty my revised ensemble.

· 'Oh, Sam, I don't know. Your mother will flip out,' she said as she straightened her crinoline.

'I know,' I said, 'that's why I also have this.' I took out a long trench coat I found on sale at the mall. I figured I would wear it over my goth ensemble on the way to the dance so my mother wouldn't see what I was wearing until we arrived. By then it would be too late to go home and change.

Mom hovered by the door as we changed, and before we exited my room, I tightly pulled the belt on the trench despite the fact that it was the warmest day in May since records were kept, according to the news. I tried to run through the living room and straight to the car but my mother would not have it.

'Sam, I want to get some pictures before we go, slow down.' Mom was wearing a kaftan made of a fabric with so many colors that it was hard to look at.

'Look at the time,' I said and pointed to the gold clock that hung above an arrangement of silk flowers on the buffet. 'We're so late. Let's just do it there.'

My mother pulled a chair from the table. 'We have plenty of time,' she said as she climbed the chair to stand in front of the clock. 'I moved the clock ahead fifteen minutes this morning because I knew you wouldn't be on time.' She stretched her arm and moved the big hand back to the correct time. The woman is a mastermind.

I looked at Patty. Her parents were totally normal, so whenever she came over to my house, she stared at my mom and me like we were exhibits in a museum for the socially bizarre. Patty shrugged her shoulders, not sure how to help me. I had no other choice. I undid the belt of my trench and let the coat drop to the floor like Lady Godiva about to defiantly ride through town. My black jeans were so shredded they had a fifty-fifty chance of making it to the dance without disintegrating completely and my faded black T-shirt with an anarchy symbol in blood red had safety pins holding together the slashes I made across the front the night before.

'Sam!' my mother shrieked. 'What in the world are you wearing? You look like you're going to a Halloween party on the bad side of town.'

'Mother, this is the bad side of town,' I said formally. It was true. Patty came from the rich end and we were broke but that wasn't the point.

'What happened to that gorgeous baby-blue tuxedo? You look so handsome in it.'

'I changed my mind. I want to wear this,' I said stubbornly.

'Sam, this is a party. Kids from all over the area are coming. You might meet someone special.' She sang the last sentence. 'You are such a handsome young man I just don't understand why you hide it with all that black dreck lately.' She wrinkled her nose and frowned.

I hated when my mom would call me a 'handsome young man'. I never felt that way. Her saying it made me feel even less handsome. I was a little chunkier back then and my skin wasn't exactly ready for the after in an Accutane commercial. I liked the baggy clothes and dark colors. They helped me feel more hidden and the fact that Matthew thought they were cool didn't hurt.

'I like what I'm wearing. Why can't I wear what I want to wear?' I was more whining than yelling. I thought about calling Aunt Shug to referee but she was sometimes too impartial and I wanted to win this fight. I had to.

'Don't you want to meet someone at the dance? It could be a special night.'

'Mom I'm fifteen,' I said and I knew exactly what she was going to say.

'I met your father when I was sixteen. It's a magical age. The love of your life could be at this and he won't ask you to dance because he'll think you're in mourning.'

Little did she know I was dressed this way because I wanted the guy I liked to ask me to dance and there was no way that was going to happen in that silly tuxedo.

'I want to wear what I want to wear.' I crossed my arms.

'Sam, no.'

We went back and forth for a while and then I made my big mistake. 'If I don't have a boyfriend by the time I'm thirty-five I'll follow all your rules until I get one but for now just let me wear what I want.' I don't know why I said it. I just picked an age that seemed so far in the future it was impossible to imagine.

I could see her mind jumping ahead. She squinted her eyes, shifted her weight, and put her arms on her hip. 'Can I have that in writing?' she asked.

'Can I wear what I want to the dance?' I parried. She nodded.

I submitted to her ludicrous request, assuming it was simply a symptom of my mother's burgeoning insanity. Mom led me to the desk in the kitchen and retrieved a pen and a piece of Snoopy writing paper. She insisted that I write down my promise, and that I sign and date it. Suddenly, I was nervous. It was an odd request even from my mother who forbade me from swimming within one hour of eating pickles of any kind. Patty, who had been silently observing the exchange, meekly piped up, 'Sam, just do it or we'll be late.' I begrudgingly took the paper and pen from my mother and scrawled out:

> *I, Sam Carmichael, being of sound mind and body, hereby promise to follow all my mother's rules for dating to get a boyfriend if I do not have one by the time I am thirty-five.*

I signed my name, dated it, and handed it to my mother.

'Fine.' She handed a colored pencil to Patty. 'You sign as a witness.'

Patty looked at me. I shrugged. I'm sure she had no idea what to do. My mother handed her the paper and she scrawled her name across the bottom. But that wasn't enough for my mother.

'Don't forget the date, Patty. I saw an episode of _Law and Order_ and the date was very important.' Patty just nodded and added the numbers. My mother smiled, folded the paper carefully, tucked it into a drawer and opened the back door. 'Let's go,' she said and we were off to the dance.

By the time we arrived, Matthew was already dancing with a tall soccer player from a school on the other side of the county, and his apparent disdain for all things conventional was lost somewhere in the soccer player's mouth, since I found him searching for it with his tongue later that evening. The fact that the object of Matthew's affection was wearing a vintage powder-blue tuxedo was difficult to overlook, but I remember distinctly trying to block out every detail of the night, including the silly ultimatum from my mother.

Twenty years later, that same exact piece of Snoopy stationery is staring me in the face like some Faustian souvenir. Snoopy looks more yellow than white and the edges of the envelope are mildly frayed. I hand the box and its contents back to my mother and stand up from the couch. 'Mom, you have got to be kidding. Is this some kind of joke? Ha. Ha. Just give me the underwear you found on clearance at Target and we can be done with the presents.'

'I'm not kidding. This is no joke. And I do have underwear for you from Target that was on clearance but this, this is your real gift.' My mother looks at me quite seriously. 'Sam, this is my present to you.'

'Mom, I wrote it almost two decades ago.'

'So what? The bra I'm wearing is older than that.'

She is not about to back down. 'Mom, I was only joking when I did it.'

'You want me to call Patty Perkins? She teaches sociology at Penn State. She knows you weren't joking.'

I can't believe she has tracked down Patty Perkins. I'm sure Patty considers her encounters with my family her first research into abnormalities. 'Look, when I wrote that I was a minor,' I say since she wants to go the legal route.

'I don't care if you were a sergeant major. A promise is a promise. And look how lucky this turned out for you! How many people have a full-time dating coach... for free? And the timing couldn't be better.'

'It couldn't be worse,' I mumble under my breath. She has no idea that the last few days have almost broken me.

'What are you talking about? The Wedding isn't until December. That's plenty of time to find you a date.'

I am about to remind her that she is not allowed to mention The Wedding until after my birthday but I suppose this is close enough. My cousin on my father's side is getting married to the 'girl of his dreams' in December just before the holidays. That side of the family is a conservative nightmare, and we generally try to avoid their judgmental stares, but my cousin is the one exception. He's gentle and sweet and about as sharp as a jellybean left out in the rain. I've been dreading every aspect of the event since we got a Save the Date card that I tore into little pieces.

'You've done such a good job not talking about The Wedding. Can't we just keep that up?'

'I don't want to go any more than you do. Who wants to be in the same room as your Uncle Donald even if it is at The Plaza in the Grand Ballroom and they reserved an entire table for us? Ziggy is your only cousin and he's a good person. We are going to support him. It's not his fault who his parents are.'

Tell me about it. 'I don't need to show up to the wedding with a date to support him.' With that side of the family, it's one thing to have an 'alternative lifestyle' but quite another to be single and in your mid-thirties.

'This isn't about the wedding. Showing up with a date for the event is just a bonus. I'm going to dedicate myself to helping you find a boyfriend. I will not rest until you find what you are looking for.' She says this like Ingrid Bergman dedicating herself to the resistance in *Casablanca*. 'Or a girlfriend or a nice couple in case you are discovering you're bi or poly. It doesn't matter to me.'

'I'm still just gay, Mom.'

'Oh well, okay then. Hold on.' She grabs her purse and takes out a notebook. She turns a few pages and then takes a pencil that I am sure she took from a miniature golf course somewhere and starts scribbling.

'What are you doing?'

'I'm just crossing out the couples. That's a shame. I met the nicest one the other day on the street. Tim and Tom. Isn't that sweet?' She sighs loudly. It's more performative than functional. 'That's too bad because you're just the right height for them.' Another sigh.

'How is someone the right height for a throuple?' I ask.

'One of them is shorter than you and one of them is taller?'

'You measured them?'

'Yes, but just with that thing on my phone.' I imagine my mother on a New York street corner trying to figure out how to turn off the flashlight on her iPhone so she can measure some random couple in case they'd be interested in her son joining their relationship. 'You would fit right in the middle, which is nice. Like steps. Boom, boom, boom.' She sings the words and waves her hand like a leaf falling off a tree.

'Mom, that is not how throuples work. Height is not important.'

'Of course it is. If two of the people are tall and one is short it can be awkward in photos to get the right composition.'

'People are not in throuples to look good in pictures.'

'I know that,' she says and rolls her eyes at me. 'What makes you an expert on throuples? You aren't even in one. Let's face it, Sam. You aren't throuple material.' She sits down and puts the notebook in her lap. 'I'm just going to tear out the page with women.' She takes a short ruler out of her purse and tears the page against it so the edge is neat. I stand over and look down at the notebook. Oh, no. This is bad. Very bad. She has color-coded tabs. When my mother is using color-coded tabs, she means business.

'Mom, I do not need your help finding a boyfriend.' She doesn't say anything. 'And who says I even want a boyfriend?' I wanted Paul as recently as earlier this morning. But that's just Paul. I want closure, I think. Not a relationship. I don't know.

'I'm your mother. Look me in the eye and tell me you don't want to meet someone.' She takes off her enormous glasses and opens her eyes as wide as she can. She stands up and stares at me like she's trying to dive into my soul, a place I have always tried to keep her out of. 'Go ahead, tell me. Say it.'

In my head I'm telling myself just to say the words. It will get her off my back and end this ridiculousness. *I don't want a boyfriend.* The words are simple enough to say. I try to conjure them in my throat. I look at my mom staring at me and the words slink back down my throat and disappear.

She sits back down. 'Now that that's settled let me tell you what I am thinking in terms of your dating profiles and—'

'Mom, no. I am not doing this. Why would I? Why would I ever agree to this?'

'Because you promised. And a promise is a promise. Also, I know what I'm doing. Remember when I put soy sauce on your vanilla ice cream because I misread the label. It turned out to be delicious. I know how to put things together.'

'It was not. It was disgusting,' I say.

'You ate the whole bowl.' She's right. But I did that because I love ice cream. 'I just want to see you find someone.'

'You just want to ruin my life.' I sit down on the couch and throw my head back in a sign of non-violent protest.

She pats my thigh. 'Oh, my sweet boy. You are just on top of your feels.'

'I'm *in* my feels. In. Not *on top*, Mom.'

'Pumpkin Pie. I know you aren't a top,' She stands up, looks me up and down and smiles to herself. 'Anyone can tell you're a bossy bottom. Now enjoy the rest of your day. Happy birthday.' She kisses me on the forehead and leaves.

Chapter 8

It takes a full day to recover from my birthday. Despite my initial objections, Omar made sure that I had access to ample tequila, pulsating dance music, and a boisterous group of friends from the neighborhood, all to help me escape my troubles. There's no shortage of queer bars in Hell's Kitchen and we hit all our favorites. I spent yesterday with a splitting headache but today I am feeling more myself. I wake up and find Omar making breakfast in my kitchen, which means his is covered in too much fabric to be functional. A foggy memory comes to me as I sit down at the table to join him.

'I had the craziest dream last night. My mother showed up here on my birthday with this idea that I let her be in charge of my dating life.' I rub my eyes trying to get to a more alert state but the dread I felt in the dream lingers.

Omar puts his coffee down, walks over to me and puts his hand on my shoulder. 'Sam, that wasn't a dream. That's your reality.' Then the memory of the morning of my birthday rushes back. My mother. The Letter. The Promise.

'She doesn't think I would seriously consider it, does she? It's not… real.'

Omar raises his thick eyebrows. 'We are talking about your mother, correct?'

I collapse on the table in the kitchen.

'Can I make you a coffee?' Omar asks.

I nod and rest my head in my hands. 'She's out of her mind. There's no way I would allow this. Like I would let my mother pick the men I date.' Omar pours an espresso from the tiny aluminum mocha pot. The rich brown liquid is capped with a tan foam that coats my spoon as I stir. I take a sip and the caffeine helps me remember the details of my current nightmare. 'Yesterday she texted six times asking for my password to SecretSlam and a bunch of apps I've never even heard of like something called FeetFanatics. My mother thinks she's going to create a sex profile for my feet?' I'm almost shouting the last bit. I guess it's going to take longer than twenty-four hours to recover.

'Well, maybe it's not such a terrible idea,' Omar says without looking at me.

I almost do a spit take, but the espresso is too good and too expensive to waste. 'You approve of my mother pimping out my feet?'

'No, not that part, although I wouldn't be so quick to judge anyone's fetish. What makes a foot so different from a bicep or an elbow? And you have very nice feet.' It's too early in the morning for me to start ranking the inherent eroticism of different body parts. 'What would be so bad about going along with her plan? Sam, you're my best friend, but let's face it. Your dating life isn't exactly...' Omar searches for the right word.

'Don't say it. I know.'

'And you can't say you don't want a boyfriend because I know you do, or else you wouldn't have put up with Paul for as long as you did,' he says in a rare moment of disapproval. Is that why I was with Paul? Just because I wanted a boyfriend? 'You just happen to pick the wrong men.' For a second, I think about protesting, but he's not wrong. Ever since Matthew back in New Jersey I've had a keen ability to pick guys who are unavailable emotionally or physically or in any other capacity in which lack of availability would apply.

I've tried to learn from my mistakes. Guys who were my age or younger than me were often sexy but almost always emotionally immature so they were off my list. Guys who didn't have gainful employment were usually fun to be with but lacked stability. They got a strike-through. But the biggest black mark I held was against artists. I dated more than my share, and they always turned out to be self-involved, and the minute I asked for something more, they dumped me. I thought someone like Paul was perfect. Older, great job, non-artist. At this point I've either created the perfect list or a room without a door.

'How much worse could she be at picking dates than you are? Because of your mom, Damola met Jimena.'

I was worried this would be entered into evidence. Our friend Damola lives on the top floor and uses Plant Daddy as the base of operations for both his dog-walking business and his music production. He remixes sounds from early hip-hop tracks. He's friendly, quiet and doesn't mind being polite to my mother when he passes her in the building. About a year ago, my mom met the most beautiful woman working at the cosmetics counter at Bloomingdale's. What my mother was doing at Bloomingdale's remains a mystery. Somehow she found out the woman was volunteering at a fundraiser for Healing Justice at the Audre Lord Project. My mom purchased a ticket for Damola so he could attend the event as well. She thought they would be a good match. Now they live together in apartment 5-b in cohabitational bliss.

'That's different. My mother sees Damola and Jimena for who they are, as adults. My mother still sees me as the little boy who needs help crossing the street and tying his shoe.'

'You did almost get hit in the bike lane last week on the way to the gym. I had to physically pull you back,' Omar says and I give him a sharp look.

'I'm an adult. I know what I'm doing.'

Omar takes a sip of his coffee. 'Do you?' My phone rings. It's her. I'm sure it's her. I'm awake enough at this point to realize it was not a nightmare. She has been calling me non-stop since she introduced her scheme. It's time to put it to an end. I will pick up and tell her in no uncertain terms that she can forget about it.

'No. No. Absolutely not. No. No way,' I say before she can even get a hello in.

'In the South we usually just answer the phone with some form of hello,' a husky voice with a laid-back drawl says. I'm still in my morning fog so I don't recognize the caller.

'Who is this?' I snap.

'This is Finn.'

'Yes. Of course,' I say and my voice cracks. I'm mortified by how I answered. I rub my eyes and try to focus.

'Right. Finn Montgomery, we were supposed to...' Suddenly I remember I asked him to meet me at Plant Daddy for a coffee this morning to get started on his rebranding. I look down at my watch and realize I'm over twenty minutes late. This is not a good way to start.

'I'm so sorry. I got very behind today. I'm sorry.' I don't know what else to do. 'Are you there now? At Plant Daddy?'

'Yeah,' he says.

'I live in the building. A few flights up. I'll be down in five minutes. Tell Kai that you're waiting for me and they'll take care of you. Short, grey whiskers. Stunning wrinkles around his eyes. He's usually wearing a paisley shirt and watering something.'

'Met him. Made me an oat milk matcha latte and scolded me for touching the leaves of a rhododendron he was watering.'

'Yes, that sounds like him. I'll be right down.'

I run to my room and don't even change. The sleep pants and T-shirt I'm wearing can double as streetwear. As I brush my teeth, I notice that my hair is sticking up like a collection of stalagmites in a cave so I grab a baseball cap from the back of my door.

I race down the stairs, walk out of the building, and stand outside Plant Daddy to look through the window. I see a few of the regulars at various tables. Damola is hunched over his laptop with his headphones on, with Jimena next to him working on her beaded jewelry. Madame Angelika is doing a Tarot card reading. Maggie is next to the register with her foot on her opposite knee in some kind of yoga pose.

I keep scanning the room until my eyes stop on Finn. He's at a table in a back corner, away from everyone, with his laptop opened in front of him like a shield. I can tell he's observing people but keeping his distance. Maybe he's not sure what to make of the denizens of Plant Daddy.

I open the door and Kai rolls past me with a container of coffee beans on the tray of his wheelchair. 'Thanks for taking care of Finn,' I say as I pass. He nods, and I can tell he's still stinging from the leaf-touching situation. I give quick hellos to the friends I saw through the window and take a seat across from the man I'm going to be working with for the next few months.

'Finn, I'm so sorry for being late. I apologize.'

He looks at me for a few seconds. I'm suddenly wishing I took an extra minute to change or take a shower or comb my hair or anything that might help my appearance. He's wearing tight jeans and a black T-shirt that clings to his body in the right areas. His attractiveness seems so effortless. It takes an act of Congress to make me presentable.

'This is a great place,' Finn says breaking the silence as he looks around Plant Daddy. 'I love the vibe here.' Kai has created a Hell's Kitchen version of Barnaby Lane. People meet friends here, do work, hang out and sometimes buy coffee or plants. There's always something going on, and I'm grateful to live a few floors up, even if my studio sometimes has water that looks like acid rain. Old pipes are a small price to pay.

'Kai is a great guy but don't let him hear me say that. He prides himself on being a cranky old man but we all know better. Just be careful around the plants. He takes them very seriously.'

'So I learned. He slapped my hand.' He rubs his left hand with his right which must still sting. 'Hard.'

'Maggie overwatered a bonsai a year ago, and she still hears about it. But he's the one who makes this place special. A bunch of us just sort of hang out here and he never cares if we nurse a cup of coffee all day and work on a gig or even if we don't buy coffee at all. He says humans give off CO_2, so he only puts up with us to help the plants, but no one believes him.'

'I watched you walk in. Looks like you know everyone in here.' Finn is keenly observant.

'I do,' I say with a shrug. 'I mean not everyone.' I look around, and there's one woman with a stroller who I don't know. 'Not her.' I nod my head in the young mother's direction and then I remember I chatted with her last week about a friend of mine who sells organic baby food upstate. 'I've lived upstairs a while, and Hell's Kitchen is like a queer, diverse small town inside a big city.'

'Yeah, I get that vibe, but small towns can be just as intimidating as big cities,' he says with a bit of apprehension in his voice. He seemed so confident when we met in the office the other day but less so here. 'New York is overwhelming. Inspiring but it's a lot. Still, it's a great place for artists. Is that why you're here?'

I thought I came to New York to become an artist but instead the opposite seems to have happened. I've slowly become something else. What exactly? I'm not sure. I knew when I was ghosting for Justine I was artist adjacent. I thought if I could get something published in my own name... *Why is he even asking me these things?* Most people I work with for Brands love to talk about themselves. I once did a profile on a startup guy who called me Frank for the entire month. I never corrected him.

'What makes you think I'm an artist and not just some guy doing his job?' I ask.

'I looked you up. I take my career seriously and I didn't want to put it in the hands of just anyone. You won a Seggerman award for a short story. Very impressive. Tried to find a copy of it online but couldn't. Maybe you can send it to me?' That damn short story award still comes up when you search my name. It's so embarrassing. I was

65

proud at the time but now it just reminds me that I peaked too early.

'Sure,' I mumble without any intention of doing so.

'Tell me what you're working on now?'

Why does he want to know anything about me? I guess this is the price for being assigned someone who does documentary photography instead of someone who's overcome nausea.

'Right now, I'm working on building your brand. I'm the one who is supposed to be asking the questions.'

'I'm sorry. I can't help it. When I meet someone and I get a vibe that there's more than what's on the surface I want to know more. I can't turn off my instinct.' When I first came in, he seemed uncomfortable, but now that we're talking about work, he's confident again. At least he's talking about himself. I use the opening to refocus the meeting. 'Tell me about what *you* are working on?' I ask, emphasizing the pronoun *you* so that he understands I am throwing the ball to his court.

'Sure,' he says. 'I'm not scared to talk about *my* work.' Is he poking fun at me? Is he implying that I'm scared to talk about my work? I'm not scared – I just don't have anything to talk about. Then, for a split-second, I wonder if the reason I don't have anything to talk about is because I'm scared. Luckily, he begins talking, and I start taking notes.

Finn Montgomery has been working as a photographer since he got an MFA at Cal Arts. He is well-known for his series of photographs documenting queer cultures and sub-cultures in the South. He uses a combination of portraiture, abstraction, and ethnography. I saw some of the images at Brands to the Rescue and they have been in my mind ever since. Soulful portraits that are simultaneously beautiful and painful. His latest work focuses on the lives of queer immigrants who have come to this country to escape persecution and, in some instances, threats of death in their homeland. He's relocated to New York for the project.

'It's a very serious subject matter and I try to give it the respect it deserves,' he says.

'Of course,' I say. 'I take other people's work very seriously. It's only myself I don't do that with.'

'Queer refugees often escape a life of darkness. They want their lives in this country to be full of light and hope.'

I write down what he says and I try to capture that last bit as accurately as possible. I re-read my words. He has this way of talking about himself and his work that isn't cocky or boasting. He talks about the people he photographs and how he works with them to tell their story. It's very humble but not self-effacing. A balance I've never understood. 'You should meet them,' he says and closes his laptop.

'Who?'

'Some of the people sharing their story.'

'That would be great but, ah, where are you going? We're just getting started. I have a lot more I need to know.'

'I've got an appointment. Sorry,' he says. 'I have a rule. I don't keep people waiting.' *Ouch.* I think that's a dig but it's not undeserved. 'Text me and we can set something up.' He grabs his bag and heads out. I look down at my notebook and realize I barely have enough to get started.

Kai suddenly appears at my side pulling the brake on his chair. 'Did he tell you?'

'Tell me what?' I ask Kai.

'Guess who Finn asked to be in his latest documentary project? None other than everyone's favorite queer disabled he/they plant-loving, coffee-serving Indonesian immigrant. He wants me to tell my story.' Kai's usually prickly tone takes a back seat to enthusiasm.

'That's great, Kai.' I was thinking about their story when Finn was talking. Kai puts Finn's empty latte glass on his tray and then wheels over to the window and takes down the 'Help Wanted' sign.

'You found someone?'

'Yep. I think this person is going to be a great fit. They've been in here before and they were looking for something in this area. On this block actually.'

'That's pretty specific. Is it someone I know?'

'You could say that.' His eyes dart down to the floor.

I wonder if it's Tony, that guy who only drinks tea with three teabags. I think I heard him say he was looking for an extra gig.

'Is it Tony?'

'Someone you know better than that,' he says. 'They're going to be here any minute for their first shift.'

The bells above the door ring and there in the doorway wearing her *Sounds Gay I'm In* T-shirt and aqua high-tops is…

'Gloria Carmichael reporting for duty.' She holds her arm above her forehead in a sharp salute.

'Mom, what are you doing here?' This must be a nightmare. I thought I was having one earlier but maybe this is one of those dreams within a dream.

'I work here now. Didn't Kai tell you?' she asks turning toward him.

'I thought it would be more fun as a surprise.' A sneaky grin crosses his face.

'Kai, what have you done?' I think about grabbing the 'Help Wanted' sign he took down and taping it back to the window.

'What he has done, my son, is make a very smart choice. I know a lot about plants and I can learn to make the matchie mucha mochas or whatever they are,' my mother says proudly.

'But… I live upstairs.' I point to the ceiling. 'I'm here all the time. This is where I work. It's where I hang out.'

'I know,' my mother says, joy oozing out of her. 'And they just changed the bus schedule, so I can take an express on Tuesdays and Thursdays, unless there's a religious holiday. In that case, I'll have to change buses, but it will still only take thirty minutes. Unless there's traffic, but I figure there won't be much on religious holidays. Isn't it wonderful how this all worked out?' She rushes toward me and wraps her arms around my body in one of her trademark squeezes; the smell of her rose-scented perfume envelops me.

'Yes, wonderful,' I say giving Kai the dirtiest look I can make. 'I have an appointment I have to get to.' I release myself from my mother's grip.

'Oh,' she says, excitement running through her voice. 'Is it a date?' She looks at me and then scrunches her face in disapproval. 'Because you'll need to change. As long as I'm in charge you are not going on a date wearing… that.'

'There is nothing wrong with what I'm wearing.' There is a lot wrong with what I'm wearing. I ran down here in glorified pajamas. 'It's not a date. And more importantly you're not in charge of anything in my life. I am a full-grown person. I am able to choose my own dates and my own life!'

She is silent and then looks toward Kai. 'See, this is why you're so smart. Plants don't mind when you are just trying to help them.'

'True,' he says. 'Though I do have a ficus that can get a bit fresh with me. Let me show you.' He gestures for my mom and they head to the group of plants by the window and the ficus that I know in fact can be a bit saucy.

'Mom, you can forget about your ridiculous plan,' I shout back to them as I pack up my stuff to leave but they both ignore me as they head to the other side of Plant Daddy. 'I mean it,' I say knowing they can still hear me. 'That contract won't hold up in a court of law.' At least, I don't think it would. Would it?

Chapter 9

I practice my smile in the mirror before I head out to meet Paul. No. Too dopey. I try again. I want to appear sexy and confident. 'Hello, Paul,' I say lowering my voice as far as I can. Too Samuel L. Jackson in *Pulp Fiction*. 'Hi Paul!' I say, upbeat and chipper. No. Too Shirley Temple. 'Ugh!' Maybe this was a big mistake. I could just text him and cancel. But I'm too curious to see what he wants and to find out why he's back in New York. And maybe there's a chance things have changed. Maybe I could make things work with Paul. Again.

I walk out of my apartment and the sticky evening air of early September embraces me. It's too warm for the tight, deep olive textured T-shirt with a plaid button-up shirt and chunky sweater I'm wearing. I wanted to have enough layers on to metaphorically suggest that I am a complex person who has changed over the past nine months since he's been gone.

I peer down the block to make sure my mother isn't lurking. Now that she's working downstairs I'll have to walk out the front door and turn away from Plant Daddy so she doesn't see me, and then head all the way down to Tenth Avenue and U-turn on the next block so I can get on a train to meet Paul at a cafe by his old apartment in Tribeca.

The whole train ride, I'm telling myself to turn around, but there's something about Paul that I can't resist. I met him after a bad breakup with a guy I had been seeing for over a year named Anders. Contrary to what my mother thinks, I can, in fact, find a boyfriend. I've had a ton of them. None of them have really stuck, but I did think after Anders, Paul was the one. Anders didn't so much break my heart as much as he broke my spirit. He was my TA in college but we didn't start seeing each other until after I graduated. Still, it was a bad idea from the start. He was also a writer but worked mainly in creative non-fiction, which I thought made him a perfect match. I told him about this story idea I was working on and he thought it was amazing and that we should write it together. I wrote an outline and we would bang out a few scenes before or after banging each other. He went away to some writing retreat and I was busy working on my latest ghostwriting project for Justine 'Divorce Hamptons-style'. But after Anders left for the retreat, I never saw him again. I was ghosted while ghostwriting. A few weeks after that I saw that he had sold *our* screenplay, which was really my screenplay, to a major studio. I should have sued. I should have confronted him. But I didn't. I thought it was my fault. I told myself that he didn't think I was talented enough to pull it off so he left because it would have been hard to tell me the truth. The whole thing stung so bad I swore off all artists and all romances.

But along came Paul and he seemed like the perfect antidote. He was a patent attorney in a large firm and had wanted to be a patent attorney since he was a kid, which is odd but also kind of nice. He was more than a dozen years older than me. I liked that. Being with a guy who is more mature makes me feel safe and taken care of. Not in any financial way exactly. Paul was able to pay for a lot of things I could never have afforded, but it was more about feeling like I was with someone who had already figured out so much of what I was still struggling to get a hold of.

When we first started dating, he told me that he and his husband had been separated for more than a year and they were working on a divorce but it was complicated. He told me they still lived in the same apartment because, well, you know New York real estate. He told me lie after lie after lie and I believed every last one. I told myself I believed his lies because I was stupid but that wasn't the only reason. I'm ashamed to admit I believed them because I wanted to believe them.

When he told me that he and Todd were moving to California and going into therapy to save their marriage, I was devastated. I thought Paul loved me. He'd surprise me with flowers. He'd take me to a lodge upstate for the weekend and stock the room with my favorite cookies, fulfilling my Old Hollywood-based romantic fantasies and satisfying my sweet tooth. He was always trying to impress me. It made me feel important to him. I thought I had a future with Paul. It's horrible to be dumped but even worse to be dumped and feel stupid and ashamed.

I'm intentionally late to my coffee with Paul. I didn't want to be the one waiting for him again. Let him wait for me. I planned to walk in all cold and calculated – Louise Fletcher as Nurse Ratched in *One Flew Over the Cuckoo's Nest* but slightly less criminally insane. I'll show him that his leaving didn't have any impact on me at all. Most importantly, I will not be emotional.

I walk in and hide behind a column so I can survey the room but I don't see him.

'Sammy!'

I jump hearing that name. Only one person in the world calls me Sammy, and as soon as I hear it, my heart melts just a bit. He taps me on the shoulder. I turn around, and I can't help but hug him. It's an involuntary reaction like when the doctor hits your knee with that rubber triangle hammer.

'Oh, Paul,' I say. 'It's great to see you.' I can't hold back how nice it feels to be here with him. This is the opposite of what I was planning to do. I can't help it. I'm a hugger. I see something that makes me feel a certain way and I hug it. I get that from my mother.

'Sammy, sorry I got held up. Let me get us a table.'

'Oh sure,' I say. 'No problem. I understand.' I follow Paul to the table and make sure there aren't any mirrors where he can see me smack myself in the forehead for being so weak. I promise myself that when I sit down I will not be the doormat I was back when we were dating... or when I met him at the door of the cafe a minute ago.

We sit down and Paul orders his usual. 'May I please have a dark roast ristretto ground at the finest setting with a side of oat milk heated to 120 degrees and a shot of seltzer. *Grazie.*' He spent a month in Florence two years ago and sprinkles Italian into his conversation often.

At this place I usually order something so sweet and creamy that it's more of a hot milkshake than a coffee but today I say, 'Just black coffee, thank you.'

Paul wrinkles his nose. 'Black coffee? Sammy, it's close enough to PSL time. Why not get yourself some pumpkin, cinnamon, vanilla, hazelnut thing like you like?' His voice is almost condescending, and if his description didn't make my mouth water, I would call him on it.

'No, thank you. Coffee. Black,' I say to the server and smile wondering how I'm going to choke that down.

74

'Paul, I did not decide to meet you to have you review my coffee order. You're lucky I showed up at all. I'm only here because Omar said I should find out what you want in order to be on guard.' Not true at all but the last thing I owe Paul is honesty. 'Now, what do you want?' I ask, shooting my words across the table, finally proud of myself for displaying the attitude I wanted. I knew it was deep down there somewhere.

Paul looks at me and pushes his round tortoiseshell glasses up his nose. It feels so good to be in his gaze again, to have his attention. The grey scruff on his face makes him look distinguished and important. I loved the way it felt against my cheek. Then his mouth opens and he says the two words I thought I would never hear him say: 'I'm sorry.'

'You're what?' I ask. I genuinely don't believe what I've heard. Paul always had an excuse. I've heard him say 'It's not my fault' hundreds of times but 'I'm sorry' is a new one.

'When I got to California...'

And as soon as I hear him say *I*, I find the strength to challenge him.

'No, Paul. Use the correct pronoun. Not *I*. You mean *we*. When *we* got to California.' I'm not going to let him use grammar to hide his deceit.

'You're right. When Todd and I got to California. When *we* were there.' He says *we* like he's learning a new language. 'I realized how much I missed you. How much I missed us. That's why I got this.' He takes out an envelope from his jacket and pushes it across the table the way they pretend to show salary numbers on TV.

'What's that?' I fold my arms over my chest. I have no intention of taking the bait.

'The proof that I am serious this time. I've retained a lawyer. I'm getting a divorce.'

'Really?' I ask with way too much hope in my voice as my eyebrows rise to the top of my forehead.

'Yes, this is the retainer. Proof. Open it. Please.' His eyes turn soft, and my hands reach across the table for the envelope. I open it and read that Paul has retained Marcia Woo as his lawyer in the case of Diller vs Pearson. It's true. It's real. Paul is finally getting the divorce he had promised me he was getting for years. I don't know what to say. I have so many questions. Why now? Why not before he left over nine months ago? Is he getting bored or is this really, truly happening? But I can't get any of those questions out of my mouth. I just sit in silence.

'I hurt you. I messed things up. I thought I could make things work with Todd but the further I got from you, the more I missed you. I missed you so much Sammy. You have to believe that.' I want to believe it, and wanting it makes believing easier.

'I missed you too, Paul,' I say. I'm speaking from my heart. I have missed him. I haven't missed feeling like his second choice, but if I'm not second choice anymore, maybe none of that matters? He moves his hands across the table for mine but I'm not ready for that. 'Tell me why you're here?'

'To apologize, to explain everything to you.'

'No, I mean, why are you here in New York? I thought you were taking a position at the Los Angeles office. You said New York is over.' The very thought that New York is over fills me with rage like I'm Carrie Bradshaw circa 2002. I came to conquer this city. It has beaten me, but I'm still here.

He shakes his head. 'I'm coming back. As soon as the divorce is final, I'll be back in New York. I've already arranged it with the firm. Had a few meetings with the New York office this week. The subletter leaves at the end of the year, and I'll move back in, but I'm hoping it will be "We'll move back in." I want us to live together.'

'What?' I ask so loudly it surprises me and the woman at the next table who looks over to see what the commotion is. 'Paul, you can't seriously think I'm going to believe you this time. How stupid do you think I am?'

He raises his hand to his chest. 'I think I'm stupid. Not you. I think you are exactly what I need. I'm an idiot for not realizing it. I had to leave here to see it. The summer has been miserable. I thought about you all the time.' He tilts his chin down a bit and then asks, 'Did you think about me?' The words come out slowly. Is this vulnerability or the performance of vulnerability? I can never tell with Paul.

Over the nine months since our breakup, I thought about Paul more than I'd like to admit. Poor Omar has sat on the couch with me so many nights as I cried my eyes out over another broken promise but once Paul was gone I could only remember the good times. All summer, I've replayed in my mind the dinners where we talked about our favorite places to travel or when we would meet at the gym to work out together, followed by a different kind of workout back at my apartment. Paul was so easy to be with. He asked almost nothing of me except that I put up with his lies.

'No, I did not think about you. Not at all.' I look down at the document he pushed in front of me. Could he be telling the truth? What if this time really is different and I'm being too stubborn to see it? What if I really could have a future with Paul? I look down at the paper again and hold it up to him.

'Is this for real?' I ask.

'Yes. In fact, you can keep that one. It's a copy but it's real. I have to fly back to Cali in two days but I want to use that time to show you how sorry I am. Let me make everything up to you and convince you to move in with me in January.'

'Paul, I don't know what to say.' That's only a few months away. I'm not sure this is a good idea.

'Don't say anything. Not yet. Just give me two days to show you I'm serious.' He reaches his hand out and puts it on my knee, and the sensation of his thick, strong hand on my leg makes me shut my eyes so I can prevent my groin from showing him that everything from my waist down does not need two days to make a decision. It's ready now.

He keeps his hand on my leg but slowly moves his gaze up to my eyes. 'I have a suite at The Simpson just a few blocks away. It has a great view. Do you still love to watch the traffic enter and exit the Holland Tunnel?'

He makes it sound sexual, but my obsession with Holland Tunnel is anything but. Most people wax romantic over bridges but I've always preferred tunnels. All that energy rushing out of those humongous tubes. Scratch that, maybe it is sexual or maybe I'm so desperate for Paul in this moment that everything is sexual.

I know I should tell him to get lost, but I'm in such a bad place that I don't have the strength. Paul wants me, and he wants me right now. It feels so good that the parts of my brain that tell me I'll never succeed are temporarily silenced. Maybe I need one last romp with Paul to get him out of my system.

He keeps his one hand on my leg and reaches his other hand across the table to grab mine. I see the familiar hairy knuckles that always turned me on so much. His wedding ring is not there.

'What do you say we get out of here? Let me use each hour I have here to show you how much I want you back. I'll be back in four months and we can finally have everything we both wanted. It's time for us to both grow up.' He takes his hand off my knee but holds my hand more tightly as he stands up. I don't say anything. I stand up. He throws some money on the table and then puts his arm around me and leads me out the door. The humid air from earlier has been replaced with the first whisper of autumn coolness. We walk down the street toward his hotel. Maybe I'm not headed in the right direction but at least I know where I'm going.

Chapter 10

Two days later I'm finally on the train uptown headed back to my apartment. The only baggage in the room was Paul's Hermes luggage. Things have really changed. He's getting a divorce, so there's no reason this can't work out, and if there is a reason, I don't want to think about it. I just want my life to make sense and feel settled. Having Paul back could do that.

I didn't tell him that every publisher, including Hurlington, passed on my submission. It still hurts too much. But I did tell him about the full-time opening at Brands to the Rescue and he thought it was a great idea. I die at the thought of working nine to five every day, but he said it would work better with his schedule, which is true. When I had deadlines with Justine, I had to work through the weekends or at night sometimes to juggle my part-time work and writing for her. It was hard to be spontaneous when he wanted to drive out to the Hamptons for the weekend or spend the afternoon at his favorite suite at The Carlyle.

The train stops and passengers shove their way in but I'm so much in my fantasy I barely notice that someone is standing on my foot. All I can think about is living as a couple with Paul in Tribeca. It feels so adult, so stable, so... expensive. I don't know how much he pays in rent, but I'm sure even half is more than I pay for my tiny apartment, and I will not let him pay more than his share. How much sense does it make to live my big adult dream with my boyfriend paying my rent? The full-time position at Brands couldn't have come at a better time. A Senior Brand Manager salary will make me more solvent; otherwise, I don't think I could do it. I've got to get that job.

'Please stand clear of the closing doors,' the robot conductor announces as the train pulls out of the next station and I stay in my fantasy about Paul. As he was getting in his car for the airport he pulled me toward him and said, 'One hundred and nine.' I didn't know what he was talking about and then he explained. 'That's how many days until my divorce is final and I'll be back in New York with you.' Then he pulled me toward him for one last long lingering kiss. Before I had even gotten to the end of the block he texted me telling me how much he already missed me. It was so romantic and thoughtful.

At least it should have been romantic and thoughtful. Now I can't help thinking about the fact that the sex was a bit of a disappointment. Everything worked and went where it was supposed to go with the intended consequences, but still, it wasn't mind-blowing like it used to be. Is the fact that he's actually getting divorced lessening the thrill? Did I spend so much time trying to get over him that I actually did without knowing it? Paul is still exactly the type of guy I want to be with so I'm sure it was just something about being apart all summer and maybe even the pressure from only having two days together. It used to be amazing and I know it can't be that way every time but this weekend it was just sort of ho-hum.

The train rumbles along, trying to push me back to reality, but I resist it. Paul's getting a divorce and we are going to make things work. The sex will get better. I stand up as we approach my stop, but instead of the train slowing down, it speeds up. We zoom forward. The loudspeaker crackles and an MTA person says something like the train is being re-routed to an express track and that annoyingly chipper pre-recorded voice comes on and apologizes for 'the unavoidable delay'. I sit back down and accept my fate. Station after station rushes by in a blur of grit and color. Sometimes the MTA takes you to a station you aren't planning on and you have to get home on your own. That's part of living in New York.

Forty minutes later I'm on my block walking toward my building when reality barges in. 'Excuse me, young man, I'm late for work,' a woman says, racing past me. She turns and says, 'Oh, you aren't a young man. You're my son.' She throws her arms around me squeezing out all the oxygen from my lungs.

'Mom, Plant Daddy doesn't open for another hour. How can you be late?'

'I need to study. I want to be ready for anything.'

'It's only your second week. You have worked a total of three shifts. I'm sure you'll figure out all the coffee drinks and what plants need what.' I walk with her and try to stifle a yawn. I don't want her asking any questions about why I'm so tired or where I'm coming from.

'I already know all that. I'm trying to learn these,' she says pulling out a stack of cards from her purse and handing them to me.

I thumb through the cards with blocks of color on one side. 'I have no idea what these are.'

'They're flash cards. On one side, I have the colors of the flag, and on the other side, the group that flag represents. Oh, see that one on the top is tricky. Gray, white, purple, and black can mean asexual, but when it has the little triangle, that means demisexual. I don't want to mess them up.' She repeats the names of the colors to herself and then the group like she's studying for the bar exam.

'Mom, no one is going to quiz you on this. People just want to chill and drink coffee and buy plants that they'll bring home and kill.' I discreetly rub my eyes so she doesn't see how tired I am.

'That's not how it works at all. I want to make sure everyone feels comfortable and welcome and...' She stops walking and turns toward me. 'Wait? Why are you on your way home. Where were you?'

This woman does not miss a trick. I scramble for a cover story. 'I was helping Omar with a fitting at Vanata. He had a big deadline for a show and we hung out there all weekend.'

'Uh huh,' she says and starts walking again. I'm not entirely sure she believes my story but at least she isn't hounding me about it. She looks at her watch and then runs ahead of me. 'Come down once you've had a shower and conditioned your hair. It's looking a little dry. You can help quiz me on the flags during my shift.'

She heads into Plant Daddy and I run upstairs to Omar's apartment.

'Tell me everything,' he instructs, standing up from his sewing machine.

'First, I told my mom I was helping you at work all weekend.'

'Got it. What did we have for lunch?' He grabs a pen and a piece of paper to take notes.

'I had a tuna melt and you had a bowl of vegan chili. We split a slice of pie.'

'What kind? You know she'll ask and compare our answers.'

'Oh, I know. We wanted cherry but they were out so blueberry.'

'Tuna. Chili. Cherry to Blueberry,' he races through the list. 'Got it. Now tell me everything.' He moves a few bolts of fabric off his couch and makes a place for us both to sit.

I know he doesn't approve of anything to do with Paul but he's my best friend so I also know he won't judge me too harshly. I go over every detail with him although I slightly exaggerate my opening resolve and don't let him know how quickly I gave in. I make sure to emphasize the retainer for the divorce Paul showed me and how great everything felt with Paul. I don't mention that the physical stuff was less than overwhelming.

'Well,' he says and takes a big breath in and out followed by, 'I see.' I didn't think he would jump in with me on the enthusiasm train. Omar had a front row seat to the drama so of course he's a bit leery.

'It's really happening this time,' I say and hand the copy of the retainer to Omar, who rubs his thick beard and looks it over. It feels silly to be so procedural but it's evidence that things are different.

'I guess this is legit but, Sam, a piece of paper is only worth as much as the paper it's written on if the intention isn't there.'

'You're right. I know this isn't a guarantee but this is more than he has ever done before and he made me feel good about myself. That's not a feeling I've been having lately. And his marriage was the biggest obstacle. Now that he's finally ending it, there aren't any other mountains to move.'

'What about the mountain downstairs currently learning to make cappuccino without using a heaping teaspoon from the jar of instant coffee she carries around?' Omar asks standing up and putting his hands on his hips.

I had forgotten about that one hurdle. When I ran into her downstairs I was still on my high from being with Paul so I didn't think through her reaction.

'She'll never accept him as your boyfriend. You know that.'

'You're right.' My mother despises everything about Paul. He's too stuffy, too old, and lives in Tribeca, a highly respectable neighborhood that, for some reason, my mother finds suspect. They met once and my mother was polite if not a bit standoffish. She said she just did not get a good 'vibe' from him but then when I let it slip that he was separated she tried to hold in how she felt but she couldn't.

'Sam don't break up a marriage,' she chided me. 'You deserve better.'

'Mom, it's over between them. He'll be divorced in a month... or so,' I said, and at the time, I believed it. It didn't happen then but this time it will.

I can hear my mother's final words on the subject: 'Sam, just remember, how you meet them is how you lose them. Stay away from him. Promise me you will.' I never promised her anything but I did promise myself to never mention him to her again.

'It's not her life. It's mine and she's going to have to accept that.' I fold my arms.

'Have you met your mother? Gravity is less determined than she is. That will never happen.' I can live with the disapproval but it's the nagging that will destroy me. I want to be able to invite Paul to holidays without my mom making us miserable with her polite yet lethal shade.

'I'm thirty-five years old. It's time for her to understand that she doesn't get a say in my life. She's going to have to accept the fact that Paul and I will be a couple.' I don't mention the fact that he asked me to move in with him. Leaving Omar and this building will be impossible but that's what growing up means: moving forward.

'You'd have to make a deal in hell to have your mother accept Paul.' Omar says and sits down at his sewing machine.

'What did you just say?' I ask as I ponder the idea.

'You'd have to make a deal in hell to have that happen,' he repeats slowly.

'Exactly! That's exactly what I'm going to do.' I leap up from the couch energized by his brilliant idea. 'She has this insane plan to be in charge of my dating life, right?' He nods but is still not sure where this is going. 'What if I agree to let her be in charge. I do whatever she wants. Go out with the parade of lunatics she prepares, and if I haven't fallen in love with whatever random she has selected, she has to agree to accept whoever I date. No questions asked. Even... Paul. But I don't tell her Paul is waiting in the wings. I leave that as a surprise.'

'You are going to trick her?' Omar asks.

'I don't want to trick her, exactly. I'll do what she says and the truth is, I'm helping her. You know how much losing Aunt Shug has affected her.'

'I do,' Omar says. 'I liked her a lot. She balanced the two of you like an isosceles triangle.'

'Right, so this is something to keep her mind off all that. Really it's a win-win.' The more I think about it the more I think it could work. Maybe I can even take Paul to my cousin's wedding in December. 'It's brilliant, right?'

Omar stares at me and blinks. 'I'm never sure which of you is crazier. You or your mother.'

Chapter 11

What's so terrible about being a 'normal'? I grab the pole on the 2 train as it rumbles toward Wall Street and look around at my people and their khakis – oatmeal, biscotti, cafe con leche. It's an entire breakfast buffet of tan. At Chambers Street I follow the other working professionals up to street level where we each make our way to our respective offices. Now that I've stopped resisting my transformation, I'm learning to accept it. Being a 'normal' means not staring at a blank page worrying about coming up with my own ideas and wondering if they're any good. It means not feeling like a failure every time I get another rejection. At Brands, I just need to finish the assignments I'm given and that's that. I'm on track for a full-time job by the end of the year and I even have a plan for a full-time boyfriend that my mother will accept. Totally normal.

I told myself that if I didn't get my break by the time I was thirty I would stop writing and find another job. Then my agent Loretta set me up ghostwriting with Justine and I thought it would be a good stepping stone to my own work but instead I was in a sort of limbo. I wasn't moving forward but I wasn't moving backward either. Sometimes Justine came up with very broad outlines and sometimes just a few scenes or a title. It was work for hire. It may have been my words inside the book but it wasn't my name on the cover. Fans already loved Justine so I just had to keep doing what she was doing. Sometimes I'd go to a signing and overhear a reader gush about her books. Once a woman told her that what she wrote gave her the courage to change her life. I thought, *she didn't change your life. I did.* But it also felt safe to be in that position. I didn't have to perform at a reading with an audience of people judging me. I got to write but I never really had to put myself out there. Maybe taking the full-time job at Brands is a way to finally become an adult or maybe it's another form of avoidance.

I'm about to walk into the building and up to the office when my mother calls. 'I'm late,' I say as I push through the revolving door into the lobby to answer the phone.

'I'm just calling to make sure you're getting enough fiber,' she says.

'Yes, I am. Thank you for your call. Nice chatting. Goodbye,' I say, knowing this is not the end of the conversation.

'What kind? I read an article that you need thirty grams a day of *soluble* fiber at least, for heart health, and then I heard that it can also help with bottoming.'

'Mom!' I shout into the phone, and the guy at the security desk, who usually waves me in, gives me a concerned look.

'What? I never taught you to be ashamed of your body. Don't be so uptight. Maybe the fiber will help with that too.'

'I am not uptight,' I growl into the phone.

'Whatever you say. I'll see you later. I love you.'

'I love you too,' I say and hang up. I agreed to meet my mother at Plant Daddy after work. That's when her 'legal team' is available. Anyone else would think their mother is kidding about a 'legal team', but my mother says incredibly outrageous things that turn out to be true.

I head up and as soon as I'm out of the elevator at Brands, Robert spots me. He's wearing his usual blue suit and toothy smile.

'Sam, loved the ideas you shot over for Finn and the gallery. Excellent.'

'Thanks,' I say. Take that Hurlington Press and every mid to large publisher who rejected me this summer. I'm good at this job. It feels nice to get positive feedback for a change.

I reached out to Robert with some ideas and found a way to slip in that I wanted to be considered for the full-time position. I was in the middle of my make-up weekend with my once and future boyfriend and emailed Robert in a moment of haste. 'Senior Brand Manager is a great title,' Paul said. 'And you don't want to be a struggling writer your whole life.' He's not wrong.

I grab a desk in the open workspace ready to begin my shift at the 'email factory' as I sometimes call it. Before I do anything else today, I need to reach out to Finn and review the spreadsheet of opportunities I have in the works, but I'm reluctant to pick up the phone and dial. Something about Finn pushes my buttons. The way he flipped the script on me, asking me about myself when I was there to interview him at Plant Daddy. He assumed I was just doing this job until something better came along. Granted, that's the same assumption I had about this job, but still, the way he zeroed in on it made me feel exposed. I remind myself this is work. I can reset the boundaries and if I want to stay on track for the full-time position, I don't have a choice.

I call Finn and he picks up on the first ring. 'Hey, Sam,' he says. 'How's it hanging?' His voice is casual and friendly.

That shadow of a Southern accent makes it sound like he doesn't have a care in the world.

'It hangs fine, thank you,' I say. I never know how to answer that question and this is a business call. 'I wanted to walk you through the spreadsheet I sent over this morning if now is a good time.' I'm trying to be hyper-professional.

'I just finished post-processing some images. Shoot.' I can almost see him leaning back in his chair and putting his hands behind his head in a stretch.

This is the part of my job I like, finding opportunities and connecting people. For the Surentox campaign I was able to hire a graphic designer who lived down the hall from me in college. It wound up being a great gig for him, the Surentox people loved him and he sent me a lovely box of my favorite brownies. I like being able to help people like that. A rising tide lifts all boats I would like to be one of the boats but I need to find a way to be happy just being the tide. Sadly, this fun part accounts for maybe five per cent of my work. Mostly I write boring press releases, arrange schedules, and follow up on details.

I've scheduled Finn on some podcasts that a woman I know from Plant Daddy produces, and a friend of Omar's who works at the Met suggested some social media accounts that look seriously at queer art, so I was able to make some connections there. I've secured interviews with a few established old-guard media outlets as well. A social studies teacher I met at a party in the East Village told me about a school in Coney Island that focuses on social justice. I snagged Finn an invitation to a panel they're doing next week.

'And that's everything I have so far,' I say when I get to the end of the spreadsheet. Finn is silent. 'What do you think?'

'You put this all together really fast?'

'In full disclosure, most of my contacts are friends or acquaintances from other parts of my life. But they're all legit, I swear.'

'I believe you. I'm just shocked you know that many people. It's impressive.' Is it? I've always been able to meet people and make friends. Romantic partners are in a whole other category. I suck at that.

'Next week is a magnet school focused on social justice change makers. It's a big event. They had a cancellation and I was able to get you in. There'll be some nice press coverage. It's in Coney Island,' I say in case that's a deal breaker. 'It's a bit of a trek to the outer edges of Brooklyn, but it's a great school with a worthwhile mission.'

'Coney Island? Like with the roller coaster and the hot dogs? That Coney Island?'

'That's the one,' I say. I forgot he's only been in New York a short time.

'Hot damn, yeah. I've been wanting to go there since I landed but I've been too busy to check it out. But it's gonna cost ya,' he says and I can hear the playfulness in his voice. 'Isn't that where they have the famous hot dogs? I'll need one, no, better make it two hot dogs.'

'I think I can swing that,' I say unable to resist his invitation to play.

'It's a deal but honestly as soon as you told me high school students I was in. The whole reason I went into photography is because of a teacher. Mrs Perez.'

'Was she a photographer?'

'No, she taught algebra.'

'How did you go from algebra to photos?' I should be taking notes because some of this might be useful later for building some press materials, but instead, I just listen.

'I was going through a pretty rough time and really struggling in her class. I couldn't tell sine from a cosine.'

'I think that's trig, not algebra,' I say.

'I told you I wasn't good at it. But Mrs Perez, she never made me feel stupid or like a bad kid. She would invite me to her classroom after school and make me a snack and go over the homework. But what really helped is that she talked to me and she really listened. About what was going on. I never really had someone do that before. She let me talk about whatever I wanted. I was kind of a loner as a kid. I guess I still am.'

'But you work with people in your photos. I've seen them. You can't get photos like that without having a connection to the people.'

'Thanks. I guess it's easier when I have a camera or a purpose, you know? Like Mrs Perez had with me.'

I can understand. It's not the way I move in the world but his photos are incredible and he is undoubtedly successful so he's doing something right.

'Sounds like she's amazing.'

'She is. I mean she was. She died about a year ago,' he says.

'Oh, I'm sorry.'

'Thank you,' he says softly. 'Losing someone you're close to like that, who's been a mentor, is hard. You know what I mean?'

'My aunt died last year.' I wouldn't usually reveal something so personal to a client but he has this way of getting inside me.

'I'm sorry. What was her name?'

'Her name was Gertrude but she hated that. So, everyone called her Sugar or Shug after the Marilyn Monroe character in *Gentlemen Prefer Blondes*.' As soon as I mention the movie I hold my breath. Guys his age usually have no idea what I'm talking about when I mention any movie with characters who don't wear capes or shoot lasers.

'I love that movie. It really had some complicated gender politics. Way ahead of its time.'

'I like the way Marilyn plays the ukulele. Shug used to do a great impression of her singing,' I say and smile to myself. 'I understand what it means to miss someone who has helped shape who you are, but I'm still not exactly sure how you went from algebra to documentary photography.'

'Mrs Perez taught me how important it is to listen to people because she listened to me and because of that I started getting really into documentaries and hearing people's stories. I love the way taking a photo can create an occasion for a connection. It creates a situation for listening and I get to make people feel seen. The way I felt with Mrs Perez. Did someone inspire you to become a writer?'

He just told me this beautiful story about this important teacher but I'm not sure how to answer his question. I want to tell him more about Aunt Shug and my mom taking me to old movies and coming home and putting on plays with the characters we just saw or writing stories about them. But I've made such an effort to put that all away and focus on a real future. I don't want to bring it up now and certainly not at work.

'Finn, I've got a meeting I have to head to.' It's a lame excuse but not entirely untrue. I need to keep a boundary with this guy. 'I'll email you all the details about Coney Island. Hot dogs are on me.'

I answer some final questions and hang up glad to be off the phone with him. He makes me nervous. There's something so raw about him and he crashes through my usual defenses. I don't like it but maybe I'm not giving him a chance.

Chapter 12

My mother has been working at Plant Daddy for almost two weeks, but when I walk in, it's still a shock to see her working behind the counter. She's wearing her *We're Here, We're Queer, Our Joint Pain is Moderate to Severe* T-shirt and a pair of rainbow-framed reading glasses dangle from a chain around her neck. Another pair is on top of her head, holding down her auburn curls. She's steaming milk and grinding beans like she's competing in a barista competition, too focused to notice me come in.

'Hey Sam,' Angelika says. She pushes her long platinum dreads back into the paisley scarf she always wears. Then she waves her hand over her scattered pile of Tarot cards. 'Want a reading?'

'My future is too complicated – even for your powerful energy. Has my mom told you about her crazy idea?' I ask and nod to a few of the regulars I spot around the cafe. I see Kai through the up-cycled stained-glass screen that separates his potting table from the rest of the cafe.

'Oh yes.' Angelika smiles. 'Astrologically speaking, this couldn't be a better time. Your mom asked me to pull some cards.'

'I'm sorry she's bothering you.' I hope she isn't getting into trouble with Kai for annoying the customers. 'I'll tell her to stick to coffee and plants.' My mom could insert herself into a concrete wall. She has no boundaries. I could handle this when she stayed on her side of the Hudson River in New Jersey, but now she's punching the clock at a job two floors below where I live. I'll never be able to manage her.

'Your mom's not bothering me. I adore her. Everyone does. She even walked one of Damola's dogs yesterday.'

We've all been helping fill the gap for Damola, who is short-staffed and trying to finish some music he's working on. Last week, I walked a bossy dachshund named Tuna. Really, Tuna walked me since I didn't have much choice in the speed or direction of the walk.

'Sam,' Angelika says in a sweet and gentle voice. 'Kai told me about the thing with the publisher. I'm sorry. I know you wanted it. But if there's one thing I've learned, the path we are given always leads us to the place we need to be.'

I guess my path is away from writing and toward Brands to the Rescue. Maybe she's saying I just have to stop resisting it and be open to becoming a full-time 'normal'.

Angelika's next client comes in, a frail woman with an anxious look, so I say goodbye and walk over to the counter. I watch my mom serve a frothy drink to a man with multiple piercings on one ear lobe and a tattoo across his neck. He leaves and my mom smiles and waves when she spots me. No matter the circumstances my mom is always thrilled to see me and that feels good. 'Kai is it okay if I take my break now?' she shouts over her shoulder.

Kai looks up from the bonsai they are working on and nods. My mother takes off her apron and comes around the counter to hug me. I'm about to trick her into giving me what I want. When her plan fails miserably, I'll have Paul on standby. I wonder if she can smell it on me – the combination of deception and guilt.

'Rajesh, we're ready,' she says and leads me to a table where a boy no older than eighteen in a bright blue hoodie is sitting reading a textbook.

'Who is this?' I whisper to her as she leads me over.

'My legal counsel,' she says.

'Hello Mrs Carmichael.'

'Good afternoon, Rajesh. Did you get a chance to ask Jessica out?' He shakes his head and looks down. 'Confidence. Remember what we talked about. You're a handsome and charming young man. She'd be lucky to hang a chill with you.' The kid smiles meekly.

'I think you mean "to have a chill hang",' I say.

'That's what I said.' She shrugs.

'Mom, what's going on?'

'I told you. Rajesh is my legal counsel. He's a first-year student at NYU and he's taking a course called legal something-or-other. What's it called again, dear?'

'It's called Law and Ethics,' he says, his voice cracking.

'That's great,' I say. 'So, since it's the beginning of September, that means you are in what? Week three?' I ask. He nods. 'I'm sure he's qualified.' I want to tell Rajesh to blink twice if he needs help but I'm not sure how I would help him. My mother would be too formidable even if we teamed up.

'Rajesh is very bright, and he also taught me how much matcha powder to use in the latte.'

'Oh, what was I thinking? Let's get him a spot on the Supreme Court,' I say.

'No, thanks,' he says as if I was going to promote him this afternoon. 'I might want to go into game design. I'm not sure yet.'

'Rajesh, I told you.' She puts her hand on his shoulder for encouragement. 'You have to follow your passion.' She sits down at the table and I take the seat next to Rajesh. 'Now, let's begin. I only have a short break,' my mother starts. 'I thought we should have an impartial third party to discuss the rules.' She pulls a napkin from the holder and wipes something off Rajesh's face. Then she takes the letter I wrote from a million years ago out of her pocket and unfolds it on the table. 'Rajesh has already reviewed a copy of the contract, and he agrees with me that it is legally binding.'

'Mom, this piece of paper does not give you carte blanche over my life.'

'I don't need carte blanche. I'm your mother. I gave birth to you. I already have that.'

I cover my face with my hand. 'The fact that you think that is exactly why we need some limits here.' I sit up in my chair. 'That's part of a legal contract. Isn't it, Rajesh?'

Rajesh nods. 'We learned that in week one. It's called the terms of the contract.'

'Thank you, Rajesh. Very helpful,' I say. 'We need to discuss *the terms*. For example, how long will this last? For the rest of my life?' I want to make sure this is a limited-time offer.

'Don't be ridiculous. Let's just say a year.'

'A year? No. No way. Are you...' I'm about to get up and walk away from the whole crazy mess. There is no way I am giving up a year of my life. I was thinking a month at the most. But then I look over at my mom and see how invested she is. A spark is returning to her eyes that I haven't seen since Aunt Shug passed, so I try to control my feelings. 'Mother,' I say, my voice calm. 'That seems excessive. A more reasonable duration would be a few weeks.'

'Son,' she says in her schoolteacher's voice. 'I'm trying to find you the love of your life. I need at least a few months.' She pauses and puts a finger to her chin. 'I know. Until Valentine's Day. That's so romantic.' She throws her hands together, pleased with her idea.

I can't think of anything more depressing than including Valentine's Day in this deranged plan. By January, I expect to be living with Paul, so that's too late. 'Let's pick something in this calendar year,' I suggest. 'Until Cousin Ziggy's wedding. That's near the end of December. You want me to have a date for that, so it's perfect. Unless you think you can't deliver by then?' I egg her on, hoping it will make her surrender. There is no way I can last into January.

'I always deliver. I know what I'm doing,' she fires back. 'That's fine. Cousin Ziggy's wedding. Are you getting all this Rajesh?' my mother asks.

'Yes. I think so. I'll put it all in the add-dead-da, a-dead-dah...'

He stumbles with the word, so I help him finish it. 'Addendum,' I say slowly, making sure I can get it out myself. 'It's a tricky word.' He nods, his pen poised for further instruction.

'I think we also need some ground rules about what exactly you'll be doing. For example, none of this shall dissolve the Bedroom Treaty,' I say.

'Fine,' my mother says. 'The Bedroom Treaty is still in effect.' She rolls her eyes, having never quite gotten over that defeat.

'What's that?' Rajesh asks. 'Should I write it down?'

'Rajesh, this isn't our first formal negotiation. When I was nine, my mother received a lifetime ban from my bedroom, excluding fire, acts of God, and laundry return.'

'I have no intention of breaking my word on that. But write down that I am in charge of everything.' She taps her finger on his notebook.

'Everything?' Rajesh asks.

'Do not write that down, Rajesh,' I say, and he looks at me.

'Write it down,' my mother says, tapping again, and Rajesh turns his head back to her. We are going to break this kid's neck.

'Mom, you can't be in charge of everything.'

'Matchmaking is an art. I can't nail it down. Does anyone ask Julia Child how many eggs go into her soufflé?'

'As a matter of fact, they do,' I say. 'It's called a recipe. She has books and books of them.'

'Sam,' she sighs. 'Think of me as your personal dating coach. All you have to do is show up and follow a few simple rules.'

'What kind of rules?' I ask, knowing she must have a list longer than the train on Princess Diana's wedding gown.

She wrinkles her nose. 'Look at what you're wearing.'

'What's wrong with it?' I'm in my Brands to the Rescue uniform of khaki pants and light blue Oxford.

'Boring. You could put someone to sleep in that. When you go on a date you have to dress appropriately. You're a funny, vivacious person. You need bright colors that reflect who you are. A little color never hurt anyone.'

Rajesh looks at me. 'That outfit is kind of boring.' He picks up the letter and examines it. 'Actually, you say here that you will "follow all my mother's rules for dating". It's in the contract.'

My mother smiles, knowing I've been beaten. I look her in the eye. She genuinely wants to help me, but why can't I make her understand that I don't need help? Maybe if I just go along with her and prove to her once and for all that I don't need her managing my life, she will stop trying to interfere. If I let her be in charge of *everything*, there'll be more opportunities for her to get it wrong and prove my point. Not to mention that I plan to get something out of the whole situation myself – a happy ever after with Paul that she can't protest. I know I'll regret this later but I'm too eager to shift to my own agenda to go back and forth with her. She's going to do what she wants anyway.

'Fine,' I say. 'But if I agree – and it remains a big if – what do I get out of this arrangement? I have to get something, too.'

My mother gives her famous poo-poo face like I'm being ridiculous. 'You'll meet the love of your life. All you have to do is let go and let me be in charge. You're perfect, but I just need to tweak a few things,' she says, squinting at my hairline.

The fact that she seriously believes she can do this is almost too much to take in. I just sail right past her confidence. 'But let's say something happens, and you can't deliver by our established deadline – Cousin Ziggy's wedding.'

'I always deliver,' she says.

'I am aware. But legally, it needs consideration. Isn't that right, Rajesh?'

He's in way over his head, with both the legalese and the interpersonal dynamic. I'm sure he has never seen a mother and child battle this type of negotiation. He shakes his head. 'I don't know. I think maybe we're covering it in week four. Maybe I should go and ask the professor.' His voice cracks, and he begins to get up.

'You stay right there, Rajesh,' my mother says. 'You still have two free lattes to work off.' She means business.

'Maybe I could just pay you for the drinks?' he asks.

'I wouldn't hear of it. Now, Sam, this contract is legal.' She grabs the letter and holds it up to my face. 'You know it, I know it. Rajesh knows it.'

'But it needs consideration. Both parties must enter the contract with an exchange of value,' I insist, trying to remember the page I read on LegalEagle.com.

'Like money?' she asks putting the letter down.

'No, not like that. If I go along with this and by the end of the contract, you haven't found me the perfect boyfriend after following all your rules...' I pause, winding up. 'You have to accept whoever I choose as a boyfriend in the future.' She doesn't flinch, so I go in for the kill. 'No matter who it is.'

Her eyes narrow. 'Fine. No matter who it is,' she says, and I wonder if she's thinking about Paul because I certainly am. My mother never breaks a promise. If she says she will accept whoever I choose, she will. She reaches her hand across the table and we shake, grinning at each other.

'Can I go now?' Rajesh asks. 'I need to do my Spanish homework before class.'

'Yes, Rajesh. Thank you. You've been very helpful. Now, make sure you ask Jessica out for coffee. Bring her here when you bring back the addendum. I want to meet her. And tell your parents about game design,' she says, and he smiles, taking in the encouragement.

Once he has left, my mother stands up. 'I'll come by tomorrow evening, and we can get started. I'll even bring some stuffed peppers I've been planning to defrost. I know how much you love them. This is going to be so much fun,' she says and heads back to the counter in a burst of giddy enthusiasm.

I should be dreading all of this, but the truth is I haven't seen her this happy in a very long time. I can almost feel some of her grief lifting and some of mine, too. If it means spending the next few months being her dating guinea pig, then so be it.

I go to leave and Angelika calls me over. 'I want to show you something.'

'What?' I ask. I look down at her table and admire the faded backs of the cards strewn about. Each has a swirly blue and gold design with moons, suns, and stars.

'I pulled a card when you were talking with your mom. Good news.' Angelika moves her fingers over her cards and then picks one up. 'I got this,' she says, revealing an image of a person dressed in colorful clothes on the edge of a cliff by the water. At the bottom, it reads: 'The Fool'.

'The Fool?' I ask. 'That can't be a good one.'

'Oh, but it is. It means new beginnings and letting go of the past. But see that dog by the cliff?' I look more closely and see the little pup. 'That dog is a warning.' Her voice shifts to something more serious than her usual lilt. 'You have to let go of the past and see what's in front of you in the present, or you'll fall right off that cliff.' I study the card for a second. The central figure is looking up at the sky, and it's unclear if he sees the danger in front of him. Will he stop, or will he tumble off the edge?

Is this a warning about Paul? Sure, he's part of my past, but he's also part of my future. Or is this about something else entirely? I have no idea, but Angelika is very sweet to offer me assurance. 'Thanks. I appreciate you looking out for me. Have a great day.' I wave goodbye and head out of Plant Daddy. When I get outside, I see that the edges of the leaves of the gingko trees that line the block are beginning to transform from the gentle green of summer to shimmering autumn gold. The summer heat still lingers, but nothing can stop the cycle of change.

Chapter 13

I can't remember the last time I went to Coney Island. I think Omar wanted to check out the famous Mermaid Parade one summer so we put on some ridiculous green sequined halters he found at the Housing Works thrift, decorated our faces with ocean-themed stickers and strolled the boardwalk with all the other sea creatures. Omar quickly hooked up with a hunky King Neptune and I rode the train home by myself relieved to be out of the summer heat.

I remember making notes on the way home for a story about a merman who falls in love with a lifeguard but doesn't know how to fake drowning in the waves so the merman can never get the lifeguard's attention. I wonder what happened to that story. I think I was working on something for Justine so either I got distracted or discouraged. Maybe both. I go to my jacket pocket now to pull out the small notebook where I jot down ideas. Then I remember: I consciously uncoupled with my moleskin a week after I got the bad news from my agent. What was the point? I'm literally turning the page on all that and starting another chapter.

A drizzle this morning gave way to a gray autumn sky and the first chilly morning of the fall. It's the perfect September day to indulge in a frothy pumpkin spice cookie mocha, but I could fly to the Bahamas faster than the N train takes to get to the last stop in Brooklyn, so I skip it in order to be on time.

I'm officially representing Brands to the Rescue at this event and I want to make sure everything goes smoothly. Press will be there and even someone from the mayor's office since this school was just awarded a big grant. I have something to prove today, not just to Robert, but to myself. And if I'm being honest to Paul too. I want the world to see me as a functioning adult instead of a wannabe writer.

When I told Paul about all the events I've been working on he said he was impressed and that Robert would be out of his mind not to hire me. He sent me a vintage mid-seventies burgundy Coach briefcase with little combination locks on each side to celebrate our new future. It's elegant and refined, just like Paul. Even though it's not my style and too impractical to bring with me on the subway, I love it. Paul's making an effort and that means a lot to me.

I enter the school auditorium but can't find Finn. Sometimes I travel to events with clients but I wanted to give Finn his space. I hope he didn't get lost. As I pass by a window, I see Finn sitting on a curb in an alley. I reach for the door to head out to him but before I do I pause. I'm hyper-aware that he makes me feel like I'm on my back foot, and it's not just that he's effortlessly sexy. It's the way he zeroes in on me with those tough questions and hazel eyes.

I hear the students approaching the auditorium. I take a deep breath and channel my best Melanie Griffith in *Working Girl*, telling myself I can do this. I open the side door and head outside to tell him where the presentation will be. 'Thanks for showing up this morning. Did you have any trouble finding your way?'

'A little. Manhattan is a grid but out here in Brooklyn, it's a maze,' he says, trying to be pleasant but his attention is elsewhere.

'I think they're about to start. Maybe you should get on stage?' I ask, trying not to push him.

'I haven't been in a high school for a long time.' He takes a long breath in and then out. I notice him rubbing his hands together tightly.

'I know. It's weird, huh?' I open the side door, hoping that will signal him enough to get inside. The panel is about to start, and it will look bad if he walks on stage after it's begun.

'I gotta be honest – it's a bit more than weird.' His chin tilts back and his eyes look up at the sky. Something heavy is going on. I close the door. It will take a few minutes for everyone to settle.

'You okay?'

'It's funny how a school auditorium in Brooklyn can remind me so much of the same space back home on the other side of the country.' Finn moves his bangs off his face. 'I'm sorry. I needed air. Some not-great memories came back when I got here. Had to get a grip on them.'

'I know high school can be rough for a lot of queer kids,' I say and take a seat next to him on the curb.

'Were you teased a lot?' he asks, turning to look at me.

'Relentlessly,' I say, thinking about how I learned the class schedule of my bullies every year so I could make sure we were never in the same hallway. School was a nightmare, but I tried to be over-involved like a lot of young gay kids, hoping that so much activity would help me be more of a blur to the people around me than a target. I learned to make friends who would be allies so I could hide behind them. I wanted nothing more than to be invisible back then. That was my strategy but it didn't always work.

'I'm sorry you had to go through that,' he says.

'Thanks. Were you? Teased at school?' I ask. I'm the kind of person who never really had to come out. Everyone assumed I was gay long before I did. I mean it's not every sixth grader who has a shrine to Joan Crawford in their locker. But Finn strikes me as the kind of person who had to tell people he was gay. I'm not sure anyone would guess he is but I'm making a lot of assumptions.

'I wasn't out in high school. I mean I didn't know I was bi. I didn't really think about it. I told you I wasn't good in algebra. I wasn't good in anything,' he says with a slight tremble in his voice. 'I lashed out a lot. I couldn't get control of my emotions. I didn't have any friends. Didn't want them. I was a quote "anti-social juvenile delinquent" end quote. That's what my parents called me.' He rubs his eyes and then mutters under his breath, 'At least when they were around.' I had imagined he'd had a great childhood – how else could he walk around with so much confidence? But I guess even the strongest structures can have cracks in the foundation. I nod and try to show him that I'm listening.

'My parents were always working,' he continues. 'I was alone a lot and always getting into trouble. A bunch of different schools kicked me out. I never had any friends because my parents never fought to keep me in one place. They'd just send me to a new school thinking it would solve the problem but it never did. Sometimes I just did something stupid and sometimes I did something bad. I sat in the principal's office more than I ever sat in a classroom.

No record but I have seen the back seat of a cop car more than once. Anyway that was a long time ago.'

He seems so accomplished and talented. It's hard to imagine him any other way but it's clear he's struggling with some unpleasant memories.

'I did a lot of things in high school that I'm not very proud of. I mean, I never hurt anyone except myself, I guess, and a lot of public property. I might not have had any friends but I always had a crowbar and cans of spray paint. I couldn't help but remember a lot of bad feelings walking in today.' His eyes focus on the ground as his head hangs down.

I was apprehensive coming out here to talk to him. I thought he'd make me nervous again but instead he's the one on edge. I want to help him at this moment, and I'm aware that it's more than a professional obligation. I want to listen to him and understand more.

'You were just a kid,' I say.

'That's what I tell myself. But I was pretty messed up until Mrs Perez. I learned to put my energy into my work. I tried to drop the destructive part but the loner part has always stuck.' He rubs his hands together like he is trying to change the channel on what he's thinking but can't. 'What would my parents say if I told them I was speaking at a high school to inspire kids?' He shakes his head and his hair falls back in front of his eyes. 'They'd never believe it.'

'They don't know you're here today?' I ask. My mother's constant inquiries about my whereabouts never stop. I wouldn't be surprised if she has put a tracking device on me, but I have no way to prove it.

Finn laughs. 'They don't know I'm in New York. They don't have any idea where I am. They kicked me out after

I was thrown out of the last school. Haven't spoken to them in years.'

My mom and I are so connected. I can't even imagine how that must feel. He puts his hand over his mouth and then looks at me seriously. 'Let me guess. Student Council, National Honors Society, French Club.' His tone is playful so I am assuming he doesn't want to talk about what he just said.

'You're wrong,' I say. 'I wasn't in the French Club. I was vice president of the Spanish Club. So there.' I was involved in too many things, never settling on any one interest. Always hiding behind a different door.

'Oh excuse, me,' he laughs but it's only a temporary break from his apprehension.

I can hear the crowd growing, and even though Robert will push me off the top of the building if I don't get him in there, I say, 'You don't have to do this if you don't want to. If being inside that auditorium makes you too stressed out we can just walk away. I'll make up some excuse. I'm making them up to my mother all the time.'

He grins. 'That's sweet. But I know this is a big event. I saw all the Board of Education bigwigs and the press in there. The gallery expects me to do a good job.'

'So what? The only big wigs I care about are the ones at My Own Private Eye Shadow.'

He laughs. 'What's that?'

'Only the most amazing drag show in Hell's Kitchen. I can't believe you haven't heard of it.' He shakes his head. 'You should come with.' He perks up, giving me a look that makes me add, 'A bunch of people go. It's really an informal thing. Usually, a group gathers at Plant Daddy before heading over.' For a second I wonder if I can set him up with one of my friends, and then I realize I'm as bad as my mother. Still my mind scrolls through a list of people who might be into him. For a second I think maybe I'd be... but I wipe that thought from my head. A sexy artist like Finn would never be interested in a corporate drone like me, even if it's only a role I pretend to play. He's not my type and I'm not looking. I'll be living with Paul in a few months.

'Do you want to get out of here and ditch this?' I ask, getting up from the curb.

'No,' he says. 'I'm good. Thank you. For listening. I think in my field of work I get too comfortable being the one asking the questions. I don't really get to be on the other side. I think I need that sometimes.' He gets up and stretches his neck to look through the window, unintentionally showing off his lithe frame. He watches the kids fooling around and being rowdy. 'Look at that. Might be some fellow juvenile delinquents in there. Maybe I can say something that will help them figure out what to do with their lives.'

'Are you sure?' I ask. I'd be grateful if he went through with it, but my offer to ditch was genuine. I want the full-time position, but I'm not going to cause harm to get it.

'Absolutely. Let's go,' he says and opens the door for me. We walk back into the auditorium together and I watch him walk up to the stage to take a seat.

Chapter 14

'Well done,' I say walking up to the stage to congratulate Finn. He was wonderful, so much passion about his work. The students started off unable to settle down, but once Finn got going, he had them hooked. I'm sure the event will get very flattering coverage, which is good news for the Carlos Wong Gallery and good news for me.

'That was exhilarating,' Finn says and I can almost feel the energy radiating from him. 'Sorry about that small freak-out before. I love the enthusiasm these kids have.'

'Did I just hear you say you love the enthusiasm here?' Superintendent Jones asks as she steps closer to join us.

'I was nervous being back in a school. But Sam helped me through it.' He smiles at me and I pray my face isn't turning red. 'I loved hearing their questions.'

'In that case, I'm hoping you'd consider being a part of our "Artists in the School" program. We find artists to work with students. It's smaller than this event. More intimate. But it's a very impactful program. I have an opening in December I need to fill at Harvey Milk School near Astor Place. Principal Chan would be thrilled to have you.'

'They're affiliated with the Hetrick-Martin Institute, right? For LGBTQ youth,' I say.

'Exactly. Under-resourced of course so we really need volunteers. Usually, we have two artists select a clip from a film or work of art to introduce and host a dialogue. What do you say?'

'I didn't even know a school like that existed. That's amazing. I'd be honored,' Finn says. Then he says something I do not expect. 'We could both do it. What do you say, Sam?'

'We could both do what?' He can't possibly think I would join him.

'The Artists in the School program. Sam is a fantastic writer. He won an award for his short story. We could choose a film and talk about it together.'

'I... ah...' I can't form words. What is he talking about? I'm not an artist. Certainly not an artist like Finn. Not anymore. I wouldn't be any good with kids. They'll see right through me and know I'm a fraud.

'Thank you both. I'll put you in touch with Principal Chan,' the superintendent says and she walks away.

'What did you just do?' I ask as we walk out of the auditorium together.

'You don't want to help queer kids?' I'm aware that he's baiting me.

'I want them to be helped, of course. I'm not sure I'm the right person to do the helping. She asked *you* to do it. Not me.' The bell rings for classes to change and students pour out of the classrooms. Whatever hesitation he had about being back inside a school has lifted, but it doesn't mean I can help with the Artists in the School program.

We exit the building and start walking down the street as the kerfuffle of kids changes from stereophonic to background noise. I'll write a very sweet email to Superintendent Jones and explain that I'd love to make a donation but I'm not able to be part of the program at this time.

'You know how to get back to the city?' I ask.

'Sure, but we aren't going back just yet,' he says and keeps walking. 'I believe the deal was I speak at this event and you treat me to a famous hot dog. Two, if I have my facts straight. According to my map, it's just that way.' He swings his arm around and then points toward the ocean. I'm not sure spending more time with Finn is a good idea, but I did promise him hot dogs. Robert always says the easiest way to create a great brand is to get to know the client and keep them happy, so hot dogs it is.

Within a few minutes we go from walking down an urban thoroughfare to strolling down a boardwalk along the Atlantic Ocean. The salt air suffocates the smell of exhaust and anger that lingers on the Brooklyn streets. The Wonder Wheel with its swinging cars slowly rotates and the wireframe of the defunct parachute drop looms over Luna Park just ahead of us. I suddenly remember something my mother told me.

'My parents had their first date here,' I say as the wind brushes my face. 'I forgot about it until I saw Luna Park and the roller coaster there.' I point ahead to the wooden structure in the distance beyond the Ferris wheel.

'Is that the Cyclone?' Finn asks.

'Yeah. My father said he wanted to give my mother the thrill of a lifetime. She was terrified but she thought she couldn't disappoint him since they came all the way out here. She said she had a feeling that she would be safe with my dad so she did it.' I think about Paul and how the on-again, off-again thing made me feel like we were always in jeopardy. Once his divorce is final all of that will change.

'Do your parents still come out here?' Finn asks.

'No. My dad died soon after I was born.'

'I'm sorry,' he says. That's what people say when they find out you lost your dad as a kid. It was so long ago and being a dad-less kid is just part of who I am. Maybe I miss the *idea* of a dad. I try not to think about it but I'm sure it's the reason I date older guys. I guess it's kind of obvious to everyone else even if it doesn't always sink in with me.

'It's always just been this way so it doesn't feel unusual to me. It feels normal.'

We walk for a few seconds and he says, 'We should do it. We should ride the Cyclone.'

'No,' I say quickly. 'I'm going to eat a hot dog filled with so many carcinogens I couldn't count them all. One life-threatening event a day is my limit.' We're close enough to the roller coaster that we can hear the click-click of the car as it climbs the first hill and then the screams of people as they whip around the creaking track. I have no idea how that thing is still standing. I'd never risk my life on it. I hate any kind of 'thrill ride'. Life is scary enough, thank you.

'But it looks like fun,' he says tilting his head. Damn, he's charming. I wonder if I should nip this in the bud.

'My ex-boyfriend is coming to visit in a few weeks. I want to make sure I'm in one piece,' I say as we arrive at Nathan's.

'An ex-boyfriend?' he asks.

Did I say ex? I don't think I did, but maybe. I'm so used to thinking about him as my ex-boyfriend over the past nine months I guess it just slipped out. 'It's complicated,' I say, hoping the documentarian in him won't press further. At least I let him know, and the fact is Paul and I won't actually be a couple officially again until January when his divorce is final. 'What about you? Are you with someone?'

There's no denying he's hot. I'm sure he has people lined up to date him.

'Nope. I was seeing someone in New Orleans but he cheated on me with a bartender,' he says.

'I'm sorry. That sucks.'

'I wasn't surprised when it happened. You have to bring your whole self to a relationship to make it work. We couldn't connect.' I'm shocked. He's been so easy to connect with. Too easy. I find myself holding on to my seat when we're together.

'In the end it all helped me get out of New Orleans and move up here. I always wanted to try living in New York and now I am and I'm even about to eat one of the famous Nathan's Hot Dogs.' He points above him to the green-and-yellow awning with the name of the establishment in green script outlined by a red oval. A neon sign of a hot dog dressed in a chef's hat and wearing a bun flashes, *Take Home Food*.

'You know you can buy these at any grocery store,' I say realizing I'm being a total downer.

'I know but that's not the point. We're here in Coney Island. Look at the waves, the rides. Smell that sea air and the steam from the grill. This is something people dream about. Being right here. Right, where we have the privilege of standing.'

I look around trying to see it through his eyes, putting my jaded New Yorker lens aside. Even in September, Coney Island is a magical place. But not in a shiny Disney way. In a gritty, more authentic style. I watch an older couple walk hand in hand down the boardwalk and then a woman roller-skates past us blaring disco hits out of the speaker she's carrying. Beyond that the waves keep the rhythm of everything rolling in and out just like they did when my parents were here on their first date.

'Right at this moment,' Finn says, looking out across the boardwalk and seeing the same view I am, 'there is probably someone in some place you've never even thought about.' His voice is soft and dreamy. His Southern accent noticeable around the edges. 'That person is so far away but they're wondering what it would be like to be right here. Right now. On the boardwalk in famous Coney Island, and you're the one actually here. How lucky are you?'

I haven't felt very lucky lately. First Paul dumped me and then all the rejections from the publishers. But with Paul back and the possibility of escaping the black hole of publishing with a full-time job at Brands, maybe my luck is changing.

A woman in a housecoat, with her hair in a kerchief and smoking a cigar, walks a yappy Chihuahua in front of us. The dog barks and then stops and looks right at me. The pup is silent for a second and then lets out an even louder barrage of barks. 'Woof, woof, woof, woof!' The woman shrugs, puffs on her cigar and they continue down the boardwalk.

I can see Angelika back at Plant Daddy in my mind. Her Tarot card with the barking dog at the edge of a cliff. What was that card warning? I'm sure the Chihuahua is only telling me not to eat too many hot dogs. Right now, that's the only real danger in my life as far as I can see.

'Mustard and sauerkraut or ketchup and relish?' I ask turning to Finn.

'How about one of each?' He walks toward the yellow-and-green awning but I can still hear the Chihuahua barking in the distance.

Chapter 15

Omar takes a piece of crusty bread and soaks up the last bit of sauce on his plate. My mother is beaming. She puts her hand to her mouth and whispers to Omar, 'Raisins. That's my secret. I puree them and add them into the sauce. It makes everything sweeter. Sam thinks he hates raisins.'

'No, Sam actually hates raisins,' I say in a loud stage whisper. In grade school, Ben Barton tricked me into eating a fly hidden in a handful of granola by telling me it was a raisin. A combination of youthful gullibility and hunger worked against me. I have been vehemently anti-raisin ever since.

'You've been eating them for years and you don't even know it,' she says. I tear off a piece of bread and copy what Omar just did. The sauce is spicy with just a touch of sweetness to balance it out. My mother makes amazing stuffed peppers even if she sneaks raisins into them.

Omar announces: 'I have to run to a fitting at Vanata. The model is only available in the evenings.'

'I can't wait for your own show this spring,' Mom says. 'I wear the skirt you made me all the time. I get so many compliments on it. That color is like a pistachio sundae.' She thanks him for the skirt at least once a week and Omar always smiles politely and takes the compliments like a champ. She slowly turns her gaze toward me. 'There's so much passion in your designs. Following your dream like that is something anyone would admire.' By anyone my mother does not mean anyone. She means a specific someone. She means me.

Omar grabs his jacket from a hook next to the door. 'Do you want me to stay and referee?' he asks with great sincerity.

'Yes,' I say quickly.

'No,' my mother says a second later. 'We've already come to a mutual understanding. Haven't we son?' Her tone echoes years of asking me if I have washed my hands before dinner.

'Yes, Mom,' I say but my eyes reach out to Omar for help. She will be so much better behaved if he's here, but that's not a reason to make him miss his appointment. 'Bye, Omar,' I say. I got myself into this mess. Omar closes the door behind him as he leaves. My mom insists on clearing the table but I insist on her sitting in the living room while I wash the dishes. Eventually, she surrenders, and I go into the kitchen alone.

I'm standing at the sink rinsing the plates and trying to gather my strength for dealing with what is about to come. I need to stay focused on the fact that if I put up with her being my 'dating coach' for the next few months, I'll then be able to live my life without her constant judgment. She won't be able to say a word as I walk into my cousin's wedding with Paul on my arm.

I turn off the water and look back at her in the living room carefully flipping through her notebook. She looked so excited when she walked in the door tonight holding a casserole covered in foil – very Jane Fonda on her first day of work in 9 to 5. I think between her job downstairs at Plant Daddy and her obsession with finding me a boyfriend, she hasn't had time to think about all the sadness from last year. I go back to finishing the dishes and remind myself to stay focused on the fact this whole situation is good for both of us no matter how hard she pushes my buttons.

I'm drying the last dish when I hear my mother talking to someone. I assume she's on her phone, but when I look in the living room, I see she isn't. She's talking *at* my phone. Her back is to me.

'Ways to meet men. Hair conditioners. Skin moisturizers. Clothes that fit properly. Tight clothes. Ideas for writers. Hot men. Sexy men. Single men.' She is reading from a piece of paper in her notebook. 'Yes. Good,' she says to herself and then goes back to her list. 'Single men. Single men. Single men.' She keeps repeating the phrase like she's chanting. She stops suddenly. 'Oh, wait. Gay men. Gay hot single men. Very hot. Very single. Very men.'

'Mom!' I interrupt and she spins toward me.

'Oh, you finished the dishes. I was just getting started helping you.'

'Who are you talking to?'

'The robot,' she says like it's our neighbor in New Jersey. 'You know, in your phone. If you say things you want around your phone all the ads and stuff will change. Remember Mrs Geisler? She lives down the corner with that hairless cat. She told me she was talking to her husband about a new dishwasher and the next day all over her computer there were these ads for dishwashers. Boom. Just like that. The robot knows. It listens.'

'Mom, please don't corrupt my phone with your ideas of what you think I'm looking for.' I dry my hands with the towel I carried in and put it on the table.

'Sam, that's why I'm here – to listen to you.' She opens her multi-tabbed notebook. I sit on the couch and take a deep breath like I'm about to get a painful injection from my nurse practitioner. 'First I want you to know that I'm open to your ideas.'

'Uh huh,' I say. I don't argue with her. I don't tell her that I have already found a guy who I want to be with and that we're moving in together at the end of the year. I don't tell her that Paul is finally leaving his husband. She'd never believe it. To be honest, it's hard for me to believe too. But his text and phone calls this past week have been so thoughtful. He really does miss me.

'Tell me, what kind of guy are you looking for?'

This could be a trick question but this whole thing is counterespionage so I use the opportunity to describe Paul. 'I see myself with someone definitely older. Someone who is serious, practical, and straightforward. Someone who is well-organized.'

My mom waves her pencil at me. 'Sam, you're describing a candidate for Congress, not someone who's going to sweep you off your feet and become the love of your life.' She puts her pencil down. 'Now I want you to close your eyes. Think about the man of your dreams and tell me what you see,' she instructs.

My eyes remain open. 'How someone looks isn't that important to me.'

'Son, I know it's considered cool to say looks don't matter but come on. When I first saw your father outside the library, my heart went boom, boom, boom,' she says, patting her chest. 'He was so handsome. Dark wavy hair and beautiful eyes. Just like you.'

'Did you know right away you'd get married?' I ask. I've asked this a hundred times but I love hearing about how they met and when they dated.

'No, not right away. At least that's what I always told him, but you know, I had this voice in my head that there was something special about this boy. That's the little voice I want you to hear and I want your heart to go boom, boom, boom.' She repeats patting her chest.

I get up from the couch and look out the window facing the street. For a brief second I think about a moment when my eyes locked with Finn when he was speaking at the event yesterday and how it made something stir inside me. But that was just some kind of physical response. He's hot but he's not the kind of guy I want to be with for the long term. If you're way into someone's looks, it makes things unbalanced. I wipe the thought of Finn from my brain and continue describing a masqueraded Paul as I turn back to my mom.

'I'm looking for a professional person with a very stable job. They should have experience in their career and be competent at it.' I am about to say a lawyer, but I figure that's too on the nose, and she may catch on, so I change it up a bit to throw her off the scent. 'An accountant,' I say and she writes it down. She's been taking notes the whole time. For the next few minutes, I continue describing Paul as best I can with some red herrings.

'Let me get this right,' she says and then re-reads her notes aloud to me. Surprisingly, she has done an excellent job of listening. She has written down almost precisely what I have described.

'Yes. That's it,' I say. 'That's exactly what I'm looking for.' Maybe this is going to be easier than I thought.

'Great,' she says and then puts down her notebook. She grabs the top of the page she has just been writing on and with a single motion rips it out. She crumples the paper into a ball, gets up, and throws it into the wastepaper basket.

'What are you doing? You just wrote down everything I'm looking for and now you just threw it away. I thought you said you wanted to find out what I wanted.'

'I said I would *listen* to what you wanted and I did that, didn't I? I even took notes. I listened to every word.' She's shocked that I would be so incredulous.

'But you threw them out.' I consider pulling the paper from the trash and smoothing out the wrinkles on the counter.

'Sam, I love you, but this is another raisin situation.' She has her notebook open, ready to move on.

'What's that supposed to mean?'

'You think you know what you like but you don't really. That's why I'm here. To help you with what you don't know you don't know about yourself.'

'What is it that you know that I don't know, I know, about myself?' I ask.

'You think you know what you don't know but how could you know what you don't know?' she asks. I shake my head trying to erase the word 'know' from my brain. 'I've got a great guy for you.' She taps her finger on the top of her notebook.

I go to the couch to sit down. I knew we were heading toward actually having to go on dates with the men my mother selected but the reality of it is making me nauseous. It's one thing to have to deal with her endless rules and suggestions but another to see it all materialize in flesh and blood.

'I think his name is Kevin or Denim or something like that.' She thumbs through some pages.

'He's great for me but you're not sure of his name,' I say.

'Don't be so hung up on labels.'

'It's not a label. I'm asking about his name. I think I should know that before I go out on a date with him.' The thought of being out on a date that my mother has set me up on makes another wave of nausea pass through me. This is becoming too real.

'You need someone with passion.' She puts her notebook to the side and looks at me. 'That's the first rule and an important one. This guy is very passionate about everything he does.'

'You're not sure about his name but you are sure that he has passion? How did you meet this Denim-Kevin person?' I ask wondering if there is a way I can cut off her supply of single gay men.

'I haven't met him.' She casually touches her soft curls.

'You want me to go out with a stranger?'

'He's not a stranger. Edwina met him. You know Edwina, she lives in that house with the red shutters. I think red was the wrong choice but she's a good person despite her flawed color choices. She bought a leather change purse from him a few weeks ago at some kind of fair and she told me all about him. I told her my rule about dating someone with passion and she suggested him.'

'Mom...' I do not want to go on a date with a leather crafter her neighbor met at a fair but if I want to get what I want, I have to just go along with this for a little while. She has been taking this very seriously and it has certainly been a distraction for her, like I was hoping.

'Do you know anything about him?' I ask.

'Of course. He's twenty-seven and—'

'Twenty-seven? I am not dating some kid.' I specifically tried to emphasize to her that I'm never interested in guys younger than I am. We never hit off. I need someone older and more mature like Paul. No wait. Not someone like Paul. I need Paul. I want Paul, but I can't tell her that.

'You are so uptight. So what? He's a little younger. What's the big deal? Age doesn't matter. That's a rule. I mean, unless you're both born on the same day at the same time, one is going to be younger than the other. It's a mathematical fact. You want to argue numbers with me?'

Her logic is almost making sense which means she's wearing down my defenses. 'You are not sure of his name but you know his age. Anything else?'

'I told you he makes stuff and Edwina said he was very passionate about it.' She grabs her notebook and takes a second to look over her notes. 'He also does something with some kind of wine. Maybe he's one of those wine people, whatever they're called.'

'He's a sommelier?' I ask. That sounds impressive. I don't know a great deal about wine so maybe the evening won't be a total loss. I could learn something beyond the difference that the red is darker than the white, which is the cornerstone of what I know now. 'Do you have a picture or anything?'

'I thought you said looks weren't important to you?' She removes her reading glasses and gives me a look that says *Gotcha*.

'Fine, Mom. Set me up with the twenty-seven-year-old passionate crafter wine person. Maybe next week,' I say hoping I can gather my courage before then.

'Tomorrow,' she says.

'What's that now?' I wished I had just taken a sip of water so I could do a spit take.

'He's meeting you at eight, tomorrow night. So, I'll be here around seven.'

'Mom, I'm not going to be ready to go out with some rando by tomorrow.'

'I know that. That's why I'm coming over to help you.' She smiles from ear to ear.

'I mean mentally. I need to warm up to the idea.'

'Well then you should have given me more time to do what I need to do.' Her smile shifts from joy to determination. 'It's already the middle of September and I only have until your cousin's wedding in December. I need to maximize my time.'

'Fine, tomorrow.' I sigh. The sooner I get started the sooner this comes to an end. 'But I do not need your help getting ready for a date. I know what I'm doing.'

She slowly looks me over, her eyes judging each inch. 'No, son, you don't.' She grabs her notebook and thumbs through it until she stops at a tab she has labeled 'Contract'. 'The rules clearly state that I am in charge of everything. I'll be here tomorrow at seven o'clock on the dot.'

I'm trapped. I wonder what Matthew Davidson would say if he knew the price I'm paying for the stupid crush I had on him in eighth grade.

Chapter 16

I look at myself in the mirror and shake my head. There is no way I can leave my apartment looking like this. I lean closer, scrutinizing the way the dayglow green T-shirt stretches tightly over my torso. The bright, rainbow-colored *Say Gay* slogan in giant letters across my chest seems to be shouting. The shirt needs to come with an off switch.

My mother looks at my reflection and smiles. 'You look so handsome,' she says. 'And this outfit says you care about people.'

'This outfit says if you beat me with a stick I will bleed candy. I look like a piñata. Did you have to go all out on the neon? And the rainbow socks? Really?' I hike up my pants to see my ankles decorated for a Pride float. I look in the mirror and mumble, trying to see if the shirt looks any less garish from a different angle. It doesn't. I support people waving rainbow flags but wearing them on your chest and ankles is so not me.

'Mom, I know you like T-shirts with messages on them but I don't and this one is way too bright and too tight? He's a sommelier, isn't he? This is… wrong,' I say gesturing to myself.

'Not at all. You have to show people who you are. That's the first rule of dating.'

'I thought the first rule was something about passion?' I ask.

'The first rule is never ordering soup on a first date.'

'Why?' I can't imagine how that could be important.

'I'd explain it to you but you wouldn't understand. Don't you worry about the rules. I've got them all up here.' She taps the side of her head with her finger and then grabs the bottom of the T-shirt and yanks it down so it feels even tighter. 'Everything you wear is so baggy. It's like you're hiding inside your clothing. This is much better.'

My face contorts into a disapproving grimace. I've always had very prominent nipples so I make sure nothing really clings to me. 'It's too tight, Mom. Do I have to show people who I am on an anatomical level?' I emphasize my point by stretching the fabric away from two very noticeable points on my chest. I go to take off the shirt and my mom stops me.

'Just what do you think you're doing?'

'Mom, this makes certain parts of my body look too...'

'Okay, okay,' she concedes, reaching into the seemingly endless pit of her purse. Out comes a roll of black tape. 'For emergencies,' she says.

'What emergencies require duct tape?'

Her laughter fills the room. 'Life is unpredictable, my dear. That's another rule you need to learn. You think I don't know you're embarrassed of your nipples. You have been since you were a teenager and I have no idea why. They're a natural part of you. I used to think that my left nipple was too high. Look.'

She is about to grab her breast to show me and I stop her. 'Mom, please.'

129

She rips off a piece of tape, lifts my shirt and covers my left nipple with a sticky small black square. She pulls the T-shirt down again and my left pectoral is smooth like a marble statue.

'Great, if you hear screaming coming from my apartment later it's just your son trying to rip off the tape and not disfigure himself.'

'Don't get so worried. It's not that sticky. I bought it at that BDSM store in the village. It's for some kind of fetish thing. I don't remember. You'll be fine.' She lifts my shirt and secures the other nipple.

'It's not just that, Mom. It's what's on the T-shirt.' I point to the words squished between two hideously bright rainbows, *Say Gay*.

'Are you suddenly a right-wing nut? You don't think we should say gay?' She puts her hands on her hips.

'Of course, I believe we should say gay...'

'I think it's important that a date knows your politics. Another important rule.' She points at me. 'Maybe you should be writing these down.'

'Well, technically they're learning *your* politics. I would like mine to be revealed during the conversation. I don't want to walk in wearing them across my chest over my now smooth nipples. Why do I have to force it down someone's throat?'

'How is it forcing anything down anyone's throat? You're just being yourself. That's the most important rule of all.' She throws up her hands.

Being myself is not something I've ever been comfortable being. I learned early on that being yourself can get you in a lot of trouble. Every time I was 'myself' I got picked on or bullied and it was awful. I learned to be myself when it was safe and all other times I was a smaller and more muted version of myself. Eventually the smaller version just took over until I wasn't even sure what the real version was. Now as an adult I feel all this pressure to be *gayer* and I'm not sure how I feel about it. I think it's great that it's an option but I'm less enthused when it feels like a mandate. Can't I just be me at whatever volume I choose?

I look at myself in the mirror with the words *Say Gay* across my chest, the rainbow glowing from my ankles, and my nipples suppressed. I see my mother in the mirror beaming at me as happy as Dr Frankenstein.

'Fine,' I say. Then she pulls an entire drugstore shelf of hair products out her bag, each promising 'natural shine' or 'sculpted perfection'.

'What until you see what I got for your hair. All of these are organic and none of them have been tested on animals.'

'That's great but I don't really use anything on my hair. I just sort of wash it and that's it.' I run my hand through my shaggy mop and let my bangs stick up.

'Son, you're so handsome but you have to put in a little effort.'

'Let me guess. That's another rule?' I ask rolling my eyes.

'No, that's just common sense. Now sit down and let me figure out how all this works.' She starts reading some of the labels and then she puts on a pair of reading glasses to see something on her phone.

'Mom, are you sure you know what you're doing?'

'Of course, I've been doing my own hair for years.'

She is not unattractive. She looks a bit like Dustin Hoffman in *Tootsie* and she has had the same hair as the title character my entire life. Everyday it looks exactly the same but I'm not sure that qualifies her to...

'Mom, what are you doing?' I ask. She suddenly has my entire head covered in some gloopy slime. I try to look in the mirror to survey the damage but she pulls my shoulders back.

'This is supposed to give you a finished look. It's called hair clay.' It feels like a pint of ice cream is melting on top of me.

'Are you supposed to use that much?' I wince.

'More is always better.'

'No, it's not.' I go to get up, but she pushes my head down gently with her hand. 'And what is that smell?'

'I think that's seaweed or kelp. Are they the same thing? I can never remember.' Even my mom gags a little as the odor grows.

'It smells like the ocean has thrown up on me.'

'It's not that bad,' she says stifling a cough. 'It's organic.'

'Manure is organic but I don't want to put it on my head,' I say.

'Now stay still,' she says ignoring my comment with a confused look on her face. It's clear she doesn't know what she's doing. She puts on another pair of reading glasses, forgetting that she already had a pair on top of her head. 'It looked so easy in those videos online. I don't know what happened.' She moves her hands around my head and then tries combing my hairbut I can feel the goop tangling it up. She keeps having to wipe her hands with a towel which is not a good sign. The more she spreads it around the more it stinks up the apartment.

The intercom buzzes. My mother goes to answer it. 'Helloooo?' she sings into the speaker.

A theatrical voice floats in, 'Sam? It's Kevin. Your valiant date for the evening.' Great, he sounds even worse that she described.

'What's he doing here? I thought I'd be meeting him somewhere.'

'Of course not. A gentleman picks up their date at their home. Kevin insisted. I thought it was very sweet.' I get up to open the door and when I pass by a mirror I see that I look like a landslide victim.

'Mom, I can't leave the apartment like this,' I say staring at the mess on the top of my head.

'Oh, it's not that bad. Maybe I used a little too much. Let me grab one of your baseball hats,' she says. 'You've got so many of them.' She grabs a Yankees cap from the hooks by the door. I'm not a baseball fan but I play one on the streets. 'Quick fix. Voila. You look great.'

Kevin knocks on the door. I open it and I'm immediately not worried about my strange appearance. He looks like he time-traveled from a Shakespearean drama gone wrong. 'Hark! Fair maiden and noble man, it is I, Kevin of deepest Brooklyn.' He's wearing the pouffiest ruffled shirt that ever pouffed and a pair of glittery velvet burgundy wide-leg pants.

'Oh, Kevin. What a unique style. I love it,' my mom coos.

'I was at work, milady,' Kevin declares, bowing dramatically. 'I serve at the esteemed tavern of Guinevere's Head in Greenpoint, purveyor of mead and medieval vibes. But I made all the leather accessories you see.' He waves his hand around his body showing off a belt and some leather pouches that dangle off him.

'Hey there, I'm Sam.' I'm trying to make this situation as normal as possible. 'What is a mead?'

'You haven't tried it? Oh, I do wish I had brought some with me. It's an ancient drink made from fermented honey. I can't believe you haven't heard of it. It's having an incredible resurgence.'

'Oh,' I say, grabbing my jacket since I don't want to blind anyone with my mother's wardrobe choice. I open the door for Kevin, he passes into the hallway and I glare at my mother.

'You two have fun,' my mom says waving from the doorway. 'Don't worry. I'll lock up.'

'I can't believe you've never heard of mead,' Kevin says as soon as we exit the building. 'During the Golden Age of Greece mead was preferred over wine. It's incredible how wine gets all this attention. It makes me so mad.' His voice is high-pitched and theatrical. I'm not sure I can get through an entire night hearing it but luckily I have a secret weapon arriving.

My plan is to grab a drink at a bar on Fifty-Third Street, only a few blocks away. I told Omar where we would be so he could show up around an hour into the date and help me end it humanely. It's the oldest trick in the book, but this guy seems like he's from another century, so he might predate it.

'Sam, do you know the most peculiar thing about mead?' he asks as we walk down the block.

I hesitate, caught off guard by the sudden question and clear obsession with this beverage. 'Um, I do not.'

His laughter rings out as if I said something hysterical. 'There is actually a blue mead.'

'Made with blueberries?' I ask trying to keep the conversation flowing. It's that or blue cheese. How much blue food is there?

'I knew you would think that. But no. Not blueberries. They add fungal spores to the first fermentation so that the final product has a blue tint.'

'Sounds delicious,' I say trying not to gag. Maybe he's nervous and all this mead talk is just a way of getting through it.

We walk into Nitty Gritty, a dive bar just beyond the theater district. I order a beer and he orders a sweet red wine since mead is not on the menu, which disappoints Kevin but he handles it bravely.

I'm beginning to think he will act more normal once we have sat down and gotten over the awkward first moments, but as we find two empty seats, he says, 'I'm sad Wayne couldn't join us tonight.' He slumps down a bit and frowns. I told my mother I was not interested in dating any couples. This is proof that she does not listen to me.

'Have you been together long?' I ask. I assume it's an appropriate question.

'Since he was born,' Kevin says.

'A real soulmate.' I nod and drink my beer.

'Yes. He goes with me everywhere, but he's in a timeout because he was chewing on the cord of his terrarium.'

It takes a few more questions to realize that Wayne is not his romantic partner. Wayne is a ten-pound, four-foot-long iguana that usually travels around the city sitting on Kevin's shoulder. I'm sure the iguana was chewing on the cord trying to escape hearing anything more about mead.

A respectable hour later, I have learned all about Wayne's eating habits and even more about Kevin's beloved ancient beverage. I'm ready to get out of there.

I casually glance at my watch, and when I look up, I see Omar walking in, pretending to be in a panic.

'Sam, I'm so glad I found you. You didn't pick up your phone.' Omar is many things, but a gifted thespian is not one of them. He sounds like he's in a high school production of *Peter Pan*.

'I turned it off. Is everything okay?' I ask.

'No, you need to...' His nose twitches. 'Oh, my gawd. What is that horrible...' He moves his head closer to mine. 'It's your head. What is that smell?'

'Never mind,' I say. I guess Kevin was being polite not mentioning it, or maybe living with an iguana you get used to unusual odors. 'What were you saying? It sounded like an emergency?' I prompt.

'Yes, your apartment. Go back to your apartment. There is an emergency. Something is wrong with your blender.'

'My blender?'

'His blender?' Kevin echoes. I told Omar he could make up whatever excuse he wanted and I realize now I should have had more oversight.

'Yes, your blender. I was making a smoothie and there was smoke and a terrible smell.'

'That sounds dangerous,' I say, showing concern.

'You need to go home,' Omar says. He's so proud of his acting. A sly smile crosses his lips.

'Oh, no. I was hoping we could grab a drink after this at Guinevere's Head.' Kevin sounds disappointed and I feel bad for concocting this charade.

But Omar pipes in. 'Is that the place in Greenpoint? Where they ferment their own mead?'

'Yes, yes. It is!' Kevin says erasing any disappointment and replacing it with excitement.

'Oh, I've heard of that place,' Omar says.

I hate doing this to Omar but I can't take any more mead or iguana talk. 'I have to get home and check on my blender,' I say getting up as Omar goes to sit down. I tell Kevin how nice it was to meet him, and I appreciate him going along with the setup and then I get the hell out of there. I really owe Omar for helping me with this. I promise I'll be his human mannequin and let him stick me with pins for the next year.

Chapter 17

Finn has asked to meet to talk about plans for the upcoming 'Artist in the School' event since the principal wants to start promoting it to students. I want to tell Finn that I'd be better suited for something like 'Corporate Communications Drone in the School', but since I forgot to email the superintendent to back out, I'm stuck being a part of the event. I'm scheduled to meet him this afternoon after he finishes some edits he's working on.

I've been avoiding Finn since spending the day with him on Coney Island. All of our communication has been through email and the occasional text. After a dozen phone calls, I was able to get him a meeting with Bruce Barnes, a curator at the Museum of Modern Art who wants to have Finn lead an artist's tour of a new exhibit for some high-end donors. It's the kind of thing the art press will cover and the museum will certainly feature him on their website. Robert was thrilled and the bonus was that it's kept Finn busy and at arm's length. Until today.

Luckily, my mother is not working at Plant Daddy this afternoon. I checked and double checked the schedule in Kai's office. I don't want to have to worry about her coming over to fix my hair or passing me a napkin with the words 'Sit up straight!' scrawled across it. She's currently working on the 'logistics' of setting me up on my next date.

She grilled me about Kevin last week. He wasn't an awful person, just an awful match. I had to tell her what we ordered and where we sat. She wanted to know what I said about myself during the date and I told her I didn't have a chance to say anything. 'Sam, you have to at the very least tell them you're a writer,' she said. 'That's an important rule.' Despite nodding, I chose to remain silent. That's one rule I have no intention of following.

I did enjoy coming home and calling Paul and telling him all about the crazy date. He's a great audience for my self-deprecating humor. He even appreciates that I'm going through all this so it will be easier for us to be together when he comes back to New York. At first I thought he might not like the idea of me going on all these dates but it didn't seem to matter to him. I'm not sure if it's the fact that he isn't the jealous type or that we're on opposite sides of the country and not really together until he comes back. In any case, I'm glad I can share my misery with him.

As soon as I walk into Plant Daddy I head to the counter and to place five dollars in the tip jar. I'm hoping to make my deposit before Omar sees me but I'm too slow.

'You have got to stop doing that,' he says placing his hand over the jar.

'I owe you big time. Making you spend the evening with that guy. It's the least I can do.'

'It wasn't so bad. He was nice and not like anyone I've met before really.' That's Omar. The endless optimist. 'Are you coming over tonight? I need to finish the hem on that skirt.'

'Yes and I promise I won't let out a peep when you stab my ankles with your pins.'

I have a brief chat with Damola, who tells me that he and Jimena are planning a romantic getaway to celebrate their anniversary. 'I'm making your mom a playlist with some classic hip-hop and Jimena is working on a beautiful broach for her. It's copper with little ruby beads. We really want to thank her for setting us up,' Damola says.

'Very thoughtful of you.' I wonder if my mom has told him to remind me about her role in their relationship. I wouldn't put it past her.

The bells above the door ring and Finn walks in. He pulls off his sunglasses and squints for a second as his eyes adjust to the light and he unwraps his plaid silky scarf so the ends fall across his chest. I notice almost everyone in the cafe either consciously or unconsciously shifts their attention toward him. He has a kind of magnetism that goes beyond great looks – a combination of attractiveness and something else. I'm about to ponder what that something else is when I stop myself short. I don't want to know. Why is water wet? What makes hot guys hot? Who knows? This is exactly why I wanted to keep our communication electronic.

He waves and joins me at my favorite table near a tall yet unassuming fiddle leaf fig plant with lovely green leaves the size of dinner plates.

'How are your edits going?' I ask.

'Hard,' he says putting his camera on the table and pushing his hair back behind his ear. 'I kept pushing to make this photo happen with this great person I interviewed a few weeks ago. I want the image to flow. They have such a powerful story but I just could not find the right way to put it all together.'

'I'm sorry,' I say.

'I kept trying to muscle through, but the more I tried to do that, the worse it got, so I finally shut down my laptop and went out for a walk last night. Sometimes that's the only thing that helps.'

'But it was pouring?' Last night some crazy storm passed through the area dumping so much rain on the city that the F train shut down. Not that the F train is a Profile in Courage. It pretty much shuts down without a reason, but still, it was not the type of weather anyone would take a stroll in.

'It's just a little water. You need to find inspiration wherever you can. Walking helps me focus. Helps me see a problem in a new way. Everyone has something that gets their creative flow out of a rut. Aren't you like that? What inspires you?'

I shrug. I have no idea. I used to think I wanted to tell stories that weren't around when I was a kid. But lately there have been so many new voices I think I got lost in the crowd. Writing for Justine meant I didn't have to think about any of that. I wrote to her market. I knew her readers well, even if I wasn't exactly part of the demographic – divorcees living on the Upper West Side. Now, I'm not sure where I fit in. Sometimes, I think I'm not gay enough, and I always think I am not cool enough. So, what's the story I want to tell? Is there an audience for the characters I want to write. Everyone wants likable leads but how can I do that when I struggle so much with liking myself?

'Oh, this and that,' I say hoping he won't investigate further. I'm severely embarrassed by such a lame answer. I jump up and ask, 'Can I get you a latte?' He nods. 'Be right back.' I head to the counter and place the order with Maggie.

'Are you on a date with that guy? Did your mom set you up?' she asks over the espresso machine as she grinds the beans.

'No and no. And I hope my mom isn't annoying you,' I say.

'I love your mom. Did you know I'm a summer? I've been wearing the wrong colors my whole life. Your mom knew it the minute she saw me in a red sweater. She has forbidden me from wearing that shade ever again. I'm so grateful.'

'That sounds like her,' I say. Maggie finishes steaming the milk and hands me the drinks in the white standard-issue latte mugs that have a few chips on them. I walk back to join Finn.

'I spoke to the principal at Harvey Milk School and she gave me a date in December. Is that still okay for you?' I ask as I sit down.

'Yep. I've got it on my calendar. Did she say more about what she wanted us to do?' He has a notebook and a pencil. I can tell he's taking this seriously, which I admire.

'I was thinking we could start with a screening of a great classic film. Something these kids might not have seen before. No superheroes,' I say and he laughs.

'I get it,' he says. 'I think we should inspire them with the power of what a story can do.'

I take a second to think and then say, 'Something classic like Billy Wilder's *Sunset Boulevard*.' I just saw that it was playing at one of the last screening rooms in the city that still shows classic movies. The drama of Gloria Swanson's eyes alone is enough reason to show it. I grew up loving this movie. Finn scrunches his lips from side to side. 'I don't know. Maybe, I guess.'

My suggestion has not inspired him.

'I was thinking something more contemporary.' His eyes brighten. 'Maybe something serious like *Moonlight*. Mahershala Ali gives an amazing performance and it hits on so many important issues. Or maybe something fun like *Priscilla Queen of the Desert*.' I roll my eyes and don't try to hide it since his mouth scrunching was so obvious. 'What, you don't like those?'

'They're good movies. Especially *Moonlight* and *Priscilla* is fun.' As a kid, I memorized multiple lip-syncs from *Priscilla* and performed them in front of my mirror to scores of enthusiastic audiences in my imagination. 'It's just that these kids already go to an LGBTQ school. I think it's too on the nose to show them films like that. Let's build up their knowledge and show them something classic.'

'Are you kidding? Those films *are* classic. *Moonlight* won Best Picture.'

'So what? Awards are meaningless.' I quickly remember he has been nominated for multiple awards for his photos over the past year. 'I mean, not all awards.'

'Smooth. Nice cover, Sam,' he laughs and he makes me laugh too. 'I don't really care about awards either. But I care about representation. Don't you?'

'Sure.'

'Then let's show something that features that,' he says, his tone growing more insistent.

'But does it have to be representation all the time? Twenty-four-seven? I think these kids need something different. They need to see the roots of queer sensibility, not just a mirror all the time.' My agitation begins to show through my voice.

'I don't get it. Why don't you want to show queer films to queer kids? That doesn't make any sense to me,' he says with a huff. I can tell he's getting irritated also.

'That's not what I'm saying at all.' I raise my hands in the air to show my frustration. 'It has nothing to do with *not* wanting to show them.'

'But you don't want to show them.' Finn crosses his arms in front of him.

'No, I don't,' I say although my point is that I would like to explore other options but I'm not going to give him a way out. My movie choice is just as valid as his.

'Maybe the problem is you aren't comfortable with those films.'

'Don't be ridiculous. I've seen *Moonlight* more times than you and I own *Priscilla* on DVD. You don't get to decide what I am and am not comfortable with.' My volume is louder than called for. This is why I hate guys like this. Artists always think they have the market cornered on originality and creativity. It's so annoying.

'Now you aren't being fair. I'm not doing that at all,' Finn says. His pitch and tone match mine.

'Yes you are!' I'm almost shouting – in fact, I am shouting.

'No, I'm not,' he shouts back like we are two toddlers fighting over a toy. Before I can get the next retort out Kai is suddenly rolling over to our table to pull the brake sharply.

'Excuse me folks. This is a quiet, friendly place and your shouting has a very negative effect on the African violets. I will have to ask you both to keep your voices down. Please think of the plants!'

'Sorry, Kai,' I say in a hushed tone. Finn says the same.

Kai takes a second to stare us down and then nods and goes back to his watering.

I take a deep breath and try reapproaching with a calmer attitude.

'All I'm saying is that I think these kids could learn a lot from *Sunset Boulevard*. It's brilliant and camp. I think they need to learn about what came *before* there was any type of representation. Being gay isn't just about this moment. It's about all the moments that led to now when the world was less tolerant and we still existed. Don't you think it's a great film?'

'I've never seen it.' He shrugs and some of his swagger fades.

'It's playing at St Marks Cinema,' I blurt out.

'How about Saturday? I could do...' He swipes through his phone. 'There's one at 9:15.'

'Wait. What? I wasn't suggesting we go out and see it this week. Together?' We have suddenly swung from an argument to planning a movie night and I'm not sure how it happened.

'I know. I'm suggesting it. We'll both go with open minds and take in the evidence and that way we can decide what movie we should screen. Can you do Saturday? The 9:15?'

'I guess that can work,' I say mindlessly. But the fact is I haven't been to that cinema in a long time and I'd love to return.

'Sounds like a plan.' He shuts his notebook and grabs his camera. 'I have to get back to my edits but I'll see you Saturday.' He gets ups and I watch him walk out the door.

I take a second to let the conversation-argument settle in my brain. Finn has this way of getting right to the heart of a situation. He's direct in a way that's exciting but also makes me nervous. I take our empty mugs up to the counter and I see the door to the back storage area is cracked open. A pair of large sequined glasses are peering out. I'd recognize those rainbow frames anywhere. I drop off the dirty latte mugs and walk over to the door.

'Mom, what are you doing here?'

'I work here,' she says defiantly.

'I know that, but today is supposed to be your day off.'

'Don't you worry about my schedule. I'm working on a project in the back.'

'What kind of project?' I ask.

'Just cleaning up a closet that hasn't been used for years and... never mind,' she says coming out into the cafe. 'Who was that young man you were talking to? He's very handsome.'

'Is he?' I pretend I haven't noticed.

She sighs. 'Son, your life would be so much easier if you were a better liar. And I saw you were arguing. Very passionately, I might add.'

'You were watching from behind the door? Mom, that's super creepy. Even for you.'

'It's not like I was reviewing security camera footage. What did you say his name was again?' She walks over to the shelf under the counter and grabs her huge purse.

'I didn't,' I say.

Kai wheels past us and my mom stops him. 'Did you see the man my son was talking to.'

'Talking to? When I went over there, they were more than talking. He was having a full-blown argument with Finn.'

'Oh, that's his name? Finn?'

'Yeah, Finn Montgomery. I met him the other day when Sam was late. Finn's a very talented artist,' Kai says and I can see the wheels in my mom's head start spinning. 'How are things going back there, Gloria? You finding what you need?'

'I sure am, Kai. Thank you.'

'Anything for you Gloria.'

Kai goes to his office and my mother pulls out a small notebook from her purse and begins to write. I move toward her and grab the pen out of her hand.

'No,' I say firmly.

'Hey, that's a very expensive pen. It's one of those German magic markers. Well, a fake version but still it's—'

'No. No. No. You are not writing down Finn Montgomery as one of my possible dates. I work with him. It's unethical.'

'Give me that pen,' she says reachingfor it. I yank it away. 'It is not unethical. It's complicated, maybe, but people can work together and fall in love. It happens all the time. One of your favorite movies is *The Desk Set*.'

I do love the Katharine Hepburn and Spencer Tracy workplace romance but I will not have it used against me. 'Mom, that's a movie. This is real life.'

'I knew you'd say that but don't forget they were a couple both onscreen and off.'

'Mom, be reasonable. You saw him, right? With your glasses on? The ones for distance, not reading?'

'Yes, of course. He's gorgeous.'

'Exactly. A guy like that is not going to be interested in a guy like me.' I can feel her revving up for some manufactured pep talk. 'No,' I say, holding up my hand to stop her. 'I'm not saying I should leave society and work in a Russian troll farm but I also know I'm not in that guy's league. Not even close.'

I've been with a few super-hot guys but I was always wondering why they were with me and what they saw in me. Maybe that's why older, more average guys like Paul are so much easier. I have my youth to fall back on with Paul, although that's a dwindling resource with each passing year.

In one quick move she grabs the pen from my hand and writes down 'Finn Montgomery' in her notebook.

'Fine. Write down whatever you want. I would never date Finn. Never.'

Chapter 18

I'm so relieved that my mother has not set me up with Finn that when she suggests I go on not one but two dates this week, I agree. Of course I have a date, or rather an appointment, to see a movie with Finn on Saturday but she doesn't know that. It's a work commitment. We are merely researching a film for our presentation.

I try to remember that each date gets me closer to my goal of being done with her silly plan but I admit she's really thriving in her role as my dating coach. I think after decades of being in the classroom, it was hard for her to find a purpose when she retired. Then Shug passed and she began to fade into the background a bit. Personally, I love the thought of blending into the world around me but it does not suit my mother. She enjoys being in the center of things, and taking charge of my dating life and working at Plant Daddy has helped her reclaim her spotlight.

Last night's date wasn't even terrible. I had an early coffee on the Upper West Side with a perfectly fine landscape architect with glasses that were so severely horizontal it looked like he was wearing a shelf on his eyebrows. He was an intelligent guy with a graduate degree in Environmental Engineering from Seoul National University, but the conversation had too many awkward silences and monologues that didn't go anywhere. My mind wandered, and I kept thinking about being at the boardwalk on

Coney Island with Finn and the ease of chatting with him. That said, I learned about the importance of rainwater conservation for irrigation from my coffee date, and I even put the guy in touch with a person I interviewed on the Surentox campaign who had just bought a property in Bucks County to do some sustainable farming. This morning, the Horizontal Glasses guy sent me a very polite 'We're not a match' text which was followed by a 'Thank you so much' text from the guy with the farm who had already contacted Horizontal Glasses to discuss some soil irrigation projects.

This evening I'm scheduled to meet Keshawn Fulani – a man my mother met at the Apple Store when she went to the Genius Barn to update them on her ongoing saga with a printer she's been on bad terms with for over a decade. When I agreed to let her be my dating coach, I had no idea she would have such an endless supply of available gay men. It's like she spent the summer selling reserved seating for the Fire Island ferry. By now, I should have learned never to underestimate my mother.

We planned to meet in Gramercy Park, a charming neighborhood packed with small, intimate cafes. Keshawn was keen on the location, but it was difficult to nail him down on a specific restaurant. We agreed to meet on the south side of the park in front of the flickering gas streetlamps. The wrought iron balconies on the brownstones that line the block are decorated with pumpkins and gourds, making the historic buildings feel cozy and inviting.

Meeting a blind date is always awkward, even under the best of circumstances, and these are far from that. Now that Mom isn't having them meet me at the apartment like she did with Kevin, I confirm a date and time and she has the prospective date text me. I imagine arranging illegal outcall massage is not so different from this.

On the other end of the block, I make out a handsome guy with a flattop and close fade. He's wearing black jeans and a red shirt matching the description Keshawn gave me. As he approaches me, I notice he's holding his phone in front of him and maybe taking a selfie as he walks, which seems both strange and incredibly dangerous. I wave, and the guy waves back, so he must be Keshawn, but he doesn't move his outstretched arm. It's clear now that he's on some kind of video chat. I assume he'll hang up by the time he reaches me, but he doesn't.

'Hello, I'm Sam.'

'Hey guys!' he says, looking up at his phone with that awful cadence you hear on social media videos. 'So, like I said, I'm about to meet my date. I put the two restaurants in the Vibe chat. What do you think? Italian or Thai? Voting begins now and don't forget to like and follow.' His voice is super upbeat and loud. He taps something on the screen and finally lowers his arm to his side. 'Hi Sam. I'm Keshawn,' he says with none of the sparkle I heard a second ago and no explanation for his strange behavior.

'Who were you talking to?' I ask.

'My VibePool,' he sighs. His phone makes a cheering sound, and he stretches his arm in front of him again, stares at the lens, and says, 'Hey guys. Results are in.' The chipper TV host voice is back. 'It's Italian tonight. Good job. Now, head over to the menu and start voting on my app and entree. Oh, and don't forget, I need to reach one thousand Vibe Points, and I'll let you all get a look at my date for the night.' He looks over at me. 'And he's cute in a very interesting way. You'll definitely want to take a peek, so vibe it in. Back in a few.' He lowers his arm.

Am I being auctioned off on some website? I have got to review my mother's screening process.

'Looks like they voted for Cafe Rosso,' he says, limply gesturing toward the restaurant's red-and-white awning across the street. 'You down with that? It was a super strong vibe – like an eighty-twenty split.'

'Sure.' I don't know what else to say so I follow him into the place.

Inside Cafe Rosso, we sit at a table in the outdoor courtyard. Checkered tablecloths and bottles of red wine wrapped with wicker on the bottom add to the charm. It's a totally normal place to go on a date – except maybe with this guy.

'Keshawn, I'm sorry,' I begin as he scrolls through his phone. 'I have no idea what Vibe Points are?'

'Oh no,' he says, looking up from his phone. 'Did my assistant not email you? Marta was supposed to brief you and have you sign the NDA. Crap. Let me check Slack. This must seem so weird.'

'Yeah, actually super weird.' At least he acknowledges the situation, so it's a step in the right direction.

'Dang. I forgot she's in Taiwan this week.' He taps his forehead with his fingers. Hard. 'It's my fault. I'm sorry. I'm screwing everything up this week.' He taps his forehead again, even harder.

'It's okay,' I say. 'We all have weeks like that.' I notice a pronounced vein on his forehead is quivering.

'No, it's not okay,' he says, gritting his teeth and clenching his hands into tight fists. 'I'm the founder of VibeTyme. Have you heard of it?' he asks. I shake my head, which freaks him out more. 'Really? It's *tyme* with a *y*. T–Y–M–E.'

'Cute,' I say. 'But no.'

'Crap,' he says and hits his forehead again. My lack of awareness of VibeTyme is clearly stressing him out.

'I'm barely on social media. You can't go by me. I have an AOL account I still use.'

'VibeTyme is an online social media platform where users get to determine the everyday actions of the people they follow. Damn, I asked my assistant to brief you on all this.'

'It's okay,' I say, which is the opposite of the truth, but this guy is clearly on the brink of a meltdown, and I don't want to contribute to some kind of stroke.

His phone cheers, and he lifts his arm above him. 'Hey, guys!' he says, his voice elevated. 'The Vibes are in, and it looks like we're having the calamari frito to start and penne ala vodka for me and eggplant parm for my date. Now keep those Vibe Points coming in if you want to get a look at him.'

'Your followers are voting on what we eat and if they get to see me?'

'I hope that's okay. Do you like eggplant parm? You can order something else. You'll just have to eat it off-camera so they don't see. The chicken marsala came in third if you want to try that.' The server comes over and Keshawn orders a bottle of wine. 'Do you want anything to drink?' he asks.

'I'm fine with wine,' I say.

'That bottle is for me. I can get you your own bottle if you want,' he says, turning to the server. 'Please make that two of the pinot noir. Thank you.'

'You ordered us each an entire bottle of wine?' I ask.

'Running this startup is really, really stressful.' I look more closely at Keshawn who is very attractive but on further inspection I notice his brown eyes look bloodshot from staring at a monitor, no doubt, and he's chewed his fingernails down to an unhealthy level. 'I'll need a bottle of wine to get through tonight. I have investors hounding me. They're looking at the numbers of each interaction. I was trending up but then I started to trend down. I thought seeing me on a date might help but these numbers are weak.'

'I'm not sure I want to have this entire night on social media. Can't we just have dinner?'

'Bro, no,' he says, his voice a desperate plea. 'I can't do that. Please. It's October. I can't start the quarter down.' His face looks like he might explode. 'Bro, please. Seriously. I'm begging you.'

The server comes back, and he pours a glass of wine for each of us from the first of two bottles he places on the table. Keshawn grabs his glass and chugs the entire thing, and then fills it up again. 'I need to get some traction on this app or else...' His phone makes that cheering sound, and he picks it up, stretches his arm out, and his entire demeanor changes. He's no longer on the brink of a breakdown. 'Hey, guys! Looks like we just broke 900, but we need at least a hundred more to get to the next Vibe Point. So, keep them coming, and I'll be back.' His shiny, sunny personality switches off. He lowers his arm, and then his entire upper body slumps forward until his head is on the table in front of me. I think maybe he's crying, but I can't tell.

I look around the restaurant and notice a few people glance over at us with looks of concern. I smile pleasantly, as if to say my date has not had a cardiac episode before the antipasto. Then I hear gentle sobs coming from Keshawn. He is definitely crying. I have no idea what to do. I just met this guy, and I want to get out of this whole situation, but I can't leave him here like this. Then I hear that weird cheering sound coming from his phone. I expect that to perk him up, but it doesn't. He remains face down, weeping into the tablecloth. His phone cheers again. Then again. And again.

'Don't you want to get that? Maybe you reached your goal,' I say but he just lets out a burst of tears without sitting up. The phone cheers. He is either too distraught to get up or the wine is kicking in, but I don't want him to screw up his entire business, so I pick up his phone and see a big *1k* badge glowing. I tap it, and suddenly, I'm staring into the camera, and I see my face through a stream of chat messages that people are sending. *Are you the date? He's kind of cute. He's mid. Where's Keshawn? Order the tiramisu!* The phone rings with each message. At first, the rhythm is slow, but then it grows faster and faster.

The sounds must make Keshawn realize what's going on. He picks up his head, wipes the tears from his eyes, looks at me and mouths, 'Thank you.' I hand him the phone and he transforms himself again. 'Hey guys! Awesome. You did it! But we need to keep raising the Vibe...'

Keshawn spends the rest of the night alternately rousing his followers into 'making more vibe', whatever that means, and weeping loudly with his head on the table. In between bouts of cheers and tears, he explains that he's been working on developing the platform since he graduated from MIT and has sunk his entire life into it. I admire his dedication and sympathize with his distress, so I go along with it. I'm just trying to get through this night but somewhere after the calamari Keshawn leaps up from the table and screams, 'Crap!' Everyone in the restaurant stops to look over at us.

'What's wrong? Did something happen to the vibe?' The words sound as ridiculous coming out of my mouth as I thought they would.

'The server crashed. I told Gary we needed to take it offline before we...' He looks at his phone, tapping the screen so hard I think it might break. 'No, no, no.' Keshawn keeps staring at his phone and walks out the door without so much as a glance in my direction. He leaves me alone at the table with everyone's eyes still on me, a bottle and a half of wine, two entrees and one big fat check.

Chapter 19

'Who's your date for tonight?' Paul asks. I suddenly stop putting on my shoes to head out the door and switch my phone from one ear to the other. I don't mind telling him about my mother's setups, but for some reason I don't immediately tell him about Finn. Not that he would be jealous or have any right to be. Paul would never understand a guy like Finn. Attorneys think artists are goofing off until a real job comes along. Or is that just what Paul thought about me?

'It's not a date. It's a work thing. Some background research.' Vague but accurate.

'Way to go, Sammy. You're really taking your work at Brands seriously. Robert would be a fool not to hire you.'

'Thanks.' I appreciate the compliment, but it feels a bit cold, more like it's coming from the school headmaster than from my future live-in boyfriend.

We say goodbye and I hop on the 6 train and head to St Marks Cinema in the East Village to meet Finn for our screening of *Sunset Boulevard*. I walk down the streets around NYU where I hung out when I was in school. There are more cell phone stores and fewer used bookstores sadly, but the feeling is the same. College kids from all over the city come down here for cheap drinks and eats that look better on social media than they taste. I pass by a bar where Omar and I used to hang out, trying to meet guys. I'd sit at the booth by the pinball machine, too scared to approach anyone, while Omar was hit on by every person who entered the place. So many nights I'd leave him to it and escape to exactly where I'm headed now.

As I approach the theater, I see Finn standing in front. The blinking colored lights from the marquee bathe him in soft pink and amber light. St Marks Cinema is one of the last remaining old movie houses in Manhattan. The owners have painstakingly kept the original features in pristine shape, like the red neon sign above the letter board of the theater, so the experience is the exact opposite of a multiplex and so much more elevated than sitting on your couch at home. Finn's staring up at the marquee. He's wearing a vintage black leather jacket that perfectly hugs his shoulders and falls to his hips like it was made just for his body. I have on a chunky cardigan from a thrift store that my mother has forbidden me from wearing. One of her rules is that I don't dress 'so old' but this isn't one of her setups. She doesn't even know I'm here.

Finn turns around and gives me a big smile that quickly changes to a dramatic expression. 'I'm ready for my close-up, Mr DeMille,' he says, framing his face with his hands.

'Someone has done their research,' I say with a laugh.

'I want to make sure we're giving these kids a great experience.' It's nice to know he has an open mind, especially considering how heated our last conversation was. I walk over to the small glass ticket booth and pass my credit card to the woman with frizzy gray hair I recognize as the wife of the couple that owns the place. 'Hey, Marlena,' I say and she looks up from the counter where she's tearing off tickets.

'Well, look what the cat dragged in,' she says in a New York accent so thick I wonder if Finn can even understand her. 'Hey, Murray! Look who it is,' she shouts over her shoulder.

An elderly man with suspenders pops his head from behind the curtain that separates the box office from the lobby. 'If it isn't our old friend, Sam. Where you been?' he asks. He eyes Finn, who stands to the side, curiously.

I started coming here in my first week of college. I love the vintage velvet chairs, the Art Deco wall sconces, the respect for Hollywood's Golden Age that permeates the atmosphere, but most of all, Marlena and Murray, who would often let me sneak in for free when I spent too much money on DVDs or burritos.

'I've been busy,' I say. It's a feeble excuse but the only one I can think of at the moment. The truth is, I haven't been for at least two years. Paul hates black-and-white movies almost as much as he hates the East Village, so once we were together, I stopped coming down.

'Don't make yourself a stranger,' Murray says. 'And you're in for a treat tonight. Norma has never looked better.'

'You just focus on the projector and don't worry about making eyes at Gloria Swanson,' Marlena scolds. She pushes the tickets through the glass opening and I promise to stop by more regularly.

'They seem very sweet. Do you know how long they've been together?' Finn asks. I love his natural curiosity. It makes it so easy to talk to him. But I noticed as I chatted with Marlena he hung back a bit. I've seen him at Plant Daddy a few times when I've been heading up to my apartment. He's always sitting alone. He's not a misanthrope at all but someone who is more comfortable observing.

'They were high school sweethearts. They went on their first date here and fell in love over a screening of *West Side Story*. Now they're in their eighties and they've spent their whole life together.'

'I'd love to hear their whole story.' I go to take two seats in the middle of the theater. He stops. 'Are you sure you want to sit there?'

'Yes,' I say, scooting toward the middle.

'I like examining the detail. Don't you want to sit closer?'

'No,' I say. 'I like to sit in the middle so I can get lost in the drama. If I'm too close, I can't get the whole picture.' A nearby man with his hand in a box of popcorn gives me a dirty look.

'But you can't get the whole picture if you can't examine the detail,' Finn insists. We are in a standoff and beginning to attract the attention of the people around us. The lights dim and I can hear the familiar sound of the projector starting up.

'These are the best seats,' I say, and about a dozen regulars over the age of seventy shush me, and they have every right to do so.

'Please just sit down,' a woman behind us says and literally shakes her cane at us. The rest of the audience mumbles in agreement. I give Finn an exasperated look and he follows me to the seat I've selected.

'The next movie we see, we sit in front,' he whispers, though I have no idea what makes him think we are going to see another movie together.

Once the lights dim and the screen starts to flicker, I'm transported. There is no here and now, there is no Finn and no conflict over seating. There is only the sprawling story in front of me. I've always used movies to escape and they've never failed me. Tonight is no different.

–

We stay until the very last name on the very last credit rolls and the lights come up. Most of the audience has already left. My mind is still lingering in the monochromatic world of old Los Angeles. I can't help but get emotional. Norma wanted it so deeply. She had been the world's biggest star, but everyone forgot about her. She was desperate to make it big again. I connect so much with her desire – the wanting. But also, the not getting. I've seen the film dozens of times but each time it has a different impact on me. Tonight, it makes me feel raw and vulnerable. I think about sitting on the couch crying after hearing that Hurlington passed. I think about how much I wanted it and how much it defeated me.

We head out of the theater but I make sure to say goodbye to Marlena and Murray before we exit. 'What did you think?' I ask.

'It was dramatic. I'll give you that,' he says as we make our way down the block. 'But wouldn't a documentary about Gloria Swanson be... more authentic?'

I stiffen. 'Do we always need authenticity? Can't we just get lost in the story sometimes?'

He considers my comment as we walk in silence past a bodega and a laundromat with bright LED signs. 'It's a masterpiece, no doubt,' he says. 'A great film. But don't you ever crave something... more contemporary? Something that reflects *our* stories?'

I tilt my head, taken aback. 'It's a classic, Finn. The storytelling, the character depth...'

'But where are the queer characters? Where's the representation? We live in a different era now. Shouldn't our films reflect that? I think we should use something more current.'

It's just after midnight and the East Village is finally coming alive, even on a chilly October night. College kids swarm the sidewalks and the doorways. The endless amount of bars in the neighborhood overflow with people despite the temperature dropping while we were inside the movie house. It's one big party in the East Village every night but I'm not feeling a part of it having to defend one of my favorite films.

'This movie is one of the foundations of the queer culture that you are so rhapsodic about,' I say, trying to keep my tone level. I've never had anyone argue against one of my favorite movies of all time. Besides – how can he not get it? 'It's pure camp,' I continue. 'Do you have any idea how many gay people have watched this film and understood it as a gay film without there being any out queer characters in it? For decades, gay people have decoded and understood it as a gay classic. The relation-ship between Norma and Max? If that's not queer, I don't know what is. The way Cecil B. DeMille calls her "Little Fellow"? The way Norma looks at William Holden in a swimsuit is gayer than an episode of *Drag Race*.' I'm riling up for a fight and I'm not sure why. Is it because I identify with old Norma too much? Joe Gillis does accuse her of not adapting to the times.

'But there aren't actual queer people represented in it,' he says, challenging me.

'Not every classic needs to be dissected for repres-entation. Sometimes what isn't said is more powerful,' I continue, more defensive than I intended. I'm not even sure how much I believe what I'm saying. It's not a very popular opinion. But he challenges me in ways that get me wound up.

'We don't have to do that anymore,' Finn says. 'We've worked hard for equality, so why not watch something that mirrors our struggles, our lives, our love?'

I laugh, but it's laced with sarcasm. 'So now, every film we watch has to check the contemporary and queer representation box?' I think back to my mom making me wear that *Say Gay* T-shirt and how much I resisted. Am I the problem?

'Sam, I respect classics. I do. But sometimes, I want to watch stories where people like us aren't just subtext, where our narratives are the story. Where the lives of queer people, people of color, and disabled people are shown authentically. We don't need to hide anymore.' He stops, turns and his eyes stare right at me, maybe inside me.

'You think I hide?' I ask. The question makes my chest wince. I stop walking and try to fight the discomfort of his accusation. It's a question I don't want to think about at all. I knew I shouldn't have agreed to going to a movie with him like this. He's too intense. He says whatever he thinks and asks whatever he wants. I feel like I'm constantly being interviewed, observed, and asked uncomfortable questions that should be none of his business.

'That's not what I said. Not exactly.'

'That's not a no,' I snap back.

'Sam, I'm just trying to figure out why...'

I can feel myself moving from annoyance to anger with tinges of self-doubt and confusion. I don't want to feel any of these things. For a second I think about the easy detachment of my mom's setups. The guys are bizarre but they don't challenge who I am at my core. I just want to get out of this conversation. That's really the only way to stop the feelings from bubbling up to the surface and making me feel out of control.

'I don't want to talk about it anymore,' I say and start walking again. His steps match mine. 'You want to show something else to the students? Fine. You can decide. I'll show up and talk about whatever you want.' He's a client and I have to start treating him like any other client. From now on I'm going to treat him the same way I treated the Surentox campaign – detached and emotionless.

Finn stops walking and turns toward me. I want to keep going but I know I can't just run away. 'We're just having a debate. Why are you getting so worked up?'

'I'm not getting worked up. But this is something that's important to me.' I shove my hands in my pockets. It's only the middle of October but the wind is making me shiver.

He's quiet for a second but his eyes are directly on me. I think he's let it go but then he says, 'Maybe you should be telling your own story instead of hiding behind old movies.'

'Hiding behind old movies!' Now I am shouting at him in the middle of Second Avenue. Again, he goes to that word: hiding. I do *not* like it. 'You don't have any idea what those movies have meant to me. I'm not hiding behind anything. In fact, they make me feel seen.' I make sure to look him right in the eyes when I say this. It's not the first time I've been accused of hiding behind something. When you make most of your living writing as someone else, it comes with the territory. But he has hit a nerve and now all the emotions I have been trying to keep under control start racing to the surface. I turn away from him. I don't want him to see how close to tears I am.

'Sam,' he says softly. 'I'm sorry. I used the wrong word. I pushed too hard. I'm sorry. I do that. I don't know how to just...' He smashes his fist into his other open hand and lets out a grunt like he's trying to control himself. 'I don't know when to stop. I get into it with people about the things I'm passionate about. I try to stay on the sidelines but I couldn't do that with you.' He pushes his hair back but keeps his hazel eyes on me as he does.

'I'm passionate about it, too,' I say, swallowing hard and trying to regain my composure but I think it's too late.

'I can see that. That's what made me push harder. I want to know. I want to know more about—'

'Don't,' I say, cutting him off. I finally have myself under control and I don't want to lose it. I made a decision to give it up – all this emotion and disappointment about telling stories and sharing stories. I need to move on with my life because if I don't I *will* become Norma Desmond, desperate to have her big break but having a nervous breakdown. I thought if I could get a publisher to bite on something with my own name on it I could have my comeback but that didn't happen. I keep hearing Paul telling me it's time to grow up, and now I'm even more sure he's right. I need to find a mature distance from all this stuff, but Finn is trying to pull me back into it. I don't want to feel the pain and anguish of not being able to do it anymore.

'I'm serious, Finn,' I say. 'We can show whatever movie you want. Just promise me we don't have to talk about it anymore. Goodnight.' His eyebrows are pushed together and he opens his mouth to say something but there is nothing else to say. I pick up my pace and walk away from him without looking back.

Chapter 20

The next day I'm in my apartment still stinging over my exchange with Finn. I hate the way he puts documentaries over other forms of film. He completely dismisses the entire Golden Age of Hollywood. It's infuriating. Growing up, those films inspired me and gave me comfort. He categorically believes that we need to focus on 'real' stories. Well, those stories were real to me. I lived with them in my head most of my life. My phone rings and I hope it's Finn just so I can tell him how wrong he is.

'Hey Sammy,' Paul coos into the phone.

'Paul, ugh. I am so angry.'

'Aw, babe. What's wrong?' I explain the whole thing, how Finn and I have to pick a film to show and how Finn is so pig-headed about his genre and how important classic films are to me. 'Can you believe him?' I ask when I finish my diatribe.

Silence on the other end of the phone.

'Hello, did you hear all that?' I ask, assuming he's driving through an area without a signal.

'Yeah, Sammy. You guys like different movies,' he says matter-of-factly. I guess he's right. It's not a huge deal, but it feels like a huge deal. Paul has a way of putting things in perspective, I guess. He's so chill. Nothing bothers him and I like that. I can get overly emotional when I'm feeling vulnerable and I hate that feeling. It reminds me of when I was a kid in school, and I'd cry so easily, making me an instant target for teasing.

'How are things there?' I ask. He tells me about a contract that he had to revise with a client and how they kept asking for the smallest changes but he didn't care because each change meant more billable hours.

I'm not very interested in his job but it's clear he does it well so I listen and ask questions. I want to find out how the divorce is going but I'm not sure it's a topic I should approach. He showed me the retainer and I don't want him to think I doubt him. Paul says he has to head to a client and then tells me how much he misses me and how he can't wait to come back and be with me and that makes me feel better. I tell him I can't wait either.

Usually when I hang up with Paul I feel this longing but today I can't shake my feelings of frustration over Finn. I see my laptop on the table. For a second I think about running over to it and pounding out a scene just to prove my point about how fictional stories with time-honored tropes can have as much emotional depth as anything 'real'. Why not? Maybe I still have it in me. I open my laptop and think about how to begin, but then I see the submission folder that got rejected on my desktop, and it stops me in my tracks. What makes me think I can write anything better than the stuff I already submitted? My self-doubt takes over and I leave my laptop on the table in my apartment and decide to walk to the next date my mother has scheduled for me. At least her setups are a distraction from facing a blank screen.

I get so used to living in the grid of midtown Manhattan that coming down to the West Village is like visiting another country. The buildings are shorter, with windowed storefronts and instead of numbers the streets here have actual names – Jane, Perry, and even Gay. I enter the Cuddle Cup Cafe past a festive scarecrow wearing an *I Heart NY* T-shirt and an arrangement of red, green, and yellow apples that look more ornamental than edible. I'm grateful to be forty blocks away from my neighborhood to minimize the risk of running into anyone from Plant Daddy or, worse, Finn.

It's easy to spot my date, Nathaniel Lee Abernathy IV. He texted me at least a dozen headshots of himself. Not candids. Actual studio lighting and backdrops, each with a different expression, from joyful to serious. Sometimes with props. He's handsome in a shiny, overly polished way with a well-toned body and perfectly coiffed chestnut brown hair that could be in a shampoo commercial.

'Hello, I'm Sam,' I say as I walk over to the table where he's seated.

'Look at you, pretty as a peach blossom in June. You're even more handsome than the photo your mama sent me,' he says. At first, I think his Southern accent is a joke. It's as thick as tar. Nothing like Finn, who just has the slightest drawl around the edges of his deep bass. My mom told me today's match was born and raised in Alabama and has a new client in New York. She met him when he made the colossal mistake of asking her for directions. You ask my mom for directions, and you've made a friend for life. She keeps in touch with a woman she met decades ago at a rest stop on the Garden State Parkway who couldn't find Atlantic City. My mother said this guy has 'pizazz'. I told her I'm not sure what pizazz is and again reminded her what a disaster all her setups have been so far.

'Sit yourself down Mister Sam and tell me all about what makes you tick.' He stands up and pulls out the chair for me.

'Thanks.' He's very polite. 'Can I get you something?' I ask but then I look down and see he already has a mug in front of him.

'No, thank you, but let me get you something. I got here earlier to finish up some work before our—' His phone buzzes. 'Excuse me. A work emergency and then I will put this thing away.' At least this guy has no plans to livestream the entire date. 'I'm so sorry. This is so rude. Not a way to make a good first impression.' He puts his finger up to indicate this will only take a second.

'No problem,' I say. I totally understand. I've spent many a dinner studying the wine menu while I waited for Paul to get off an important call with high-end clients who simply couldn't wait. Once, he even took a call from a senator, which impressed me.

Nathaniel answers his phone and says, 'Tiffany Renee Sunshine O'Leary-Chang y'all are on my last nerve. I told y'all. You are not wearing the tulip blue taffeta until the Little Miss Crab Cakes Pageant this spring. I want you in Sunset Orange and Sunflower Yella. What part of Little Miss Candy Corn do you not understand?' He pulls the phone away from his mouth to speak to me. 'My apologies. She's only eight, but she is the most stubborn eight-year-old in the world and not the brightest.' He goes back to his phone. 'Now, Miss O'Leary-Chang, your Uncle Nate is at an important personal engagement. I want you to put on the Candy Corn dress and video chat me the second you have it on. I have not approved your hair just yet young lady.'

He hangs up. 'Apologies. I'm up here working Miss Stacey Lynn Cavatelli for the big Little Miss Outer Boroughs Pageant. Her parents are big spenders, so it means I need to work remotely with some of my Southern gals.'

'My mom said you were a coach,' I say. At first, I thought it was some kind of sport, but now I think I may have made a wrong assumption.

'I am the East Coast's foremost Pageant Coach, specializing in toddlers up to pre-teens. Once they hit thirteen, I'm done. Teenagers are too hard.'

'I see,' I say. When Tiffany calls back I offer to get him a refill and he declines. I head up to the counter so he can sort out the dress situation, and so I can figure out how long I have to stay on this date to qualify as a date in the eyes of my mother. I order something on ice. That way, I can gulp it down and be finished sooner than I would with something steamed. I take my iced passion fruit tea back to the table, and apparently Tiffany is wearing the correct dress.

'Gorgeous, Honeybee. You look absolutely gorgeous. Don't you agree, Miss Mommy?' Out of the corner of my eye I see an adult woman pop her face into the video chat and nod enthusiastically. 'Let me ask my new boyfriend what he thinks?' Nathaniel smiles at me revealing teeth that are a few shades too white for any human. I'm assuming he called me his boyfriend ironically or facetiously, or maybe metaphorically. He can't have done it seriously. We met five minutes ago. He shows me the screen of his phone which is thirty per cent pouffy dress, sixty per cent big hair and ten per cent little girl.

'Doesn't she look like Calhoun County's next Little Miss Candy Corn?' he asks.

I nod and grab my drink, seeing how much I can chug without my bladder bursting. He smiles at me, and I think he reaches for my hand, which I quickly pull away. He takes his chair and moves it right next to me, so our legs are almost touching.

'Now look you two, I need to give this handsome man my full attention. I will call you back. Goodbye, now. See y'all.' He puts his phone down and turns to me. 'Your mama said you were a successful writer. I always thought it would be wonderful to be married to a writer ever since I came out. Something about all that creative energy.'

'When did you come out?' I ask. It's not an uncommon question in these types of situations.

'Just three weeks ago. It was a shock to everyone.'

I almost spit out my iced tea. 'I'm sure it was.' Are the people in Calhoun County headless?

'But I'm not good at being single. I broke off with my fiancé just before my birthday. Amy Sue was devastated. We had been engaged for fifteen years. I thought while I'm up here I would find myself a Yankee boy and bring him back home.'

'Oh, did you?' My eyes stay on the clock on the wall behind him.

'The country club does gay weddings, you know. They won't allow them in the main ballroom, but they will let you use the carriage house during the week, which is quite darling.' He reaches for my hand again and I yank it away.

'I'm not really looking to get married,' I say. 'At least not right away.'

He moves his chair a few inches away from me. 'Then what are you doing here on this date?' He is highly offended. Maybe he should be. It's a fair question. What am I doing on this date with this guy I have no intention of dating? On the other hand, it's just coffee. Does it mean I have to be ready to pick out china patterns and debate the benefits of a chocolate fountain at the reception?

'I just thought we could talk and...' How am I supposed to respond? I watch the minute hand tick.

'Just talk? Good sir, where I am from, you do not enter your horse in the race if you don't expect him to win.'

'Do you have a horse?' I ask. I am just trying to make small talk. 'That's nice, I've always liked horses.' I have no idea what to say.

Nathaniel stands up, brushes some imaginary dust off his chest and shoulders as if I have infected him with Northern stupidity. 'Good day, Sam. I'm sorry to have to say this is not a relationship I can continue to pursue. Please give my best to your sweet mama and let her know I asked after her.' He nods to me and walks out.

I will definitely let her know about this, no question about it.

Chapter 21

I'm at lunch with Robert talking about Finn but after our night at *Sunset Boulevard* last week it feels weird. It's not as weird as the brief coffee experience I had with Nathaniel Lee Abernathy IV, but it's weird, nonetheless. Robert only thinks of Finn as a product connected to the Carlos Wong Gallery. I need to do more of that and less thinking about Finn as the guy who is constantly pushing my buttons and hangs out at Plant Daddy working his way into my circle of friends.

It's almost impossible to believe that Plant Daddy is a few long blocks west of where I'm sitting with my boss Robert at the elegant restaurant on the second floor of the Seagram Building on Park Avenue. The Grill is famous for hosting media power brokers. Modern light fixtures that look like bronze icicles hover above us, and metallic wall sconces illuminate the wood paneling that makes the place feel like the inner sanctum of some private club. It's the exact opposite of the overgrown greenery and mismatched chairs of the charming cafe I call my second home.

'Are you sure you don't want a drink?' Robert asks me as the waiter stands attentively next to our table. He has already finished one drink and orders his second.

I respond with a polite, 'No, thank you.'

The waiter leaves and Robert says, 'The Carlos Wong people have a booth at the New International show for Art Week in Miami and they want Finn to be down there. I don't have to tell you how huge an event Art Week is. Everyone wants to be there in December.'

'I'm sure Finn will have a great time in Miami. I know he had a studio down there. I'll block those dates out on my calendar so I know he won't be available.'

The waiter returns with the drink and Robert takes a small sip and then another. I imagine the pressure involved in Robert's job makes an afternoon indulgence a necessity.

'Actually, you won't be available either,' Robert says. 'I want you to go to Miami with him.'

'Miami? Like "thank-you-for-being-a-friend", Miami?'

'I'm not sure what that means but the one in Florida. Yes. Our travel team will set it up.'

'But... but. Robert, I have to be honest with you, I burn very easily and...' I'm not sure I want to go to Miami. I suddenly get an image of Finn in a tank top and this is not a good idea. Then I remember an even better excuse. 'I have a family wedding middle of the month.' I can't miss my cousin's wedding. My mother would explode into a million pieces and expect me to use her Dyson stick to vacuum them up.

'Don't worry it's just after Thanksgiving. I wouldn't need you there the entire week just for the kick-off weekend. You'll be back in plenty of time.' Robert's hairy knuckles wrap around the stem of his glass as he lifts it to his mouth and finishes it with one swallow. 'I wouldn't normally ask a part-time staffer but Finn insisted and since the chances are good you'll be full-time soon it seemed like the right opportunity.'

He insisted? I don't even know what to think about that. I guess he's happy with the work I've been doing for him.

'And they want you to write the copy for the gallery catalog. A behind-the-scenes look at the artist. Spend a day watching him work and write it up. Like the Surentox stuff.' Working with Finn is nothing like working on Surentox. That was steady, boring work with some very nice people. Working with Finn is like a roller coaster I can't seem to get off.

'If that's where you need me.' I can't really say no to Robert when I'm trying to get him to hire me full-time.

'Great. I think this trip will be a good way to help you think about your future at Brands to the Rescue.'

My eyes wander around the dining room taking in all the people in conservative suits looking stressed and clutching gimlets or other cocktails. I had to search my apartment for a tie and finally had to borrow one of Omar's. I'm not sure this is the type of place where I will ever fit in but Robert is here asking me about 'my future'. Will this place be a part of it?

'Sam, your work is excellent. You pay attention to detail, the clients like you and your writing is quite good,' he says. Quite good. It's not exactly Michiko Kakutani in *The New York Times* but that's the most praise I've gotten for my writing in a long time so I'll take it. 'But is this what you want to do? Do you want to be a Senior Brand Manager? I thought you had other interests when you started? I need someone who's committed and passionate about the job. Is that you?'

'Yes. Yes, that's me,' I say but I have no idea if that's true or not. My first instinct is to give him the answer he wants to hear. Am I passionate about writing press releases and scheduling publicity for people? Is that even something one *can* have passion for? I don't mind doing it but I wouldn't say I'm passionate about it.

I blame Oprah. She's the one who got everyone all into their passion. I hate that word. What does it even mean? If we all follow our passion, who is collecting the garbage, driving the buses, or emailing the press releases? Not every job can have passion, right?

'I'm glad to hear it. But I have to be honest there are a number of external candidates who look quite promising.' Robert nods to a thin man in his late fifties with short grey hair who could be his twin. The man nods back.

'Oh,' I say and grab my water glass to avoid having to say anything else.

'With so many shifts in the landscape, there are a lot of great people looking for new positions.' This might not be the slam dunk I thought it was. If it weren't for the fact that I'll be moving in with Paul in a few months I would happily stay part-time. I make just enough to support myself but splitting the rent on Paul's terraced one-bedroom in Tribeca would be impossible. Not to mention the dinners out and anything else we might do for fun. If it's going to work with Paul I have to come into the relationship as his equal. I can't have him paying and throwing around his money.

'I understand,' I say realizing I will need to sell myself to Robert, something I know I'm not very good at. 'I think I bring a lot to the table.' Even I can hear how lame I sound.

'I'd love to promote someone from the part-time ranks. You know you remind me of myself when I was younger.' He smiles to himself. 'I was working part-time at Kleinman way before I started Brands. I thought I could write the next great American novel. I finally got a short story published and I counted the beans and you know how much I made from it. Less than a penny a word.' He signals for the waiter and politely requests another martini.

'What was it about?' I ask. I knew Robert had moved from some literary background into corporate but I've never heard him talk about it before.

'Oh, some nonsense about a guy who gets his girl-friend pregnant, and he joins the military so they can get healthcare. Then he dies before the baby is born. All very sad and serious.' The drink arrives and he takes a large swallow. 'The point is in the end I wasn't making any money. It wasn't a serious way to earn a living. It wasn't something I could do as a real adult.'

Is this what it looks like to be a real adult? Liquid lunches? Client demands? Suddenly it feels like Robert is The Ghost of Christmas Yet to Come and he's showing me Kermit and Miss Piggy weeping in a corner. The Muppet version of the classic is really the only one worth watching. Still, it's an unpleasant future.

By the time we finish lunch, I expect Robert to be a bit tipsy, but he isn't at all. We get up from the table, and we walk through the sea of 'normals' in dark blue and charcoal grey suits. I wonder how they got here. Am I passing through a room of former sculptors, dancers and poets or did everyone here set out plotting this destination? Maybe life is more about where you end up rather than where you planned to go.

Chapter 22

This one was the last straw. I do not even go up to my apartment after my aborted evening with Riesling. No last name. Just Riesling. These blind dates are getting out of control. It's one thing to force me to play laser tag in Jersey City with an orthodontist from Poughkeepsie but another to endure what happened tonight. At least the orthodontist gave me a free toothbrush. I walk right into Plant Daddy and straight to the counter, which is unusually busy for this time of night.

I move closer and realize my mom is holding court. 'Now, Morgan,' she says raising her voice to be heard over the steaming wand. 'You have to embrace body positivity. You're a beautiful person inside and out and that's what matters. I want you to write a love letter to your own body. Telling it everything you love.'

'That's a wonderful idea. Thank you, Gloria,' Morgan says with a shy smile and the crowd around my mother thins.

'Mother, may I speak with you,' I say stiffly.

'Uh oh, Maggie. He only calls me mother when I'm in trouble. Mind if I go spray the tropicals and chat with my beautiful son?'

'No problem,' Maggie says, stretching her arms above her head. My mother grabs a vintage brass atomizer and I meet her by the shelf with the orchids and bromeliads.

'How did it go with Riesling? I thought you were going to dinner tonight.'

'That is what I'm here to talk to you about,' I say sharply but she's oblivious.

'Riesling seems so interesting. And he has both passion and pizazz. He helped me find the most perfect shade of apricot lipstick at Sephora. What an eye for color. I thought you two might hit it off. He's a very gifted cosmetologist.' She spritzes a tall yellow and violet orchid before carefully examining the leaves.

'So you said. He told me he had to finish up with a client and asked if I wouldn't mind meeting him at work before dinner. I thought I'd be going to some photo studio or behind the scenes of a runway show, so imagine my surprise when my Uber drops me off at Peaceful Meadows.' I try to remain calm and follow her as she shuffles to the next plant.

'I hear that's a lovely place,' my mother says without the slightest bit of remorse.

'If you're dead. It's a funeral home. Riesling is a *mortuary* cosmetologist. He works on dead people. You seemed to have left that part out.'

'Did I?' She puts her finger to her mouth and then shrugs. 'So what? It's a job.'

'Sure, I get that, but he made me wait for him in the lobby while he put blush on a corpse. I had to sit *shiva* with a family from Canarsie. Then he wanted to drive to the restaurant using the company car – a refrigerated hearse.'

'It's not like there were bodies in it,' she says spraying a plant. Then she stops, holds the mister in both hands and tilts her head toward me. 'Were there?'

'We'll never know, Mom, because I made up a very polite excuse to get out of there and avoid being stuck in the Midtown Tunnel a few inches away from a dead body in need of fresh eye liner. And don't get me started about the pageant coach. Mom, seriously, how are you screening these people?'

'Nathaniel? Yeah. He's a bit desperate but you have to admit he has amazing skin. Riesling was a strong candidate. And they're both very passionate about what they do. You know that is such an important rule. I thought there might be a little spark. That's what you need. Someone to ignite that in you.'

'I do not need to be ignited. Thank you.' Is that what she thinks I need? How can she know so little about me? I need the exact opposite. I need someone stable. Someone who keeps me calm and makes my life easier, not harder. I have her for that. Then I hear a weird sound from her phone sitting on the table between us. It's a cross between a growl and a moan. Then it happens again and again. 'Mom, can't you hear those notifications?'

'Are they going off again? I can't really hear them. Too high or too low, I think.' She grabs her phone and turns it over to look at the screen. 'Fabulous. Look at all these possibilities!' She shows me the screen and I see a cascading stream of notifications from SecretSlam, a hookup app.

'What are you doing on SecretSlam?'

'I'm not on SecretSalm. You are.' She takes back her phone and swipes a few times until she finds a picture of me from at least five years ago at some formal event I don't even remember. I look like I should be selling insurance. I swipe through and she has a picture of me from a production of *Godspell* in college. I'm wearing glitter on my face and overalls that are a few sizes too big. But what's more awful is the name she has selected.

'JoyBoy793!'

'Isn't that adorable? I came up with that myself. I think it says that you bring happiness and vigor and that number is just our street address. You know, to make it more memorable.' She swipes to show me my profile. There are a bunch of check boxes for types and sex stuff and she has checked all of them. All of them. Fetishes and sexual things I have never heard of. Some of them I'm not sure I can even pronounce.

'Mom, delete this profile immediately,' I demand but I stop myself from shouting since we are so close to the tropicals. Kai would have a fit if I spoke any louder so close to his precious orchids.

'Don't worry. I tell everyone I chat with that I'm your mother.'

'Oh, that makes me feel so much better.' I worry the intensity of my sarcasm will make the blossoms wilt.

'No one thinks they're talking to you. That would be goldfishing and unethical.' I do not correct her. She puts the atomizer on the shelf and takes a seat at the closest table. She pulls out a seat for me and pats it sharply. 'Now that you're here, we can go over some of these profiles together. I've met some very nice people, and I even helped one with his chronic rosacea. I know a dermatologist on the Upper West Side who can work wonders, and this guy has already seen an improvement.' She wipes her hands on her apron and pushes her curly hair back behind her ears before swiping through more profiles. 'Are you still eating meat?'

'Yes. Why?'

She frowns. 'That's too bad. So many of these guys are vegan. They all have these eggplants in their profiles or peaches.'

'That's not what those mean.' I put my elbows on the table so I can hold my head in my hands. She ignores me so I let her go on thinking that most of gay New York is just looking for a healthy dose of fruits and vegetables. My mother is a minefield of knowledge. She knows a ton about some things and is completely oblivious to others.

'What do you think about this guy?' she asks, holding her phone toward me.

'No,' I say without looking at the picture.

She swipes again. 'This one? He's in Bahrain at the moment but flies to Atlanta next week and then New York.'

'No,' I say. What kind of filter is she using to meet guys in Bahrain? We repeat this a half dozen more times.

She eventually throws up her hands and says, 'I have a delivery scheduled out back. Look through all of these messages and choose at least one guy who seems interesting. I've hand-selected each boy on that list. Some of them are super sweet and all of them have passion.' She starts walking away but she stops and turns back. 'But OscarTime44 does some weird thing with Q-tips. I think it's sexual but I'm not totally sure. I'm not saying cross him off the list; I just want you to be aware, and if that's what you're into, I say go for it.'

She walks away to deal with the delivery, squirming out of responding to my complaint about Riesling. Just for kicks, I scroll through the list she has created. It's a parade of shiny torsos and other pleasantly filtered R-rated body parts. At least she isn't asking for dick pics.

My mom comes back, wipes her hands on her apron and cranes her neck to look at the profiles with me. 'Oooh, what about that one? He's been very polite in the messages. I think he works in graphic design.' She points to a guy wearing a wide-brimmed felt hat and huge sunglasses.

'You can't even see what his face looks like.'

'So what? He said he likes the beach.'

'Mom, I hate the beach. You know that.' All that sand in places it shouldn't be.

'Of course I do. That's why I figured someone who loves the beach would be a good match. You'd get to see it through their eyes. Opposites attract. That's a rule everyone knows. It's not mine. It's science.'

Kai comes over with a very sad-looking pot of dirt with something that used to be green on the top of it. 'Poor thing. They were once a blooming camelia, all full of life. Now look at them.'

'Oh, Kai, I'm so sorry,' my mother says. 'Camelia can sometimes need re-rooting.'

'Good idea. I'll be out back in the potting shed if you need me.' He rolls away but turns back. 'Gloria, did the shipment that we were waiting for come in?'

'Just now. I'll get it set up later.'

'What's going on back there?' I ask Kai. For all I know, my mom is building me a husband out of discounted parts she finds online.

'Don't you worry about it, Mr Nosey.' Kai leaves and I think I almost catch him wink at my mom but it's more likely Kai has dirt in his eye.

'So, none of those guys float your boat?' my mom asks, resting her elbows on the counter.

'Not a one.' I hope that will be the end of it. 'I do not want to be on SecretSlam. Can you please delete my profile?' I ask even though it's a demand.

'Not a problem.' I know enough to trust that when my mother says something *isn't* a problem, it means a big problem is coming. 'I checked your calendar and I see you are free this coming Sunday.'

'Oh, Lord. Another blind date? I don't think I have the strength. Who is it? Your butcher's friend's neighbor's plumber?'

'A plumber!' She puts her hands together and kisses them before raising them up to the sky. 'From your lips to God's ears. What I wouldn't give to have a plumber for a son-in-law. But no, it's not a blind date. Those have a very low ROI. That's return on investment.'

'I know.'

'I need to start casting a wider net.' I pray she is using a metaphor and doesn't plan to stand on Ninth Avenue with some kind of webbed sack. 'Your cousin's wedding is less than two months away. I want you to walk into The Plaza Hotel with the man of your dreams on your arm. And I've found out about something even better than blind dates. Better than the apps. It's called Speed Dating. You spend a few minutes with dozens and dozens of men. It's making a huge comeback according to an article I read in *The New York Times*. Your generation is tired of hiding behind screens. They want to go out and meet people face to face.'

'Is that what I want? I'm so glad you have a digital subscription to *The New York Times* so you can play Wordle and find out what I want.'

She pats her apron pockets, and then pushes her hands into the gauzy green bohemian-style skirt Omar made for her before pulling out a piece of paper and showing it to me. 'I knew you wouldn't believe me so I printed out the article and I underlined all the important passages.' She folds the piece of paper for safekeeping and puts it back in her pocket. 'That's not me Gloria Carmichael. That's *The*

New York Times speaking. Surely you'll trust them if you don't trust your own mother.'

She has me cornered. 'If I go to the speed dating thing then we put a pause on the blind dates?'

'That's fair. And look, I'm not a monster. I'm going to let you wear whatever you want to wear as long as it isn't too baggy and not so much black. You're going to speed dating, not cleaning the garage. And nothing yellow. Makes you look jaundiced. And no hats. But whatever you want, really.'

'You must really think I'm a loser,' I say to her seriously and sink into the chair. The whole experience is draining me.

'What?' she exclaims and raises her hands to her cheeks in shock. She fake spits on the ground. Twice. 'Don't even say such a thing. Don't even think it. What in the world would make you say that, Sam? I love you. I think you are the most wonderful, handsome, and best son a mother could ever have. I say that all the time.'

'I know you say it. You say it a lot but that's different than expressing it through actions. Look at all this crazy stuff you're doing...'

'What? I'm just helping. That's what mothers do. And, Sam, don't use crazy that way. A lot of people could be offended.'

I look at her in her lavender T-shirt with bold white lettering that says 'Moms for Equality' and a small yellow and blue flag in the corner. I love her dedication to the cause but I am not one of her social issues.

'Maybe you think you're just helping but it's more than that. You think I can't find someone on my own.' I don't tell her that I already have found someone, that his name is

Paul and she already hates him. 'You think I am so poorly presented that I need your help to get a date.'

'That's not true at all. Not at all,' she says, shaking her head and rolling her eyes. Serious conversations are not our strength. I want to sit her down and ask why she is obsessed with helping me. I don't get it. I want her to understand who I am as a person, not just who I am as her son, but we don't really operate on that wavelength. I guess I don't really understand her as a person either. Our connection is strong but not always deep, and there's a difference. Despite the torture I've had to endure since this plan started, the fact is we are slowly learning more about one another even if there are some dead-ends and head-on collisions.

Her phone makes that growl/moan sound and she takes it out and pulls down her reading glasses from over her head, despite the fact that she has a pair hanging from her neck. 'I'm going to have to tell Desperate2Love that you aren't interested. That's going to be rough for him. He just got over a bad breakup and was looking forward to meeting you... but maybe I can set him up with InsatiableBtm444.' She looks away for a moment deep in thought. 'You know that just might work. I'm getting so good at this.' A customer appears at the counter register with a snake plant and a small bag of dirt. 'I wrote all the information down here.' She hands me a piece of paper. 'And I emailed it to you in case you lose the paper. You know we never did find that glove.'

'What glove?' I ask.

'The ones I bought you for your tenth birthday. You barely had them a week when you lost the left one. So be careful with this. I know you can misplace things. You don't mean to but you do. I love you. I think you are wonderful. Forehead,' she says and I bend toward her over the counter. She kisses me above my eyebrows and says, 'I love you times a million billion.'

'I love you a billion more,' I say and she heads to the other end of the counter to take an order. She tosses a fresh dish towel over her shoulder and greets the customer with an easy smile. I can tell she's enjoying working here as much as she's enjoying interfering in my life. But it's hard to be too upset with her meddling since she genuinely wants what's best for me, or at least what she *thinks* is best. Everything she's doing is done from a place of love and it makes me feel guilty because I'm just going through the motions. It reminds me of the time I agreed to take one of Maggie's yoga classes. I thought I would humor her and casually move through the poses but I could barely walk for a week.

Chapter 23

Speed dating takes place on Sunday between brunch and dinner at a club in Greenpoint Brooklyn. As soon as I walk in, I see the host, an older man known around the city as the drag queen Clams Casino. Along with two other drag queens, he forms the Giblet Triplets, a trio famous for their bawdy songs and general fabulousness. Today he's out of drag but sporting a Pucci-inspired scarf over a corduroy jacket. He's as enthusiastic as I am unenthused for the event.

'Once you sign up, write your number on your name tag big and bold. We want big and bold. Remember not everyone has the eyes of a twenty-four-year-old twink from Massachusetts.' He points to his eyes and then points to a muscular jock-type blushing in the corner. 'That's right, I'm talking to you Number 38.'

I've always been good at following directions. I sign up, grab a name tag and write 47 in big bold numerals across my name. The idea is that you go on a series of ten-minute dates, and you write down the number of the guys who want to get to know you better, and if they write down your number too, at the end of the event, you exchange contact information. It seems harmless enough. It's so crowded in the room that I can only see the guys who are standing around me. Most of them are in their twenties but there are a few older guys in their forties that look kind of interesting. Not that I'm looking. I'm just hoping that when the big speed dating wheel begins to spin I'm not stuck talking to some kid obsessed with a music genre I've never heard of. I'd like to spend the ten-minute session at least connecting with someone old enough to hold a conversation.

Clams has the back of the room set up so that there are two lines of chairs. You're supposed to have your back turned before you sit down so that when you see your speed dater, you can have a visceral response to their physical presence. It's a lot of work to create some ah-ha moment that might never happen but Clams is so incredibly excited about it that everyone goes along. He rings a loud, high-pitched bell over his head.

'Now, take your seats and do not turn around until you hear this bell. Even numbers go toward the door after the bell rings and odd numbers toward the bar to keep things interesting.' He rings the bell. 'Now hurry up. Sunday Supper with Drags Stars of the Apocalypse starts right after this and Hell Fire Fantasia will have my head if we run over.' He rings the bell again, and I stand behind my assigned chair, dreading the rest of the afternoon. This is such a humiliating way to meet people. What happened to normal encounters like one-night stands?

I have my back to my chair and when I turn around it's the muscle twink from Massachusetts, Number 38.

'What's up, bruh?'

'Hello,' I say. I'm sure most of the guys here are drooling over him. He's wearing a tight tank top despite the fact that it's the first week in November and most people are wearing jackets and scarves. His arms look like a boa constrictor swallowed a few softballs – bumpy yet hard. His hair is sculpted perfectly. Although I do not use any facial moisturizers myself, you can tell he has an entire bathroom full of lotions and serums. His skin is actually dewy. It's so moist I think he should worry about mold.

'What do you bench?' he asks.

'What do I what?' I ask. 'Is bench a verb? I only know it as a noun.'

'Oh, wow, you're funny too. That's funny.' It is? At least he didn't ask me what a noun is.

'Thanks,' I say.

'So really what do you bench?' he asks again. 'You know, like on the bench press, bro? What do you bench?'

'Oh, I see,' I say. I go to the gym with Omar but it's mostly a social activity. I don't pay attention to the weights since Omar keeps track of everything. I do it like someone who learns a prayer in Latin and sort of mumbles through it phonetically. 'I don't know. I mean one of the weights is usually red and sometimes my friend adds a blue. At least I think it's blue. The blues are used a lot so they're very chipped. I think it was blue once so yeah, a blue and red maybe. Blue and red. Final answer,' I say. Now I think I'm being a bit funny or at least humorous but it's clear Number 38 doesn't think so. The blank smile and forced laughter that were the sum total of his personality just a minute ago have vanished. He takes the little pencil we were given at the start of the event and I watch him draw a line across my number and put his pencil down. Then he folds his hands across his chest and stares just above my head for the remaining time. I ask a few questions to help make the time stop going backward, but he either doesn't answer or grunts.

Clams rings his bell; the lines move and we all turn around before meeting our next 'date' for the evening.

Number 72 is a perfectly nice social worker who I have a lot in common with. He's got a soft voice and a mop of curly brown hair that goes to his eyebrows. We chat for a bit about restaurants but there is a lot of silence in the conversation and long pauses thinking of something to say. He might circle my number, and for a second, I think about circling his to appease my mother. The bell rings, and we move along, but Clams makes an announcement before the next 'date'.

'Listen, dolls,' Clam says dramatically. 'I see a lot of blank papers and I will not accept that. I expect to see at least one number circled on your sheet. Violators will be prosecuted to the full extent of the law. Well, drag queen law, and you all know that is much more severe than any other jurisdiction.' Chuckles are heard around the room and he rings the bell.

The next guys starts off asking me how much money I make. Then he corrects himself. 'I'm sorry. I shouldn't have said it that way. I meant how much money do you make *after taxes*?' That one gets a big no on my sheet. One guy cleans his ear with the end of his keys and another guy almost cries when I tell him I have no idea what comes out of a Vanderpump.

The next few 'dates' are fine but ultimately boring with stilted conversations about mundane matters. Each is eager to make a connection, and I suddenly feel bad for being here at all. Not that I am some great catch, but I am putting myself out there with the assumption that I'm available. Technically, Paul and I are in limbo. He has promised to come back, and we'll move in together, but for the time being, I'm technically a free agent since he's sharing a place with his soon-to-be ex-husband. Sitting across from 18 and 26 I feel that pull of desire from them. That feeling of wanting to make a connection with someone and have it returned. I think about writing down 72 from earlier on my list. We may not be a love connection but I could see us being friends. Nothing wrong with having more friends.

'Hey folks,' Clams yells above the din of the room before grabbing his bell. 'This is the last match of the night. The very next face you see may be the love of your life.' I go to the next position and turn around waiting for the signal. At least this whole event will be over soon and I can tell my mother I honored our agreement. The bell rings, I turn around to see the next date and gasp.

Chapter 24

Our eyes connect and for a half-second I feel the room stop. A smile spreads across my face but I quickly shut it down. I don't know what to say. He's the very last person I expected to see here. I'm shocked, confused and, although I don't want to admit it, excited.

'Hello, Finn,' I say, my voice cracking a bit.

'Hey, Sam.' He grins and his hazel eyes are so twinkly I have to look away. He shouldn't be so charming and handsome.

'What are you doing here?' I hope my tone isn't too aggressive. The last time we were alone I was walking away from him in the East Village after the movie. I was so angry that night, and so embarrassed of my reaction, that I wasn't sure what to say to him. I've relentlessly focused any communication with him on work and shut down any attempt to move beyond that. I even had the person at Brands who books travel work with him directly to arrange the trip to Miami. When I see him at Plant Daddy I'll make up any excuse to keep him at arm's length, from volunteering for a dog walking shift for Damola to emptying the container of grounds.

'I'm here for the same reason as you,' Finn says simply.

'I doubt it,' I say, thinking about the latest negotiation with my mother.

'Everyone's here to make a connection. I'm not always great with things outside my art. Correction – I mean with people, of course.' He looks down, breaking eye contact like he's suddenly nervous. I can tell it's something he doesn't love to reveal. At the school in Coney Island, he confessed he was kind of a loner as a kid, but I assumed that was a stage he passed through. He looks up at me again. 'That nice woman at Plant Daddy who is always telling me I should cut my hair shorter suggested I check this out. She even printed out a newspaper article about it.'

'The one with the jokey gay T-shirts and high tops who sometimes has multiple reading glasses attached to different parts of her body?' I ask, although I don't have to. I've purposely avoided being there when my mom and Finn are both around. I'm afraid she'll sniff out something between us that isn't there.

'Yeah, do you know her?'

'A little bit,' I say without elaborating.

Finn leans forward, placing his forearms on the table. 'Sam, I wanted to…' He begins quickly and then pulls the brakes. His voice is more shallow and less playful than when I turned around. He wipes some sweat off his forehead and tries to reboot. 'Sam, I've been wanting to talk to you. Not about work or whatever. I wanted to apologize for what happened after *Sunset Boulevard*.'

His eyes are soft and almost pleading. He doesn't look anything like the know-it-all who steamrolled me after the movie. Maybe this is a new language for him. 'I get too worked up about stuff like that.' He rubs his hands together in a slow, calming way. 'My emotions take over. I'm sorry I pushed you. Not everyone I meet is a subject for a documentary. I'm trying to learn that.' He's not being aggressive or demanding like he was after the movie and it makes me want to explain.

'It's my fault,' I say before I can even process how kind he's being. 'I shouldn't have been so defensive. I get in this funk after a screening. My feelings are all on the surface. Especially at that theater with a movie I love.' The film had an impact on me but it was his probing that put my stomach in knots. But sitting here with him after his apology my stomach feels more like happy butterflies fluttering.

'I thought more about *Sunset Boulevard*,' Finn says. 'I even watched it again on my own. A few times in fact. I think you're right. It has the core elements of good filmmaking and it's camp as hell. I should have gone into it with more of an open mind.'

'Wow. Thank you.' It was generous of him to do that for me. Not that he did it for me per se. He really did it for the kids, but the generosity is there, nonetheless. 'That was very kind.' I lean a bit closer to him. 'I have a confession. I stayed up the other night to watch *Moonlight*.' I don't tell him that I also watched it before our screening in the East Village. 'You're right. It's complex and important. It really speaks to this moment. The kids in the program should see it. I guess we have both been doing some secret movie watching.'

We laugh and the tension from the other night fades. We quickly move to a conversation about both of the films and how much we admire and appreciate them.

'What do you think about showing a black-and-white film to kids? Are you worried they'll get bored?' he asks. It's a fair question.

'I think they see so much high-tech HD. Super-rich color. Special effects. Black-and-white can open the door to their creativity without some high-end slick production. It invites imagination.' I remember my fascination with these films when I was a kid. I close my eyes for just a second, and a memory of sitting on our beat-up couch mouthing the lines through my hundredth viewing of *All About Eve* while my mom made dinner comes to mind.

'Sounds like you've done that,' he says.

'I have. The library down the street from our house had a whole stack of classic Hollywood movies on VHS tape. Do you even know what that is?' I ask seriously. I just made the cutoff for analog technology; I'm pretty sure Finn was born into the digital age.

'Of course. I wasn't raised into the simulation,' Finn says, putting his hands behind his head. He's comfortable with me and that makes me feel good.

'I grew up without cable, and we only had an ancient VCR to play worn-out tapes from the library,' I say. 'We didn't have a ton of extra money. My mom was a schoolteacher and a single parent.'

'That's rough,' he says.

'She made sure I had a great childhood,' I say, ignoring the fact that my mother has forced me to be at this speed dating event and is currently ruining my life. 'She'd do anything for me. I don't think I appreciated it enough. School was a nightmare. Being overly involved wasn't enough. Kids teased me mercilessly so my mom would drive me over an hour each way to the LGBTQ youth center just to make sure I had a safe place to be.' Maybe that's why I'm going along with her plan. To say thank you? Which is incredibly twisted but suits our dynamic.

'I can sort of tell that you had a great mom from talking to you.'

'You can?'

'Yeah. You're used to being around people, and you're easy to talk to. Both my parents are lawyers. Everything is by the book with them. No coloring out of the lines.' He makes a scowl and wags his finger. 'They don't know how to talk to each other let alone talk to me. Lots of polite conversation. No real connection. It's easier for me to get to know someone through the lens of my camera. Just talking like this is hard for me. My parents never really taught me that. It sounds like your mom did.'

'I have another confession,' I say, fidgeting in my chair. 'That woman who keeps telling you to get a haircut and suggested you come here is not just some rando; she's my mother.'

His eyes widen and he leans in. 'No way. I bet there's a story there.' His documentarian instinct kicks in.

'I'll tell you, but you won't believe it.' I explain the whole thing, from the contract I signed to the meeting with Rajesh to the dating profile for my feet. I don't tell him I'm doing it to be with my ex, Paul. Maybe I should but it's complicated enough. I don't want to overwhelm him. Or maybe it's something else.

'Wow,' he says because I'm sure he doesn't know what to say.

'I hope it doesn't make you think my mother is nuts. She's really very nice, in her own way.'

'I think it's amazing. She must love you a lot.'

'Yes, she does,' I say. Sometimes too much, but seeing it through Finn's reaction doesn't feel like too much – in fact, it feels pretty good. Is there even such a thing as too much love?

Clams ring the bell. Ten minutes could not have already gone by. It feels like ten seconds. 'That's your one-minute warning,' Clams calls. 'Now make sure you have at least one number on your sheet. Come on, dolls. Give love a chance.'

I look down at my card and see nothing but blank spaces. 'My mom is not going to be pleased when she finds out I didn't write down any matches. She'll insist on making another profile for me on some horrible app.' I look across the room and see 72, who seemed like such a nice guy. 'What do you think of that guy over there? Do you think if I wrote down his number and explained to him that my mother is obsessed, he might understand? I have to write down someone.'

'Write down 24,' he says and I look around the room for the number but don't see it.

'Which one is...' I start to ask and then realize he has a great big twenty-four on his name tag.

'Write my number down. I already know the story, and you can tell her you had at least one match because I'll write you down too.'

'Thanks,' I say, caught up in the moment. We write down each other's number and smile as Clams rings the final bell. Sometimes the only thing that solves a problem is creating a bigger problem.

Chapter 25

I walk into Plant Daddy and Kai is busy transforming the place from late summer paradise to early November fall fantasy. Artfully placed limbs of brightly colored leaves adorn the window facing the street. Across the cafe vibrant sunflowers, dark purple sweet potato vines, and ivory and rust mums, infuse autumn color into the usual greenery. I say hello to Damola who waves at me and bounces his head along to some beat coming in from his headphones. I nod to Angelika who is in the middle of a reading with a woman with straight black hair who is weeping into a cup of tea as Angelika pats her on the back.

Rajesh has become a regular with his new girlfriend Jessica, an equally shy blond girl with thick glasses. They always sit at a booth in the corner so they can hold hands as they study. I notice Kai has made sure there are always a few tall snake plants near the table for privacy.

My mother spots me before I'm even able to put down my bag.

'Pumpkin Pie, how did it go?' she shouts from across the room. Everyone in line turns to see who in the world could be called that name. I'm sure they are expecting an orange cat but it's just me. I see her finish a drink and then ask Maggie something. Maggie nods which is my mother's cue to come out from behind the counter and sit next to me. Line of early-morning commuters be dammed.

'I want to hear everything,' she says, handing me a mug with a perfect spiral of whipped cream and chocolate and orange sprinkles. She sits down next to me.

'Is this a bribe?'

'It's a Mocha Salted Pumpkin Dulce de Leche latte with extra sprinkles. Call it what you want.' I take a sip and enjoy the super sweet mix of flavors.

'How did speed dating go? Tell me. The Wedding is just a month away and you've rejected every wonderful candidate I've brought you. If I have to put up with your horrible Aunt Mary telling me how she wishes you would find someone special in that condescending tone, I will throw myself on the wedding cake no matter how much I like your sweet cousin Ziggy.'

'Mom, Ziggy doesn't care if I have a date or not. He's already agreed to let us bring Omar and whoever we want to be at our table.'

'But won't it be more fun with someone special? Now tell me all about it. How many guys did you meet and did you get their social media names? I want to weed out the wackos.'

'Present company excepted.' I nod toward her.

'I'm not sure if you mean you or me but I don't think either of us are wackos or maybe we both are so the statement is moot.'

A few people come in and pass by our table. They must be regulars because my mom greets each of them by name and tells them to let her know if Maggie needs help.

'Sure thing, Glory,' a tall guy in a thick flannel shirt says.

'See you later, Glory,' his companion in a similar flannel says and they head to the counter.

'Who the hell is Glory?' I ask.

She straightens her blouse and adjusts the multi-colored scarf she is wearing around her neck. 'Me, of course. I'm Glory.'

'Since when?'

'Since I had a wonderful conversation with Kai.' She glances toward the back of the cafe where Kai is carefully trimming a bonsai. He notices her, puts down his clippers and gives her a small wave and a big smile. She raises her hand and closes her fingers to her palm a few times to wave back. 'You know he chose the name Kai after his transition. It's such a beautiful name. He says there is no reason I couldn't change my name if I wanted to.' She looks at Kai again and I notice her eyes soften. 'I've always hated the name Gloria. Blech. It's such an old-lady name.'

'But you are an old lady,' I remind her.

'Please, you're much more of an old lady than I am,' she fires back. She's not wrong.

'I withdraw the accusation.' We tease each other all the time, so I know she isn't offended, and I'm not either. She does seem very happy with her new name.

'The name Glory suits me much better, don't you think?'

'As a matter of fact, I do. It suits you perfectly.'

'It's never too late to become who you were always meant to be.' I disagree with her, but I don't want to get into it. 'Who did you match at speed dating?' she asks. She has a remarkable ability to stay on message.

'No one,' I say despite the fact that I woke up this morning thinking about my conversation with Finn at the event.

'What?' she asks loud enough so that everyone turns to look at her except Maggie, who I'm sure is acclimated to my mother's outbursts. 'How is that possible? There had to be at least a hundred people going in there on Sunday. Some of them were very handsome. Alright, I saw one guy wearing a beret. That's a deal breaker. Even I can't put up with a beret. But that was only one out of so many. Are you sure?' She looks me in the eye like she knows I'm fibbing.

'How do you know how many people there were? And how do you know someone was wearing a beret?'

'I was there, of course. I mean, not inside the actual room. That would be butting in and I would never do that.'

'Oh, no, not you,' I say as sarcastically as humanly possible.

'It's still a free country the last time I checked, Sam. A human being can hang out on a street corner across from a gay speed dating event and tag each of the participants if she wants to,' she says like it's the most natural thing in the world.

'Tag the participants? They aren't birds migrating for the winter. You do not need to tag anyone.'

'I saw a lot of very interesting folk. Surely there was at least one who caught your eye?'

Then the one who caught my eye walks in. Finn opens the door and looks over his green-tinted aviator glasses to survey the room before making an entrance. He doesn't have to do much to have every single person in the cafe turn their attention to him.

My mother jumps up from her seat and waves. 'Yoo-hoo,' she sings. 'Over here.'

'Mom do not call him over here,' I say hiding my mouth with my hand. She ignores me. Finn walks over and kisses her on both cheeks. It's clear she has already gotten her claws into him.

'Hi, Glory. Good morning, Sam,' he says. I wave hello. I'm not sure what to say.

'How did it go at speed dating?' she asks him. 'Did you get any great matches?'

'Mom, do you really need to interfere in Finn's life too? Isn't trying to destroy mine keeping you busy enough?'

'Sam,' my mother sighs. 'Finn is new to New York. He's looking to meet people. And I'll add, it took very little convincing with him. Unlike some people, Finn knows a good thing when it's staring him in the face.'

Is that what she thinks my problem is? I know she thinks something in me must be broken but I've never been exactly sure what she thinks it is. It's got to be more than just my hair and how I dress.

'Finn, word on the street is that a lot of people wrote down your number but you only wrote down one.' She fluffs her curly hair with one hand.

'Word on the street?' I repeat. 'What's that supposed to mean? Are you telling us that there's a buzz across New York City about a speed dating event at a dive bar in Brooklyn? I find that hard to believe.'

'I may or may not have been texting with Clams.' She grins.

'What? How do you know Clams?' I ask.

'Pumpkin Pie,' she starts and I shudder a bit being called that in front of Finn. It's embarrassing. 'When two people are in the same business, they tend to know each other. We're both matchmakers. Of course we know each other. Clams is a lovely person and Kai used to date a member of the Giblet Triplets.'

'Mom, what happens at speed dating, stays at speed dating. That business is private and personal. It's one thing to invade my privacy. I'm used to it. It's another to do it to someone like Finn who you just met.'

'Stop being so uptight,' she says and then turns to Finn. 'He's always been a little tightly wound. He doesn't get enough fiber. I think he tends to be constipated but he's really got so much potential.'

'Mom! Stop. Please.' I cover my face with my hands.

'Fine. It's not like Clams handed over the data. That would be unethical. At least that's what he told me when I asked for it.'

'I went. I did what you wanted. Can we just stop talking about the whole thing? You are embarrassing Finn,' I say.

'I don't mind.' Finn shrugs.

'You aren't helping,' I say and shoot him a look.

'In fact,' Finn says, pulling out a chair and sitting down with us. 'I did match with one person at the event.'

'Oh, that's wonderful. How fabulous.' My mother responds like money is falling from the sky. 'Have you arranged the next date yet?'

'I haven't yet. I don't know when he's free. Sam, when are you free?' He raises his eyebrows in a way that makes me almost forget he is not a viable match for me. He's just doing this to entertain my mother, I tell myself.

'I knew it!' She slaps her hand on the table so hard the sugar falls over.

'You did not know it,' I say. 'Finn and I work together. We are not a match. Not in that way.' The words are more challenging to get out than I thought they would be. I notice Finn's face shift downward slightly.

'Finn, my son has no idea what he wants. He's still finding himself.'

'Mom, enough,' I interrupt. I'm about to remind them both again that Finn and I work together. I've told her this but she doesn't listen. Still, I can't help but wonder what a date with Finn Montgomery would be like?

'I think it's nice that you're helping, Glory,' Finn says firmly planting himself on my mother's good side. 'My parents would never be that interested in my life.'

'Again, Finn. Not helping. But if your mom is looking to do a late-stage adoption please give her my contact information.'

'Sam, you don't understand what a gift this is. Finn understands,' Mom says, and pauses putting her finger to chin. 'I've got an idea. You two are so busy. I'll plan the whole thing, soup to nuts; how does that sound? All you both do is show up. What do you think Finn?'

'Sure,' he says. 'That sounds like an adventure.'

'Um, you didn't ask me what I think,' I interject.

'You don't get a choice. Do you need me to call Rajesh over or bring out Exhibit A, The Letter, and the addendum? I keep a photocopy behind the counter for moments exactly like this.'

'No, Mother. Plan away. It's not like anyone can stop you.'

I look at Finn and he seems to be enjoying the whole thing. I wish I could see more things through his eyes.

Chapter 26

The last time I went to the Statue of Liberty I threw up on Patty Perkins' brand-new Skechers. Each June the fifth-grade class at Longview Elementary went to visit Lady Liberty as a special end-of-the-year celebration. Patty and I even bought matching bright red Gap logo T-shirts to wear during the prerequisite class photo at the base of the statue. But the morning of the trip I was so amped up that I ate three bowls of Lucky Charms with chocolate milk. My mother warned me, said I'd get sick, but I refused to listen to her, and even ate the third bowl just to show her I could do it. But as we rode across the choppy Hudson River on a tiny ferry, Patty and I stared up at the golden torch above the pale green-blue statue, and I started to regret my morning meal. As soon as I stepped off the ferry and on to Liberty Island, I felt my stomach swish violently, and Patty's shoes were in the wrong place at the wrong time.

This morning I've only had half an everything bagel with a schmear of low-fat cream cheese, so I should be fine but I'm still apprehensive. I can't tell if that's because of my past history or the fact that I'm going to spend the morning observing Finn in action. When Robert asked me to write the copy for the artists' catalog, I hadn't yet gone to speed dating with the client and my mother wasn't chaffing at the bit to see the two of us go out on a date designed by her. Still, I need to observe him in order to do my work. So, I'm on the 9:48 a.m. ferry to Liberty Island where Finn is interviewing a subject and getting some footage.

I step off the ferry without any stomach grumbles and go to find Finn. The stark pale aqua patina of the statue that looms overhead sharply contrasts with the gold, orange, and red of the trees that shimmer in the autumn sun. In Manhattan, the traffic and noise make it easy to forget that you're on an island. But here, on this large rock, halfway between the state where I grew up and the city I now call home, the briny air and sound of waves crashing remind me that I'm in a very special place. The image of the Statue of Liberty has to be one of the most well-known in the world, but nothing really prepares you for the experience of being at the hem of her gown. I crane my neck to see the crown and I'm humbled by how massive she is.

Gaggles of tour groups and students crowd the pathways and line up to see inside the statue. I walk past them through the garden paths that surround the base until I find the quieter part of the park where Finn said he would be set up. I locate him at a picnic table with incredible views of Manhattan behind it. The skyline looks like an erratic EKG with random spires stretching above at regular intervals. Finn has a complicated-looking camera connected to his laptop and a light on a tripod. He's talking with a young woman with short blond hair that's shaved on one side.

'Hey, Sam,' Finn says as soon as he sees me. 'I'd like you to meet Ekaterina. Ekaterina, this is the man I mentioned who would be joining us today. Is that still okay with you? You can change your mind, of course.'

Ekaterina looks at me and bites her lower lip. I'm dressed conservatively and I wonder if that's making her put up her guard or if she is just unsure about meeting a stranger. 'He is your friend?' she asks, her voice shaky.

'Yes,' Finn says. 'Sam is a new friend. He's also an artist. A writer.' My instinct is to bristle, but in this moment, I don't. Ekaterina looks at the ground. Finn adds, 'He's also queer.' I usually say I'm gay but I'm getting more comfortable with that identity as well.

I watch as Ekaterina takes in this statement. Her shoulders and jaw seem to visibly relax, and then a smile spreads across her face. 'Hello, Sam. Is nice to meet you.' Her accent is thick and reminds me of a film professor from Moscow I adored.

'Thank you,' I say, grateful that she's allowing me to witness her story. I take a seat and let them get back to it.

Finn asks her simple but thoughtful questions about how she escaped Russia and what her life was like there. He always gives her a way of getting out of answering a question so she doesn't feel trapped or intimidated. He doesn't command, 'Tell me what happened when you were in school.' Instead, he maintains eye contact and nods his head. He repeats back some small detail that shows he's been listening and then asks something like, 'What parts of school were enjoyable?' or 'What do you remember about the parts that were hard?' He's snapping photos the whole time but he never takes his eyes off of her. From all outward appearances it looks like two friends having a conversation.

Ekaterina comes from the suburbs of St Petersburg. Her parents were both doctors and didn't have any problem with her being a lesbian but she was harassed at school so her parents moved. 'I acted like regular schoolgirl at new town. I tried to like boy but is not that easy when that is not who you are on inside.' She touches her hand to her chest. 'People this time is more violent.'

She pulls back the blond bangs on the side of her head and reveals a thick scar above her ear. I inwardly cringe, almost as if I can physically feel the pain of it, but I try not to react because I don't want to interfere with her story or make her self-conscious. Seeing the scar makes it all too easy to imagine what's responsible for it. I want to reach out to her and tell her she's safe now. At least safer in the US, I think. Maybe. My mom always tells me to stay vigilant in the fight for equality. Usually, I just dismiss it as her being overly eager, but in his moment, I see a way in. I see how Finn connects his activism to his art and I wonder if there is ever any way I could do something like that.

'They took a rock to the back of my head,' she says. 'Not a throw. A hit. Teachers do nothing.'

Finn stops. The moment needs attention more than anything else and he says, 'I'm sorry that happened to you. I'm so glad you found your way out.' He slowly approaches her making sure she welcomes him into her physical space. He puts his hand gently on her shoulder and she raises her hand up to join his. 'Maybe we should stop for today.'

'No,' she says, looking up at the sky. She doesn't allow a single tear to fall down her face. 'I want to tell my story.' When she begins again, there's a new resolve in her voice. 'Yes. I tried to be like they wanted girl to be but I could not. I try every day. That person always want to come out. That real person Ekaterina. To live. To be who they need to be. That is why I come here. To be. Just, to be.'

To be. Just to be. The words have oceans of meaning for me and I let them sink in. It's so hard just 'to be' for so many people in this world. I'm fully engaged in listening and taking in her story. I'd wanted to take some notes about Finn and his work process for the catalog but I'm willing to rely on my memory so that I can stay in this moment with them. I'm caught up in Ekaterina's story, and the proud way she tells it. It's beautiful. The way she's able to express herself and the emotion behind each word is so strong it could topple the statue that towers above.

I look at Finn, and he has this soft, caring focus on her. I love that he created a safe space for her to tell her story. How does he make it seem so effortless? Maybe because he genuinely cares about Ekaterina, and all the people he documents. I look at the laptop and see the image he's somehow managed to capture: the beauty of her emotion and the magnificence of the statue in one frame that is distinctly queer. They created it together, right here in front of me. I feel privileged to have witnessed it.

The mood shifts to lighthearted easily. They talk about bands they like, Russian and Southern slang, and what it's like to meet queer people here versus back in Russia. Ekaterina tells Finn that she started seeing a very special woman just a few weeks ago named Lil and that Lil has made her happier, and more like her authentic self, than she ever thought possible. 'Do you have someone special?' she asks Finn.

Finn's eyes dart toward mine. 'The American expression is, "it's complicated."' He looks away quickly.

'What about you?' she asks, nodding toward me.

'It's complicated,' I echo. I try not to look at Finn but I can't help it. Our eyes connect for a half second, which stops my heart. When he looks away, I feel the loss.

'Let's just get some fun shots. Do whatever you want,' Finn says, and we're suddenly back to work, shaking off the complex emotional stuff between us. Ekaterina nods enthusiastically, straightening her collar and brushing back her hair. I grin – she seems to like the idea of being on camera.

'You said the Statue of Liberty was the thing that most felt like New York to you, right?' Finn asks. Now he splits his attention between Ekaterina and the lens of his camera.

'Yes,' she says, her eyes gazing up at the tall beauty and her beautifully draped robe. 'I would see pictures sometimes, but she seemed so far away, so out of my reach, that I started to think maybe she wasn't even real. Then I saw from the city, a small blue-green dot in the distance, and it still seems like a dream. But now here we are and there it is.' She takes in Lady Liberty, from the top of her crown to the pedestal she stands on. '*Oy da.*'

Finn gets up and starts moving around so he can get both Ekaterina and Lady Liberty in the shot. He moves like a cat, lightly and gently, and I watch her slowly become freer and more open as they talk. She even dances around a little and explains that she took ballet in Russia for years, which explains her elegant movement.

Once he has the shots of Ekaterina, he thanks her for sharing her story. 'I know there's going to be so many kids who identify with what you went through. They'll know they're not alone.' Ekaterina, who I thought was so steely when I first saw her, now melts into a hug with Finn.

'Thank you,' she tells him, 'for letting me be me.'

When they part, he tells her, 'Any time.'

'So nice to meet you Ekaterina,' I say as she picks up her bag to leave.

'*Da svidania*,' she says, and walks away still carrying the energy and grace of a dancer and with a bit more lightness than she had earlier.

'Wow,' I say and turn to Finn.

'I know, her story is incredible and she has been so great to work with. What she had to endure in Russia was a nightmare. I hope when I'm finished creating the final collage with her portrait and her words that people understand what it's like to be queer there. No one should have to live that way.'

'No,' I say firmly. 'Her story is important, not to mention brave. She seemed somehow relieved after.'

'Yeah, that happens a lot,' he says and then moves back to the table where Ekaterina was sitting when I first came over. 'Telling your story can be powerful for the audience, but it can also be just as intense for the storyteller.'

'We should invite her to stop by Plant Daddy.' I could see her finding her footing in the Hell's Kitchen community.

'Oh, so you do it too,' he says. 'You're like your mom.'

'Do what? I love my mom but we are nothing alike.'

'You're a helper like her. Introducing her to Plant Daddy. Like your mom suggesting I go to speed dating. You're really good at connecting people.' It feels weird for him to understand that about me. It is part of who I am, I think, but I'm not even sure I've ever said it to myself in those terms. 'I admire it,' he says. 'But in a way, it helps you stay in the background.'

Does it? Now he's going a bit too far. I think about what he's saying. Maybe he's not wrong. 'What are you scared of?' he asks.

'Nothing,' I say but the real answer is *everything*. I'm scared of failure. I'm scared of finding out that I really suck at what I've wanted to do my whole life. I'm scared of rejection – professional and personal. I'm scared of being on a competition reality show and being eliminated first. The list goes on and on. I'm sure Finn isn't scared of anything.

'I'm scared all the time when I'm working,' Finn confesses.

This surprises me. 'But you're so successful,' I say in disbelief. 'You were named one of the "Thirty Under Thirty to Watch".'

'So what? That's all just PR BS.' Then he realizes his audience. 'No offense.'

'None taken,' I say.

'But honestly,' he says moving his face closer toward me. 'I couldn't sleep last night. I was so worried I might say the wrong thing to Ekaterina, or I wouldn't find the right way to shoot it, or she'd think my questions were lame. Or she wouldn't show up at all. But this morning I woke up and my desire to hear Ekaterina's story was greater than my fear. I always try to find that balance.'

I like that. When I worked with Justine, it was easy because her name was on the book, and if she didn't like what I had submitted, I would simply rewrite it or toss it out. But it was one person responding, not a larger audience. I need to balance my fear with my desire to tell my story. But I don't know what that story is, so how can I find balance?

'Can I ask a question?' Finn asks.

'That's sort of what you've been doing since I met you,' I say and he laughs gently. He's not unaware that he has a way of getting inside my thoughts.

'Why won't you talk about your writing more? I've asked you about it a bunch of times, but you change the subject or just ignore the question.'

'That's ridiculous,' I say, and heat flares up in my cheeks, but it doesn't feel like it did at the movie when he was pushing me. That fire was outward rage at him. Today's boiling point is internal. Why won't I talk about it? 'Listen, we really should get going. It's supposed to storm and I don't want to ride the ferry when it gets windy.'

'You just did it! Right now,' he says, almost like he can't believe I played into him so easily. But I can't let him get to me.

I look up at the clouds. They are still fluffy and white. No sign of impending danger.

'Maybe I do, but we really need to get going. I need to handle some logistics for the Miami trip today and...'

Then, at the same exact moment, both of our phones sound an alert. At first, I hope it's a special bulletin from the National Weather Service about my fictional storm, but when I look at my phone, I see it's just the very real Hurricane Mom.

Please see attached itinerary. That's all it says, with a link to a file.

'Did you get this too?' I ask hoping it's a strange coincidence. Finn holds up his phone and shows me his screen. It looks exactly like mine.

'I'm sorry. My mother is not very good with personal boundaries...'

Our phones buzz again. I don't even need to ask if he got the same new message that I did, because now his name is on the group chat list. I open the link and see a reservation for two has been made at 'Swingers'.

'What?' I gasp and feel my entire body clench 'I'm really, really sorry. She wants us to go to some swingers club?'

Finn stops me. 'Did you open the link?' he asks.

I shake my head, and when I click to open it, I see that Swingers is not, in fact, some kind of free love orgy. It's worse. Much, much worse.

Chapter 27

'Swingers!' I say after I storm through the front door of Plant Daddy and march directly toward my mother, who is with Kai carefully examining some leafy plant in a macramé hanger.

'Shhh,' my mother says, swatting her hand at me. As I get closer I see that Kai has a speaker hanging on the side of his wheelchair and my mother is adjusting the volume. Familiar classical music streams toward the plants in front of them.

'We're playing Vivaldi for the heartleaf philodendron,' Kai says. The music swells and comes to an end. They both stare at the plant. I think they are expecting it to applaud. Poor Kai. He was a perfectly normal person before she started working here. Grumpy but sane. Now he's smiling at customers and playing classical music to plants.

'Why are you doing that? Was this her idea?'

'No, mine. I've always wanted to try this,' Kai says and I can tell he is a bit protective of her. My mother needs about as much protection as a bear in the woods. 'Research shows that it can help open the stomata on the plant.'

'That's where the plant breathes. Tiny holes that allow oxygen in,' my mother says, and she holds up her fingers, indicating the size. Kai looks over at her and smiles.

'Fascinating,' I say, my sarcasm volume at an eleven. 'Mother, can I speak with you for a minute?'

'You'll have to wait for my break,' she says.

'It's fine Glory. Go ahead. It's slow. I was thinking of trying out some disco on the monstera plant in the corner.' He fiddles with the speaker and then his phone before 'Stayin' Alive' by the Bee Gees starts playing. He heads toward the large potted plant on the other side of the cafe.

'Did you get my text?' she asks as she uses a spray bottle to wipe the leaves of a plant.

'That's exactly why I'm here. Swingers? No way. I looked it up. I was hoping it was something other than what I thought it was, but it was exactly what I was scared of.'

She puts down her spray bottle. 'I had to pull a few strings to get you both in. It's a very popular place but luckily Pierre was easily swayed by some free lattes and my usual charm. Soon you and that very handsome young man will be swinging. That's the deal.'

I hate that she calls him 'that very handsome young man'. I am painfully aware of how attractive he is.

'Mom, I'm not about to risk my life and dangle from a trapeze just because I made some deal with you almost twenty years ago.' I swallow hard and try to imagine it. I can't. There is no way.

'Swingers has an excellent safety record for circus arts. I spoke to a very nice young woman at the Better Business Bureau, and I told her that my son has a teeny-tiny fear of anything involving the circus and all that kind of stuff. She assured me that there have been very few reports of people falling off the trapeze and breaking their neck or getting tangled in the net and losing an arm or a leg. It's very rare. Sam, it's time.'

'Time for what? Bodily injury?' I have always been terrified of any kind of aerial acrobatics. When I was a kid, we went to the circus for a class trip – the trapeze and the high wire terrified me. The clowns running around in oversized shoes and sloppy make-up didn't help either. The thought of falling into some bouncy net from high up makes my knees shake.

'A deal is a deal and it's time you got over your fear. You can do it. I know you can.' The bell above the door rings and a small group of customers line up at the register. 'I have to go help Kai. I'll text you both everything you need to know. And don't worry about the trapeze. It'll be fun. You need to be fearless on your dates,' she says.

'Is that one of your rules?' I ask calling after her, hoping she can hear my eyes rolling in my tone.

'It's one of them,' she says and walks to the line of customers. But when she gets there she turns and shouts back to me, 'Maybe, just to be safe, wear two pairs of underwear in case you have an accident. Love you!' She steps behind the counter, and Damola, who for once is not wearing his headphones, just stares at me. I cover my face with my hand and walk out.

I start walking down the street and notice a black car with tinted windows following me. At first, I think I'm being paranoid, but each time I turn back, the car is right at my heels. When I get to the end of the block, I stop, and the car stops, too. The tinted back window rolls down, and it's Paul.

I run over to the car. I can't believe it.

'What are you doing here? And why are you following me? Is everything okay?' I rattle off the questions.

'I wanted to wait until you were safely away from the cafe and any prying eyes. I think I saw your mother in there.'

'But what are you doing here?' I bend down to make sure he's alone and not with a business associate. 'Did I mess up the dates of a visit or something?' I would absolutely have written down a visit from Paul. No way I would forget it. He claims I'm a scatterbrain but I'm not.

'Drove in to take my guy to lunch. I booked a flight with a long layover. Just enough time to drive in from JFK and take you out before I head on my way to London for two days.' His charming smile oozes with charisma. 'Let's go.' He opens the door for me.

I hop in the car and push my head into his shoulder to cuddle but he retreats just enough to remind me how uncomfortable he is with any public displays of affection. Paul is very out but from a generation where two men simply did not ever do that kind of thing in public and I've had to get used to that. I'm always aware of my surroundings, but I'm also comfortable showing affection toward the person I'm with, no matter the gender.

The car flies down the West Side Highway and we enter the maze of short streets and pencil skyscrapers that make up the financial district. Paul says, 'I made a reservation at your favorite restaurant,' as the car pulls up to Delmonico's – his favorite restaurant. It's a well-known steakhouse frequented by bankers and lawyers with stuffy, over-done decor and meat squeezed into every conceivable menu item. Not my style at all but I know Paul enjoys walking through the dining room and nodding to legal counsel from other firms.

But when we arrive, I remember they are one of the last restaurants in New York to have a strict dress code.

'Paul, I'm not really dressed for this.' I'm wearing a pair of light green cords and a thermal I threw on this morning. Way too casual for this place. 'Maybe somewhere else?'

'I'll take care of it,' he says and we walk in. We head to the coat check where I see Paul slip the attendant some cash. He looks me up and down before heading to the back and returning with a navy sports jacket. 'Problem solved,' Paul says as he holds open the jacket. I feel like a little kid getting dressed for his first formal event. I've often felt this way with Paul, like he's taking care of me by teaching me how to do something or giving me advice, but usually it makes me feel safe and taken care of. I'm not feeling all of that this afternoon. I'm thinking about being in Liberty Island with Finn and how he treats me like a peer, someone who has something to contribute. But that makes me anxious, too, because then I feel like I should contribute something. Being with Paul doesn't have that kind of pressure at least.

I push my arms through the jacket and face the full-length mirror next to the coat check. The jacket is way too big for me in the shoulders but too short in the sleeves. Still, it's enough to get us to a table so I follow Paul to a private booth in the corner.

'Are you able to come back to my place after lunch? I could sneak you up somehow and we could...' I trail off. I don't want to be too explicit.

'I wish. I go right from here back to JFK and you know what the traffic can be like on the Belt Parkway in the afternoon.'

'Oh.' I look down at the table. So much of our relationship in the past was made of brief snippets of time. I was hoping that with this new chapter, I wouldn't have to settle for the interstitial moments sandwiched into the rest of his life.

'But I'll be back in a few weeks. We're still on for Thanksgiving?'

'Absolutely,' I say although I'm not entirely sure how I'm going to pull it off. My plan was to reintroduce him to my mother after demonstrating that her plan has been a complete failure.

'You think your mother is ready to meet me? How will she handle the news about us moving in together?' I want to say, *The same way Patti LuPone handles people using their cell phones while she's performing*. But I don't.

'Leave that to me,' is all I say. I push the thought out of my head as the waiter arrives to take our order. Paul orders his usual steak rare and I search for something on the menu that won't sink to the bottom of my stomach like the Titanic. The Cobb salad here has so much bacon on it they should list it as bacon with a garnish of lettuce; still, I order it with plans to edit the meal when it arrives.

'I've got a surprise for you,' Paul says pulling out his tablet. 'I thought we would redecorate the entire apartment before you move in. Top to bottom. I've even asked a landscape designer to give the terrace new trees and plants. But I want to make sure you like everything. It's going to be our place.'

The very idea of moving in with him to 'our place' makes me feel wonderful. This is the Paul I cried over for all those months when we were broken up. This is the Paul I want to be with. He scrolls through the different options for kitchen cabinets, shower fixtures and antique rugs. He even has a few paint chips and fabric swatches in his bag. We discuss and debate each option in great detail and the conversation is easy. Unlike talking with

Finn. The intense conversation at the statue the other day creeps into my thoughts and I shut it out along with my concern about how much all this redecorating is going to cost. I just want to enjoy my time with Paul and not let the details get in the way.

Lunch is quicker than I would like, but he doesn't want to miss his flight back to London; the little leather folder with the check arrives, and the waiter hands it to Paul without hesitation. I guess that sort of thing happens when you show up to the table in a rental jacket. Paul almost always paid in the past, and I'm sure he thinks that's how things will go in the future, but I don't want that. Even half of the bill will make a serious dent in my monthly credit card payment this month. I don't have a ton of income coming in at the moment to be able to afford surprise splurges like this. Once I get the full-time job at Brands this won't be as much of an issue. I'll have more cash flow so I hope I'll be able to hold my own. I reach in my pocket for my wallet and Paul stops me.

'I've got this, Sammy,' he says and places his heavy high-end credit card on the folio.

'Let's split it,' I say and I take out the credit card I think has the most room on it.

'Don't be silly. I've got this. I invited you to lunch,' Paul says. He thinks I'm just making a show of pretending to pay but I want him to understand that is not the case.

'I insist,' I say and look him firmly in the eye and put down my cheap plastic alumni credit union card next to his. The waiter splits the bill and we both sign but I triple my gratuity because I know Paul is such a lousy tipper.

'Well, then,' he says and he nods his head. 'I hate that we don't get more time together but I can't miss my flight. I snagged the last business class seat.' He looks around the corner of the dining room where we are tucked away and then leans over to give me a quick peck. 'I'll call you,' he says and I watch his elegant frame exit through the dining room.

I take a few moments to finish my coffee and brush my fingers over the fabric samples Paul left for me. I'm deeply focused on a plush forest green swatch and the image of cozying up together on a new couch in front of a resurfaced fireplace when the server returns. 'Sir, thank you for the generous gratuity but...' He looks down at the ground. 'I'm afraid this amount was declined. Do you have another card? Or perhaps I can put the difference on your friend's card?'

'No, don't do that,' I say quickly. My daydream fades and I shake my head to help adjust to the reality of the moment. I start shuffling through my wallet to find the right combination of credit, cash, and desperation to pay my half of the bill.

Chapter 28

'Why won't you tell me anything about your date?' I ask Omar. We are up at his place going through his endless wardrobe. The fact is Omar looks good in everything so that makes the decision harder. His apartment is identical to mine, just two floors up, but at this moment, his is hidden beneath an avalanche of shirts, pants, and shoes that he has tried on and discarded.

'I told you I don't want to jinx it.'

'But this is the third date with this guy and I don't know anything about him.'

'That's only because I've been so busy pattern cutting at Vanata, and I have to get my own stuff ready for the spring shows. I'm grateful your mom has been covering my shifts.'

'At least tell me something?' I beg.

'What do you think of this?' He holds up an earring with a dangling arrow beneath the post.

'You don't have a pierced ear,' I remind him.

'I thought you could pierce it for me before I go. I've got a needle somewhere.' He starts opening a few drawers and looking under a pile of shirts.

'We are not the Pink Ladies and this is not *Grease*. I'm already overcoming one of my fears tonight. I think conquering my fainting response to blood can wait.'

'Fine,' he says and puts the earring on the top of his dresser. 'I've heard Swingers is a blast. You'll have a great time and at least you're going with someone you like. Finn seems wonderful. He's always very friendly at Plant Daddy. Angelika adores him and Damola lets him wear his headphones to listen to stuff and you know he lets almost no one do that. Even Kai likes him.'

'Yes, I like Finn but I don't like-like him,' I say and wonder when my life became an episode of *The Gilmore Girls*. 'He's a very nice person, I guess. A little too into his art and a bit too intense.'

'All I'm saying is you should approach the evening with an open mind,' Omar says.

'You're starting to sound just like my mom.'

'At least she's letting you wear what you want. That's your favorite shirt.'

It is. I usually save it for special events where I'm trying to impress someone. It's a simple black denim shirt with mother-of-pearl buttons up the front. I was surprised when I impulsively grabbed it, but it's such a cool shirt. If I'm gonna die falling off a trapeze, might as well do it in something I like.

'She's not entirely letting me pick my own wardrobe.' I pull down my jeans just enough to show a hideous rainbow peeking out from my backside. They match the socks she got me last month.

'Ooooh. I love those.'

'She made me send her a picture to confirm.'

'I have to ask her where she got them.' He brushes his face with some kind of powder and looks in the mirror.

'You look fantastic. Let's go,' I say, and we walk downstairs and out of the building together where the car he ordered is waiting for him.

'Do I at least get to know this guy's name?' I ask as he confirms with the driver and opens the door.

'I'll tell you later,' he says and closes the door. Omar's mysterious behavior is out of character, but I'm certain that once his busy schedule eases up, he'll spill all the details.

—

Swingers is a converted warehouse on the West Side Highway that houses a school for the circus arts. It's become a date destination in the city, although I have no idea why. Who wants to see their date dangling from some swinging bar in the sky unless the date is really not going well. I walk in at the time my mother has designated and look for Finn but he sees me first.

'Great shirt,' he says and I'm immediately glad I chose to wear it. It's always nice to be complimented.

'Yours too,' I say. He's wearing a sky blue vintage bowling shirt that hugs his chest tightly and looks great with his hazel-green eyes. I wouldn't have thought it was his style.

'Yeah, I like it too, but I can't take credit for it,' he says adjusting the buttons.

'Why not?'

'Your mom told me to wear it. In fact, she insisted. It was part of the package she gave me.'

'She gave you a package?' I ask and my mind reels at what manner of rules and instructions were included.

'Yeah, and don't worry. No dairy tonight. She was pretty clear about that rule.'

I cover my face with my hands and rub my eyes. 'I'm sorry. It's the only way to get her off my back and make her happy. But I signed up for this. There's no reason you need to get tangled up in our crazy stuff. Your situation is complicated. My situation is complicated. If you wanted to walk out right now, I'd understand. I mean this isn't even an actual date.'

I look up at the trapeze and see people swinging. It looks terrifying but it also looks like everyone is having fun.

'I'm game if you are. I'd love to get up there.' He looks up at the ladder and platform. His face is full of excitement. 'A purely platonic, kinetic experience. What do you think?'

I look up, and all the hopeful anticipation from a few seconds ago has been replaced with a generalized anxiety, but I'm in too deep to say no, and it looks like Finn wants to do this. 'Let's fly,' I say and we head over to get suited up.

Our instructor is a young woman so effervescent I find it hard to believe she needs a trapeze to fly at all. Her name is Mindi Kim and you can hear the hearts over the i's in her name. I was hoping for someone with more gravitas who approached the entire thing like a plan to escape a prison, but Mindi Kim it is. She explains how all the riggings work, and we do some practice exercises from the beloved safety of the ground. Finn is incredibly good at each challenge. It's clear he's a natural athlete. When it's time to grab the practice bar that hangs at eye level, he has no problem leaning forward and shifting his weight correctly so he can grab and swing in one fluid motion.

Then it's my turn. 'You got this,' he says. 'It's not as hard as it looks.' He has no idea what it is like to live in my body. Sports are something I've avoided my entire life. Mindi goes over the instructions again, explaining that I hold on to the end of the ladder with one hand, lean forward, and then release my other hand as I shift my weight – a series of instructions that seem impossible.

'Ready? Go,' she says. I try to remember the proper order, and I let go of the pole that stands in for the ladder and lean forward, but my weight is too much to keep me balanced, so I try to shift back, but it's too late and I fall smack on my face on the mat. I stay on the ground for a second, too embarrassed to get up.

Finn kneels down next to me and puts his mouth close to my ear. 'You okay, Sam?' I can feel his breath on my face and his concern. It's very sweet and makes me feel like maybe I can do it. I start to get up and he offers his hand. I grab it and I feel a jolt of something, maybe confidence. The feeling must have something to do with the fact that I am minutes away from repeating this fall from a much greater height. I look into Finn's eyes and wonder if the feeling has anything to do with him.

'I'm fine. Nothing hurt except my ego. I don't know. Maybe I should watch you from down here.'

'Is that what you want?' he asks.

'What I want is to not fall from a hundred feet in the air and break my neck as I get tangled in that net. I think I can accomplish that better by watching from down here.' I point to the ground to make my point.

'You'd rather watch from the sidelines instead of being up there?' He points toward the tower platform.

I want to yell, 'Yes, yes, yes!' Of course, I do. I'm much more comfortable on the sidelines, near the action but not part of it. I like to be behind-the-scenes holding the ropes. It's where I'm always the most comfortable, but something about the way Finn is looking at me makes me think that maybe I should change that. At least for tonight. Mindi explained that there's a safety net to catch me if I fall. Maybe that's what I have been waiting for my whole life — a safety net.

'I'm not going to make you do anything you don't want to do. If you want we can take off all this stuff and grab a beer. Should we just get out of here?' he asks. When he says he is going to take off all this stuff for a second I feel something stir in me like I wouldn't mind him taking off all that stuff at all. Maybe he should start with the harness and only stop when he gets to his underwear.

What am I thinking? I tell myself it's just my brain trying to find a way to avoid the situation. This is an opportunity for me to do exactly what I've been saying I want to do lately: grow up.

'No. It looks like fun. Let's do it,' I say, trying to convince myself. 'But you go first? Okay?'

'No problem,' he says.

Mindi promises she will be with us the whole time. She starts crawling up the ladder to the platform and then Finn follows her. I take one foot and put it on the first rung and stop. I give my other foot a quick pep talk that convinces it to join the first and I begin my ascent with a great deal less enthusiasm than Mindi or Finn.

From up here, I can see the entire building, and everyone is watching us, which makes me more nervous. There is a man already swinging way on the other side of the trapeze scaffolding, waiting to catch us.

'You okay?' Finn asks.

I shake my head slowly from side to side. I'm scared talking will make the platform sway more than it is. Mindi goes over the instructions again, and then it's Finn's turn. He has no hesitation whatsoever. He grabs the swing, gives a countdown and he's off. Finn is all ease and confidence. His body arches and flows in ways that make him look like an elegant bird. An elegant, sexy bird – but I try to stay focused on watching his technique. After the first swing, he's ready to turn upside down and get up to speed. He's effortless on the trapeze and soon he has the speed needed for the release. I watch as the catcher matches his tempo and energy. Finn releases from his trapeze and the man across the way catches him.

Finn shouts, 'Yes!' And I notice a few people doing the ground exercises are watching and applauding. Finn releases his hands and gently falls to the net. He immediately looks up at me with a big thumbs up. 'You can do it!' he shouts and then rolls off the net to watch from down below.

No, I can't! I yell back in my head.

Mindi goes over everything one more time. She hands me the trapeze bar. I grab the end of the ladder with my other hand. I lean forward like we were taught to do and begin to shift my bodyweight until my other hand releases its grip on the ladder. I lean forward until the platform is no longer under my feet and I'm flying. It's exhilarating. Everything around me is a blur which allows the sensation to be more focused. The part of my brain that has been holding me back is silent. I suddenly feel confident and able to do anything. I get my speed up and go through the steps in my head. I'm able to hook my legs around the bar without too much difficulty and that makes me feel even more confident.

I hear Finn screaming, 'Yes, yes, yes!' And he's pumping his fists in the air with each step I accomplish. 'Gooooo Sam!' he screams but he doesn't make me feel pressure. I feel like I can do it, so I signal to the catcher and let my body take over. My brain butts in and says, *Will he catch you? Will this stranger catch you?* but I shut it down. I focus on the energy Finn is sending me from the ground.

I take another swing using all my bodyweight to get as high as I can and then I release my legs from the trapeze and stretch out my arms hoping someone will be there. For a few seconds, I am literally flying. I've released the trapeze, and I'm not yet caught. I'm just in this moment of being alone in the ether. I realize this is the exact sensation I have spent so much of my life avoiding. But before I can give it another thought, I reach for the catcher, and he grabs me.

I did it. We swing together and the momentum carries me from one side of the building to the other. I let go and fall gently to the net and just lay on my back and let the satisfaction of the experience come over me. I did it.

My entire body is nothing but adrenaline. I can feel every part pulsing on the net as I stare up at the ceiling and the platform where I stood frightened a few minutes ago. I want to do it again and again and again. I roll across the net and my excitement builds until I hop off the net and Finn is waiting for me.

'Great job. You did it, Sam! You did it!' He has this grin on his face that is a combination of excitement and pride. I can tell his body is still buzzing from his turn up there, but I can also tell he's happy for me. He saw how nervous I was and he got me through. I appreciate his support so much, but right now, my words are limited since the experience was so visceral and so corporal. I can't get my mind to make my mouth work in the way I usually do.

'Thank you,' I say and my body takes over. My lips aim for the side of his face but I'm still so revved up my aim is off and I come closer to his lips than I intended. I give him a friendly kiss but once my lips are on his face I'm not so sure how friendly it is. I press my lips against him again. This time I'm even a bit closer to his mouth and then I feel his lips move a bit closer toward mine and the edges of our mouths are connected. I know I should back away but I don't. I should move my face away from his but these brief seconds feel so intense that my mind can't do anything but feel them. His stubble brushes my lips and for a moment I think his mouth is moving closer to mine. I move mine closer to him. Our lips are touching and I feel his tongue move toward mine.

Then, my mind suddenly comes back online and shoves my heart and body to the side. What am I doing? I shake my head just enough to change the channel in my brain and push myself away from him. I try to be as subtle as possible but Finn notices.

'I'm sorry,' he says softly. I should acknowledge what just happened but I'm not sure what to say so instead I try ignoring it but he can tell I'm more than aware that something just happened between us. What exactly? I'm not sure.

'That was awesome you two!' Mindy says breaking the spell. Everything shifts again and reality enters. 'Do you want to go again?'

'Yes,' I say before she can barely finish the question. I know I want to feel what I just felt again. Only do I want to feel the sensation of swinging through the air or the one I felt on the ground with Finn? Maybe both?

Chapter 29

'There's nothing to tell,' I say to Omar with one eye on the door. My mom starts her shift at Plant Daddy in an hour but she's known for being ridiculously early to things so she could pop in at any moment. 'It was kind of Finn to go along with my mom's plan and we had a very nice time actually.' I don't say a word about what happened after my first trapeze swing, how I felt uneasy for the rest of the night and the horrible feeling of wanting the night to last longer and longer living alongside the feeling that I should leave and run back to my apartment alone. He's such a gentleman that he didn't even come close to talking about the lip touching situation and I'm too much of a scaredy cat to bring it up. I can't even bring it up to Omar.

'Are you willing to acknowledge that your mother might know what she's doing?' Omar says, putting a small succulent in a bag before entering the sale. He reminds the customer to place the plant in a sunny spot before handing them the bag and waving goodbye. 'You had a nice time. She knows how to plan a date.'

'She knows how to interfere. It wasn't a real date. He was just helping me out. He knows that.' I think he does. Maybe I should have been clearer about it but I think I was. Wasn't I?

'But why wasn't it a real date? Why couldn't it be?' Omar asks.

'You know why,' I say. I don't mention Paul's name because I don't want to hear him go off on Paul and how he's a cheater, etc. All that is going to be different. I want to tell Omar about all the plans Paul has for our apartment but I take a different approach. 'Finn is just a kid really. He's like more than five years younger. I was in high school when he was in middle school. That's weird.' I know it's a weak defense.

'Paul was in law school when you were in kinder-garten,' Omar responds.

'That's not true.' I quickly try to do the math in my head but give up. 'Well, not entirely,' I concede. 'I could never see myself with a guy like Finn.'

'He's not your type? He's one of the most beautiful, sexy, charming guys I've seen you with. How is that not your type?'

'Exactly. It would never work out. He's too cool for school and I'm an after-school special. Seriously, Omar what do people think when they see us together? I'm sure they think we're friends. Like you and me. Hot guys like Finn do not date guys like me. Sure, in the beginning, my charming personality might be enough to make a guy like that interested, but that gets boring.'

'I will not let you speak about my best friend that way and you have it completely backward. I've dated a ton of super-hot guys.'

'You are a super-hot guy,' I say.

'Thank you,' he says. 'And by the way that is how you take a compliment. But that's not my point. My point is a connection is what lasts. You and Finn have a connection.'

I can't really deny that with any plausibility. A customer comes up to the counter and orders a complicated to-go order saving me from having to explain myself further to

Omar. When he comes back from making the drinks I make sure to be the one in the driver's seat of the conversation.

'Speaking of dates, it's your turn. How did it go? Are you ready to tell me about the mystery man? Was it that guy from the gym who wears his hair pulled back in that sloppy ponytail? Or the guy who orders the London Fog latte and tips you twice the price of the drink?'

'No and no,' he says adjusting the bow of the blousy black-and-white top he has on under his apron.

'More importantly will there be another date?' I ask, raising my eyebrows. It's not like Omar to be so cagey with the details. Usually by this point in the relationship I know the guy's shoe size and his favorite post-workout drink. But I'm holding back also so I can't really push too much. It's not that I don't trust Omar. I do. I don't trust myself to describe the date without conveying the overwhelming feelings I had being with Finn.

After we left Swingers we followed my mother's directions and went to Viva! Viva! Viva! for nachos with vegan cheese and margaritas for the second part of our date. We eventually strayed from my mother's script and talked about *Sunset Boulevard* and *Moonlight* but this time the conversation was easy and productive. We made a plan for our presentation that we both like. When the night ended, I made sure to be standing at least a yard away from him to say goodbye, which made it difficult to hear him over the traffic of the West Side Highway, but it was safer than having my mouth anywhere near his. I thanked him for going along with the plan and waved goodbye.

Omar can sense I'm not being completely upfront with him but I can't help wanting to know more about his date.

'Can you at least tell me his socials so I can look your guy up?' I ask.

'Doesn't have them,' Omar says plainly but the statement is shocking. I don't think Omar has ever dated a guy without a huge social media presence. It's not uncommon to reject social media, I certainly barely pay attention to it, but the kind of guy that Omar usually falls for is a bit narcissistic, if I'm being honest.

'I understand you both had dates last night,' Kai says as he approaches us with a small aloe plant on his lap. He's carefully cutting off the parts of the plant that have turned brown.

'We did,' Omar says and I nod.

'Scale of one to ten, one being root rot and ten being blossom time, how were they?' he asks.

'Sam's sounds like it was a ten and mine was an eleven,' Omar says but before I can get more information, my mother comes in for her shift. Early, of course.

'Good morning, everyone,' she says to the entire cafe. Customers wave hello and Kai perks up when he sees her. She comes over to us and instead of greeting me first she gives Kai a friendly kiss on the cheek.

'Look at that aloe. She's doing much better.' My mom gently touches the plant but keeps her eyes on Kai.

'I think you're right, Glory. Exactly right.' He gazes up at her.

'Good morning, Omar. Good morning, Sam,' she says as she walks behind the counter, stuffs her purse on a shelf and puts her coat on a hook. 'Son, I thought you were going to that Brands Will Not Rescue You job today. Did you come to your senses and quit?'

'Oh, I see. You're saying the inside part out loud now. As a matter of fact, I'm heading into the office in a few minutes.'

'Wonderful, I can hear all about your date while I'm getting ready for my shift.' She grabs her apron off the hook near the tea tins and pulls it over her head.

This is the part I was dreading most. I knew she would grill me about that date with Finn. I could try to make a break for it and head to work but she'll see right through that.

'Omar, you go first, please.' I figure this will buy me some time and I'll get to hear more about his evening.

'I already texted Glory all the details this morning,' Omar says and then my mom points her finger at him and he points a finger back at her. It's some playful game they must have developed while pulling espressos together. My mom has always liked Omar but her relationship with him has always been through me. Now, it seems like they have their own thing going, which is not surprising considering they work together. A teeny tiny part of me is jealous, but they're the two people I love most, so it's hard not just to be happy that they're connected. Still, I worry about their alchemy.

'So, you two are texting?' I ask without judgment.

'Omar doesn't have a problem answering simple questions. Unlike you, son.'

'What do you want to know?' I ask falling right into her trap. She baited me and I swallowed it. Now I'm stuck.

'I want to know everything. Did you fly through the air and was Finn waiting for you on the ground ready to embrace? Did you finally see why he's so perfect for you? Did you make sure to order the margaritas without salt?' Then she turns to Kai. 'Sam's sodium intake is way too high.' Kai nods. 'Is that what happened?' she asks turning to me.

'No,' I say. 'That is not what happened.' At least the salt-less margarita part didn't happen. I love salt. 'Mom, we had a perfectly fine time. Finn is a nice guy. He would have to be to go along with your date plan. Did you both know she sent Finn a mile long list of rules for the date?' I stare at Kai and Omar hoping I can pull them to my side. 'Helicopter much, Mom?'

She pretends to be offended when in truth it is impossible to offend her. 'I am not a helicopter parent or a snowplow.' Her voice is defiant. 'I'm an Octopus Mom. No, wait, I mean a tiger.' She puts her hand to her chin. 'No that's wrong too. It's some kind of animal...?'

'Is it a swan? You look like a swan,' Kai says and my mom smiles.

'Maybe a cheetah. They're super-fast. Are you a Cheetah Mom?' Omar asks.

I can't take it a second longer. 'What does it matter?' My voice is a bit too loud.

'You're right, son. It doesn't matter,' she says, babying me. 'When is your next date with Finn? That's what matters. Do you think you're ready to plan one solo. I'm happy to do it, but I don't want anyone to think of me as controlling.'

'There isn't going to be a second date. He's a nice guy but there are no sparks, he's not my type, I'm not interested.' That phrase has been in my repertoire since this whole thing started. No sparks. Not my type. Not interested.

'You say that about every guy. You look me in the eyes and tell me there were no sparks with Finn. Go ahead.' She stands on her tiptoes and supports herself on the counter with her arms so she can have her face level with mine.

I look at her about to do exactly what she thinks I won't do. I bend down slightly so my face is right in front of hers, open my mouth and say, 'This is ridiculous.'

'You can't do it.'

'I can do it. I don't want to do it. There's a difference.'

'I don't think you're taking this seriously,' my mother says. 'Do either of you think he is?' She looks at Kai and Omar.

'I think you're doing a wonderful job, Glory,' Kai says.

'And you Omar? What do you think? You're Sam's best friend but I know you can be impartial. Is Sam taking this seriously?'

Omar looks at me and I stare him down so hard I think he might fall over. 'I think... there is a Boston fern that needs fertilizer on the other side of the cafe so I had better go over there.' He nods toward the fern. 'Kai will you join me?' Omar asks. Kai nods and they both get away from us as fast as they can.

'Sam, the point is if we are going to do this we have to do this right. I've presented you with an abundant buffet of wonderful matches. Each one a hand-crafted Glory Carmichael experience.' She raises her hand as if seeing each word in bright lights on a marquee. 'Surely one of these guys is worthy of a second date.'

'None of them,' I say quickly.

'That doesn't make any sense. Hold on.' She dips below the counter and grabs the boulder she carries around called a purse. She fumbles around and then pulls out her multi-tabbed notebook. Flips through it and then rips out a few sheets. 'This is a list of every guy I've set you up with since we started. I want you to review it and choose one to bring to Thanksgiving.'

'You want me to bring someone from this group of lunatics to your house for Thanksgiving.'

'Many of these boys are very nice. I have personally vetted each one.' She looks over the list. 'Oh, but cross out Ken and Teddy. They won't work.' I barely remember Teddy but Ken was about three weeks ago just before Halloween. A nice guy who taught kindergarten and smelled of crayons and paste.

'Why?' I ask out of curiosity.

'They'll be in Puerto Vallarta for the holiday. Ken just told me. As a couple! I might add. Your mother knows what she's doing.'

'Let me get this straight. You don't care who I bring but I have to bring someone to Thanksgiving dinner.' I'm creating just the loophole I need in order to bring Paul.

'Yes. Well, wait.' She thinks. 'It can't be Omar, of course.'

'Of course. Agreed,' I say formally. 'I assume he's already coming.'

'He is, with a date,' my mother adds. Omar has come to Thanksgiving at my house for years but he's only brought a date twice. The first was a bodybuilder who cried over the fact that we didn't have keto-approved cranberry sauce. The second was a twink who ate almost half the turkey and was never heard from again. But those were both a few years ago.

'Do you have anything to do with this mystery date?' I ask.

'I would never meddle in Omar's love life. Unless he asked me to, of course.'

'That's not a no,' I say. She walks back to the counter and I walk out to leave. But as I open the door I run into Rajesh.

'How did your midterm in Law and Ethics go?' I ask. I know he was studying for it last week in his favorite booth with Jessica.

'Not so great,' he says with a nervous frown. 'I think I failed. Maybe I'm not cut out for law.'

I nod and say, 'Why don't you tell that to the woman in the neon *Is It Me or Is It Gay in Here?* T-shirt?'

Chapter 30

I rush out of Plant Daddy so I can make it to work in time. As I'm waiting for the train I text Paul to confirm my little counterattack on my mother. Instead of nagging him about the plans I text, *Let me meet you at the airport. Send me your itinerary so I can hire a car.* I look at the text before I send it. Hiring a car for him feels so adult. I know it's not filing my taxes early or getting a mortgage but it's something. I hit send and wait for him to respond. I see the three dots of hope and then they disappear. I count back the hours to make sure he's awake in California. He should be heading to work by now. The three bubbles reappear and then disappear again.

The train arrives and I know once I'm inside there's little chance of a signal squeaking through so I silence my phone and put it in my pocket. As soon as I get out of the train and above ground I pull it out again. A text from Paul. *Yeah, about Thanksgiving. Let's talk. Around tomorrow?*

Tomorrow? There is no way I can wait until tomorrow to find out what he's talking about. I see the time and realize I might be late for work but this is too important to my mental stability. Maybe he's flying in early so we can spend more time together. I try to convince myself of that fantasy as I dial.

'Sammy? Hello. I guess you got my text.'

'I did. What's going on?' I ask. I know this feeling. I know how Paul delivers bad news. He delays and then he squirms out of whatever he promised. I can feel the sensation of disappointment entering my body as my throat tightens.

'This isn't a great time to talk but I wanted to tell you that I have concerns about Thanksgiving.' I hate when he talks like an attorney instead of a human being.

'I'm not worried about concerns. What I'm worried about is attendance. My mom is expecting me to bring someone and I want it to be you.' I do not like the way my voice sounds. Almost pleading. 'Are you coming or not?' I ask more assertively. I wish I had been more this way when we first started seeing each other.

'I want to. I really want to,' he says and I know it's a lie. I'm sure he does not want to go to Thanksgiving at my mother's since he knows he'll be judged and scrutinized. It's not a matter of want. It's a matter of need.

'Paul, I'll start it for you. "I want to go *but*…" I know there's a but coming.' I'm being more confrontational than I usually am with him and it feels good. I will not let him get away with his old tricks.

'They need me in Atlanta early. I can't get out of it.'

I knew he was going there from here but going early messes everything up. 'Atlanta? What the hell? It's Thanksgiving. You were just in London.' I really need him here. I can't keep up this charade with my mother. It's getting too uncomfortable and I want to just grow up already, have a boyfriend who lives in the same city and a job that contributes to a retirement account.

'I know. I know,' he says. His voice is soft and gentle. He's trying to calm me down but it's not working. I stop walking to work and find an empty doorway where I can focus on the conversation and hear him better. 'It sucks but the client is in Atlanta and they don't want to travel during the holiday so we have to go to them. That's how it works. You'll understand better when you're full-time at Brands. We cater to the client. That's part of the job.'

He blames everything on his job. I swear he only works in order to have an excuse. I guess I'm being childish but this is important to me. A rumble of thunder causes me to look up to see the clouds turning grey.

'Sammy, the trial is coming up and you know I'm only doing this for you. But I've got your cousin's wedding on my calendar in bold. I will be there. I've been looking forward to walking into the reception at The Plaza with you on my arm. We can go back to *our* apartment after the wedding. The decorators won't be done but I'll make it special. I'll light candles and get that special chocolate chip gelato you like.' He's really laying on the charm and I have to take a second to see if it's working like it used to.

I look across the street and take in the depth of the urban landscape. Directly in front of me, commuters rush past in both directions, and behind them, the traffic starts and stops at the light. Behind that, another sidewalk of pedestrians, and past that, I can see into the window of the bookstore where customers are browsing. So many lives passing in different directions barely intersecting. I thought Paul and I were finally in the same place, a crossroads where we could both meet. But this conversation doesn't feel like a new place, it feels like the old place. Maybe all he has really done is redecorate. I am so irritated with him right now and the fact that I'll need to find a new victim to endure Thanksgiving at my mom's only compounds the feeling. Apparently his old charm *isn't* working.

'Sammy, are you there?'

'I have to go, Paul. Goodbye.' I hang up. I'm furious and hurt and I don't like where this is going but I've put too much time and effort into it. Is it too late to change direction? I walk out from the protection of the doorway and into the torrential downpour which only takes a few seconds to soak me to the bone.

Chapter 31

I walk the last two blocks to Brands in the pouring rain, still mad at Paul but trying to focus on my new dilemma. If my mother thinks I'm not taking her plan seriously, it will mean all the work I've already put in will be for nothing. I have to choose one of her horrible dates to join me at Thanksgiving.

The elevator doors open at Brands, and I head over to the kitchen area to make a hot cup of tea and dry out before I start pounding away at whatever tasks have been backing up in the digital workflow. No one else is around so I sit and let the hot liquid heat me up from the inside as I use a few paper towels to wipe off my face. As I'm trying to gather myself, Robert comes in followed by... Finn. At first, I panic that I missed a meeting, and then I panic because I realize we haven't really talked since our trapeze date night, and then I panic again because I look like I swam down the Hudson to get here.

'Hello,' I say as they walk into the kitchen. 'I hope I haven't missed a meeting.' I grab a wad of paper towels and press them to my shirt, hoping they will soak up some of the wetness.

'Not at all,' Robert says, heading to the coffee station. I can tell from his wrinkled nose that he's judging my lack of an umbrella. 'I asked Finn to come in so I could convince him to be a part of our team.' I hate when Robert or anyone uses the word team to describe the workplace. A team is a group in a game or sport. It's something fun. Work is not fun. It's work. It's the very opposite.

'Hello, Sam,' Finn says. I search his eyes to get some kind of read on how he's feeling toward me, but they are inscrutable.

'Hi, Finn,' I say, and I notice the sides of his mouth turn up just a bit.

'Sam, I had absolutely no luck with him.' Robert makes himself a cup of coffee with the fancy machine that's usually broken. 'Maybe you can help convince Finn how wonderful we are here at Brands. We need someone to run visuals for a number of big clients we're taking on.'

Finn working here? He is so not a 'normal'. I can't see him putting his art on hold to create a pitch deck, logging every working hour, or wearing ugly pants. Not to mention that I don't want work to be any more stressful than it already is.

Robert looks at his watch and says, 'I've got a client who needs some extra hand holding.' He walks out leaving me alone with Finn.

I look at him and he returns my gaze but neither of us say anything. Should I say something about the other night? It feels weird to bring it up here. I'll accept any reason to avoid the topic so I ask, 'Do you want to work here?'

'Not really,' he says, shaking his head. 'Robert pressured me into coming in. I felt I had to with Miami coming up and I didn't want him to think I don't like working with you.'

'That's very nice. Thanks,' I say, blotting myself one last time before throwing the towels in the trash can and giving up.

'I'll never be rich making art but I can't see myself working full-time in an office.'

'I understand. I couldn't see myself here either...' I look around the sterile kitchen area with the prerequisite offering of vending machines. 'Until I could.'

'Why *do* you work here?' he asks and stops immediately. 'Wait. That did not come out right at all. Sorry.' He's flustered by his stumble and it's very sweet. I even hear a bit more of his Southern drawl when he's nervous. He usually keeps it under wraps. 'Everybody needs a day job. I've been lucky with my grants and gallery sales. But this place? Full-time?' He looks around at the fluorescent lighting and dull office furniture designed to be inoffensive. 'It seems so corporate and stifling. How would you find the time to write if you had to come here every day?'

'I had another gig before this where I got to do more writing, sort of. It was...' I look up at the ceiling as I search for the right word. 'Complicated.'

'Would you tell me about it?' His voice is warm and sweet like when he was working with Ekaterina. He pulls out the chair next to me and sits down. I do the same.

I take a sip of tea and debate how much I should tell him. He sits quietly, patiently, like he's ready to listen when – or if – I'm willing to talk. Truthfully, it makes me want to tell him everything. I couldn't open up about it when he asked at the Statue of Liberty. He was right. I changed the subject and avoided an honest answer. At Swingers I was too focused on not dying. I don't know if it's my conversation with Paul or the pouring rain or the fact that I'm beginning to trust him, but today his intentional softness makes me want to open up at least a tiny bit. I take a breath in and hold it for a second before I start to share my story.

'For a bunch of years,' I begin, 'I worked for this woman. I'm not sure you'd know her. She had this big breakout book in the late nineties that became a huge movie – *The Jilted Belles of Bel Air.*'

'I know that movie.' He smiles at the recollection. 'It's kind of campy and funny. Wasn't Katie Diane in it? And some other big Hollywood actors.'

'Exactly,' I say. 'That movie was based on the book written by a woman who went by the name Justine Jasmine. I wasn't around during *Jilted Belles*. Way before my time.'

'I've heard that name,' Finn says. 'I see her books all the time, like at airports and places like that. You worked for her?'

'I *was* her.' I dramatically raise my paper teacup.

He looks at me curiously, and I can practically see the cogs in his mind try to fit into place. 'Like in drag?'

'No, although we used to joke about me doing appearances as her. She was known for being a fashion icon, and I could never walk in stilettos. I've tried. I always fall over.'

'Same. Weak ankles,' he says with a chuckle and it helps me keep going.

'After some big successes she wanted to enjoy the fame and money but she didn't want to write the books. My agent knew her socially and suggested...' I lean just in case some 'normal' is in earshot. 'I write the books under her name. Like a ghostwriter.'

Understanding spreads across Finn's face. He nods slowly and says, 'So you *are* Justin Jasmine. Wait. Is Justine Jasmine a real person?'

'Very much. I mean, the name is made up. Her real name is Olivia. And we worked together mostly on the books. She taught me a lot and...' I trail off and bite my lower lip. I'm still under a non-disclosure but when I look at Finn, I have this feeling deep inside that I can trust him.

'Wait. Books plural? How many did you write for her?'

'About six,' I say matter-of-factly.

'You've written half a dozen books and you still don't consider yourself a writer?' He tilts his head to look at me with wide eyes.

'But my name was never on them. Sometimes she would thank me in the acknowledgments but not always. They were her stories. I just did the heavy lifting.' I shrug.

'You'd go to bookstores. See the book with her name on it or see people reading it, knowing you wrote it, and you could never tell anyone?'

'Yeah, that's the job,' I say. I remember Paul saying that to me just a little while ago about his work. I guess every job has its obstacles and punishments. 'I'm still not supposed to tell anyone but things changed when she decided to retire. Although I was doing most of the work she still did appearances and stuff like that. Her editors didn't know I was writing most of it.'

I realize I haven't really done a post-mortem on the whole Justine situation. When everything unfolded, I was too devastated, and then I thought I could find success independently. When that didn't happen, I felt too humiliated to truly confront everything.

'Was that hard for you?' His eyes are soft and gentle, searching my face for the answer.

'Not really,' I say, but realize that's what I always say. I always told myself that the money was good, she was a nice enough person, so it didn't bother me. But if I'm putting all that behind me, I also need to confront the truth. 'Scratch that,' I say sitting up in my chair. 'It did bother me. I was never mad at her or my agent. I knew what I signed up for, but writing a book is hard and at the end you want some kind of recognition.'

There, I said it. Out loud. I wanted people to see me as a writer. Why is it so hard for me to acknowledge it? I had to give up writing to admit it.

'But now you can write your own stuff,' he says casually, not knowing he's pushing on a wound that hasn't healed yet.

'Tried that. Didn't work out.' I grab my tea which is now cold. 'Even submitted the last book I was working on before she retired. Same exact kind of book to the imprint that published dozens of hers and they rejected it.'

'That's something I can understand. I get a lot of rejection too. Bad reviews. People who don't get what I'm trying to do with my photos. Things like that.' He shakes his head and runs his fingers through his hair. 'But maybe it sounds like it was still her stuff you submitted?'

'It was kind of. It just had my name on it. That's why I was so upset when they passed.' I'm able to talk about this with him but the feeling in my stomach is making me aware that it's not a topic that has completely lost its volatility.

'No, I mean, no wonder they passed.' He looks at me like he's not sure I understand. 'Maybe you were still writing as her even though your name was on it. Maybe it was still in her voice. Her story. You have to write your own story.'

'Oh really?' I put my elbow on the table and place my head in my hand. 'Do you think the world is waiting to hear about a thirty-five-year-old gay man with a boring job and overbearing mother who lives above a plant store cafe where his friends hang out? I don't think so.'

'Maybe *you* don't think so. Sam, you have to be the first person to believe you have something to say.' His eyes are searching mine looking for a way in. 'Sometimes when I meet a subject they're shocked that I want to interview them. They think their story isn'tworth telling. I try to help them see that their stories are important, not just to them but to others who need to hear them. Don't you think that you have your own story? Your own voice?'

I'm not sure. Or maybe I've never really had to figure it out because I was executing Justine's vision. 'All I know is I got rejection after rejection this summer and it broke me. And that was with stuff in her voice. I can't imagine...' I trail off. I've been trying to avoid these feelings but now he's making them bubble up. My heart begins to beat faster.

He scratches his temple like he's figuring it as well. 'I'm sorry that you feel broken. But you're stronger than you think. I've seen you try things you didn't think you could do. I loved watching that. Seeing you conquer your fear on the trapeze was a real turn-on,' he says, and then catches himself. He blushes, and I might also. 'I mean, it's exhilarating to see anyone do that.'

I'm thinking about the accidental kiss that happened at Swingers. I'm wondering if he is too. Do I tell him I didn't want it to happen when I'm the one who let my lips linger? Do I tell him I don't want it to happen again even though when I look at his face now I can still feel his stubble on my cheek? The conversation we are currently having is the less difficult of the two, so I stick with the topic at hand and leave my questions unanswered.

'That was a physical feat, not something creative,' I say, taking a sip of my cold tea to cover my unease. 'I just had to jump. It's totally different.'

252

'They're both leaps of faith,' Finn says. 'One is faith that the harnesses will hold you. The other is faith in yourself.'

'I've never been very good at that.' I look out the window. The rain has stopped and the sun is peeking through the clouds.

'Why don't you apply to Art Barn?' he asks. 'It's an artists' retreat upstate. I always spend a month or two in the spring. It's a great mix of creatives – painters, poets, sculptures… writers.' I can hear the excitement in his voice. 'You would have the space to take yourself seriously as a writer.'

A month away from Brands? I can't imagine Robert would allow any of the full-timers to take that much time off. Plus, Paul would never go for it, me leaving him alone for weeks. I get a flash of the anger I felt when I was on the phone with Paul earlier. I can't be pulled back and forth in different directions. I can feel my seams being torn apart.

'I appreciate the advice,' I say stiffly, trying to control my emotions. 'I've got a plan in place. There's a full-time position opening here that will keep me so busy I won't even think about writing. That's what I need.' I try to make my voice clearer and more assured.

A sadness appears across Finn's face. 'I think what you need is to take yourself seriously as a writer.'

'No, it isn't.' I say and now I feel it. Whatever I've been holding back has risen to the surface. I'm angry. This has been a friendly conversation, and I know he's been thoughtful and kind to me, but the fact is he's just a client – or maybe a new friend or something else. But whatever our connection is, I don't need him trying to pull me back to a place I made a conscious effort to leave. 'Look, Finn, I get that a job here isn't for you,' I say, 'but that doesn't mean it isn't for me.'

'I'm not talking about the job. I'm not saying you shouldn't—'

'That's exactly what it sounds like.' I interrupt him. 'It sounds like you think you know better. After all, you're one of the Thirty Under Thirty. Good for you. You're the right combination of talent, intelligence, and good looks.' As soon as I say the good looks part I wish I hadn't. 'Finn, you don't know me.'

'Argh!' he yells, standing up from his seat. 'You are one of the most frustrating guys I have ever met.' He turns his back to me and paces in the small space, his hands jammed in his pockets like he's trying to control himself.

'So are you!' I shout back.

He turns back to face me, his face pink with emotion. 'As soon as we get close to having a real conversation about your work you pull out. I see you. I think I see you better than you see yourself.'

I see myself as a failed writer who couldn't get anything published in their own name, who has to take a full-time job at a place that makes him feel like he's slowly dying. That's who I really am. Everything else is a façade. I'm not ready to go where he wants to take me. I've cracked open the door but I need to seal it shut.

'You don't know me,' I say, my voice full of indignation.

'But I'm trying to.' His voice is soft and sincere as he slowly sits back down. He's listening and he's trying. The softness in his eyes reveals a depth of patience I've never seen before.

I take a moment to regain my composure. I look down at the table to center myself and breathe in and out and to let my mind clear. Why does he push my buttons? Why did I get so angry just now when he was only trying to help?

It only takes a few seconds to I realize I'm not mad at Finn. I'm angry about a lot of things in my life, but he's not one of them. He doesn't know I've been through all this in my mind a million times and I can't find any other way forward than what I have planned. I'm really angry at Paul for canceling Thanksgiving and leaving me to deal with finding someone else to take to dinner. Paul is the one who left me feeling raw and on edge this morning. But the more I think about it, it's not just Paul. I realize it's the first Thanksgiving my mom and I will have without Shug, and all my emotions are coming to the surface. Maybe that's why I'm so upset about Paul's cancellation. Maybe it was a bad idea to spring him on my mom during the holiday anyway.

The point is, I shouldn't take all this out on Finn. He doesn't deserve it.

'Finn, I'm sorry,' I say. 'I shouldn't have gotten so worked up. I don't want to go any further with this topic.' I try to find words that are more professional than emotional. 'It's not an excuse but I have a lot going on at the moment.'

'I push too much. I'm trying to do this thing where I have a normal conversation with a person instead of turning it into an interview.' He covers his face with his hands and then moves them up pushing his hair back. 'I'm sorry.'

'No, it's not you. I have a lot of pressure with Art Week and I have to figure out Thanksgiving with my mother. I still don't have a...'

'Oh, yeah, Thanksgiving.' He chuckles. 'I keep forgetting about it.'

That's when I remember: Finn isn't close with his family, plus he's new in town. I put my hand to my chin to think for a moment. It just might work, and it'll show him that I'm not the jerk I just revealed myself to be.

'You know,' I say. 'If you don't have any plans for Thanksgiving, you could join me at my mom's. It'll just be her and Kai and Omar. And I think Omar's bringing a date.'

I watch him carefully to see if I can predict his answer, but before I can render a guess he says, 'Yes. Thank you. I'd like that. I'd like that a lot.' A big smile stretches across his face, and it's like his happiness transfers to me, and suddenly I'm smiling too. Whatever emotions were threatening to erupt a few minutes ago have been subdued.

'Then it's a date,' I say. Through the window behind him, I can see that the rain has stopped, and the clouds have given way to clear blue skies with sharp rays of autumn sunshine. It's turning out to be a beautiful day.

Chapter 32

Two days later I'm at my favorite table at Plant Daddy trying to get through a stack of edits on some material for the Carlos Wong Gallery but my mind keeps wandering. All I can think about is my conversation with Finn and, if I am being honest, Finn himself. The way he pushed back at Brands the other day. It was annoying but also very sweet. Maybe he's right. Maybe my problem is that I don't take myself seriously as a writer.

I switch screens on my laptop from the spreadsheet for Brands to a document I started after my last encounter with Finn. It's just a collection of notes and ideas for a story. More my point of view than just being a copy of Justine Jasmine. I should be organizing columns on the other screen, but instead, I start writing a scene that's been in my head since I climbed up the ladder to the top of the trapeze last week. My fingers fly over the keyboard. There's no deadline for Justine, no particular audience I'm imagining. The words keep coming. It's all very rough but I'm enjoying it enough that I notice I have a few pages down before I lift my head up from the screen. I start to re-read what I've written when I feel someone's eyes over my shoulder.

'Are you writing something? Oh, that's wonderful. What are you writing? Can I read it?'

I slam the screen of my laptop down. I turn around and my mother comes from behind me and sits at my table. 'Show me,' she says rubbing her hands together in anticipation. 'Or read it to me. Do you remember when you would come into my room and act out those stories for me? You had that one about the squirrel who thought he was related to Judy Garland and he went to Hollywood to find her. It was so adorable and you were so cute reading it.' She smiles and touches my hand with hers.

I do remember that story. I used to write weird little skits as a kid, and I liked performing them for my mom and sometimes Aunt Shug, when she was over. Mom would always laugh and tell me how good they were. I loved that feeling, but somewhere along the way I worried they weren't good enough. I never wanted to disappoint her, so I stopped showing her what I was working on. I know my mom believes in me and if you do the math it should mean I have all the confidence in the world but it doesn't work that way. I think she believes in me so much that I never had to make room to believe in myself.

'Mom, it's not a story. It's just work for Brands. That's all.'

'Fine. You don't have to show me if you don't want to but I don't understand why you don't just keep writing and...'

I signal to Kai. 'Excuse me. One of your employees is bothering me.' I wave my hand to get his attention and he comes over to us.

'Glory, please remember,' Kai says, 'we reserve the right to withhold service from anyone.' He turns to me. 'Sir, consider this a warning?' He smiles at my mom and they both giggle before Kai heads off to water a plant.

I sink down in my chair. I'm glad they have become friends since she started working here. I like Kai a lot, and of course, I love my mother, and the fact that it might keep her more occupied with less time to interfere in my life is only a bonus.

'It's been nice having you here,' I say.

She kisses me on the forehead and I immediately rub the spot to remove her pink lipstick. 'I love you for saying that and I love that I raised you to be such a horrible liar. It shows good character. I know I annoy you. That's normal. That's what a mother is supposed to do.'

'Is it?' I ask tilting my head sharply.

'In our case, yes. Now let me grab my notebook so we can nail down an escort for Thanksgiving since you're ignoring the obvious.' She says the last part with her eyebrows raised and then goes to get up but I stop her.

'Mom, you don't have to do that.'

'Yes, I do. I don't have that much time—'

'You don't have to do it because I've already invited someone,' I say coyly and lean back in the chair. Now I'm the one instigating.

'Who? Who?' Her excitement is palpable.

'Oh, someone…' I say playing with her.

'Tell me!' she demands.

I wait a few seconds longer watching her face contort trying to be patient before saying, 'Finn.'

'Finn? I knew it. I just knew it.' She leaps up from the table, unable to contain herself. 'He's perfect for you. He's so handsome and smart and he's a real artist. He has passion and pizazz. He checks all the boxes on my rules.' She sits back down and leans in toward me. 'Did you know he's taking pictures of Kai? He does documentary photos and they are just wonderful. He was here the other day and he showed me his portfolio. It's fabulous.'

'Mom, calm down.'

'It's working. My plan is working.' She stamps her feet on the floor. 'I knew it. The minute I saw you sitting with him. I knew he was the one.'

'You mean the day I forbade you from putting him on your list?' I remember her eyes peeking from behind the door to the storage area.

'Oh, please. You think I'm going to be stopped by a technicality. I found a way. A mother always does.'

'I invited him to Thanksgiving. It's nothing more than that.'

'Whatever you say, Sam,' my mom says, her excitement bubbling.

Then the bells above the door ring and Finn walks in. I try to keep my face neutral but I can't. A smile stretches across my mouth. 'Hi, Sam,' he says. 'Hey, Glory.'

'Play it cool, Mom,' I say quickly, but before I can get the words out, she leaps up from the chair and has her arms around him, squeezing all the air out of his body in one of her famous hugs – but on steroids.

'You're coming to Thanksgiving,' she says with her face still buried in his chest. Finn accepts the hug and even returns it. His long arms wrap around her tiny body.

'Yes, sure do appreciate being invited. Please let me know what I can bring or how I can help.' He knows how to lay on the Southern charm for my mother.

She steps out of the hug and changes gears. 'I'm going to make my rye bread stuffing. It has r-a-i-s-i-n-s in it but don't tell You Know Who.' She points at me.

'You Know Who can spell, Mom, and he can also hear you. I'm sitting right here.'

'Do you have any allergies, Finn? Hold on.' She runs to the counter and pulls out her notebook to rip out a page. She runs back and hands it to Finn with a pencil. 'I want you to make a list of two columns. Write all the things you like at Thanksgiving on one side and then on the other write down any allergies or things you don't like. Oh, and use different colors just to make it look fun. Wait, I know, I'll start a new tab in my notebook. Oh, this is wonderful,' she says and heads back to the counter to wait on a customer.

Once she's gone I say to Finn, 'Thank you. This will make her very happy. I owe you for it.'

'I can't wait. But I do have a way for you to return the favor if you want. No pressure.'

'How?' I ask.

'During Art Week a lot of the artists from Art Barn have kind of an end-of-year reunion. A bunch of people I know from the residency are usually down there. Luis hosts it at his place, an old cigar factory he converted into an amazing studio. Come with me?' he asks.

'A fabulous loft in Miami in exchange for a Thanksgiving at the suburban split-level where my mom still has plastic slipcovers on the furniture?' I pretend to mull over the offer. 'It's the least I can do.'

Chapter 33

Thanksgiving morning in New York is magic. I can feel the energy of the parade a few blocks away from my apartment but the streets surrounding the building are unusually peaceful and calm. The air is crisp and still, and there's a sense of hushed anticipation, as if the city itself is holding its breath before the celebrations begin.

Plant Daddy is closed for the holiday so Kai is driving the adaptable van he uses for plant pickups to get to my mother's house on the other side of the George Washington Bridge. When I get downstairs, Omar and Finn are helping retract the collapsible ramp, and Kai is in the driver's seat, clearly ready to go. When he sees me he honks the horn and yells out the window, 'Hurry up! Glory is waiting.' Then he honks again.

'Are those your world-famous Rice Krispie treats?' Omar asks looking at the square of rumbled tinfoil I'm carrying. He thinks they're revolting, so I know he's being sarcastic.

'Don't make fun,' I admonish him and turn to Finn who looks more preppy than arty today. He's wearing a cable-knit sweater that hugs his chest and a tweed newsboy hat. 'Omar sneers at my low-brow taste in food,' I say to him, handing the treats to Omar to put in the van.

'Are those really Rice Krispie treats?' Finn asks with some surprise in his voice.

'With peanut butter. That's my little trick.' I wink.

'That is my absolute favorite dessert,' Finn says, his voice a mix of playful eagerness and sincerity that makes me smile from ear to ear.

'Thank you for coming today, Finn. It means a lot to my mom. She likes you.'

'I like her,' he says. The cold late morning air is making his cheeks redder than usual.

'Remember, my mom knows I'm going to Florida, but she has no idea that you're going to be there too. Can we keep it that way? At least for now. I'll spring it on her just before I leave to minimize the nagging.'

'I'm not going to lie to her but I promise I won't bring it up.'

I guess that's the most I can ask for. Kai honks the horn. 'Stop gabbing. Glory is expecting us.' We do as we're told and hop in. Kai pulls out and we're on our way.

'Where's your mystery date?' I ask Omar, who is sitting up front and adjusting the orange-and-green striped bow of his flouncy shirt in the vanity mirror above the windshield.

'He had to take care of something this morning but he'll be there. I gave him directions.'

I wonder what he's hiding. We drive through midtown and up the Henry Hudson Parkway. A few pine wreaths and red bows have been put up in store windows and on streetlamps, but the feeling in the city is still autumn. The trees that line Riverside Drive and the Hudson River are at their peak with colors that radiate deep jewel tones of ruby and topaz.

'I love autumn,' Finn says. He can't take his eyes off the trees as we pass. 'I've never lived any place with seasons that change so dramatically. One day all the trees are leafy and green and the next they're totally different.'

'The colors are beautiful,' I say looking out the window with him.

'But it's not just that. It's the change that's so striking. So dramatic. I look at those massive trees with all those green leaves and it feels like they'll be that way forever but then suddenly they turn into something new or maybe something they were always meant to be.'

I try to look at the trees and see them as he does. I like trying to understand his perspective because it's so different from my own.

We hit a pothole on the road and everyone shifts in their seats. Kai says, 'One of you look back there and make sure the potted palm I'm bringing for Glory is alright. It's fragile and special.'

Omar twists his head behind him. 'It's fine.'

'Are you sure?' Kai says keeping his eyes on the road.

'It's just a plant,' I say without thinking.

'Just a plant? Keep talking that way and you won't make it over the George Washington Bridge.'

'Sorry, Kai.' I forget how protective he is of his plants. And my mother for that matter.

Once we're over the bridge we take the exit for the town I grew up in avoiding the highway that is currently under construction We are less than thirty minutes from Hell's Kitchen but the crowded suburb of Leonia, New Jersey, is almost another universe. Kai drives past the public school I attended for most of my teenage years. The parking lot is empty, and the building is silent, but in my memory I can hear the crowded halls filled with students.

I see myself trying to be invisible as I went from class to class, praying that one of the idiots who taunted me wouldn't be bored and seek me out to make their day more interesting. Trying to be overly involved in school activities since a moving target is harder to aim for. I can feel my body stiffen. It's an automatic response. I wonder if Finn is having a reaction to seeing the school, but before I can find out, he must sense my discomfort.

'You okay?' he asks. I can't immediately break my gaze from staring at the school and I have to consciously turn toward him.

'Yeah, I'm fine. That's the school I went to.' My words come out flat and emotionless. 'I know your school years weren't the best either.'

'No, but we didn't just drive by mine,' he says. I look down, and for a second, I think I see his hand move toward me, but then it stops. Or maybe it was my imagination. I'm not trying to lead him on at all. I don't want to do that. But a part of me wouldn't mind if he reached out for me in this moment. I'm sure feeling my hand in his would make the stress melt. I'm about to edge my fingers toward his when Kai slams on the brakes.

'Sam, which way? You know how I hate driving in the country.'

'Kai, this is not the country. You can still see the Manhattan skyline. We're in a suburb. Turn left up ahead by that drug store.'

'The only person I'd leave Manhattan for is your mother,' he says accelerating slowly. 'Everyone be on the lookout for cows or Republicans. Anything that might attack us.'

The van pulls up in front of the house I was born and raised in, a golden-rod yellow, split-level with black shutters. My mother has an assortment of flags, signs, and garden statuary across the front lawn. As a kid, the tackiness of our house embarrassed me. I would beg my mother to have more tasteful curb appeal but then she would find a gnome with a particularly radical look or a lawn sign with a new clever way to say, 'everyone is welcome here' and our front lawn would turn into a combination safe haven/zoning violation.

We use the back entrance so Kai can easily enter and as soon as I open the door my mom runs over and gives each of us a kiss on the cheek and one of her famous hugs. I let the rest of the crew get their greeting as I walk into the kitchen. The first thing that hits me is the smell of turkey roasting in the oven with my mother's unique blend of spices and garlic. Everything still looks exactly the same as it did when I was in school. Across the kitchen counter, she has various side dishes in the weird brightly painted handmade pottery I grew up with. I'm sure she has been working on this meal for the past week.

The dark brown cabinets with dark powder-blue accents haven't changed. Drawings from elementary school, yellow with age, still hang on the fridge, and there are many pictures of me scattered about. Too many.

'Is that you?' Finn asks pointing to a yearbook photo from fifth grade in a wooden frame. I'm wearing a Spice Girls T-shirt and I was at my heaviest that year. I should have arrived early to do a sweep of the place.

'Yeah,' I say. 'I have no idea why she keeps that picture up. We had such an argument over wearing that T-shirt.' I shake my head.

'She wanted you to wear something more formal?' he asks.

'No, not at all. She wanted me to wear my Destiny's Child T-shirt.'

Finn laughs and picks up the frame. 'You look adorable.' There's no way he's being honest.

'Finn, I'm busting out of that T-shirt, my hair is a frizzled mess, my braces caught the flash of the camera, and my skin looks like the surface of the moon. I do not look adorable.'

'You had a glow up at some point. There's no doubt about that,' he says looking me up and down. 'But the kid in that picture is adorable.'

I'm thinking about what he said the other day about how I see myself. I felt the opposite of adorable at that age. I wanted to hide from everyone and everything. I barely had any friends beside Patty and I sat in my room, watched old movies and ate Cheetos and chocolate milk, a combination of flavors I still love.

Finn heads out to the van to help Omar carry in even more food and I peek into the dining room where my mother has squeezed just enough chairs around the tiny dining table. In the center of the table is the turkey pineapple that has been a part of my world since I was a kid. Every year, my mother would purchase a pineapple and use it as the body for a turkey head she made out of felt and googly eyes. It has been the centerpiece for as long as I can remember. The house feels trapped in time but it's comforting. My mom finds me alone in the dining room.

'I can hear them both, you know,' she says quietly as she puts her hand on my back.

'*La Traviata* or *Carmen*?' I ask.

'*La Bohème*,' she says and closes her eyes, listening to the music only she can hear. My aunt and father loved to sing opera in the kitchen every holiday. I don't remember my father doing it, I was too young, but my aunt kept the tradition alive, serenading us as we stuffed the turkey or peeled potatoes. She was a horrible singer and it was hard even to figure out the tune but that didn't stop her. Sometimes my mother joined in but she said she wanted to listen more than she wanted to sing so Aunt Shug would belt out arias and fill the air with music while we cooked and laughed.

'She's here today, you know. She wouldn't miss Thanksgiving. She would love this crowd so much.' My mom closes her eyes gently.

'She really would,' I say thinking about how Kai would like Shug as much as he seems to like my mom. 'She'd be thrilled to see so many people here squeezed into the dining room.'

'Thank you, Sam. For bringing everyone here. I had been dreading today, but knowing everyone was coming made me look forward to it.'

'You invited them,' I remind her.

'Maybe, but you're the hub of the wheel here. You're the person that helps people connect. You're like me that way.'

'I guess I am,' I say. I was angry when Paul couldn't make it, but right now, I'm glad he couldn't. It would have been a very different day for us if he had been here. We texted this morning and he's planning to stay parked in front of the TV in his room in Atlanta watching football.

'I thanked Shug for bringing you Finn,' my mom says interrupting my thoughts. 'He looks so handsome today, I don't know how you don't jump his bones right now.'

'Mom, stop it. I am not jumping anyone's bones, and certainly not Finn.' I look out the window to make sure he's still on the back deck with Omar setting up chairs.

'Why not? He's perfect for you. He checks all the boxes on the list.'

'*Your* list.' He's her fantasy of what my boyfriend should be.

She rolls her eyes. 'Finn is handsome, passionate about his work, about life, and I think he's really falling for you. He's what you're looking for.'

'No, Mom,' I say. Finn is not falling for me. We are becoming friends. That's it. 'You have no idea what I'm looking for.' When she finds out I'm moving in with Paul, she won't take it well, but at least she will finally understand once and for all what I need in a boyfriend, and this entire topic will be closed.

'You just don't want to admit you like him because that means admitting I'm right.' Didn't Omar claim this theory a few weeks ago? There must be something in the coffee beans at Plant Daddy.

'That's outrageous. It's not true at all. Not even a little bit. No, no, no. No way, Mom.' I stop my tirade, thinking my protestation might be making a case for the opposite. Luckily, the doorbell rings, so I can temporarily avoid the conversation.

'Will you get that? I need to check on the turkey,' my mom says and steps back into the kitchen. I walk through the living room and open the front door to find the last person I thought I would see today.

Chapter 34

'Kevin!' I say shocked to see my former date and mead expert at the door with his pet iguana.

He bows at the waist and tips his hat grandly, but the iguana, Wayne, stays on his shoulder somehow. 'What are you doing here?' Did my mother invite him by accident before I told her Finn was coming, and she forgot to cancel? 'I'm sorry. There must have been some crossed wires. I already have a date for Thanksgiving,' I say trying to be as gentle as possible. This poor guy came all the way out to New Jersey just to see me and on a holiday. I didn't feel anything for him except a strange fascination but I guess he really fell for me.

'Good sir, I think the joyous season of gratitude has clouded your brain. I'm not your date for today's festivities.'

'He's mine,' Omar says coming in from the kitchen. He walks past me and kisses Kevin on each cheek and then Kevin bends a bit so Omar can do the same to Wayne. I can't stop my body from displaying an intense shudder. My mom comes out of the kitchen and hugs Kevin but thankfully she only waves to Wayne. I swear if I saw her lips on that animal I'd explode.

'Would someone please explain what's going on here?' I ask. I'm too confused to hazard a guess.

'Just your mother doing what she does best.' She pinches my cheek like I'm seven.

'Sam,' Omar steps in. 'I've wanted to tell you this for a while but I've been busy and you've been busy. Then your mom and I thought it would make a fun surprise,' Omar says as he reaches for Kevin's hand.

'Everyone. I have some appa-teasers in the kitchen and I made a lovely salad for Wayne. Omar, I'll let you explain to Sam. Son, maybe you'll finally understand...' Mom says, ushering everyone out of the room leaving me and Omar alone. 'That I know what I'm doing.' She sings the last part as a triumphant operatic march and closes the door behind her.

I sit on the couch with Omar. 'This is the mystery guy you've been seeing?' I still can't believe it.

'I didn't know how to tell you.' He scratches his beard with his hand. 'I mean I was sure you weren't interested in him. You know I would never try to steal a guy from you.'

'I know that, and I wasn't interested in him, but I'm surprised you are.' I try not to sound too judgmental.

'I know. He's not my type at all. But your mother thought...'

'This has her fingerprints all over it.' I can hear her chatting and laughing in the kitchen with everyone.

'Your mother thought we would hit it off. Kevin and I started talking after I showed up at your date with him. I told your mom about it during one of our shifts and before I knew it, she set up a real date for us. At first, I did it to be nice to your mom, but the truth is we had such a great time. Did you know he brews his own mead?' Omar puts his hand on his chest and his head kicks back in awe.

'I am aware,' I say, emotionless.

'He's super sweet and he loves his iguana so dearly and he's just so nice. He makes these fabulous leather pouches. He loves to watch me sew and thinks my designs are incredible,' Omar says. I can see his fondness for Kevin in his face. His eyes are doing their own happy dance.

'Well, your designs are incredible.'

'Thank you. Kevin loves them and it means so much to me and he's such a nice guy.' Omar cannot keep the smile off his face but then he pauses. 'Unlike so many of the jerks we've both dated.'

'If you like him that's all that matters.' But then I realize he said jerks *we have both dated*. Omar has dated some real creeps and I've tried to be supportive but also protective of him. But does he think I have the same problem? 'You think I date as many jerks as you do?' I ask. The question comes off ruder and more intrusive than I had planned but that's the benefit of having a best friend. You never assume malice.

'No, I don't,' he says and I feel a moment of relief. Then he adds, plainly, 'I think you date more.'

'What?'

'Maybe not more, but certainly the jerks you date are more intense,' he says, and I know he's talking about one jerk specifically. He looks toward the kitchen to make sure no one is coming in. 'I mean, I thought you said Paul would be here today,' he whispers. 'Not that I want to see him, but I know you were counting on him.'

I told Omar Paul was coming when I thought Paul was coming and when he cancelled I sort of let the topic fall off the radar. I didn't want to admit to Omar or myself that Paul had disappointed me once again. 'He had an important meeting in Atlanta. He couldn't get out of it. It wasn't his fault.'

'Sam that's what you say all the time about him. That it's not his fault.'

'But it isn't,' I say and feel childish as soon as I do.

'Paul is a jerk. He was a jerk before and he remains a jerk.' I want to tell Omar about the plans for the re-design of the apartment and the thoughtful messages and gifts I've been receiving. I want to show him the piece of paper about retaining the lawyer, but I know he will tell me again that it's only a piece of paper. Could he be right? Omar looks me in the eye and says, 'I was hoping that if you can't see what a jerk Paul is, you would see how wonderful Finn is.'

'What? This isn't about him. I don't like him. I could never be with a guy like Finn.'

'Why? Because he's talented? Because he cares about the people around him? Because he's super sexy?'

'No,' I say quickly but without a great deal of firmness. It would never work with a guy like Finn because… my brain gets ahead of me and sends a message way before my heart is ready to receive it. I would never be with a guy like Finn because I would resent his talent. It would make me feel like even more of a flop. Being with a guy like Paul means I never have to worry about not reaching my potential or fulfilling some creative desire. It also means never having to find out if I can achieve anything. Maybe that's just as good or maybe I'm beginning to realize that won't be enough.

'Let's table this,' I say. I don't want to get in my head and if Omar has found someone he really likes, I want to celebrate that. 'Tell me more about you and Kevin and…' I swallow hard just to get the last word out. 'Wayne.'

'It's all kind of new but he makes me laugh and the sex is amazing.'

'Please tell me the iguana is not in the room when that happens.' I cover my face with my hand.

'Oh no. Wayne gets very jealous. We have to put him in his home. But he does sleep in the bed sometimes, which is very comforting. And I sewed Wayne the cutest little waistcoat to wear with some leftover leather from the pouches that Kevin makes and sells at the Renaissance fairs.' Omar holds his hands up to indicate the miniature size.

'Rara,' Kevin says, poking his head in. 'Come see how much Wayne loves Glory's sweet potatoes.'

'I will Kevs,' he says. 'Be right there?'

'Rara and Kevs?' I ask. 'You already have pet names for each other?' I take a moment to examine his face. 'This is more serious than you're letting on but go ahead. We're good and I don't want to miss Wayne eating my mom's sweet potatoes.'

—

It's warm enough in the afternoon to have some drinks and appetizers on the deck off the kitchen. The ancient apple trees that line the yard have small pieces of misshapen red and green fruit. A bright, multicolored blanket of fallen leaves surrounds each one. In the distance, I can hear people cheering at the annual Turkey Trot down Main Street.

Kai is explaining how he first got interested in plants after his divorce from his first husband decades ago when he came to the US. 'I figured if I could take care of someone who sits around all day and is totally useless, plants would be easy.' Everyone laughs but I notice my mom laughs even harder than everyone else. I'm sure today is hard for her, but I'm relieved to know that she has found such a good friend in Kai. They're so different in some ways but from the same generation so I guess they understand each other.

The Thanksgiving meal is wonderful as always. My mom brines the turkey for two days before she roasts it and she's also made a vegan roast out of lentils that she shaped into a heart with mushroom gravy as a garnish. Omar has made a traditional *bademjan* with eggplant and tomato and Kevin's mead-braised shallots with apples are surprisingly delicious. Of course, my mom raves about Finn's Cajun rice, which is spicy and sweet at the same time.

At dinner I can't help thinking about how natural it feels for the six of us to be together. At times, we're all laughing so hard we're trying not to choke, but at other moments, the conversation turns more serious as we discuss politics and current events, each person contributing a thoughtful point of view.

If Paul were here, it would have been a very different table. He doesn't laugh easily, and we rarely discuss politics, if ever. I make a lot of assumptions about his beliefs but part of me fears his political leanings are not the same as mine. He would have been a conspicuous outsider while Finn has effortlessly become one of the group.

After dinner, we insist that Kai and my mom relax in the living room while the rest of us do the dishes. My mother argues that she can do them, but Finn won't hear of it, so the four of us create an assembly line of scraping, washing, and drying. Omar puts on some pop music and the time passes quickly.

My mom packs leftovers for each of us and wraps them in foil with our names on each. We're driving Kevin –

and Wayne – home, so they get in the van with Finn and Omar.

I head back into the house to get Kai and give my mom one last goodbye. I walk in through the front door, but they aren't in the living room, so I head to the kitchen. I'm about to announce to them that we're ready to go, but when I look through to the kitchen, I receive my second big surprise of the day.

My mother is seated across from Kai and she's kissing him goodbye but it looks like more than a friendly kiss. Is my mother involved with Kai? I think it's impossible, but then I remember all the little looks between them at Plant Daddy, how Kai thinks my mom invented Miracle-Gro.

I wait in the living room and give them a few moments before I cough loudly and say, 'Hello, we are all set with the van.' They spring away from each other as if they were caught, confirming my suspicions.

Kai is suddenly in a rush to get out. 'Thank you very much Glory. It was a very nice meal and I think everyone enjoyed it. I will see you at work. Goodbye,' he says pushing the words out.

'Yes, at work. Thank you,' my mom says in a weird soprano she only uses when she is guilty. She opens the door and Kai heads out of the house and down the ramp toward the van.

'What did I just walk in on?' I ask, slowly walking toward her.

'What?' Her voice is still unnaturally high.

'Is there something you want to tell me young lady?' I taunt her.

'Stop it. I was just saying goodbye to my friend.' She waits a few seconds and then adds, 'A very special friend.'

'So, the two of you are a couple?' I ask, trying to keep an image of them together in any romantic way out of my brain. The woman is my mother. Still, if she and Kai are happy, then I'm happy for her.

'How did I raise a son to be so conservative in his thinking about relationships?'

'We are not talking about me; we are talking about you.'

'Couple is such a limited term. I like Kai. I care for him deeply. And he cares for me. When you come back from Florida, I'll show you what he made for me at Plant Daddy.'

He's probably potted a bonsai for her or made a terrarium. Very sweet of him. I want to know more but I also want to model good boundaries, so I say goodbye and bend down to have her kiss my forehead then I head to the van. I open the door to get in and she comes out of the house.

'Wait,' she yells out after me. She's running toward the van. 'This was on sale and I bought it for your trip to Florida.'

She hands me the largest bottle of Pepto-Bismol that has ever been created. Finn looks at the jug of pink liquid and then at me and we drive back to Manhattan.

Chapter 35

I had to leave so early for the aiport that I was a zombie during boarding and slept for most of the flight to Miami. But as I get into the car to take me to the hotel a blast of warm air engulfs me and it's clear I'm not in New York City anymore. I put on my sunglasses and let the rays penetrate my face as I roll down the window to smell the distant sea air.

It's been a week since I saw Finn at Thanksgiving. He flew down the day after the holiday to have some time with the artists he knows before the weekend kick-off for Art Week. We've had a few texts but nothing more.

Before the car is even out of the airport, I see that my mother has texted me at least a dozen times. It's a small opera in alphanumeric. It starts with: *Landed?* And then: *Where are you!!!???* Finally: *OMG WHAT HAPPENED?* I call her to make sure she doesn't have a heart attack. 'Hi, Mom. I'm fine. The plane didn't crash.'

She doesn't answer me. I can hear her put the phone to her bosom and say, 'Kai, he's fine. He's not dead.'

'Tell him not to give you such a scare,' I hear Kai say in the background.

'Is Finn with you?' she asks, her voice full of mischief.

'No, I told you he came down earlier.'

'When will you see him? At the hotel? I wish you were sharing a room. I called the hotel to see if maybe they were overbooked and you two would have to squeeze into a single together.' I should not have told her where we are staying.

'Mom, this is not *It Happened One Night*,' I say, although I'd love to be in that movie. It's one of my favorites. 'For the millionth time, this is not a romantic weekend.' I kept the fact that Finn would be down here at the same time a secret for as long as I could, but the truth came out forty-eight hours before my flight. 'This is a work event,' I say but I'm sure she's not listening.

'Did you bring enough sunblock? You're so pale I'm worried the gamma rays will go right through you. I slid some extra Pepto tablets into your carry-on when you came down with your luggage this morning. The liquid is better, but sometimes the chewables are more convenient. Also, some condoms because you never know. I got the big ones. For Finn, of course, not for you. I got you the regular ones but I didn't get ribbed because—'

'Mom, you know the rules. Any references to my penis or anyone else's, and I hang up. Goodbye,' I say, and as I put the phone back in my pocket, I notice the driver looking at me suspiciously in the rearview mirror. I'm sure this isn't the first time he's overheard someone in his car talking about penis size, although less likely that the person was talking to their mother.

After a few minutes of highways and palm trees, we zoom past the high-rises of downtown Miami and across the intercoastal to Miami Beach. New York is a vintage black-and-white photo but Miami is a dayglow pinball machine. Each Art Deco building is more stunning than the next, with pastel embellishments and geometric windows that make them look like ocean liners from another century. We pull up to The Lafayette, a bright yellow-and-pink building across from the beach where massive white tents for Art Week are already set up.

A front desk clerk with way more muscles than a front desk clerk needs checks me in and chats me up in a way that simply does not happen in New York. 'Enjoy your stay,' he finally says and hands me my key card. 'You're in 403.'

'Look at that. We're neighbors,' I hear and don't have to turn around to see who it is. 'I'm in 405.'

'Finn. Hello,' I say. He's wearing bright neon green sunglasses to hold back his hair, cut-off shorts and a tank top. I haven't seen this much of his body before. He's only been here a few days but his skin is already bronzed to perfection.

He looks at what I'm wearing and frowns. 'No, no, no. This will not do. You're in Miami. Enough with these heavy jeans and your coat. Get on some trunks and flip-flops and meet me at the pool bar.'

'Thanks, Finn, but I just landed. I should catch up on some emails and maybe take a nap before I...' It's a nice offer but I want to keep this purely professional. 'Art Week starts tomorrow, and the gallery booth will be open in the afternoon. I want to proofread the catalog again. We have press events in the morning,' I say, and then I open the side pocket of my bag where I packed a printout of the schedule for the weekend the night before. I zip open the pocket without looking and pull out the schedule, but when I do I realize the pocket is fuller than I remember. I yank out the paper and over a dozen condoms that fall to the floor.

'Whoa. Buddy, slow down. Didn't know you were going so hardcore this weekend,' Finn says as we both bend down to pick them up so the hotel guests don't trip over them.

'These are not mine,' I say. 'My mother put them in here.'

'Sure, she did,' he says teasing me. He holds up one of the XXXL ones.

'Those aren't for me. Those are for you,' I say, flustered and remembering my conversation with her in the car.

'Excuse me?' A devilish grin crosses his lips.

'I mean she packed them for me – I mean for you – I mean—'

'I'll tell you what,' he says as we both stand. 'You go up and change and meet me at the pool. And I won't spend the weekend making you explain why you have enough condoms for all of Provincetown during Bear Week in your carry-on, deal?'

'Fine,' I say and head up to my room to change.

–

Thirty minutes later, I'm staring at myself in the mirror of the elevator wishing I had thought about a tanning salon or maybe a bronzer before I left. I'm not just pale, I'm almost translucent. I'm gripping a printout of the events for the weekend, hoping I can use the schedule to emphasize the fact that this is a business trip.

The pool at The Lafayette is a small kidney-shaped puddle of glittering aqua tiles surrounded by a jungle of lush tropical plants and a sea of gorgeous people. They recline on loungers, sip cocktails at the bar and push their sunglasses down their noses so they can check out the people who are checking them out. My immediate reaction is to want to flee to my room, hide under the covers, watch an episode of *The Golden Girls*, and wait for work to begin.

Unfortunately, before I can make my escape Finn spots me and waves. He's changed into a square-cut Lycra swimsuit in sea-foam green. Whatever was left to the imagination seeing him in a tank top in the lobby has now evaporated. I can't help staring. I hate to admit it, but my mother was right about the condom sizing.

I clutch the papers in my hand tightly, reminding myself that I'm here for a work event as I walk over to him at the bar.

'Sam, you made it.' He kisses me on both cheeks. It's a friendly greeting and not uncommon, but still having his lips anywhere near my face when he's so naked is not a good idea. I wonder if I will need to adjust my trunks.

'Just wanted to go over some of the details for tomorrow.'

'That's tomorrow. Right, now I want you to meet Luis.' He points to a table under an umbrella on the far side of the pool. 'Do you want a margarita or a mojito?'

I notice a server carrying a tray with glasses of fizzy clear liquid and green leaves floating on top, so I order a mojito and take a big sip before I follow Finn over to the table.

'Luis, this is Sam. The writer in New York I told you about.'

His intro is false advertising at best but I smile and extend my hand to Luis, who is a bit younger than my mom with a thick black beard that covers his neck, covered in faded but still beautiful mermaid and octopus tattoos.

'So nice to meet you.' I'm expecting a handshake but he gives me a big hug so I hug him back. I step out of the hug and Luis nods his head toward Finn. 'This one says you are something else.' I immediately see Finn shoot him a look.

'Does he?' I ask. I'm so used to being on alert with my mother around back in New York, I'm enjoying Finn being the one on the back foot for a change. I take a sip of my drink and the mint leaves tickle my nose. I can feel the rum starting a gentle buzz and I let the pulsating music flow over me. The three of us hang out by the pool talking about Art Week some, but also movies, music and where to get the best fried catfish in Dade County. I begin to feel some of my overall stress melt. I offer to get the next round of drinks and head up to the bar. When I return, Luis asks Finn, 'You'll be at Art Barn this spring?' Finn nods as I hand him his drink. 'The board bought the property next to the studios on the hill so there'll be a lot more people. I think it'll be stimulating.' Luis strokes his beard and takes a sip of his beer. I sit back down under the umbrella.

Finn turns to me and says, 'You should go.'

'That's the artists' retreat upstate, right?' I remember him mentioning it that day at Brands but one and a half mojitos in, everything is a bit fuzzy. 'Sure, I could do a day trip to visit you up there. I'm sure your gallery would love the coverage.'

'No, not to visit. You should come up and do a residency,' Finn says, swirling his drink with the swivel stick and grinning at me.

'You should,' Luis says nodding. 'Too many visual artists complaining about the light and needing enormous rooms for their canvases.' He points at Finn who pretends he has no idea what he's talking about. 'We need more writers.' Luis looks at me. 'They're so easy up there. They only need a room and a place to be.'

'I think Luis forgot to mention that he's on the board,' Finn adds.

'Actually, I'm the chair,' he says sticking his chest out in pretend formality. 'But Finn is very involved in the organization, too. He's on the artist advisory panel. I'll introduce you to Beverly. She works with the writers.'

Finn nods and puts his hand on my back. I hear Luis' words in my head again – *a room and a place to be.* Usually, a conversation like this makes me want to run away. I can't tell if it's the sunshine, the music, the mojitos, or the fact that Finn has his hand touching me, but at this moment, I don't want to go anywhere.

Chapter 36

The next morning, I wake up as early as possible to prepare for the day. The sunshine and tropical vibes make me feel like I'm shedding a layer of anxiety as easily as I stored my coat in the closet when I arrived. From the balcony of my room, I can see the massive tents that have been set up for Art Week. Each one would cover almost an entire block in New York. Galleries from all over the world have booths in the posh, air-conditioned pavilions with cocktails bars and lounges. Everyone is trying to promote their artists and create a buzz.

After a quick breakfast in my room, I head down to meet Finn in the lobby. I thought he couldn't look any sexier than he did in his swim trunks but he's standing in the lobby in a tight-fitting suit with a T-shirt and no socks. It's a spicy mix of formal and casual that takes my breath away. I'm wearing my 'normal' costume, which bears some distant resemblance to what he's wearing – a boring blue shirt and dull khaki pants.

The day starts with Finn speaking at a panel on the role of the arts in activism. He has lunch with a curator from a museum in Dusseldorf after that and then there's a screening of a short film he made last year and a talkback. He does a ton of interviews with everything from garage-produced podcasts to glossy international art magazines. The day is a great success but also exhausting. There are so many press obligations that I don't get to visit the Carlos Wong Gallery booth until the afternoon, while Finn is still finishing interviews.

The main tent is even more crowded than it was in the morning. There is an enormous blue horse that reaches at least two stories above the beach to the top of the tent. When I get closer, I see that it's made entirely of recycled materials – plastic bottles, wrappers, and old toys. I smile as I admire it and think about the lives the empty containers had before they became art.

I had my doubts when Robert gave me this assignment. I was hoping for a routine pharmaceutical campaign. But being in Miami surrounded by so many people living creative lives makes me think I might not need to always make the safe choice. Of course, being around Finn so much these past few months may have something to do with my change of attitude as well. Still, I'm safely on my side of the road. Changing lanes at this point might not be possible. I think I missed the last exit.

I walk past rows and rows of temporary white walls set up to create individual gallery spaces with abstract sculpture, vibrant painting and provocative photography. I see artists talking about their work to potential collectors, proud of what they've accomplished.

I have to look at my printed map to find the Carlos Wong booth. I take a few turns and then I see the most stunning collection of photos I have ever seen in my life. I've seen images of Finn's work before but only in his portfolio or on a screen. This is entirely different. The portraits are huge – at least a few yards wide and tall. Larger than life with hyper-focused detail and a composition that draws you in and makes you want to understand the person in the picture. Immediately, I recognize Ekaterina with the

Statue of Liberty behind her. I smile thinking about that fall afternoon watching Finn in his element. I stand a few feet from the glossy photo to take it in. The image captures her sense of freedom and energy in a way I didn't think was possible. He has taken parts of the conversation and used collage to make her words a subtle but vital part of the image. The entire image has a network of lines and bursts of colors super-imposed on it that pull you in and help you understand. I could gaze at it for days, taking in details and appreciating the words. I focus on a smaller section and read the words I see out loud: 'That is why I come here. To be. Just, to be.' Then, in my head, I hear Luis talking about Art Barn – *a room, a place to be.*

I stand a few feet back from the glossy image and just take it all in when I sense someone standing very close to me. I don't have to turn and look to know exactly who it is. 'Finn, it's beautiful. Your work is really gorgeous.' I hope he knows how much I mean it.

'Thank you,' he says. 'I'm proud of how everything turned out and Ekaterina loves it so that's a good feeling.' He looks at his photos hung across the white wall and I can tell it makes him feel good. I love how he's able to take pride in his work and not be a jerk about it. So many of the artists I've met feel insecure and have the need to inflate their egos, which is so annoying. My reaction to being insecure is to deflate mine.

'The catalog looks great. Carlos is thrilled with what you wrote and...' He pauses and turns to look me in the eye. 'So am I. It's wonderful. You really captured that day.'

'Just doing my job,' I say, brushing off the compliment but inside I truly appreciate it. It means a lot to me that he liked it even if it is standard-issue press catalog copy. Writing about him was easy. Finn gives me a look that says he isn't quite satisfied with my response but he doesn't push it.

We back away from the image so that others can get a closer look. People wander into the gallery and most stop in front of Finn's work to admire it. He watches the people looking but then turns to me and says, 'We better head back to the hotel to get ready for Luis.'

'Don't you want to stay and enjoy people admiring your work?' I ask.

'I've done my part. The rest is up to them.' He discreetly points toward the couple standing in front of the photo of Ekaterina. I put my finger to my chin and turn my gaze from the image to the artist. I'm not sure which is more fascinating.

'Let's go,' he says and unbuttons his suit jacket before walking toward the exit. I get a glimpse of the tight T-shirt clinging to his body and it stops me in my tracks. My mind races thinking of excuses to stay in my room tonight so that I don't have to leave my comfort zone.

'Finn, Art Week is a lot,' I say a step behind him. 'So many people, so many galleries, so much color and sunshine. Everyone oohing and ahhing over things. It's sensory overload. Maybe I've had too much art for today.' I hope he will accept my excuse.

'Today was about galleries selling. Tonight is a totally different scene. I promise. Everyone is looking forward to meeting you. Luis texted me to make sure you're coming.' He smiles but keeps walking, shutting down any further protest.

What can I say? I agreed to go earlier. I take a quick step to catch up to him and realize I want to go tonight. I don't want to be alone in my room. I want to be at the party with Finn.

Back at the hotel I take a long shower to help me reenergize. While I'm letting the water wash away the work of the afternoon I can see my phone on the vanity buzzing. It's Paul but I don't want to dry off and answer it right now. I'll call him later this evening when I get back from the cocktail party.

I meet Finn in the lobby and he's back to his effortless casual chic look. Despite the fact that we were inside all day and only looking at the beach, he seems to have gotten more tan. I catch myself in the mirror and think I'm maybe even paler but at least I am wearing something more interesting – a pair of black gauzy harem pants that Omar made for me and a bright pink shirt with orange swirls on it. It's perfect for Miami. It's not my usual style but I like the way it looks and I like the way I feel in it.

Since we'd been inside all day, we decide to walk to Luis' place. We step out of the hotel and the atmosphere of South Beach embraces us. Candy-colored convertibles and souped-up hot rods cruise down Ocean Drive. Salsa music plays from a speaker somewhere competing with a few other speakers creating a cacophonous soundtrack of Latin beats for our walk.

'I think your gallery will be pleased with today. I saw a lot of great coverage and heard a good buzz.' I'm trying to keep the pretense of business.

'Sam, it's Friday in Miami. The sun is about to set. Can't you feel the energy?' He gestures toward the crowds of people around us laughing, dancing, and hanging out. Everyone is ready to let go. 'It's time for the business of art to stop. I want you to meet everyone from Art Barn.'

We pass by some shops and Art Deco apartment buildings until we get to a more industrial part of town closer to the intercoastal. 'This is it,' Finn says in front of a four-story warehouse with a flat roof and large multi-paned windows. The loft is far enough from the busy South Beach atmosphere to have a calmer vibe but still feel part of the action. On the side of the building, I see the remnants of an old ad for Santiago Cigars that must have been painted on the brick. I can hear pulsing music inside and the sounds of laughter and conversation spill out of the open windows. We head in and I recognize some people from the art fair today. The vibe is chill but intense, kind of like Finn.

'You made it,' Luis says, giving us both a kiss on each cheek. 'I'm so glad. There's someone I want you to meet.'

'Who?' Finn asks.

'Not you, *tonto*,' he says playfully, bopping Finn on the nose. 'You already know everyone. This one.' He points to me. 'I want you to meet Beverly – she's looking for writers who want to be a part of Art Barn. In the new cabins.'

'That sounds great,' I say. 'But I'm not really looking for a retreat. I could never get that much time off work and—'

'Beverly!' Luis shouts and then stands on his tiptoes waving to a tall woman with aggressive bangs and a long black ponytail. She comes over. 'This is the person I was talking about. Finn's *friend*.' I think he says the word friend like there is something more but I'm not sure. 'Beverly is one of the advisory artists at Art Barn. Like Finn,' Luis says as I shake Beverly's hand.

'Oh yes, you're the writer. Come tell us what you're working on,' she says and grabs my hand, leading me away from Luis and Finn. I look back at them. This is not how I thought the evening would start.

'I'll catch up with you later,' Finn says and I follow Beverly. She leads me to where a few people are sitting on overstuffed cushions scattered across the floor. I grab a mojito, my new favorite, off a tray of drinks and plop down to join them. Beverly introduces me as a writer and they accept it. No questions. No third degree. There are about six of us on the floor. They each talk about what they're working on, but it's not competitive. One person is trying to solve a problem with advancing her plot when the action moves to a European city and another is trying to decide how a character might react when she gets a big inheritance. I haven't been in a group like this for a very long time but I'm comfortable participating and sharing ideas because they make me feel so welcome. When I suggest Stacey, who is working on a historical novel about Trinidad, consider combining two of her characters, she's thrilled with the idea.

'Are you going to be at Art Barn this spring?' Stacey asks, taking a sip of her drink.

'Oh, no. I don't think so. I'm not...' I'm about to do my whole stupid monologue. *I'm not a real writer.* My same sad refrain over and over again. I'm tired of it. I simply say, 'I'm not sure.' It's a sufficient placeholder for now.

Beverly pops in: 'We still have a few spaces open. The committee would love to see your application.'

The very thought of having to submit a portfolio, have it reviewed and then be told I'm not good enough is the entire reason I don't want to even tell anyone I'm a writer. The rejection is too humiliating.

'It's less about a portfolio review and more about engagement,' Beverly says tossing her hair to her other shoulder. 'Art Barn wants people who want to be a part of the community and respond and give feedback just as much as they want to create.' Everyone in the group nods enthusiastically.

'I see.' I close my eyes for a brief moment and wonder what it would be like to spend a month writing and hanging out with other artists. I picture myself in some snow-covered cabin, my laptop open, sipping hot chocolate as I write each morning and sharing drafts with colleagues in the evening.

I open my eyes before I get lost in the fantasy and when I do I see Finn halfway up the metal staircase that hugs the brick wall. He gestures for me to join him. I haven't seen him since we walked in. It's warm inside the loft and his face is shiny with perspiration that makes his skin glow in the soft light.

I stand up and say goodbye to the people I just met. I begin to walk across the room toward Finn but it's so crowded I can't seem to find a path through. I look up and he tilts his head and rubs his chin in a way that makes me laugh. He waves both arms and then points to my left. I walk through an opening and then his gestures guide me through the maze of people. I'm under his command. I get to the bottom of the staircase and since I've had a few drinks, I steady myself with the railing as I begin to climb the steps, but I never lose eye contact with Finn.

'I want to show you something,' Finn says when I get closer. I'm high enough up in the loft to take in the entire party – a world of color and creativity so different from the standard-issue corporate office I go to in Manhattan. I look back at the spot where I sat with the circle of writers and smile before looking up at Finn who has his tanned arm stretched toward me. 'Let's go,' he says and I put my hand in his, ready to see what's next.

Chapter 37

We climb all the way up to the top of the building and when we get to the landing he says, 'Wait until you see this view.'

He pushes open the thick metal door and lets me walk through. The percussive sound and energy of the party mute and I'm suddenly in an alternate universe of sky, stars, and ocean. On one side, the intercoastal shimmers in the setting sun with vibrant streaks of red-orange and yellow-magenta; above us, stars begin to dot the purple-blue sky, and on the other side of us is nothing but a vast ocean.

We're alone on the roof so we stroll around near the edges to take in the view. We walk in silence but still connected like when he guided me to the stairs – an invisible energy that's becoming harder to ignore.

'I could sleep up here. It's so beautiful,' I say stopping in the middle of the roof.

'I've done that,' he says. 'The loft doesn't have great AC, so one night, we all brought up sheets and pillows and slept up here to catch the breeze.' He closes his eyes and raises his chin so he can feel the air on his cheeks.

'That must have been incredible.' I try to imagine sleeping under the stars, hearing the ocean, sharing a blanket with Finn.

'It was until it wasn't'. A seagull relieved himself right on Luis and I don't think he's spent more than a few seconds up here since.' Finn laughs and walks over to a pair of vintage lawn chairs that are tattered and faded from the sun. He sits down and I sit next to him. A gentle wind weaves around us and makes the humid air less sticky. Above us an airplane moves smoothly through the sky but other than that the evening is calm.

'What did you think about the folks from Art Barn?' he asks without looking at me.

'It was energizing.' I liked getting into it with them about the craft of writing, but then I think about how my throat tightened when Beverly mentioned the application. 'But I'm sure they've all published a lot more than I have. They're real writers.'

Now he's looking at me. 'Why do you do that?' he asks but his tone isn't demanding. It's almost pleading. He really wants to know. 'I'm not trying to push but I want to understand. You get so close to accepting the fact that you are a writer. A real writer. And then you back away.'

I don't say anything. I stare out at the ocean in the distance and then turn my head to the other side to watch the setting sun. During the day, the sun barely seems to move, but as night approaches, it seems to rush like the final grains of sand in an hourglass. I could tell him he doesn't know what he's talking about, but he does. He knows exactly what he's talking about, so I need to find another way out.

'You think I'm a real writer when you've never even read anything I've written,' I say. I'm just laying out the facts. He hasn't. I have no idea where his belief in my talent comes from.

'That's not true,' he says moving his gaze from the streaky red-purple light of the sky to me.

'The press releases and stuff like that don't count.' I look away from the view and down at the top of the roof between my feet. 'That's not writing. That's copywriting. There's a difference.'

'That's not what I'm talking about.' I can tell he's looking at me but I don't look up.

'Did you read one of my Justine Jasmine novels? *Exwives of the Upper West Side*? That stuff doesn't count either.' Why do I have so many ways of erasing myself from the conversation? Disappearing is my best trick.

'No, I don't mean that stuff either.' His voice is even and serious.

'Then what do you mean?' I ask, finally looking directly at him. I'm sure he doesn't have an answer to my question.

Then he says four words I am not expecting: '*Closer Than They Appear.*'

'What?' It's not possible. There is no way. 'I don't understand.'

'I'm not going to lie. It took more than just a quick search online but after a few hours at the New York Public Library and some help from a lovely archivist named Lindsey, I found it and I read it.' His eyes search my face for a reaction but I don't reveal anything.

I don't know if I should be honored or embarrassed. *Closer Than They Appear* is the story I wrote that won the Seggerman. I thought that was the beginning of my career. But everything was so hard after that and I took too many detours. I can barely process the fact that he not only sought it out but he found it. Any other feelings I may have give way to shock and confusion. 'Why did you do that?'

'At first, I was just curious,' he says bringing his lawn chair closer to mine. 'But once I read it I...' He stops and throws his hands up in the air with a shout. 'Oh boy! Sam, I loved it.' His face radiates joy. 'It's such a wonderful story. It's not just beautifully written. It has so much to say about being young and gay and finding yourself. It was funny but also touching.' He can't get the words out fast enough. 'The scene where he breaks into the carousel with the boy he's in love with and the boy runs and leaves him alone to get caught. It broke my heart.' He touches his hand to his chest.

'That really happened,' I say without thinking. 'Well, sort of. It wasn't a carousel. It was the community pool after dark and...' I stop and bring myself back to the roof. I can't believe he read it and he liked it. He liked it enough to remember my favorite scene in the story. But I'm sure he's just being kind.

'I really connected with Pete and Jay. And the way it was written... it just pulled me in. Reading it I sort of fell in love,' he says and I look away instinctively until he adds. 'With the story. I fell in love with the story.'

'I wrote that a long time ago and I don't think it was very good. I think I got lucky with the award, and the story is overwritten and too long, and the dialogue is...' I get up from the chair and walk away from him so I can have some distance.

'The Seggerman is highly prestigious.' He gets up and walks toward me. 'Do you think they were just being nice?'

'Yes.' For years I've told myself that they made a mistake or maybe they just wanted to give the award to a gay writer for once. I have a hundred excuses for why it happened.

'You are an amazing writer,' he says and I can feel my shoulders scrunch up by my neck.

'We should go back down to the party. It's getting late.'

He walks closer and stands directly in front of me. 'You're crawling out of your skin. It's hard for you to hear it. Isn't it?' He's being so compassionate and tender. I can't help but be honest.

I nod hoping we can talk about something else. But he walks over to some stray milk crates left in the middle of the roof. He takes two and stacks them on top of each other. 'What are you doing?' I ask but he doesn't answer me.

He takes two more crates and places them a few feet away from the first set and makes sure both structures are stable. Then he climbs on one and spreads his arms wide and screams, 'My photos are amazing! I am an amazing artist!' He is so loud that his voice echoes off the roof. He jumps off the crates, turns to me, and points to the makeshift platform. 'Now it's your turn.'

I look at him like he asked me to jump off the building and fly home to New York. That's as likely to happen as what I think he's asking me to do. 'You do not mean...'

'I do,' he says walking toward me. 'I want you to stand up on those crates and say that you are an amazing writer.'

'I am not saying that.' I shake my head at the very thought.

'I don't want you to say it. I want you to scream it at the top of your lungs!' He shouts the last few words.

'Finn, I'm not doing that.' I cross my arms.

'Why not?'

'Because I'm not.' I walk over to the crates and move them off each other, so there isn't even a possibility of getting on top of them.

'I'm serious.' He puts his hand on my forearm. 'Why do you think you can't say it?' It's a fair question. It's just a bunch of words. 'Just say it here to me quietly. *I am amazing.*' He mouths the words slowly so I can follow along.

'Fine.' I convince my mind I'm just practicing a foreign language. The words have no meaning and this will get him to drop it. 'I am...' I start and my brain takes over my motor function. I cannot seem to form the words. 'This is silly.'

'I know it's silly but it's also important,' he pleads with me.

'It feels like bragging,' I say with a wince.

'Bragging is showing off to people or over-inflating yourself. This is not bragging. This is believing in yourself. There's a difference. How did you feel when you wrote *Closer Than They Appear*? When it was nominated and then it won?'

'I felt good,' I say trying to recall the memory. 'I felt great actually. That was a long time ago.'

'Yeah, but that feeling. You had it once. You had that feeling. I want you to have the experience of feeling amazing because you are. That's more important than any of the words. The words are just for us alone together up here on the roof. It's the feeling that matters. You are what you feel. Maybe just whisper it for right now.'

I try to shut out everything except being on this roof with Finn. I swallow hard, take a breath and, as softly as I can, I say, 'I am an amazing writer.' The words escape out of my mouth like puffs of flour from an over-stuffed sack.

I'm not sure Finn can even hear me. 'I am an amazing writer.' I say the words louder and try to feel the feeling, which is so much harder than saying the words. I know Finn can hear me because I see him smile widely, and his eyes connect with mine. I like seeing him look at me this way, so I try it again. 'I am an amazing writer,' I say and for the first time the words are loud and clear. My chest suddenly expands, leaving room for the feeling to enter my spirit.

'Yes!' he says, jumping up and pumping his fist. He runs over to the crates and stacks them again. I join him and he extends his hand so I can climb up. 'You can do it,' he says and I try not to let my brain stop me. I take his hand and feel his energy supporting me, helping me find my way.

I take a step up on to the crates and I can see Miami Beach in every direction. To one side, the neon lights glow, and the distant cars play music cruising Ocean Drive. On the other side, the city of Miami rises toward the night sky, all clean lines and majesty. We are surrounded by the city yet it feels like we are the only two people that matter.

'On the count of three?' he asks.

'Well, I'm not doing it alone,' I say and point toward the other set of crates.

'You got it.' He lets go of my hand and climbs up to his perch. 'You first. Are you ready?'

I nod my head.

'One.'

I close my eyes and try to focus on the feeling.

'Two.'

I take a deep breath in so I can catapult the words out.

'Three.'

I let my arms fly out above me and the air in my lungs pushes out like a cannon ball. The words sail across the night sky. 'I am amazing! I am an amazing writer!' I feel my entire body respond. It's a complete release. I can't stop myself from doing it again it feels so good. 'I am amazing! I am an amazing writer!' This time I'm shouting as loud as I can. The words sail out of my mouth and the most amazing thing is I feel them. I really feel them.

I look over at Finn and he's beaming from ear to ear. 'Your turn,' I say.

'We are amazing,' he says.

I'm surprised that he says *we* but I like it. I join him. 'We are amazing!' I say and throw out my arms. My fingers touch his. It's not the first time we've made physical contact tonight but this sensation is different. There's an undeniable energy. Finn must feel it, too, because he grabs my hand, and I respond by grabbing his, and we both come down off the crates and stand in front of each other. The electricity is enough to power every sign in South Beach.

'I think you're amazing,' he says with his mouth only a few inches from mine.

'I think you're amazing, too,' I say.

Our lips find their way to each other, and he's pressing his against mine as I slowly go deeper with my tongue. At first, I'm unsure, but I can feel how much he wants this. How much we both want this. He puts his arms around me, and I do the same to him. We pull each other even closer so our mouths can explore further. I'm kissing his whole face. Feeling his stubble on my lips. I throw my head back as his tongue enters my mouth, exploring inside. Then I can feel his lips over my scruff and then his mouth travels up to my eyes and his lips gently press against them.

My hands start to explore his body moving from the back to his chest. I can feel his physical strength under his clothes but it's more than that. I can also feel what an incredible and kind person he is and that makes him even hotter to me. I move my hands down to his belt and I feel his hands move down my back and grab my ass. It makes me kiss him stronger and harder. He pushes his groin into me and I pull him closer. It's clear this incredibly hot guy wants me as much as I want him.

'Sam,' he says gently in my ear as he puts his hand on my cheek.

'Finn,' I whisper back in his ear, trying to be as present as possible, continuing to kiss him.

'Finn. Finn!' A voice from the stairwell to the roof is shouting his name and the spell breaks. We look at each other for a second but don't let go.

'I'm sorry,' he whispers. 'I think that's Luis. There's nowhere to hide up here.' The roof is a flat open space, nothing but shadows and moonlight now that the sun has completely set.

'I want to finish this,' he says and kisses me quickly on the mouth. 'I promised Luis I'd introduce him to—'

'There you are,' Luis says huffing as he stands in the stairwell. 'I know this view is incredible, but Sancho is leaving and I want to make sure the three of us are on the same page about the community outreach project.'

'Sure,' Finn says. 'I'll be right there.'

I think we're both hoping Luis will head back down and wait there but he doesn't.

'It's okay,' I say. 'Do what you have to do and I'll meet you outside when you're ready.'

'This won't take long. I'll order a car, and we can head back to the hotel together, maybe go for a late-night swim in the ocean and pick up where we stopped?' Suddenly he's a bit shy and I like it. It makes him even more desirable.

'I'd like that,' I say and we follow Luis down to the party where Finn goes to meet with Sancho and I head out the door to wait for him.

My head is spinning. The air is warmer on the ground and there's not nearly as much of a breeze. I'm not thinking about anything else but being on the roof with him and the sky and the stars and the ocean. I don't want to let any practical thoughts disturb where my mind is, so I push away any that dare enter. When my phone buzzes I don't have any desire to even acknowledge it.

Eventually, a black car with a rideshare light pulls up. 'Are you Finn Montgomery?' The driver asks.

'He's coming,' I say leaning into the open window.

'Oh, sure, no problem. Roads are busy tonight for Art Week. Is that what you're here for?'

'Yes.' I nod.

'Are you an artist?' the driver asks.

'Yes,' I say with an easy laugh. 'I am. I'm an amazing artist.'

'That's awesome,' she says nodding her head. Finn walks out, runs over and kisses me on the cheek. He grabs my hand and we head back to the hotel together.

Chapter 38

The rideshare driver talks to us the entire time. I was hoping to continue our make-out session in the back seat but we can't because the driver wants to know all about us. Finn happily answers each question but has no problem sneaking in a kiss right in full view of the driver.

We get to the hotel, and my instinct is to run through the lobby up to our rooms like a reverse emergency evacuation, but instead Finn opens the doors, and we walk through the lobby side by side knowing we have all night. We decide to go up and change into our swimsuits and then head to the beach for a midnight dip, but I wonder how long our swimsuits will stay on in the ocean.

'Sammy!' A voice says from the bar. I turn to see who recognizes me and it's the last person in the world I want to see right now.

'Paul!' I say as he walks toward me. I can feel Finn bristle and maybe he can feel me stiffening. Paul gives me a hug. My arms don't move to embrace him and he doesn't seem to notice. But he does notice that I just walked into the hotel with a guy.

'Who's this?' Paul asks.

'Paul Pearson this is Finn Montgomery. Finn is one of the artists here for Art Week.' Paul reaches out to shake Finn's hand not knowing that a few minutes ago it was around my waist. I'm mortified.

'Finn this is Paul,' I say and I think my voice cracks. 'Paul is my...' before I can think of how to phrase exactly what Paul is to me, he jumps in.

'Nice to meet you Finn.' Paul kisses me on the cheek quickly and I catch Finn's eyes darting away. What have I done? 'I'm the prodigal boyfriend returning to New York next month to be with this one.' Paul pulls me toward him. I close my eyes briefly hoping this isn't really happening, but it is.

'Paul what are you doing here?'

'Work ended a bit early. I was in Atlanta and it's not so far from Florida so I grabbed a flight after work, took a car from the airport and waited for you to walk through that door. I texted you.'

'You did?' I ask. Maybe he did.

'One of the partners has a place in Palm Beach. Big party tonight. I thought I'd surprise you. I know how much you like to be my plus one.'

'But Paul...' I say looking right at Finn. It feels like the evening is an express train that suddenly screeched to a halt. I was so close to getting to where I needed to go but now I'm not sure what the destination is. I shouldn't have made out with Finn. That was just a little dream brought on by the sunshine and mojitos. I can't sustain the feelings I had on the roof about him or myself. They were exquisite but ephemeral – a comet that flashes across the sky and then disintegrates. Miami was just a fantasy. Paul is reality and I have to face that. I need to explain to Finn, but I'm not sure how I can even get a few seconds alone with him.

'Looks like you two have quite a night ahead of you,' Finn says, his voice tight and cold. 'I'll just say good night to you both.'

'Finn, wait!' I call after him. He turns but I don't say anything else. I don't know what to say. He waits and our eyes lock, but when I don't say anything more, he heads to the elevator.

'Paul, just a second. I have to make sure he knows his itinerary for tomorrow,' I say thinking of an excuse to break away from him for a minute.

'No problem. I'll be at the bar. I'm sure trying to get artists to show up for things on time is almost impossible,' Paul says snidely and rolls his eyes.

'Actually, he's very prompt,' I shoot back with a bit more anger than I intended but Paul is oblivious to it. I dart over to Finn at the elevators.

'Finn, I'm sorry. I didn't know he was coming.'

'I get it.' He stares straight ahead. 'I knew your relationship status was complicated.'

'It is but I should have told you about Paul. The thing is he's been living in...' I try to wiggle out but I know that's wrong. 'I should have been clearer. It's my fault.'

'It's my fault,' Finn says biting his lip.

'No, I should never have...' I start but can't fill in the rest of the words. It was less than twenty minutes ago but the roof already feels like it's so far in the past we could never go back. It took so long to get there and only a few seconds to tumble back to reality.

'I guess this was just a big mistake,' Finn says and the bell from the elevator rings. He gets in without turning around and the doors close.

'It sure didn't feel like a mistake,' I say to the closed mirrored elevator doors and stare at myself as the words come out. I look sad, confused, and lost.

'Sammy, we better hurry,' Paul says joining me at the elevator with a glass of wine in his hand.

I bring my hands to my face and cover my nose and mouth for a second to regain my composure.

'You'll need to change,' Paul says. 'Palm Beach is much more upscale than this place.' He looks around the lobby like it's not good enough for him.

'I'm not sure I brought anything...' The words just fall out of my mouth. My body is in the lobby but my mind is still with Finn.

'I'm sure you didn't. I grabbed something for you before I left.' He holds out an expensive-looking garment bag. 'Hey, Sammy.' Paul snaps his fingers and I'm suddenly back on planet Earth. 'You okay? Too many mojitos this evening?' He laughs and then jams his finger on the elevator button. 'Let's go to the suite I got and make you presentable. I have a car waiting but traffic is going to be murder.' He walks into the elevator and I follow him because that's what I've always done.

Paul works on his laptop, and I quickly shower and change into the sandstone linen suit, crisp white shirt, and powder-blue faux-crocodile yacht loafers. He's even included a pair of high-end underwear and some boring beige socks. There was a time when I would have appreciated all of this but today I feel like a dress-up doll performing for his pleasure.

We get in the car to head to the party, and Paul doesn't ask me anything about how things have been going in Miami or about me in general. He says he's happy to see me and glad that he can take me to this party but I feel like I could be anyone in the suit he picked out. I guess when we were together, I liked being able to fade into whatever role Paul wanted me to play, but maybe I don't want to do that anymore. Maybe I want Paul to see me and understand me for who I am... the way Finn does. I look over to Paul and ask, 'Why me?'

'Sammy, what are you talking about?' he asks without looking up from his phone.

'What is it about me that you like? That makes you want to move back to New York or fly down here and take me to this party?'

He finally looks up from his phone. 'I think you spent too much time in the sun today, Sammy.' He laughs, trying to ignore my question.

'I'm serious.'

'Okaaaay,' he says slowly. 'I like you because... you're my Sammy. And we have a good time together and you're cute as hell.' I stare at him without expression and he can tell I'm not satisfied with his answer. He hasn't said a single thing that shows he really knows who I am. I go back to looking out the window and he goes back to his phone.

The party is at some stately mansion right on the water. It's exactly as you would expect it to be, in one of the most affluent and conservative areas of Florida. It's an upscale version of The Cheesecake Factory with more palm trees.

We walk past perfectly manicured topiaries and a fountain large enough to hold an Olympic backstroke final into a foyer with high ceilings and sweeping views of the Atlantic Ocean. The women are all wearing floor-length gowns that are only slight variations of one from another and the men are dressed like we are – suits, open shirt, loafers. Not sure if we are all wearing the same underwear and socks but it seems likely.

'Paul, you made it.' A woman in an peach version of the gown-uniform walks over to us. She kisses Paul on both cheeks and they each laugh but I have no idea why. Is there a joke I missed, or is this how the wealthy say hello? I knew I'd be entering Paul's world more once we moved in together, but I thought I'd have more gradual exposure. This is a deep dive off a dark cliff.

'Maxine, you look radiant. As always. Your hair is different maybe? Something.'

Maxine does not look radiant. She looks like someone has taken her face and filled it with helium. It's so plump in different areas that I expect her head to rise up to the ceiling like Linda Blair in *The Exorcist*.

'This must be your Todd. Such a pleasure to finally meet you,' she says and my entire body freezes. She grabs me and kisses me the same way she kissed Paul but I'm too much in shock to resist her. 'I want to hear all about skiing in Aspen over Thanksgiving. I heard from Agnes that you two had the Rochette Suite at the St Regis. John and I love that suite. It's so romantic. I'm sure you had a wonderful time.'

I think I might throw up. I might go out to the fountain and turn it into a cascading waterfall of vomit. What is happening?

'Maxine, I think you're confused. That wasn't me,' I can tell Paul is trying to cover. His voice quivers and I can see his hand shaking. 'You're thinking of someone else. I've been in Atlanta,' he says emphasizing the name of the city. 'This is Sam.'

This is not the first time Maxine has been caught in this particular web so she knows exactly how to play her part. 'Oh right, Sam. Atlanta. Of course. I don't know what I was thinking. You know, come to think of it, it wasn't you at all. My mistake. Planning this fundraiser has my mind completely scattered. Anyway, nice meeting you… ah…'

'Sam,' I say plainly.

'Of course, Sam. Thank you both so much for coming. Marco is saying a few words out on the beach patio in just a bit. I'm sure they'll be inspiring.' She exits quickly.

'Let's go check out the view,' Paul says putting his hand on my back and walking toward the patio like nothing has happened. I don't move. He looks back at me confused.

'Is everything okay?'

'No, Paul. Everything is not okay. What the hell was she talking about? I thought you were working in Atlanta not skiing in Aspen with Todd.'

'What? You heard her. She got the details wrong. She's in her eighties and has done so much Botox I'm sure it's creeped into her cerebral cortex. Let's just enjoy the night. You look so handsome in that suit I bought you.' He gives me a dirty grin but it has zero impact.

I look down at the lapel of the suit and hold it between my fingers. I could never afford something like this. 'I didn't ask for the suit,' I say spitting out each word.

'I know Sammy. It's a present. I bought it for you so you would look nice.' He says the words slowly like he's talking to a child. 'I know you don't have any clothes that would fit in here. What's the big deal?'

He doesn't get it, and he's just trying to distract me from the obvious. 'Why did that woman think you would be here with Todd?'

'You heard her. She said she was confused.' Paul looks nervously from side to side.

'But she knew the suite you were in.'

All this time I was worried about him getting back together with Todd. That the divorce wouldn't happen. I hadn't even considered that I would become Todd and he'd become me. I've gone from being the fun fling to the one who has to show up at parties and look the other way.

How could I have been so stupid? We never talked about being exclusive while we were waiting for his divorce to become final. I get that. If he had had a fling with some random, I could have understood, but Todd?

A man who I think is a butler of some sort walks around with a small bell and politely rings it as he announces. 'Senator Marco Azul will be delivering remarks in just a few moments. Please join us on the East Patio.' He rings the bell again.

It takes a second but then I realize how I know that name. 'Wait. Marco Azul. Isn't he that awful Republican involved in the Pray Gay Away nonsense?' I can't believe I'm attending a fundraiser for a homophobe. What is wrong with Paul? He can't possibly think this would be okay for him or for me. I think about how my mom wanted me to wear that *Say Gay* T-shirt for my first date and my resistance to it. I feel ashamed. Who cares if the colors were awful, the message was right.

'I guess that's the guy. I mean, yes, it is. But we have some big clients here, and it makes them feel good if gay people support conservative causes.'

'I don't want to make them feel good. I don't support them,' I say firmly and hear the bell ring on the other side of the room as people empty out.

'Neither do I,' Paul says like it's no big deal. 'Just remember Sammy I was gay and had a boyfriend when you were still in grade school. This is how you play the game. I've been at this a lot longer than you.'

'At what? Being a hypocrite? Being a liar? There is no way I'm going in there. You can forget it!' I'm almost shouting I'm so mad. A few people look at us and I can tell Paul is embarrassed.

'What are you getting so worked up about? It's a beautiful home, with great catering on a gorgeous night. Who cares if we disagree with the politics? Did you see that raw bar? It's a mountain of crab and shrimp. Let's go.' He laughs like he made a joke when all he did was make himself look like a fool.

'I'm leaving!' I shout.

'Keep your voice down.' He scolds me and looks around to make sure no one is watching. 'I don't need clients to see me with some kid having a temper tantrum.'

'A kid? Paul, I am a thirty-five-year-old man. I'm not a child.'

'Then stop acting like one. We all have to do things that we don't want to do sometimes. That's how the world works.' He runs his hand across his beard and closes his eyes for a second. 'I knew I should have asked Todd to come. It would have been so much easier,' he whispers under his breath but I hear every word.

'What did you just say? Are you seriously still involved with Todd. I thought you were getting a divorce. I thought you had a lawyer and we were moving in together in January.'

'Yes, that's still the plan. I'll be in New York in January. Maybe February. March at the latest. These things take time.'

I blink my eyes and stand a few feet from him to look at him. Really look at him. A few hours ago, I was on a rooftop with Finn feeling free, creative, and unlimited. But here I am with the man I thought I wanted to be with, feeling small, unseen, and trapped.

'She wasn't confused. Was she?' Paul knows exactly what I mean but plays dumb.

'I don't know what you're—'

'Tell me the truth. For once tell me the truth!' I demand in a voice I have never heard come out of my mouth before. It's strong, confident and comes from deep in my gut. It feels good to use it. 'Tell me the truth!'

I can hear the polite smatter of applause for Marco Azul and it makes me even angrier. I wouldn't want to be caught dead here.

'Were you in Aspen with Todd?' I shoot the words at him.

Paul looks at me and says, 'Yes.'

That's all I need to hear. He has never once told me the truth. He's always found a way to avoid it, to make an excuse or concoct a story. He's been lying to me this whole time. He never intended to get a divorce and I'm not sure he was even serious about moving to New York. He was probably going to just keep me as a side-piece for whenever he was bored or needed a date for some ridiculous event like the disgusting one I am standing at right now.

'Goodbye Paul.' I turn to walk out. I can hear him calling after me, telling me that it's over with Todd, that they only went to ski and that he needs me at the event tonight. It's background noise, and I keep walking without looking back. I find the driver who brought us here and ask him to hurry back to the hotel. Maybe I can still make things right with Finn.

Chapter 39

Crying in an airport after a breakup while sucking on an iced coffee the size of an infant makes me feel like the cliche of all cliches, but here I am. I'm sitting on the floor next to the only working electrical outlet in the entire Miami terminal so I can hold on to enough charge to keep talking to Omar. He's doing his best to keep me calm, but to be honest it's not working.

'It's going to be alright,' he says.

'No, it's not. I messed everything up. I was so focused on making things work with A-hole Paul and proving my mother wrong that I couldn't see what was right in front of me. I was so stupid.'

'You are not stupid. I will not let you talk about my best friend that way.' He has the same fierceness in his voice he's had the other dozen times he's said it to me today. I take a huge gulp from my drink, smush my coat into a lumpy pillow, and lay down on the floor of the airport despite the fact that it probably has more germs than a public toilet.

'I am stupid. Of course Finn was going to be gone by the time I got back to the hotel.' I wipe the tears from my eyes with my sleeve.

'Read me the note he left again,' Omar says, even though he has heard it many times since I picked it up from the concierge. I dig my hand in my pocket, past my boarding pass, to find the piece of paper with Finn's words.

'"Catching a flight back tonight. Be honest with yourself."' My throat catches before I read the last word. '"Finn".' I shove the note back in my pocket. If only I had been able to catch him, I could have explained everything, and maybe we could have even had our midnight swim. But it's a long way from the fancy private mansions in Palm Beach to the nightlife in Miami, and I'm not sure I could have found the words I needed to explain myself to Finn. I'm still not sure I can explain myself to myself.

'That note isn't so bad,' Omar says, trying to be encouraging.

'It's not so good either. I had just kissed Finn and then left him in the lobby to go be with another man. I should have been honest with Finn. Who cares about being honest with myself?' I cover my face with my hand.

'You were not *with* Paul. You were tricked into going to a fundraiser with him in a surprise ambush,' Omar says sharply.

'I should have been clearer that Paul was coming back or that I thought he was coming back. Paul did the same thing to me, always being vague about Todd.'

'It's not the same thing. Not exactly. It's not like you were living with Paul. He was on the other side of the country,' Omar says raising his voice. 'You haven't even seen him in person since, what? September?'

'More or less,' I say. I did see Paul for a few hours during his layover in New York but that was about as platonic as it could be. Not that it matters anymore. 'Paul is a complete jerk. I see that now. Hell, I saw that before. What I didn't see before is how I had any control over the situation.' My battery icon flashes from green to red and I sit up to push the plug deeper into the wall. 'I see that now. I don't have to be with Paul just because he asked me or he's the type of man I *think* I should be with. I don't need someone who just makes me feel safe because it's easy and he doesn't challenge me. I need someone who makes me feel safe enough to believe in myself. Choose the things I want and go after them even if it's hard. Even if I face rejection.'

'Stop it,' Omar says and I can hear the usual sirens in the background. 'Now you're making me cry. I've been waiting so long to hear you believe in yourself. You know I believe in you, and the people who love you do, but you had to believe it yourself.'

'I have a long way to go with my own self-confidence, but at least for one brief moment last night, during sunset, standing on a milk crate, I felt it.' My voice wobbles thinking about balancing myself on the podium Finn created. 'I felt it for that moment, and I think I can feel it again.' Maybe that's all self-confidence really is. Maybe it's not a checklist of accomplishments or something empirical that you can measure with a ruler. Maybe it's just a feeling that you have about yourself. You need to keep practicing the feeling until it's a part of you.

'Final call for OpenSkies, Flight 79 to Newark, New Jersey,' a muffled voice announces from the gate.

'I have to go,' I say and yank my phone charger out of the wall and gather my things.

'Kevin and Wayne are on their way over but I'll text and tell them to turn around,' Omar says. 'I can bring down my samovar and have tea waiting for you the minute you come back.'

'No, that's okay. But thank you. Don't change your plans.' Omar's offer is generous and kind. He's a wonderful friend who I've never needed or appreciated more than in this moment. 'I have someplace else I need to go.'

315

Chapter 40

We land in Newark, and I head directly to ground transportation, where weary travelers are lined up for ride shares into the city. But when I get in the car waiting for me, I don't give an address in Manhattan.

'Hello. I'm going to 793 Hawthorne Court in Leonia.'

'New Jersey?' he asks.

'I'm afraid so,' I say. He exits the airport and we drive up the Garden State Parkway. In less than an hour I'm knocking on my mom's front door.

'Sam!'

'Mom.' I throw my bag down and wrap my arms around her and she squeezes me with her usual combination of fierceness and love. I've messed things up so much. I don't want to let go. I want to stay in her embrace as long as I can but I have to sit down with her and come clean.

As soon as we separate she can see all the pain and confusion on my face. My cheeks are still red and stained with tears from crying throughout the flight back from Miami. 'Sam, what's wrong? What happened? Are you okay?' She sits as close to me as she can on the couch and puts her hands on mine. 'I'm your mother. I love you. You can always tell me anything. I will never *not* love you.'

I know she wants to make me feel better but hearing how much she loves me only makes the tears shoot out of

316

my face like those water pistols you use to inflate balloons at a carnival game.

'Son, what's wrong? Nothing is forever. This will pass.' She rubs my back with her hand. 'I love you.'

'I love you too, Mom,' I say wiping my eyes. 'But I have to be honest with you. I only went along with your plan so I could be with...' It's hard to even say his name at this point. My throat tightens, but I'm able to croak out, 'Paul.' I look at her face, expecting to see anger or shock but she's undisturbed. 'I thought he was getting divorced. For real this time. I thought we could make it work, but I was wrong. I was totally wrong.'

'Oh.' She shakes her head and her curls bounce. 'You think I didn't know Paul was back in the picture?' She rubs my back with her hand.

'How could you know?'

'A mother knows.' She shrugs. 'I understand, son. I do.' Her hand stays on my back, supporting me as I'm crying. Something about being with my mother makes it easier for me to release everything: all the emotion, the hurt, and the frustration.

'Paul was in Miami, and I wanted to go to Cousin Ziggy's wedding with him. I thought that after you realized you couldn't find anyone I liked, you'd have to accept Paul. But it all backfired.'

'I have to admit, I like your thinking. I respect a solid plan like that,' she says, reviewing the situation in her mind.

'And I went along with everything because I know how much you miss Aunt Shug. How much we both do. I thought it would take your mind off her.'

'Oh, my sweet boy. I miss her terribly but I don't want to take my mind off her.'

'But you seemed so sad before, whenever I would mention her name or something that reminds us of her.'

'That's part of grief. But I don't want to forget about her. I love that she's still with me in so many ways. I love talking about Shug. Kai and I talk about her all the time, and he talks about his last partner, Cheryl, who passed away, and how he misses her. It's one of the things that I love about Kai.' She leans toward me. 'He's always willing to talk and listen. I can tell him the same story five times in a row and he doesn't care.'

'It sounds like you and Kai are very close.' The thought relieves my pain a bit.

'Closer every day. We spend time at Plant Daddy and we talk on the phone and text and we're going to a protest for food equity next week. Which I would like to see you at, come to mention it.'

She never misses an opportunity to remind me that I need to be more politically aware. 'Yes, Mom.'

'Pumpkin Pie, Paul was a jerk. Good riddance to bad rubbish,' she says and flicks her hands like she's getting rid of some dirt on her fingers. 'What happened with Finn?' I knew she'd get there. But I give her credit for letting me get so much out before she did.

I put my hand in my pocket and touch the note he left me. I remember everything I felt with him in Miami and I can't help but smile. Then I remember everything I lost with him and even though I think I'm out of tears I feel them well up in my eyes. But unlike the ones when I first walked in, they aren't propelled by anger or frustration. They just hang in my eyes like weights.

'What happened with Finn?' she asks again but gently.

'Everything.' That's the only way I can describe it.

'That's wonderful.' She's not pushing. She's just happy for me.

'It was,' I say and feel the tears run down my face. 'For a little while at least but then I screwed it up. I wasn't honest about my feelings and I made all the wrong choices in Miami.'

'So what?' I thought she would be more upset by my confession. 'You see that wallpaper?' She points to the wall with a gold oval mirror. 'I put it up in the eighties. All those beautiful cabbage roses and the birds of paradise on it.'

I look at the brightly colored wallpaper that's been in the living room all my life. I never really thought about it or looked at it before. It's always just been there.

'You know what's underneath it? A thick coat of the most awful tan paint. As soon as I painted it, I hated it. So blah and boring.' I think about the khaki pants I wear to work at Brands and how blah and boring they are. 'So, I went out and found the prettiest wallpaper I could. I wanted flowers and animals. Lots of color. I came home and covered all the boring paint.'

'Are you saying I should cover up my mistakes?'

'No, son. You can't ever do that. But you can make better choices and learn from what you screwed up. Now, every time I walk into the living room and look at myself in the mirror, I'm surrounded by this beautiful flora and fauna and all this color. I changed the frame around the reflection I saw of myself.' I look over at the wall and take in the bright colors and vibrant imagery. I think about Finn's gorgeous portraits of refugees and how he has created a way of seeing their lives surrounded by beauty and hope. 'It's not just about *what* we look at in the mirror. It's *how* we see ourselves that makes a difference. Surround yourself with a world that makes you feel how you want to feel. Not one that makes you feel boring and small.'

That's exactly how I felt with Paul: small. I didn't feel that way with Finn. I felt limitless. But it scared me.

'Sam, your wallpaper is the people you've surrounded yourself with. They see who you really are. Maybe you need to start seeing yourself how the people who love you do.'

I lean toward her and then fall to horizontal to put my head in her lap. For maybe the first time in my life, I can openly admit my mother has a point.

Chapter 41

The next day, I wake up to a barrage of texts from Paul. I glance at the first few – shallow apologies sprinkled with flat endearments. I know what I want to do but I'm not sure how to do it. Eventually, after watching a video online, I figure it out. I never thought I'd be able to block someone permanently but I'm finally seeing things clearly. Unfortunately there isn't a video tutorial to guide me through what I need to do next – apologize to Finn and ask him if there is any way we can find a way back to the place we were in Miami.

I spend most of the week at Plant Daddy plugging away at my laptop, but not on anything to do with Brands to the Rescue. Everyone knows about what went down in Florida and the people around me are supportive and sympathetic. Damola has made me a 'Fight the Power' playlist and Angelika pulled a few cards for me and says new beginnings are right around the corner. Maggie taught me a stretch that's supposed to heal from the inside out. I even appreciate the bottle of mead left in my apartment with a note signed by Omar, Kevin – and Wayne.

Kai comes over as I'm working and says, 'Don't tell your mother but I can get my hands on a cholla.' He glances back toward the espresso machine to make sure she isn't paying attention to our exchange.

'What's a cholla?' I ask.

'A very dangerous cactus with painful, prickly thorns.' He grins mischievously and rubs the whiskers on his chin. 'One stick and it can really do a number on someone's stomach. We could send a whole carton to Paul from,' he looks around Plant Daddy, 'an anonymous address.'

'I appreciate it but Paul's life is miserable enough as it is. I see that now.'

'Let me know if you change your mind,' he says and wheels over to my mother at the counter. I can't hear them but she tells him something that makes him smile and then he says something that makes her laugh. I'm glad they make each other happy. I see her bend down and kiss him on the cheek and he grabs her hand.

Paul is the last thing I care about at this point. I want to make things right with Finn but I'm not sure how. I hear the bells above the door ring, and my head snaps toward the entrance, hoping it's Finn. It's not; it's only Rajesh and Jessica, but I keep hoping Finn will show up here, and I'll suddenly find the words I need.

Finn has been such a part of Plant Daddy these past few months and I know everyone misses him. He hasn't returned my calls or my texts and he has every right to be done with me. But I have to see him in a few days at Harvey Milk School. It might be the very last time I ever get to see him and that makes me sad.

—

I take the train down to the Village and arrive early for the presentation. I wait outside on the sidewalk in front of Astor Place trying to figure out what I'm going to say to Finn. I spent the afternoon writing a speech because I wanted to get it right. I wrote about how grateful I am that we met and how much he has inspired me and how wrong I was not to be more honest about Paul and how stupid I was for going with Paul that night in Miami. I printed it out, but at the last minute I threw it away. It's not that I didn't mean every word. I did. But if I want to have a chance of convincing Finn to take a chance on me, I need to speak from the heart.

Ten minutes before he's scheduled to arrive, I see him crossing Fourth Avenue and walking toward me. He's wearing a blazer and a thick scarf with jeans, looking perfectly casual and professional at the same time. I thought I'd panic when I saw him but I don't feel that way at all. I'm happy. Happy to be standing in front of the building in the freezing cold with this amazing guy.

'Hello, Sam,' he says. His tone and expression are neutral and more professional than usual.

'Finn, I wanted to talk before the event. I was hoping we could...' I trail off. Now I wish I had brought the speech I prepared.

'I'm listening.' He stuffs his hands in his pockets.

I still can't read his tone. I start off with the most important thing: an apology. 'I want you to know. I'm sorry. I'm sorry about—'

'Hello!' a booming voice says as the doors to the school open. Principal Chan's timing couldn't be worse. 'Thank you both for coming tonight. We have a great group of kids and they're very excited to meet you both. Come on in. It's cold out there.'

'We'll talk after,' Finn says and I nod. I wanted to do it before the event because I couldn't stand the thought of having to be with him in front of all these kids with so much tension between us.

We walk into the room where we're doing the screening, and there are a few dozen students waiting for us. Some kids are dressed in outrageous colors or have hair that defies gravity but others look like they could be in a school uniform catalog. It's very clear that this is a school where you can experiment with self-expression. New York is known for its diversity and that's well-represented here. There is something about the atmosphere and the community that reminds me of a place I know, but then Finn turns to me and says, 'Feels like a Plant Daddy junior in here,' with a smile.

'Exactly,' I say and I'm relieved that he's willing to keep the conversation light during the event.

The principal asks us to introduce ourselves and Finn goes first with a simple explanation of his work as a photographer and the series he's working on. 'I create portraits of queer people who have come to this country so they could be themselves. I want to show people how many different ways there are to be queer.' His words are simple and powerful and I watch the kids nod and smile.

Then Principal Chan asks me to introduce myself. I take a deep breath, ready to do something I thought I would never do. I know I want Finn to hear me, but the fact is I'm not doing it for him. I'm doing it for myself.

'Hello,' I say and press my hands together to get a hold on my nerves. 'I'm Sam and... I'm a writer.' The Earth doesn't stop spinning. None of the kids stand up, point at me and yell, 'Fraud!' The room is calm and matter of fact.

But inside my body, it's a different story. It's been so long since I have thought of myself this way and meant it. It seems like something so easy to say, and I'm sure millions of people say it every day, from bestselling authors to kids writing their first story, but somehow I lost my connection to understanding myself that way. The roof in Miami was a magic moment where I leaned on Finn to get the words out. It was fantastic but it was part of a dream, a fantasy. A school presentation with a group of strangers, kids even, is reality, and saying it here makes me think it might stick this time.

'I'm Sam,' I say again. 'And I'm a writer.' I let the feeling bubble up inside of me and just linger around my heart and throat enjoying how it feels. I look over at Finn, and I see him really looking at me for the first time this evening. He's smiling and nodding and he gives me a thumbs up. Maybe I can convince him to give me another chance.

We show a clip from *Sunset Boulevard* and we talk about camp and how it's part of gay culture. Then we show *Moonlight*, which isn't camp at all, but explains the lived experiences of queer people in this century. It's not a formal presentation like the one in Coney Island. This event is much smaller and more intimate. We're really able to connect with the kids one-on-one, and that feels great.

We work in small groups, and Finn works with some kids who want to look more closely at the images of the films. I take a group in another corner to talk more about the words. They ask me questions and really listen to my answers. I think because I introduced myself as a writer, they simply accept that I am, and it feels wonderful.

I catch Finn's eye as a kid in his group with a striped mohawk is pointing at one of the images of *Sunset Boulevard* on a tablet and then recreating the poses. The kids are laughing and Finn has no problem getting them involved.

I'm working with the script from *Moonlight* and talking about autofiction as a way of generating ideas, journaling, and getting words on the page. I was nervous about working with kids but I'm loving the experience tonight. I'm able to encourage them and make them feel like they have something to say and that feels good.

When we get to the end of the event, the kids are still buzzing about everything we discussed as they get ready to go home. Finn and I walk out of the building together and stand alone on the sidewalk in front of the school. He doesn't immediately walk away from me and I think that's a good sign. There is so much I want to tell him, but at this moment, it feels like all my thoughts are jammed like a bunch of marbles trying to squeeze through a funnel. I want to break the silence, but he does before I'm able.

'I heard you say it,' he says looking directly at me and smiling. I know immediately what he means. 'I heard you call yourself a writer.'

'I did.' I want to tell him how good it felt in that moment but whatever confidence I had just over an hour ago seems to have evaporated here on Astor Place in the middle of rush hour. I'm scared of not getting another chance with him and my mind takes over. I can't stop it. I feel the anxiety rush through my body in all the old ways. Fear makes my nervous system take control. 'But that was just for the kids.' His smile drops and I can feel him shrink away from me.

'I better get going,' he says and turns away.

'Wait,' I shout after him and try to find the courage I need. 'I want to apologize. I am truly sorry.'

'For what?' He turns back. His question is something much bigger than the two words he just uttered.

I answer with my first thought. 'I'm sorry for not being more upfront with you about Paul. For getting you involved with this whole mess with my mother.' I pull my jacket closed to protect myself from the cold.

'Who says I didn't want to get involved? I knew what I was getting into.' I don't say anything, I just stare at the puffs of cold air that vaporize coming out of his mouth. 'And I liked it. I liked spending time with you and getting to know you. I loved hanging out at Plant Daddy and that was the best Thanksgiving I've had in years. It felt like family, and I loved being there with you.' His eyes are reaching out to me but he keeps his hands in his pockets and his arms close to his body.

'I loved being there with you,' I say echoing his words. 'It's over with Paul. I'm sorry I couldn't see how wrong I was about him. I'm sorry I wasn't honest about him.' My eyes search his face for any sign that he's accepting my apology but I can't find any. 'I'm being as honest as I possibly can with you.'

'But you're not,' he says pushing his hair back off his face. 'I want to be with a guy who is honest with himself. Honest about who he is and what he wants. I've seen you do it. I've seen those parts of you poke through. Do you have any idea how hot it was watching you stand on the roof and shout out that you believe in yourself? I wanted to have you right there.'

'I wanted you too,' I say. I think about the warm air surrounding our bodies as we held each other. A cold blast of air whips around the corner and makes me shiver but I don't take my eyes off Finn. 'I loved standing up on the roof, shouting with you. Saying those words.'

'But it's not just about the words. It's about saying them and honestly believing them. It's about feeling them so it isn't just something that dissolves in the wind.' He throws his hand in the air toward the sky. 'I wish you would take yourself seriously.' He looks at me and he wants me to say something but I'm too overwhelmed. I can only think of the words we said. The feeling is still uncomfortable and evanescent. I haven't had enough practice with it. I stare back at him without saying anything. He's the one studying my face now and I think he knows exactly what I'm thinking. He takes one last look at me and then turns away to walk down the block. I watch him blend into the crowd. The cold December wind bites my exposed face and fingers. I'm surrounded by rush-hour commuters hopping on the 6 train or heading over to the N on Broadway. Throngs of people rush past me in every direction but I've never felt more alone.

Chapter 42

I have a meeting with Robert today at Brands to the Rescue and as I ride the elevator up to his office I look at myself in the mirrors that cover the walls. I'm wearing my standard-issue khakis and a blue shirt, but when I look in the mirror today, I don't see a 'normal' or even someone pretending to be a 'normal'. I see a writer with a day job and it feels correct. Everything Finn has helped me understand about myself is finally sinking in. It's time to not just feel it but to take action.

'Sam,' Robert says as I walk into his office. 'Have a seat. We're so pleased with the work you have done with Finn and the gallery.'

'Thank you. I enjoyed working with Finn.' As soon as the words come out of my mouth, I feel them in my heart. I messed everything up there but maybe I can get this part of my life on track.

'I'm glad to hear that,' Robert says. 'I wanted to talk to you today to start thinking about how we on-board you to something full-time. We have a job description HR is working on, and of course, we can negotiate salary and office space and...'

'I'm sorry Robert.' I lean forward in my seat and interrupt him. 'When I said I wanted to talk about my position I may have given you the wrong impression. I wanted to let you know that I'd like to remain part-time. In fact, I need to take the rest of the week off, and if things work out I may need more time off this spring. I'm sorry I wasn't clear in my email.'

'Oh, I see.' Robert furrows his brow. I like him, and he has been a good boss. I don't want my news to create too much of a problem. 'Is everything okay?'

'Yes, wonderful actually. I've liked my work here and you've been great to me,' I say. I look around his familiar office and take in the sleek furnishings and efficient layout. It's not a bad place to work. It just isn't a place 'to be'.

'You do excellent work, and I'd like to keep you on in any capacity we can.' He smiles at me and his words are sincere. It's nice to hear Robert say them, and it makes it easier for me to ask for what I need. 'I'm hoping I can ask you for a favor. I've been connected with the Harvey Milk School.'

'Oh yes. You and Finn did something there with the kids.' My heart aches thinking about standing with him in the cold after the presentation. Getting so much right in the school and so much wrong out on the street. But I have to stay on task and stop the memory from making me too upset.

'Right, exactly.' I sit more erect in my chair. 'They have an opening for a creative writing teacher and I've reached out to the principal about applying. I'm also in the process of applying for a residency at Art Barn, which I'm sure is very com…' I'm about to finish that sentence with my usual self-effacing statement of doubt, but instead, I catch myself. 'I'm sure it is very competitive, but I've been working hard on the application and I have a good chance.'

'I'm sure you have a great shot at both,' Robert says with an approving nod.

'I was hoping you'd write me a letter of recommendation. There's a quick turnaround and I'm sorry to be asking with such a tight timeline...'

'I'm happy to do it,' he says not needing further persuading. I've already secured a letter from my agent Loretta, who said she was thrilled to write one. I only need two so I'm one step closer to getting what I want.

Robert walks me to the elevator and we pass the conference room where I first met Finn. Through the door I can see out the window we looked out together the day we met. The December sky is a bright arctic blue today and there isn't a single cloud. I can see all the way up to midtown. The city lies in front of me, inviting me to take myself seriously and be a part of it. Maybe it was inviting me when I looked at the same view with Finn months earlier but now I'm ready to accept the invitation.

Chapter 43

Kai lets me stay at Plant Daddy after closing so I can finish my application to Art Barn. I read through my statement one last time and at 11:53 p.m. I hit send, only seven minutes before the window for applications closes. I've spent the last few hours so focused on my submission that I've barely noticed Kai has turned off the lights and shut the place down. I'm about to head upstairs and go to bed when I see a light still on in the back. I know he'd hate to waste electricity so I go to turn it off before I leave.

I walk past the counter and Kai's potting area and through the supply area. A door I've never seen open before is ajar and a shaft of light pierces the darkness. I peek my head in and I can't believe what I see.

'Mom! What are you doing? What is this?' The room I thought was just a storage closet has been turned into some kind of makeshift pottery studio. There are shelves with old jars and cans filled with tools that look like they cut through clay or embellish it in some way. On the walls she has pinned sketches of mugs, plates, and some kind of large platter. Hunks of rust-colored clay sealed in plastic bags sit waiting under the large table where my mother is carving something into a vase with a wide bottom and a skinny opening at the top. She has a rainbow headband pulling her hair back, and she's wearing her *The Future is*

Inclusive T-shirt that has stray clay marks across the vibrant rainbow design.

She pops out her AirPods to talk to me. 'Sam, I didn't know you were still here. Did you finish your application? How did it go?'

'Fine,' I say. 'What is all this? When did you...'

'I told you Kai was building something for me. This is it.' She waves her arm around the room her face a mixture of pride and gratitude. 'My very own pottery studio. He thinks the mugs he's been using are too boring for Plant Daddy, and I told him that I used to make things, and he thought I should start it up again.'

'When did you make things?' I don't have any memory of my mom working with clay or even taking a ceramics class.

'Before you were born and right after. Until Daddy passed really. Don't you remember all those plates and cups?' she asks wiping her hands with a towel.

Growing up we had the most unusual dinnerware. All of it was made of pottery and with vivid colors that didn't seem like they should go together but they did. The details slowly come back to me. The shapes were what you might call experimental. One plate had indentations on the side where you could hold a utensil, and some of the cups had edges shaped like lips, so it felt like you were kissing someone. Like so much of my life they just seemed normal but now that I think about it, there was nothing normal about them.

'I thought those came from a garage sale or something,' I say.

'They came from our garage. I loved making those things, but I had my teaching, and as you were growing up, I started taking on summer school, so there wasn't

333

really time.' She turns toward the small sink and fills a cup with water. 'I guess I lost my way but being here at Plant Daddy with you and everyone has helped me see myself again.'

'I never knew you wanted to do this,' I say. I look at my mom and try to see her with fresh eyes. 'I wish I could have supported you more.'

'That's very sweet. I'm glad you know now.' She turns the water off and places the cup next to her work surface. 'I want you to know me. Not just as a mom but as a person. And I want to know you. Our relationship is strong.' She squeezes her small hands into fists and then releases the grip and sits down at her worktable. 'There isn't a stronger one. But I also want it to be deep.' I smile to myself because I think I've wanted the same thing. 'That's what all this boyfriend stuff was about really.'

'You made me go on all those dates so you could know me better?' I ask. It doesn't make sense but I'm at a point where I think maybe she does know what she's doing.

'No, I made you go on those dates so you could know *yourself* better. I can only truly know you: if you truly know yourself. Then I can love you even more than I do right now. You're my son and I want to love all of you. It doesn't matter if you're single or married or anything like that.' She puts down the carving tool she had in her hand and looks at me. 'I thought if you could find someone who saw how wonderful you are that you would be able to see it yourself.'

Immediately I think about being on the roof with Finn and how that felt. He did make me see myself with more confidence than I had before. I could never have even thought about applying to Art Barn before I met him. Mom kept pushing me toward him and I just wanted to run in the opposite direction. She was right all along. 'But Mom I did find that person.'

'In Finn?' she asks. I pause and then nod. 'I thought so.' She nods too.

'But he doesn't want anything to do with me,' I say and squeeze my eyes to fight back a tear.

'Right now, he doesn't, and maybe he won't, but you had that connection, and you felt that feeling, and maybe that's what you needed more than anything. It's what we all need.' She stands up and carefully takes a large unfired vase with a round base and fluted opening off the shelf and places it in front of her. 'Sam, you think I have all these rules to help you find what you need. Maybe I do, but there is only one rule that matters.'

She picks up her carving tool, makes a few more marks in the wet clay and then turns the piece around to show it to me. In beautifully etched letters that cover the entire side of the vase is one word – *Love*.

Chapter 44

A week later, the night of my cousin's wedding, we gather at Plant Daddy before we head up to The Plaza for the ceremony and reception. Kai is wearing a tuxedo with a pink, blue, and white striped bow tie, and my mom is dressed in a sparkly gown with the same colors. Omar has designed matching suits for him and Kevin. I have no doubt there is a lizard somewhere in Brooklyn wearing a miniature version. Omar offered to make one for me but I declined. I'm wearing a simple vintage tuxedo but I've added my own flair with the pair of rainbow socks my mom bought me for one of my dates.

We walk into the wedding at The Plaza, and the famous Grand Ballroom is decorated with so many winter white flowers it's hard to believe there are any left in the tri-state area. White roses, lilies, tulips, and chrysanthemums fill the room, spilling out of glass vases that soar above the tables like trees frosted with fresh snow. Soft lighting bounces off the intricate gold and burgundy embellishments on the vaulted ceiling, giving the entire room a warm glow. No expense has been spared for this event. We wait in line with the other guests and then congratulate my cousin Ziggy and his new wife Hilda. We even make nice with my Uncle Donald before we head to our table.

Mom and Kai, and Omar and Kevin, look so happy to be with someone special at this event. I'm glad to be sitting with so many people I love. I'm also glad Wayne is home with a cold because I don't want to eat wedding cake sitting next to a lizard.

I know my mom didn't want me to be alone at this, but tonight I don't feel lonely. I feel like I'm with my people. But it would feel great to be here with someone special.

We get to the table reserved for the 'Carmichael Family' and I take away a chair to make morespace for Kai. Then I pull out my mom's chair and she sits down. The table seats six, so there's one empty chair remaining where my date should be.

I turn to my mom and say, 'I'm sorry. I know you wanted me to have a date for this wedding.' I can't help staring at the empty place setting. Beautiful gold-trimmed plates and elegant glassware that won't be used tonight. I think about asking the server to remove it so it doesn't taunt me.

'Sam, all I've ever wanted is for you to be happy and from where I am sitting it looks like you're almost there.'

Maybe I am. It felt like I might have been getting close but I'm still not there. 'Mom, I don't even have a date.'

'Who says?'

'Everyone at our table is with someone and I'm not. Five is an odd number I'm afraid.'

'Samuel, our agreement is valid until midnight tonight. I have no intention of relinquishing my control until the very last moment.' She checks her watch. 'Don't forget I'm still in charge of your dating life for the next six hours at least.'

Her phone buzzes inside her purse. She opens it and looks down but keeps the screen hidden. 'That's your blind date… He's out by the fountain. Go get him and show him where we are.'

'Mom, you didn't.' I cover my face with my hand. 'Please tell me you didn't set me up with some random for tonight.'

'Sam do not keep this young gentleman waiting. They're about to start serving the salad course, and you know what happens to your tummy if you don't get enough roughage.' She holds up a finger with her warning.

I roll my eyes. Some things will never change.

'I've learned a lot over these past few months about what you need,' she says. 'Anyway, you don't have a choice. I have Rajesh on speed dial. Don't make me call him to go over terms. It's rude to keep a blind date waiting. Go.'

The last thing I want to do tonight is have a date with some guy I don't know. The Plaza is so romantic it will just make everything worse. My heart is not in the right place right now. I get up from the table and my mom says, 'I love you times a million billion.'

'I love you a billion more,' I say, and I really mean it. I walk out of the ballroom past the Palm Court with its elegant green lattice and fronds stretching to the ceiling. I exit through the lobby to the front entrance where a red carpet leads out of the hotel to Fifth Avenue.

Across from me I see the iconic fountain at the foot of Central Park where Barbra Streisand brushed Robert Redford's bangs out of his eyes in *The Way We Were* – one of my favorite Hollywood classics.

I scan the area around the fountain and don't see any single guys but then the spray from the fountain shifts and through the mist I see the back of a man in a tuxedo.

A strip of color catches my attention and my eyes drop down to his ankles. He's wearing the same rainbow socks I am. My eyes move up from his socks, and my entire body responds to the handsome figure I only see in silhouette. I recognize him. His frame is strong and confident. It has to be... The man turns around, and it's Finn.

I run across the street between The Plaza and the fountain, almost causing an accident and making a few cars roll down their windows to scream at me, but I don't care. I keep going until I'm standing in front of him. 'Finn, what are you doing here?' He looks stunning in his tuxedo and I notice he must have recently gotten a haircut.

'A certain mother from New Jersey invited me to a very important family wedding.'

'And you came? Thank you. Thank you so much.' I don't know how he feels about me but the fact that he was willing to come tonight is a good indication that maybe he's had enough time to reconsider.

'I also wanted to give you this.' He opens his tuxedo jacket and pulls out an envelope from the inside pocket. He looks at it for a second and then shows it to me. I immediately recognize the Art Barn logo. He hands it to me and I rip it open and read.

'Oh my gosh. They accepted me for the residency. This spring. I just submitted the application a week ago. I can't believe... how... what?' The words fall out of my mouth and I'm not sure what I'm saying. This moment is all about feelings and I like the ones I'm having right now.

'I had nothing to do with it,' Finn says, raising his hands to show his innocence. 'I'm only the messenger. When I found out you applied, I recused myself from evaluating your application. But it was a unanimous decision, and I did read your application. It was beautiful. Not just in how it was written but because of what you said. You finally did it and I know you meant it.'

'What I said is true. It's all true.' I remember exactly how my application started:

> For most of my life, I've struggled to take myself seriously. I was always doing something else instead of just being myself because I wasn't sure who that was. Lately, I've learned that the only way to believe in yourself is to know yourself honestly, and that's what I'm determined to do.

'You taught me to do all that. Thank you,' I say.

'I knew you could get there, and maybe you were already there when we were doing the presentation at the school. When I read your statement, I knew it was more than words because I felt...' He puts his hand to his mouth and searches for the words. 'I felt connected. Connected to you. I take my art so seriously. Maybe too seriously. That world is easy for me, but this?' He gestures to the space between us and shakes his head. 'I thought my work alone could be enough but it's not. I also need to be connected to people I love. People like you.' He bites his lower lip and pauses. 'Not just people like you. You.'

He tilts his head and I do the same but the opposite way. It feels like time is slowing down as our lips are drawn together by a force neither of us wants to stop. He puts his lips on mine, and we kiss. The air is cold, but I feel his warmth, and I share mine with him as our mouths connect and he holds me in his arms. I can hear the traffic and smell the chestnuts and fresh pretzels from the food carts on the edge of the park. We don't separate. We keep kissing and smiling, and it feels like we are both letting down whatever obstacles were there before. We're finally knowing each other in the way we have both been wanting. Horse-drawn carriages, traffic, tourists, and native New Yorkers swirl around us. We are a part of it all, but we are also a part of each other.

We catch our breath, and our lips separate, but we're still holding each other. He looks at me, I look at him, and at the same time, we both say to each other, 'You're amazing.' We laugh, and I can see his breath in the cold night air. I look into his eyes and say, 'We are both amazing.' But it's not the words that are important. It's the feeling.

A letter from Philip

Dear Reader,

Many years ago, a version of the book you just read was the first manuscript I wrote after the best-selling women's fiction author I had been working with suddenly passed away. The main characters were a mother and her straight daughter. It never even occurred to me that the hero could be gay. At the time, commercial fiction rarely included gay protagonists, and if it did, those characters often met tragic endings. How could I imagine happy-ever-afters when growing up I never thought I would live past thirty and marriage equality wasn't even on the distant horizon?

It's taken me a long time to find myself in my writing and create stories that reflect my lived experience. If you've read one of my books before, you might know that I write what I call "kiki lit" – chick lit with gay leads. I write stories about becoming yourself and the power of loving yourself because that journey has been such a personal struggle.

I'm so grateful to Canelo and Hera for creating a seat at the table for authors like me who never thought there would be one. If you liked this book, I hope you will consider writing a review or rating it online. Demonstrating engagement is such an important part of keeping the seats at the table expanding.

I write to connect with people, and I'm grateful that digital media gives us so many ways to do so. I'd truly love to hear from you directly. I answer every message I see. Please find me at any of these digital waypoints.

https://www.instagram.com/philipwilliamstover/
https://www.facebook.com/philipwilliamstover/
https://www.philipwilliamstover.com/
email: philipwilliamstover@gmail.com

In MMRR4D, Sam's mom explains that she wants her son to know himself honestly, because then she can love him even more. My mom was similar. She was always trying to love me more, and although I found it endlessly irritating, it also made me feel safe. She passed away just after I graduated from college.

While writing this book, my mom would sometimes visit me in a dream. Usually we would be at our favorite diner in New Jersey. In the dream, she's wearing a hospital gown and shows off her favorite Apricot Evening press-on nails. After coffee and pie, she gets up to leave. I beg her to stay. She turns to me and says, "I'm with you. I'm always with you." I wake up and look over at my sleeping husband and our precious dog snoring, and I feel her. Not as some ghostly figure. She's a feeling. A feeling of love.

I hope you are reading this and feeling loved today. I hope you are becoming yourself and loving yourself. After all, it's not the words that are important. It's the feeling.

Philip

New York City

July 2024

Book Club Reading Guide

Growing up, my mother often said, 'When you have a book, you're never bored, and you're never lonely.' Sometimes we even read the same book and discussed it as went along.

I love the thought of *My Mother's Ridiculous Rules for Dating* being read by moms and sons, dads and daughters, elder queers and gaylings, twunks and twinks, mentors and mentees. Whatever combinations works for you. Reading with someone always deepens the experience. To get the party started, I've come up with a few questions you might want to consider.

1. Do you have any rules for dating? What are they? Do you think your rules might be helpful to someone else? Would you ever try to follow someone else's rules?

2. How involved should a parent be in an adult child's dating life? What about giving dating advice to a friend?

3. Sam says that his relationship with his mother is 'very strong but not always deep.' How do Sam and Glory deepen their relationship? What scenes show how much they care for each other? How do you show your child/parent that you care for them?

344

4. Plant Daddy is an inclusive coffee/plant shop in Hell's Kitchen. Who are the regulars at Plant Daddy? Who from the book would you like to share a table with? Is there a place where you hang out and feel accepted? If you could create a space for your found family to gather, what would it be?

5. Finn tells Sam he is a lot like his mother. How are Sam and Glory similar? How do they differ? How are you and the person you read with alike or different?

6. Sam thinks his mother is trying to fix him, but Glory thinks she's helping him. Which do you think it is? Have you ever tried to help/fix a friend/child/parent/mentor? How did it go? Would you do it again?

7. What are Sam and Finn's initial impressions of each other? What are the key moments in the story that impact how they feel about each other?

8. Sam and Finn both work in creative fields. Do you think it's easier to be with someone who is in the same field as you or with someone who does something different than you?

9. Sam struggles with confidence. What happens in the book to help him with this? How do you think people develop confidence? Finn tells Sam that confidence is a feeling you practice having. Do you think that works? Do you have any tips or tricks for believing in yourself?

10. At the wedding Glory is with Kai, Omar is with Kevin, and Sam is with Finn. What do you think of each of these couples? Do you think they're well-suited for each other? Does each couple have a happy ending?

I hope these help get the conversation started. I'd love to hear about who you read with or see a picture of your book club. Please find me on Instagram @philipwilliam-stover and let me know!